Letting In Light

ALSO BY EMMA DAVIES

Merry Mistletoe

Letting In Light

EMMA DAVIES

LAKE UNION
PUBLISHING

Text copyright © 2016 Emma Davies

Published by Lake Union Publishing, Seattle
www.apub.com

Amazon, the Amazon logo, and Lake Union Publishing are trademarks of Amazon.com, Inc., or its affiliates.

ISBN-13: 9781503935808
ISBN-10: 1503935809

Cover design by Lisa Horton

Printed in the United States of America

To my three amazing children, who every day manage to remind me why we had them, and to my wonderful husband, who just gets on with it and in so many ways, big and small, allows me to get on with it too. Fictional heroes can be wonderful, but real heroes like mine are so much harder to find.

PROLOGUE

Ellie never knew it, but it was probably the conker that saved her life. On any other day, Will McLennan would have approached the final bend below Fordham Farm at thirty-five miles an hour. As it was, the sight of the little brown nut lying in the middle of the road caused his mind to wander, resulting in an unconscious easing on his accelerator pedal, which meant that he hit the bend at twenty-seven instead. This reduction in speed gave him just enough time to bring his Land Rover to a halt without actually hitting the car already half in the ditch.

'Shit.'

He scrambled out of the truck and hit the ground running, covering the short distance in seconds.

The car had skewed sideways as it slid down the bank. It must have been coming towards him and veered straight across the road, mercifully not rolling but coming to a halt with the driver's side angled down; had the bank been any steeper, it would be on its roof. Glancing at his boots for a second, he jumped into the ditch, landing up to his ankles in muddy water. Whoever was in the car was bloody lucky; two weeks ago this area had been in flood. He gave a slight shiver.

Bracing himself with one hand on the roof of the car, Will dropped down to his haunches, doing his level best to keep his bum out of the water. The glass in the side window had shattered, gone in part, and he scooped the rest outwards, sending it tinkling into the water. A figure was slumped towards the steering wheel, and he had to take a very deep breath before reaching out and gently touching the shoulder.

Will stayed that way for a moment, breathing hard, trying to calm the rush of adrenaline. Deep in his pocket, his mobile phone vibrated insistently against his thigh. He ignored it, as he had countless times already today. He knew it would be Caroline, but at least now he really did have a good excuse for not answering her. He focused on the driver, thinking only of what to do next.

A small sigh rose from beside him, and he felt the muscles in the blue shoulder move, a little effort, but there all the same, and then a lurch as the shoulder came up, followed by a head with auburn hair. A groan then, and a release of breath.

'Oh Jesus,' came the female voice.

'Hi,' Will said simply.

There was another sigh. 'If you're not a paramedic, I'm in really deep shit.'

'My name's Will.'

'Will, the paramedic?'

He actually smiled then. 'No, just Will.'

'Well, Will, do you think you could call an ambulance? Because my arm's killing me.'

'Shit. Christ, of course, yes. I've got a mobile here . . . look – sorry – I'm going to have to stand up. Can you hang on a minute?'

Will dialled and waited.

The call made, he ducked down once more. 'I'll be back in a minute. Don't move, okay?'

'Going nowhere.'

'Yeah, right. No, I meant "don't move" as in – you know – don't move your body, in case you have a head or neck injury.'

'There's not actually that much of me that wants to move right now.'

Will scrambled up the bank and ran to his truck, throwing open the rear door and fishing about in the tumble of his belongings. There, at the bottom, was the mesh bag containing emergency equipment, none of which he had used before. He pulled out the metal triangle, and ran back around the bend to where the road was straight and set up the warning sign. At least if anything came along now, there wouldn't be another car in the pile.

Seconds later he was back in the ditch, crouching once more. 'Hi, I'm back again. Don't worry – the ambulance is on its way. It won't be long now, and I'm not going anywhere. I need to know where you're hurt, though – can I check?'

'Okay,' came the voice through clenched teeth. 'Can you do me a favour first, though, please? I can't feel my feet, so can you have a look for me, and if they're missing or anything, can you just lie to me and tell me everything's fine?'

Will reached through the window once more, placing his hand on her shoulder, splaying his fingers to make his hand bigger, more reassuring. 'Everything *is* fine,' he said. 'We are in about a foot of water, though, and bloody freezing water at that. I'm hoping that's the problem.'

'Okay, I can go with that,' she whispered.

Will was silent for a moment, adjusting his footing to stop the ferocious ache that was developing in his calves. Better balanced, he reached into the car again. 'We haven't been properly introduced, have we? Only, I can't see your face . . . do you mind if I just . . . your hair is in the way.' He tentatively tried to move aside the curtain of copper curls that separated them.

'You'll have to tie it back,' came her voice. 'Believe me, it's the only way. Just grab a handful and scoop it round the back and then tie it, like two ends of a rope.' Will followed her instructions.

'Thank you,' she whispered again. 'That's much better.'

Will still couldn't see her face properly, thrust downwards as she was, but he had the impression of slight features and pale skin. She moved slightly to turn her head, eliciting a sharp hiss. 'Christ, that hurts.'

'Don't move, okay? You need to stay still. I think you might have hurt your neck.'

'Really?' she said sarcastically. 'Actually, I think it's my collarbone . . . and my arm. I heard something snap, it might have been the car, of course . . . or it might have been me . . .' She trailed off, shoulders starting to shake now as emotion welled. 'I'm sorry. I'm being incredibly rude. I don't know what's the matter with me.'

Will moved his hand to touch her cheek. 'Don't – it'll only hurt more. It'll be okay, I promise. I swear to God that your feet haven't floated off downstream. Do you hurt anywhere else?' he asked, peering into the car and running a hand across her shoulders and down one arm.

'Not exactly. I'm not sure, really. Anyway, thank you – you're being very kind. I'm sure you must be sitting in the ditch, which can't be very comfortable. I'll be okay, if you want to go. You must have somewhere that you need to be.'

Will thought of all the things he could and should be doing. Caroline would be furious with him. A barrage of text messages had assailed him during the day, alerting him to the fact that tonight she would launch another attempt to get him to talk, but now he would be late home, which meant everything else would be late. Feeling the ache in his leg muscles building uncomfortably, he wouldn't even be in the mood for an argument later, let alone anything else. Not that that would make any difference.

'No, nowhere I need to be,' he replied lightly. 'I'm here for the duration. I might even have to start telling you my life story soon, like they do in films, just to make sure that you don't slide into unconsciousness.'

'You could, but you might be really boring. Would you want to take the risk that this might *cause* me to slide into unconsciousness?'

'You have a point there,' Will agreed. 'I could beef it up a bit, invent a few things. Although actually, I'd lay money on the fact that you've never met a sword swallower from Barnsley before, and especially not one that's run away from the circus.'

'Liar – that's never a Yorkshire accent.'

'I took elocution lessons when I was younger, just in case the sword swallowing didn't work out and I had to retrain to become a lawyer.'

A giggle. 'Are you a lawyer?'

'No, I lied about that too. I'm a teacher.'

'I think I liked it better when you were a sword swallower.'

'So did I.' Will stopped for a minute, listening, a faint wailing growing steadily stronger. 'Just stay nice and still now.'

It was nearly three hours later when Will pushed open his back door, praying that Caroline wouldn't be waiting in the kitchen. He needed a little space to acclimatise: time to get his head beyond what had happened tonight and the thoughts that had chased around it on the drive home. They'd had to cut the roof off the car to get the woman out. He'd stayed with her, holding her neck still and trying to keep her calm over the noise and the smell as they opened up the metal box that encased her. His head still rang with it. She'd be okay, though – just a bashed-up arm, feet intact. He smiled; it could have been a lot worse.

Caroline came towards him, holding out her arms, murmuring endearments. *Poor him, what a terrible evening he'd had, was he okay?*

All he could see was the girl's face, pale and drawn but still beauti-ful, as she'd lain on the stretcher inside the ambulance and held out her hand to take his fingers.

'I'm Ellie,' she'd said. 'Thank you, Will, thank you.'

'My pleasure,' he'd answered.

CHAPTER ONE

a year later – September

Jane knows I'm nervous today. She even volunteered her husband to take the children to school so that she could drive me to the training centre, and that's not something done lightly. Jack's a writer and usually at his most creative first thing, and he and Jane are two of my favourite people in the whole world.

I didn't want to turn down Jane's offer, but I had to. I have recently instigated a spirit of 'getting on with things,' which is still in its early days of resoluteness, but now as I drive, I'm beginning to regret my well-intentioned decision because I can feel the bubbles of apprehension welling up, and I'm worried about just how large they're going to get. I've been down this lane twice now since the accident, and rationally I know that the chances of me having another one are non-existent, but the thought is there, and I can't hide from it.

I'm being foolish again, muttering swear words to myself, which doesn't help in the slightest, and I mentally add this to the list of things about myself that I do not like and am going to change. It's strange, though, because today I have no trouble in summoning up a voluptuous 'fucking hell,' but back then, during the conversation that ended my six-year relationship with Robbie, I said practically nothing. I'm thirty-four years old, and I'm an English teacher, for God's sake; I'm usually irritatingly eloquent, but the one time – the only time – I have ever wanted to skewer someone with words, to pierce their skin and then drive my venom home, nothing would come.

I make it through the day, and I'm a mile and a half from Jane's house before it occurs to me that being with people again is not as bad as I thought it was going to be. I don't think I disgraced myself, but then I find it hard to tell. After what Robbie accused me of, that sense of just being yourself without even thinking about it is something that seems lost to me. I wonder if I'll ever lose the feeling that I'm acting, that I'm looking at myself from the outside in and analysing everything that I do. It's so wearing, though, being so self-conscious all the time, and I think that in the end this feeling won't be able to sustain itself and, like a dying star, will implode. I'm not quite sure what happens to me when it does.

I accepted many things about myself a long time ago: the fact that my eyes are green and not blue; the fact that my carroty hair corkscrews its way around my head whatever I try to do with it; and that my hips are practically non-existent, along with my chest. These minor irritations have niggled me at times, but as I grew up, I learned that they really made no difference to me as a person. I realise now that I never truly thought about the person I am – I was just me. Now, though, it feels as if it's the only thing I think about, and that's something I will never forgive Robbie for. I feel stolen away, a changeling.

That's why I'm longing to see Jane. I need to be immersed in her own special brand of chaos. I need her children's noise and chatter to silence my own.

The White House sits on the edge of a small hamlet burrowed into the side of the Stiperstones, and its location is perfect for Jack.

It has an air of remoteness I always think very suitable for a writer, and Jane loves the fact that her back garden can, if she wants it to, extend for miles of bracken and heather-strewn hillsides. I have always loved coming here, and now in a little over a week Shropshire will be my home too.

The kitchen is combining the functions of dining room, study and playroom all at the same time, as usual, with four-year-old Tilly flinging bits of play-dough around gaily while Grace is colouring with ferocious concentration. Jack is stirring a pan of gravy by the cooker, telephone in one hand. He looks up as I walk in and mouths, 'Hello,' a pained expression on his face, which rapidly takes on a much sharper look as both girls erupt into noisy greetings. I shush them as best I can, waving Jack away to finish his call while I take up stirring duties.

The back door opens then, blowing in debris, and Jane is home. She surveys the scene for a nanosecond, then relieves me of my spoon, puts the kettle on and brings the girls to order while giving me a huge welcoming smile. Jane in full flow is an awesome sight. She is the queen of multitasking, but she does it all with such calmness and gentleness of spirit that we lesser mortals are like moths to her flame; we bask in her warm glow.

'Is Jack about?'

'Mmm.' I nod. 'On the phone.'

'Sorry about that, folks,' says Jack, reappearing on cue. 'Simon moving my goalposts as usual.' He crosses the kitchen to where Jane and I are standing. 'Hello, gorgeous,' he says, bending to kiss Jane, and then, 'Come on, Tilly, sweet, time to clear this away now.'

'We'll all help,' I say. 'Come on, Grace, you and I can lay the table.' I look at Jane. 'What's for tea, Mum?'

'Toad-in-the-hole.'

'Ah, wicked,' I say, winking at Grace.

As we sit down to eat, I think once again how lucky I am to have such good friends. I feared that our friendship would lose something when Jane got married, but Jack has always made room for me in their lives and understood the implicit bond between us.

Jane and I have been friends for nearly thirteen years, since meeting in a rundown bookshop in Worcester, where she was working part-time around studying for a history degree. She was two years younger than me, and I was still trying to make it big in bookselling. It was probably our late-night philosophical discussions that finally helped me to decide what I wanted to do with my life, and back then, taking an English degree seemed like the culmination of all my dreams. Completing my teacher training in Worcester had also meant that our friendship continued uninterrupted, although it was me who moved away first, following my career to Cambridge, where I had lived ever since.

Cambridge seems a million miles away from this welcoming kitchen, with its golden walls adorned with the girls' pictures, and the Aga, which I had never seen unfettered from drying clothes. I remember when we painted this room, a wild weekend when Jane was heavily pregnant with Grace. It seems such a long time ago now. I was with Robbie then, but he hadn't been able to make it over that weekend. *No, I guess not,* I think bitterly, with the benefit of hindsight, with which I am now cursed. It was a good weekend. We had laughed so much that I was scared Jane would deliver the baby right there on the floor. She hadn't, of course, and Grace had arrived three weeks later, so tiny and perfect, and with a disposition so mild that after two days she had chosen her own name.

I realise that the conversations around me have become distant, and sensing that both Jane and Jack are giving each other furtive glances, I give what I hope is a natural-looking smile.

4

'So then, Grace, tell me about this fab princess party you're planning for your birthday.'

I am groaningly full when we finish and have a yearning for a chair and a book, but I've got into the habit of giving the girls their bedtime bath since I've been here, and one look at Jane convinces me that it's an effort I need to make.

The girls are a spent force now, calm and malleable. It's a lovely time of the day. Perhaps sensing my mood, they are content to play mermaids, which involves very little effort on my part.

'You could be a mermaid, Auntie Ellie,' says Tilly. 'Your hair is all long and curly,' she giggles.

'And it would cover your boobies,' adds Grace quite seriously. 'Although your boobies are only little. Mummy couldn't be a mermaid – her boobies are much bigger than yours, but her hair only goes down to here.' She points to her shoulder. 'And her eyes are brown. Everybody knows that mermaids have green eyes, like fishes.'

'Do they?' I ask. 'I always thought fish had blue eyes.'

'Oh no, fishes' eyes are green – all seaweedy, just like yours.'

'Well, perhaps I am a mermaid then. Maybe,' I start to whisper, 'when I go in the water, my legs turn into a tail, and you've never noticed before.'

Tilly and Grace give one another that *oh, aren't grown-ups silly?* look as Grace declares, 'Don't be a noggin! You took us swimming last summer, silly, and Uncle Robbie kept diving down and tickling your toes. I remember.'

'So he did. Oh well, I can't be a mermaid then after all.'

Grace holds her head to one side, looking at the water trickling through her fingers. Her eyelashes are dark and wet as she looks up at me through them.

'Could Uncle Robbie not come this time?'

'No, I'm sorry, sweetheart. He has to stay in Edinburgh.'

'How come?'

'Well,' – my mouth is suddenly dry – 'he has his own family now, and he's decided to stay with them.' Such an easy thing to say, this small death sentence.

'But I like him,' says Tilly, pulling at her lip. 'He's funny. Doesn't he like us anymore?'

'It's not that, sweetheart.' I am fighting back tears. 'I think he likes you very much, but he likes his own family too. He has a tiny little girl, even littler than you are, and she needs her daddy, just like you do.'

'I didn't know he had a little girl.'

'No, darling, neither did I.'

Tilly looks at me, an unformed question on her lips. Even her four-year-old antenna can pick up danger signals, though, and the question remains unasked. Instead, she recognizes an opportunity for gain, and I am wound comprehensively around her little finger.

'Can you read us a story before bed? Please?'

'Yes, alright, but on one condition,' I say. The girls' eyes are round and attentive. 'That we read *Room on the Broom*.'

'Oh, cool!' cries Grace.

The lamps have been switched on in the lounge, and the room is cosy and dimly welcoming. I settle into one of the big, squishy chairs, with Grace under one arm and Tilly, the other, inhaling their sweet and fragrant warmth. Their bodies yield to mine, and as I read, I feel my breathing slow, tension sliding away.

My voice is slurred as I finish the story, and neither child protests when Jane collects them to take them up to bed. I sip my tea, the day's events milling around my brain, but there is no urgency to any of my thoughts, and they drift away from me, slower and slower, ebb and flow.

When I come to, it's dark, and I start with the guilty conscience of the catnapper. I can hear muted voices in the background and get up to cross the room's threshold into the hallway. It too is dark, but at its end is the bright yellow rectangle of light from the kitchen doorway. Silhouetted inside the room are the figures of Jack and Jane. Jack is standing behind his wife with his arms around her belly, enfolding her, his hands moving slowly in caress. His head is bent into the side of her neck, and together they rock slowly as if to some unheard melody. The picture is one of such tenderness and surety that the grief I carry just under my skin rushes headlong to the surface.

I lean against the wall for a few minutes, breathing deeply. I'm not jealous. I am deeply moved and gladdened by my friends' intimacy, but my own loss stands out in stark relief: the loss of my future and the comfortable, relaxed intimacy I shared with the man I loved, but the loss of my past too. Memories rendered meaningless, my memory of them now false, altered by the knowledge I now hold. I blink away my tears furiously, wiping under my eyes and brushing the wetness against my jeans. After a few moments, I clear my throat, warning of my presence. Jack immediately steps away from Jane, knowing that they have been seen.

My voice sounds tight. 'I thought I'd come in and say hello in case you thought I was a total slob.'

'It's okay, Ellie. We were just—'

I interrupt Jack before he gets any further. 'You were just hugging your gorgeous wife. It's fine. It's allowed, you know, especially since this is your house.' I give him a look that challenges him to change the subject, which he does adroitly.

'Actually, we were just going to have a nightcap.' He smiles at Jane. 'Well, I was. I think Jane is feeling her advancing years and is going to have cocoa. What would you like, Ellie? I've got a fruity little red open.'

'Thanks, Jack, but I think I'd rather have cocoa as well. If I remember rightly, last time you and I opened a bottle, I lost three days.'

'Ah, but that was the hard stuff. This is just a drop of grape juice.' He studies my face for a moment. 'Boring,' he says, cocking his head to one side, 'but understandable.'

Jane takes hold of my hand, pulling me to sit down. 'So, how did it go today?' she asks softly, shooting Jack a look that has him busy himself with the milk pan.

'It was okay.' I smile weakly. 'No, actually, better than that. It was good. I felt fine once I'd got over the first half hour or so. There were a couple of nice people there, which helped.'

Jack raises his eyebrows. 'Nice girl people or nice boy people?'

Jane glares at him.

'Okay, okay, I know I shouldn't ask. Sorry, I'm just curious – must be my writer's nose.'

I smile in spite of myself. 'It's alright, Jack.' I nod reassuringly at Jane. 'It's what you're both thinking, and don't try to deny it, Jane,' I say pointedly as she tries to hide a smile. 'So, just for the record, it was one girl person and one boy person. The "she" in question was a really nice woman called Freya, who seemed very down to earth and easy to talk to. Actually, there were only three women, including me, but the other one, Francesca, was so perfect she was scary, so I didn't speak to her much. I'd be prepared to bet a million quid she has a perfect boyfriend as well, not one who commutes from one end of the country to the other to see his wife and their six-month-old child.'

It's a flippant comment; I probably shouldn't have said it. I can see that I've taken the wind out of Jane's sails. She doesn't know what to say, and now neither do I, for that matter.

Jack puts down two mugs on the table and sits in front of me. 'Maybe not, but I bet she actually goes home to an empty house, plays with her goldfish and then spends a lonely evening fantasizing over George Clooney.'

It's Jane who laughs first. 'Honestly, you two. The poor woman. I almost feel sorry for her now.'

Jack shifts in his chair slightly. 'But what about this nice boy person?' he teases. 'Do we get to know about him too?'

I catch his mood. 'I'm saying nothing except that his name is Ben. He's a carpenter. He has deep dark eyes you could drown in, a very sexy ponytail, and' – I let the words hang in the air – 'a girlfriend called Alex.'

'Oh fuck!' says Jane succinctly, and then snorts into her cocoa.

Jack looks at me expectantly, still smiling, but concern showing there too. 'Actually, Ellie, I wanted to talk to you about something. About Netty's house?' He looks to me for confirmation. 'I just want to be sure that it's what you want to do – that you're not going to house-sit for us because you feel you have no other option. Nothing's final, you know – we can easily ask the agent to find another tenant.'

I consider my answer carefully. 'I know,' I say slowly, 'but the reality of it is that I have nowhere to live.' I carry on before Jane can protest. 'And I know that you've offered to let me stay, but I've been here nearly a month as it is. My house is sold, my furniture is all in storage. I've got no job, and I just don't know what to do. The longer I stay here, though, however much I'd like to, I'll never get anything sorted out. I need to start somewhere, and a house is as good a place as any.'

'I haven't seen the house for a bit, though, Ellie; *you've* never seen it for that matter – you might hate it.'

'What, with me not being a country girl and used to muck and stuff?' I mock. 'It's fine, honestly,' I say, seeing Jack's sheepish look. 'We'll both be helping one another out. I get a place to start anew, and you get someone to look after the house for you while you decide what to do with it. I don't care if it's a mess; it'll give me some purpose if I can do it up a bit. After all, I may well have a lot of free time on my hands.'

'But what *are* you going to do?' asks Jane with a worried look. 'I can't imagine you not working; surely you need to do something to occupy you?' She studies me for a moment. 'There'd be schools around here that would give their eye teeth to have you.'

'I know, but I'm not even sure that I want to carry on teaching – that's the weirdest thing. I think I only did the training today because I've always held a first aid certificate, and it seemed sensible to keep it up, just in case. A year ago I thought my whole life was settled. I can't believe how fast it all unravelled, and now, far from wanting my life to pick up where it left off, I just want to throw everything up in the air and see what lands where.'

Jack looks a little like a light bulb has just gone on above his head. He nods encouragingly. 'I felt just the same when I started to write,' he begins. 'I had a good life; I was sorted, settled, earning good money, and I just couldn't understand why I was feeling the way I did. But then I found the strength to ditch the things that no longer made me happy and follow what was inside of me. I took the plunge.'

'Which worked for you, I'll admit,' I say, 'but that's because you're a bloody good writer.'

'It worked because it was the right thing for me to do. I firmly believe that.'

'But what if you don't know what you want to do?'

'Well, maybe,' says Jane, taking my hand again and giving it a squeeze, 'what you want to do will rise to the surface once all this other stuff has died down. You know, like cream to the top of the milk. It only does that if it's not shaken.'

CHAPTER TWO

At its heart, Wickford is a gentle village of mellow stone cottages dotted around a series of country lanes, the houses gradually petering out until the lanes themselves meander into the next village. At some point in its history, the council saw fit to allow what, no doubt, they termed a 'select development,' and so on one edge of the village stands a gated cul-de-sac of twelve very large and modern red brick houses. This naturally spawned a couple of other developments, not quite as grand, but houses with a definite executive air to them. It renders this part of the village as distinct and separate as if it were another place entirely.

No doubt this all caused considerable uproar amongst the locals, but I wonder if they can also see that it may well have been their salvation. On my first visit here two weeks ago, I expected to find a pub and a church, but was surprised to see a village school, a good-sized local shop, a tea room and, incongruously, a designer dress shop. These incomers may have disrupted a rural idyll, but they brought money and children, two commodities vital for any community.

As I drive past the school playground, reassuringly loud on this bright autumnal morning, I realise that I'm about to find out what this little community is all about. If I'm lucky, I might become a tiny part of it. I negotiate a tricky turning, through a high wall onto a long driveway, before pulling in beside a patch of grass that belongs to Rowan Hill Lodge. Home. At least by the end of tomorrow it will be.

When I first visited my new home with Jane two weeks ago, I was astounded when she pulled into a lay-by just off the main road and commanded me to get out of the car. I'd been looking at the view the whole way over with steadily growing excitement, and this stretch of hills looked just the same as the last six miles or so, a patchwork of dips and rises – beautiful, yes, but why had we stopped here? Jane came up behind me and angled my body slightly to the left. She pointed out a collection of houses some distance away, a church spire rising out of their midst.

'That's Wickford,' she said, 'and that big house there is Rowan Hill.' I followed her finger to an impressive array of buildings, one topped with a bell tower, standing to one side of which was the kind of house you buy when you win the lottery.

'Beautiful, isn't it?' said Jane. 'You don't get quite the same sense of it when you're up close. That's why we stopped here; it's quite the best view of it.'

'Right,' I said slowly, trying to work out Jane's logic. 'So I guess that's where the lord of the manor lives then. I'll be sure to practise tugging my forelock. The village looks very pretty, though, Jane. Come on – I want to see the house.'

I turned back to the car before realising that Jane was still standing there with her hands on her hips, grinning at me.

'You don't get it yet, do you?' she asked.

'Get what?' I replied, getting out of the car again.

She turned me round once more. 'See where the bell tower is? Well, look to the right of it. The white house standing forward is Rowan Hill Lodge.'

I looked, a smile creasing up the corners of my mouth as realisation dawned. 'That's the Lodge? My lodge? Jane, why didn't you say so before? Get in the car, now!'

Jane started the car again, laughing at my haste. 'I just wanted to show you before we got there. It looks impressive doesn't it? But actually the house is quite shit.' She burst into a full-blown gale of laughter. 'It looks so much better from a distance!'

I wouldn't describe it as shit exactly, but the Lodge has somewhat fallen on hard times. Rowan Hill was originally a farm, but most of its land has been sold off over the years; in fact, I'd hazard a guess that half the village has been built on it. Up close, the main house is not as big as it looks from a distance, but it's a handsome place, all different roof lines with picturesque mullioned windows and an air of permanency about it.

The house is flanked by an array of stables and other buildings that stand to its right, forming a courtyard. There's a pillar in the middle of the entrance, where I can see the huge hinges for what would have been some mighty impressive gates on either side of it. The courtyard is large enough to have once held several carriages, but now stands empty, watched over by the bell tower at its rear. To its right another wall extends outwards from the stable block, about two-thirds back, and thus becomes the rear boundary to the Lodge, which sits forlornly in its clearing surrounded by overgrown trees, ivy and general mayhem. It's sorely in need of some new paint.

Today, as I push open the front door (actually, I think it's the back door), I realise that I can't remember what the house is really like. I can picture the rooms, yes, but none of the detail, nothing of its character that's going to make it mine. So I stand just inside the door and breathe deeply. Tomorrow it will be chaos, hopefully of the organised variety, but I realise why I'm really here today. I had to pick the keys up from the agent, but I also want a moment with the house alone. It smells cold – not damp, but like a lingering lack of warmth. There is no smell of cooking or of wood burning in the hearth, no scent of life or of occupancy at all. Instead, I can smell the house: the tang of the cold paint on the walls, the slightly musty hall carpet and soot. In a few weeks, the house will smell of me; my perfume will linger in the bedroom; the kitchen will smell of my last meal; of a night, my candle will fill the lounge with its warm, honeyed tones – but all this is to come. For now there is nothing beyond a clean, empty coldness.

I am standing in the kitchen, which must have originally been two rooms and is now split by a massive oak beam traversing the ceiling and coming to rest on its support, which runs down one wall. The room is beautifully light (although painted a very distressing green colour) but completely empty of furniture save for a huge pine table, a stone butler sink on a wooden trestle and an enamel Aga standing in the hearth. Jane called it my 'mission impossible,' should I choose to accept it. Two weeks ago, this seemed like just the sort of project I needed. Today, as I think of the removal van piled high with all my worldly goods, it seems foolhardy in the extreme. I take a deep breath and move on.

The kitchen turns left at the top and opens into a hallway, where it passes the front door. Beyond, the sitting room seems dark by comparison, having only one window, but it's a good size and has a stone fireplace, above which sits a mantle that would appear to be made of half a tree whose other half clearly made the windowsill.

There is another door in this room, a beautiful, old oak slab, its edges worn smooth, that sits in one corner about a foot from the floor, some five feet tall overall. I took it for a cupboard on my first visit, and Jane laughed at my surprise when I pulled it open and found a flight of steps to the bedroom above instead of the dark hole I expected. It is only now that I realise with horror that none of my furniture is likely to make it up these stairs.

There is a wonderful view of the main house from the bedroom. It's a quaint room with sloping ceilings on two sides, like a little eyrie with its hidden, cut-off staircase. The bathroom is simply hideous, though. I resolve to call it an ensuite in an attempt to lend it an air of charm and luxury, although actually it's the only bathroom in the house. I see interesting times ahead for any guests I might invite around.

I wander haphazardly from room to room, trying to imagine where I might put things, what to unpack first and what might need to stay in storage, but in the end I give up, knowing that any decision I make today will probably have to be unmade next morning. I had thought I might have a wander around outside too, but I feel a little reluctant about this. The Lodge clearly has a garden, but the boundaries have become blurred over time, and I'm not sure where my bit ends and the big manor house's begins. There doesn't seem to be anyone around, but I don't want to be caught trespassing before I've even moved in.

There is a toot from below, and I cross to the other window to see Jane pulling up outside. The removal men should be here in less than an hour. There's a strange feeling in my stomach that I recognize as plain old-fashioned excitement. I'm standing in the bedroom, taking in the view, a moment of calm before the hard work of the day starts.

Jane sails into the kitchen, bringing a sunny warmth that wasn't there before and, just as importantly, a box containing a kettle, mugs, tea, sugar, milk and a packet of chocolate digestive biscuits bearing the legend '25% Extra Free!'. The only place to deposit these is the table.

'Christ, Ellie, what have we done to you? There's not a single work surface in here, is there? How are you going to manage?'

I take the kettle from the box. 'I haven't the faintest, but I will become a mistress of improvisation and have the finest array of packing-crate furniture in the Western world.' I fill the kettle and plug it in to boil, the cable mercifully long enough to allow me to stand it on the floor, where we both look at it and burst out laughing.

'Come on, Ellie, get the biscuits open. I'm starving.'

The removal men carry my furniture around with consummate skill, and eventually I end up with something in each room. The only sticking point is the bed, which is still outside, waiting to be dismantled before being carried upstairs. The mattress only made it up by dint of sheer brute force.

Now it's lunchtime, and only Jane and I remain, flopped onto one of my sofas, which is pushed up against one wall of the kitchen. A bright shaft of autumn sunlight falls on it through the window opposite, warming the cushions, which feel a little cold and damp from their journey. Jane drains her mug first, placing it carefully on my table in front of her.

'I'll just go and get lunch from the car,' she says. 'Wait here.'

I know I should get up to help, but to be honest, it's rather nice sitting in the sun, and I'm suddenly overcome by extreme lethargy.

The back door, which has a tendency to stick, is unceremoniously kicked open, and Jane reappears, carrying a cool box in one hand and a huge bunch of chrysanthemums in the other. I jump up straight away.

'Oh, Jane, these are just beautiful!' I gush, touched once again by her thoughtfulness.

She eyes the walls, which are not far off a kind of muddy pea green, and says, 'I'm not sure they really go with the decor.'

The burnished orange and yellow blooms do clash rather violently, and I resolve to place them somewhere other than the kitchen. I'm just filling the sink with water when there is a loud ta-da from behind me. Jane is flourishing a crisp white tablecloth and lays it down with a grin.

'If Madame could take her seat, please,' she says, gravely indicating one of the chairs, 'then luncheon will be served. It's all finger food,' she adds succinctly. 'I thought it might be best.'

The rest of the meal is finished in near silence, but the sort of companionable silence that doesn't need to be filled. I'm lost in thoughts of tricky storage problems, and Jane seems intent on demolishing the entire tub of olives.

The crunch of tyres on gravel brings me out of my reverie. I look up to see a dark green Land Rover crawling up the drive. It turns before it gets to the Lodge, pulling in through the wide entrance to the stable block. Lord – or lady – of the manor, I presume.

'Aye, aye.' I nod to Jane. 'Looks like his lordship's home.'

She strains to catch a glimpse, but the car is gone. 'Mr McLennan, although I can't for the life of me remember his first name. Bit of a recluse from what I can gather, although a nice enough chap. Netty used to say that he was suffering from an acute case of inheritance, whatever that means. I expect they're like all these families, skeletons falling out of the cupboard left, right and centre. I've never met him myself. There's a brother around somewhere too, but no womenfolk I'm told . . .' She gives me a lascivious wink.

'Oh, give over, Jane – I bet he's as old and crumbly as the house.'

'Yeah, but he could be *rich* and old and crumbly.'

'I hadn't thought of that. Blimey, what am I doing sitting here? I should be heading straight round there!' I sit back and survey the remains of food on the table. 'On second thoughts, I think I'll just stay here and have another almond croissant.'

'Spoilsport,' says Jane, pouting and looking at her watch. 'Hey, Ellie, I'm sorry, but I'm going to have to go soon and pick up the girls.'

'I know – it's okay. I'm just really glad you could come over this morning and see me in. I'll be fine from here; I've just got to take my time finding a home for things. Actually, I'm looking forward to seeing all my stuff again. I've forgotten about loads of things since I've been doing without them. It'll be nice rediscovering them.'

'Tempted to just not unpack and start again?'

'No, I'm not really the minimalist chic type am I? It's been a bit of a holiday the last couple of months. A lovely holiday,' I add quickly so as not to hurt Jane's feelings, 'but a holiday just the same. This is where real life kicks in.'

'Well, listen – don't let it kick you too hard. You know, I'm only on the end of the phone.'

'I know, and I promise I'll come and help with the girls at the weekend. I should be sorted by then, and if I'm not, I'll need a break.'

Jane is grinning broadly. So am I. We're both playing the jolly hockey sticks routine, neither of us wanting to say goodbye and bring an end to the weeks of shared companionship. I decide to be bold. I know it will make Jane feel less anxious, and if I am convincing enough, I might just believe myself.

'Right, come on then: sling your hook, woman. Some of us have got work to do,' I say loudly, gathering wrappers and pulling Jane's tablecloth out from under them. Jane is eyeing me closely and soon catches on.

'No need to say long goodbyes is there, not like we used to have to. Now that you live just down the road, we can pop round whenever. Sort of an *adieu* rather than an *au revoir*, isn't it?'

'Absolutely,' I reply.

'So no need to say any more, all understood,' she says. 'Small hug, though?' She grabs me and gives me an almighty squeeze and then is out the door, cool box in hand.

I watch her car until it turns out of the gates, and then turn back to the house, trying desperately hard not to feel what I so obviously am. Alone.

I can feel myself on the verge of an almighty blub, and it's tempting to just let go, but I know I'll feel worse if I do. Better for having had a good cry, yes, but worse because I've allowed myself to feel pitiful, which will give me the opportunity to despise myself all over again.

It's seeing the wooden pieces that make up my bed frame lying abandoned by the door that spurs me to action. They need a home and I need a place to sleep, so I push up my shirtsleeves and make purposefully for my toolkit.

I don't notice the cold until teatime. The physical activity has kept me warm, but the sun is going down, and I'm tired and hungry. I'm in the kitchen, flopped on the sofa, looking around the room with a critical eye. It's as good as it's going to get for the time being, and I'm pleased with my efforts. It's not until I get up to fetch some paper and a pen that I give an involuntary shiver. Of course, the house has been empty since the last tenants moved out a couple of weeks ago, so it's bound to feel cold. It's as I'm wondering where the central heating control is that I'm struck by a sinister thought, something that hadn't registered earlier, but which now arrives with a dull, foreboding clank.

I get up slowly, carrying my tea, and walk from room to room. I check upstairs as well, although I don't know why that should be any different. There are no radiators in this house. Those beautiful fireplaces, which I had admired as nothing more than a period feature, are in fact my only source of heating – or they would be if I had anything to burn in them.

A quick scout around the outside of the house confirms my predicament. I can see where the woodpile has been, but all that's there now is a scuffle of loose bits of bark and wood lice. Bollocks.

Back inside, I flick a switch to my right; at least the lights work. I head upstairs to get a jumper, and decide to make my bed. I have a feeling I might be retiring early tonight. The mattress is still on the floor where I left it, assorted pieces of wood lying beside it. Putting the bed together wouldn't ordinarily have been a problem – I've done it several times before – but it does help when all the bits are available to reassemble. Try as I might, I could not get the long pieces of wood that form the sides of the bed up the stairs; the angle through the door just wouldn't accommodate their length, so I gave up. They're currently propped up along the kitchen wall. I push the rest of the pieces aside with my foot, resolving to deal with this problem another day.

I feel a bit better when the bed is made. My beautiful Cath Kidston quilt doesn't exactly go with the brown tufty carpet, but it's cheering nonetheless. It's another little bit of my life before, my contented and seamless life. If I surround myself with as many of these little reminders as I can, then maybe I will absorb some of their quality – an osmotic peace.

Grabbing my jumper, I head back downstairs, my stomach beginning to growl. It's nearly seven o'clock, and I've been accustomed to Jane's bountiful cooking; a meal is long overdue. I'm not in the mood for anything extravagant, but I have a few basics courtesy of a fantastic farm shop near Jane's house.

A vision of a melting cheese omelette pops into my head, and the matter is settled. I unsettle it just as quickly when I remember that I haven't yet lit the Aga and as a result have nothing to cook said omelette on. I had airily dismissed Jane's offer of lighting it with a bold and – I now realise – very foolish assertion that I would do it later. In fact, I have no idea where to begin, and after warily eyeing the instruction booklet that is thoughtfully hanging above the Aga, I mentally shove this task onto tomorrow's to-do list. Alongside finding some wood, doing the shopping and totally rebuilding the kitchen.

I hack a great lump off the end of a loaf of French bread, do the same to a piece of cheese and carry these to the lounge together with a tub of Pringles. In an effort to retain some semblance of dignity, I return to the kitchen to hunt out a plate and on impulse grab a bottle of champagne that Jane brought with her. Back in the lounge I break out my collection of sentimental DVDs, which I know will do untold damage to my emotional state, but at this precise moment I don't care.

As the closing credits to *Sleepless in Seattle* roll, I am curled into a ball on the sofa, trying to retain my body heat. One cushion is clutched to my chest, and another is placed over my feet. Meg Ryan has fallen into her man's arms, whereas I am just falling.

This is not what I had planned at all. *My first night in my new home should have been better than this,* I think miserably. I had pictured a nice meal, a drink, a candlelit bath in petal-strewn water and a good book taken to bed, followed by a deep and refreshing sleep. Instead, I feel sick from having eaten too many Pringles and am contemplating a mad dash upstairs to crawl fully clothed and unwashed into my camp bed. Who am I trying to fool with my chic designer duvet cover? I'm still sleeping on a mattress on the floor. I don't even know if I have any hot water. At this thought, the tears come.

I realise I've had too much to drink when I wake in the night and my head's banging. It stops, then starts again. Stops, then starts again. I experience that odd sense of disorientation that only comes in the dark in an unfamiliar room. I forget which way I'm lying and try to get out of bed like I would have done at home – my old home, that is. All this achieves is a painful jarring of my legs against the floor, which I remember – too late – is only centimetres under me. In reverse, my bedside table seems to have grown immeasurably as I inch my hand up and grope for the light. The room isn't just dark; it is a void into which all the darkness in the world has been poured. And all the time the banging, stopping, then starting again. Finally, my fingers find the switch. Now that I can see, I realise that the banging is coming from outside the room. I get to my feet slowly and listen. It's coming from the house next door.

There's a wide pool of light in the courtyard to the main house, but there's too much reflection from the window, and I can't see clearly. I also don't want to be seen myself, so I double back and switch the lamp off.

Having the benefit of fully functioning senses again, my eyes and ears put two and two together and come up with a vision so extraordinary I'm inclined to disbelieve it. Silhouetted in the light is a solitary figure chopping logs. One log up on the block, a flash of a blade – thud, thud, down. Another up on the block – thud, thud, down. Stop, then start again. I can scarcely believe it. It's twenty to two in the morning, and my stupid bastard of a neighbour is chopping logs.

CHAPTER THREE

When I wake up the next morning, I feel inexplicably great. No headache, full of energy: in fact, I feel rather cheated – I was quite looking forward to a day of self-pitying slothdom.

I crawled back into bed following the episode with the Phantom Log Chopper and must have fallen into a deep, refreshing sleep. Now that I'm awake, my head is instantly full of all the things I have to do. First on the list has to be a cup of tea.

I fling back the covers, a little overenthusiastically as the cold air hits me, and wonder how many more clothes I can put on. I did go to bed fully dressed and am relieved that there are no mirrors in the room yet. The likes of Meg Ryan might be able to come through any situation looking stunningly tousled, but in my case I suspect the words 'train wreck' would be an accurate description. I pad through to the bathroom, muttering to myself about the whereabouts of my slippers, and to my delight discover that I have an immersion heater in the airing cupboard. I almost whoop with joy at the prospect of a bath. Tea and a bath, or tea in the bath – even better. I look at my watch; it's only eight, and in another hour I will be warm.

I'm just warming my hands around my first cup of tea of the day when I hear a series of strange rumbling noises from outside that sound like they're getting louder. It's a persistently rainy sort of a day, and I have no real inclination to investigate, but as this is not my house, I suppose that I should. The back door is stuck, and I pull it so hard that it opens with a worrying crack. I am face-to-face with a dark, wet, hooded man, who looks just about as surprised as I do.

I seem to have slopped half my tea down my trousers and am contemplating throwing the rest over the Grim Reaper when a flash of blue catches my eye.

He raises a hand to wipe the rain away from his face, and in that second I recognise him. I've thought about those hands often enough. I hardly saw his face, except for the flash of his blue eyes as we said goodbye, but as he crouched beside my car in the ditch just over a year ago, I felt as if I'd known him all my life, and now he's here, standing before me. Will. My pulse begins to quicken.

But something is not right. He doesn't appear to have shaved for days and sports a pallor that wouldn't look out of place in Broadmoor. He looks bloody awful, in fact.

I try a tentative smile. 'Hi,' I say.

He looks at me steadily, a drop of water snaking down a curl of hair on his forehead. If he recognizes me, he does not show it, nor does he offer any greeting. 'I've brought your wood,' he says flatly, his hands hanging limply by his sides. *'Hello' would be nice*, I think.

I can see a stack of logs just beyond him under the overhang of the house. A blue plastic sheet is pulled tight over the top. I am deeply confused. Maybe I've got it wrong. Perhaps this isn't my Good Samaritan after all, but in any case, what is he doing here?

'Er, thanks . . . I'm sorry, did you say *my* wood? Only I'm not sure I ordered any, exactly.' I laugh nervously.

25

He jerks his head back towards the stack. 'Keep the plastic pulled down; the wood needs to stay dry.' He rubs a hand over his face to wipe away the rain and turns to go, shoulders hunched.

A few beats of silence pass before I call out after him. 'Will . . . ?'

He has reached the end of the logs now and bends to retrieve a wheelbarrow, which he wheels back towards me. He drops the handlebars and straightens up to face me.

'Miss Hesketh, isn't it?' He doesn't wait for confirmation. 'Listen. I don't want to be rude, but I'm wet, I'm cold and I need a cup of coffee so badly it hurts. If I'm not very much mistaken, you need wood – I've brought wood, so could we please save the twenty questions for another time? I'll come back later to ease the door.'

My jaw, already slack, drops another foot or so. I can feel my face beginning to burn. *Who the fuck does he think he is! Waltzing over here at some ungodly hour of the morning. 'Brought my wood' indeed. He'll probably charge me some exorbitant price for it as well, as if I can't get my own wood.* My mind rumbles on in this fashion as I watch his back retreating, until, like a train cannoning into a buffer, my thoughts come to a sudden, abrupt and not very pleasant halt. Oh my God, he lives here. If I'm right, this man – perfectly normal teacher, or so I thought, and who had seemed like a nice guy; after all he did kind of save my life – has just turned into Mr McLennan, lord of the manor, rude, unwashed, idiot, middle-of-the-night-log-chopping bastard of a neighbour. Fan-bloody-tastic. I slam the back door dramatically and then have to go and nudge it closed.

The bath is as wonderful as I'd imagined. I lie there, trying to come up with a solution to the storage problem in the kitchen, when it occurs to me that I could use my bookcase and a load of baskets to create more space. I remember going to a wonderful shop with Jane that sold just what I needed. A quick trip later and I have a boot load of basketry.

It's still raining as I head back into the village. It's only lunchtime, but the sky is incredibly dark, the streets gloomy and rain soaked. On a whim, I decide to stop at the little tea room; the lights are on inside, and the windows are steamed up, making it look warm and cosy. It's called Perfect Setting, and it's really rather pleasant inside. It used to be someone's front room, I would guess, and it's a pretty place, not overly big, but with a cosy charm. There are plates everywhere, mostly on the walls, but a large dresser holds quite a collection, along with some lovely blue-and-white china.

I go and sit at a small table at the back of the room and pick up the menu.

A waitress is clearing plates from a nearby table. She catches my eye and offers a smile. One or two nonchalant glances are made in my direction, but the general air of conversation hasn't stopped dead, which I take to be a good sign. The waitress reappears from the door somewhere behind me. She's very slight, older than I first thought, with jet-black, spiky hair and the biggest pair of hoop earrings I've ever seen. I order soup, a roll, a flapjack and hot chocolate. Rather an odd combination, but comfort food of the highest order.

A sudden raised voice breaks into my thoughts. An older woman has called the waitress over and is gesticulating wildly at her plate. Her voice is assertive, to say the least. It matches her checked skirt, which is also rather formidable. Judging by the rather grovelling apology she receives, I would hazard a guess that not only is she well known, but she's also an accomplished maker of complaints. I decide to reserve judgement until my own food arrives. Unfortunately, the flapjack has been overcooked and is dry and brittle (although the soup is obviously homemade and beautifully seasoned).

By the time I'm ready to leave, I'm the only customer left, and I'm conscious of hurrying, as I'd rather not sit here by myself. The waitress asks if everything was all right.

'Yes, fine, thank you,' I lie, not wanting to be rude.

She smiles. 'So we might see you again?' She pauses to count out my change. 'Or are you just visiting?'

'Well, no, actually, I just moved here, to the Lodge up by Rowan Hill.'

The smile becomes broader. 'I've never known Alice Tweedy to be wrong. She said someone new had moved in. How are you finding things?'

'Well, I only just moved in yesterday, but . . . good, thanks, getting straight, you know,' I say, nodding.

'And have you met Mr McLennan yet?' She leans in conspiratorially. 'Mr McLennan Junior, that is.'

I've never heard a more loaded question. 'Um, Will, is it? Well, only briefly this morning.' I can't bring myself to say any more.

'That's good. I'm Gina, by the way.' She holds out her hand. 'Welcome to the village. Come in again, won't you. Mrs Tweedy is here most days.' She motions with her head towards where the old lady was sitting. 'I'm sure she'd be very willing to tell you all the history from the big house' – she winks cheekily – 'if you know what I mean!' Her amusement is infectious.

Manhandling an assortment of baskets through a door while trying to hurry out of the rain is not that easy, I discover. I have one knee bent up, braced against the door for support, with the baskets wedged precariously under one arm. I turn the key in the lock, ready to mount an assault on the door with my shoulder, but when I push the handle down, I am propelled through the door and into the side of my kitchen table, where a chair gives my kneecap a vicious blow.

It's while I'm dancing around, clutching my knee, crying, sniffing and uttering expletives, that I become aware of two things. The first is warmth, and the second is the smell of smoke.

I stop and look around, the expletives slowing to a whimper, fully expecting to see one side of the house on fire, but everything is just how I left it. Except that it isn't. I hobble to the other side of the table. The Aga is lit and radiating such delicious heat I could hug it. I sniff it cautiously: there is no smell, so where is the smoke coming from? I move into the lounge as fast as I can and stand, open-mouthed, staring. It's beautiful. The fireplace is dancing with flame. A bed of glowing ashes supports two logs that are merrily ablaze and reflected in a glass fire screen that stands on the hearth. It's yellow and red with flashes of orange, pale pink and marbled white that swirl together across the surface, catching the light and turning it this way and that as the logs burn.

I don't know what to think. I'm struggling to take everything in, let alone work out what it all means. My first thought is of Jane, but there's no sign of her car outside, and the door was locked when I came in. The house is still, and I feel I am alone. Besides, what kind of burglar breaks in, lights the fires and then leaves everything untouched? And then it comes to me: the door. The door that was sticking fast earlier but that now swings freely. A voice coming back to me: *'I'll come back later to ease the door.'* Will. Fucking hell.

I have no idea where I'm going, but I'm not about to let a little thing like that stop me. I get to the courtyard of the stable block and look around for signs of life. Immediately on the left is a door into a room on the front of the house. I hammer on the door, and when there is no reply, I hammer again.

The door opens instantly this time, revealing a rather more together-looking Will than the one from this morning. He breaks into a broad grin which momentarily disarms me. There's not a trace of the surly manner of earlier either, which confuses me even more.

'Hi, how's it going?' He pulls the door a little wider, as if to invite me in. He obviously thinks I'm about to throw myself at his feet in fawning gratitude. Arrogant sod. I take two steps towards him, leaving him with no option but to retreat inside the house as I follow him. He's looking slightly less welcoming now, a little disconcerted. We come to rest in what is obviously the kitchen.

'Have you been in my house?'

He doesn't reply, but there is a look of surprised understanding on his face, which is all the confirmation I need.

'Don't you think it would be polite to ask first, instead of coming into my house when I'm not there and doing whatever you please? You keep me up half the night, chopping logs, which you deposit at my door at some ungodly hour – not to mention that I didn't ask for any – and then you think you can just swan around—'

Will holds up his hands suddenly, as if warding off blows. 'Look, will you just let me get a word in? Bloody hell, I was coming around to apologise.'

'I should think so. You might have set fire to the house, leaving the logs burning like that.'

'I meant,' he says forcefully, 'I meant about this morning. I must have seemed a bit odd, I realise. I wasn't at my best.' He pauses for a minute, anger flickering in his eyes.

'So you don't think it's wrong to come into my house when I'm not there?'

'I didn't say that.'

'But you didn't apologise either. I bet you thought I'd come over here and throw myself at your feet, didn't you? In gushing thanks for having lit the Aga and a fire, because naturally I would never have managed to do that myself.'

Will looks like he's been slapped. 'Sit down,' he says angrily.

'What?'

'I said, sit down,' he repeats, 'please,' pointing at the kitchen table, where I can see the remains of a meal. There is something in his voice that brooks no argument. I do as I'm told.

Will waits a second or two, never taking his eyes off me, before finally coming to join me, sitting in a seat on the opposite side of the table. He holds his head in his hands, as if it hurts, and lets out a long slow breath.

'Look, can we just wind this back a bit? It's Ellie, isn't it?'

It's the first time that he's acknowledged my name, I notice; so he does remember me.

He sounds exhausted, and I feel my irritation beginning to cool.

'I tell you what: I'll apologise for trespassing, wantonly lighting fires and giving the impression that I think you're a helpless female, which wasn't my intention at all, and you can thank me for fixing the door, lighting the Aga – which is a bitch to get going from cold, not that you'd know that – warming the house and leaving a welcoming gift as a surprise.'

His eyes never leave mine. I am in such trouble, and I have no idea what to say. I offer a conciliatory smile.

'Shit,' I say.

Will leans back in his chair, shaking his head slowly. 'And I thought I was fucked up.' There are small crinkles at the corner of his mouth. He stands up.

'Tea?'

'Yes, please.'

He slides an enamel kettle across the hot plate of an Aga, which looks identical to mine, and busies himself with mugs and a teapot. It's the first opportunity I've had to look around; the room is gorgeous.

'So tell me,' Will starts, his back still to me. 'I have an excuse for my irrational behaviour, but what about you? I'm guessing a broken heart, right?'

He turns around, a broad smile on his face. 'You don't have to answer that, of course. I'm just curious to know if I was right.'

His smile is infectious. I want to remain cross with him, but he's right after all; my behaviour is totally out of character. I find I'm laughing.

'Okay, his name was – is – Robbie, but that's all you get to know, for now anyway. I owe you enough of an apology already without adding to my burden by crying all over the place as well.'

'Fair enough. I should apologise too. I'm sorry I woke you up last night. Some nights . . . well, I don't sleep much, and I didn't think you'd hear me.'

Most people I know don't chop logs to help them sleep. I'm not sure how that could possibly help, but if it works for Will, I think I'm prepared to go with it in the spirit of reconciliation.

'Ordinarily, I doubt whether I would,' I reply. 'I think it was a case of first night in a new house – that and the thick end of a bottle of champagne. You'd think it would help, wouldn't you? But it never does.'

'I wouldn't know; never touch the hard stuff myself.'

I've already taken in the open bottle of whisky on the dresser. I make a small noise, which Will takes for derision. There's a twinkle in his eye.

'You've tried the more traditional remedies, I suppose?' I ask. 'You know, bit of telly, cup of camomile tea?'

'Yes, and, variously, a bit more telly, something a bit stronger than PG Tips, the collected works of Shakespeare, yoga, *Ulysses*, transcendental meditation and *Paradise Lost*. Now I just chop logs, which seems to do the trick and actually serves some kind of purpose.'

'So reading Milton is supposed to put you to sleep, is it?' I counter. He gives me a quizzical look. 'I never told you, but I'm a teacher too – an English teacher. You're on very dangerous ground.'

Will takes a slug of tea. 'So *Paradise Lost* is one of your favourites is it?'

'Not my most favourite, no,' I say with care.

Will studies me for a moment, his blue eyes missing nothing. 'Thought not,' he says, smiling. 'Remind me to lend you my copy any time you can't sleep.'

I raise my mug to him. 'Touché.'

'And how's the arm now? I read all about it in the paper; it sounded quite an ordeal.'

'It's much better, thank you. I did a spectacularly good job on it – broke it in two places and bust my collarbone as well. I now have a lovely chunk of metal holding it all together. I can't believe you actually live here, though. What are the chances of that? I wanted to thank you properly, but I never got the chance. I realised when I got to hospital that all I knew was your first name, and I had no idea how to contact you. And now here you are.'

There is silence for a moment, Will considering whether he should add any more to the mix. 'It was a bit of a surprise finding out you were moving in,' he says finally, batting the conversation back in my direction. 'Didn't I read you lived in Cambridge? What made you move here?'

'I have friends up this way. The Lodge is their house, actually. I'm just house-sitting for a while. You used to look after Netty when she was alive, didn't you? My friend mentioned you'd kept an eye on things. They were very grateful that she was able to stay in her own house right up to the end.'

Will looks somewhat surprised at this. 'I liked her. I was a neighbour – that's all. But her grandson sent me a nice letter when she died, thanking me. Sorry, I can't remember his name?'

'It's Jack. Jack Manning.'

'Yeah, that's it. Anyway, it was nice of him. Netty was fiercely independent; she did everything for herself. I just used to go in and light the fires for her – that's all. She wouldn't let me get away with anything else, used to threaten to throw me out of the house. You're not related, are you?'

'Very funny,' I say with as much sarcasm as I can throw at it. 'So how come you're not at school today, then? Term's already started, hasn't it?' I ask, changing the subject.

Will's eyes flicker away. 'I don't teach anymore,' he answers benignly.

'So what do you do then?'

The reply is a long time in coming, and I get the distinct feeling that I've strayed where I shouldn't. I wonder if he's unemployed; I've probably touched a nerve. But then Will throws up his hands in an expansive gesture.

'This place,' he says simply. 'I'm its caretaker, I suppose. I try and keep the estate ticking over, keep the old family firm in business.'

I'm suddenly conscious of the size of the room I'm sitting in, and remember what Jack's nan had said about Will suffering from an acute case of inheritance.

'That must be quite a tall order. What does the estate produce?'

'Not much, if I'm honest,' says Will with a resigned tone. 'The present caretaker isn't much of a gentleman farmer, I'm afraid – should have got the sack years ago. Fortunately for me, I have a very clever older brother who is shit hot at his job and currently building half of Dubai. He comes home every few months and deposits an inordinately large amount of money into the bank, which I then pour into the bottomless pit that is Rowan Hill.' He drains his mug and replaces it on the table with slightly more force than is necessary.

I'm torn between wanting to know more and obeying Will's warning signals. I'm not being entirely forthcoming myself, so it's hardly fair to delve any deeper. I decide to back off and return to what I hope is a safe question.

'Have your family lived here long – owned the estate, I mean?'

'Not really, no, in the grand scheme of things. You'll notice McLennan is not of English descent? My great-grandfather came here as a lad, a lowly stable boy, and had the temerity to fall in love with the daughter of the house, a comely and rather brazen lass, if the tales are true. Lucky bugger, though.'

'Why? What happened?'

'Usual story: he got the lass pregnant and was just about to have his prospects cut off when her father became ill and died. Turned out the old man was bedding half the village, had contracted syphilis and died a gruesome death, leaving no son and heir. Not wanting the truth to come out, the mistress of the house welcomed young Willie into the family, threw a lavish wedding breakfast for the happy couple and declared Willie the new head of the household in a wonderfully orchestrated bit of PR. Much to everyone's surprise, he rather grew into the role, and the rest, as they say, is history.'

'It's rather a nice story, though.'

'It is, yes, if you hold with tradition. Makes it rather hard for us mere mortals to live up to, however.'

'A blessing and a burden then?'

Will nods his head. 'Definitely.'

I study him for a minute; his face is weary. 'And are you burdened or blessed?'

'Right now?' He pauses for a moment to consider the question and then lays his hands flat on the table, leaning forward slightly. 'Too bloody knackered to know the difference.' He pushes the chair back suddenly. 'I've got something here,' he adds, crossing to the dresser and taking down something from a hook. He lays it on the table in front of me.

It's a key, and I instinctively know it's the pair for my own back door key. 'You should have this back.'

I lay a hand over it guiltily. 'Maybe you should keep it, just in case,' I say, pushing it back slightly towards him.

'Listen, you can tell me to piss off if you like, but your Aga is probably up to temperature by now. Shall I give you a quick tour?'

I drain the last of my tea, smiling. 'Lead on, Macduff.'

Will puts on a fake but nevertheless accurate Scots accent. 'Have ye no' listened to a word I've said, woman? Ma name's McLennan, not Macduff.'

CHAPTER FOUR

'Hi, Ellie.' I can hear the smile in Jane's voice as I pick up the phone. 'Are you bored yet?'

'How did you know? Oh God, Jane, I'm having one of those days, dithering about, and it's driving me mad.'

'Well then, are you up for visitors yet?'

'Oh, definitely,' I say, laughing. 'How soon can you get here? Not that I'm desperate or anything.'

'It's that sort of day, isn't it? Bloody rain. Now I don't want you to think that I'm checking up on you or that I'm going to make a nuisance of myself, constantly turning up on your doorstep.'

'Jane! How could I ever think that? Stop being so considerate and just come on over,' I laugh.

I check my watch: it's a quarter to eleven. All thoughts of painting go out of my head as I check my stock of cooking ingredients, which I know are practically non-existent. I'll definitely make shortbread, but what else? I've only got a small amount of ordinary flour, and no rice flour at all. Caster sugar, but no soft brown. No fruit either. I scribble a quick list to cover most possibilities, snatch up my mac and hunt for my bag. I just hope that the village shop will have what I need.

I actually can't remember the last time I did any baking, and yet I used to do it all the time when I was younger, before I met Robbie. It became a bit of a standing joke amongst family and friends – whatever the occasion, be it life, death or anything in between, there I would be, bearing shortbread. I put it down to it being one of the first things I ever learned to make and to my mother having taught me never to go visiting empty-handed.

I check the dial on the Aga; the line is bang on the black – perfect. I'll pop a couple more logs in when I get back. I think of Will then. We've not spoken since I blundered into his house two days ago, and perhaps because I'm still feeling guilty about losing my temper, he pops into my head with disconcerting regularity – particularly those eyes.

I had been woken in the night by the sound of the rhythmic chopping of logs again but had found it rather soothing, oddly. This morning I noticed my woodpile had been replenished, although I don't know when, and yesterday a bucket of kindling had been left by the back door. Of Will, however, there had been no sign, not even when I knocked on his door, so my thanks have been left unsaid. He seems to spend the entire day outdoors, as lights only appear in the big house about seven o'clock, even though it gets dark much earlier now.

I drag my thoughts back to the present and away from what is none of my business. My horizons have simply narrowed over the last few days, I conclude. The Lodge is tucked behind the estate boundary wall, and I can see nothing of the village beyond, so it's natural that Rowan Hill and its occupant have been on my mind. I pull the door shut behind me, make a dash for the car and am gone.

The village shop is something of a surprise. I was expecting a rather tired and dusty selection of cornflakes, tinned peaches and packets of Whitworth's split peas. Instead, although half of the shop caters for traditional needs, the other half is a rather glamorous delicatessen-cum-bakery, with bowls of juicy olives with feta cheese, and a honey-and-sunflower-seed loaf that found its way into my basket, though I had no need for it. There is a reassuring hum of conversation from the till at the front that allows me to browse unpressured.

I stop in front of a wide island offering a beautiful selection of fruit and vegetables, and my eye is caught by a red cabbage with suede-like leaves so dark that they're almost black. Braised cabbage is one of my favourites. I find some Bramleys too, which settles the matter of what to make today – apple cake. Having gathered together the other bits I need, I make my way to the till, where two older women are deep in conversation with a third, slightly younger, whom I assume to be the owner. She is propped on a stool behind the counter, elbows resting on its surface, a mug of something steaming gently beside her.

She straightens up when she sees me and smiles, flashing her other customers a warning. The lady nearest me is clutching a box of eggs and turns slightly, also smiling, rather apologetically, I think, leaving the third customer to carry on talking, unabashed. I see that it's Alice Tweedy, from the tea room, her voice loud and strident.

'Well, if it makes them lower their prices, I'm all for it. Do them good to come down to our level. Flitting about with all those fancy restaurants is giving them nothing but an inflated opinion of themselves, if you ask me, and we're the ones that are paying for it.'

I hold back, not wanting to interrupt and, if I'm honest, not wishing to become embroiled in village politics, but the woman behind the counter holds out her arms for my basket, and I have no choice but to move forward. Not getting any reply, Alice falls silent and finally turns, fixing me with an appraising look that I find rather unnerving.

'Morning, love,' says the shopkeeper. 'Let me take those from you.'

I hand over my basket, returning her smile as I watch my items being added up and wait for the predictable statement that I know is coming, sooner or later. Two, three items go through, and then:

'Just moved in, have you, love?'

'Oh yes, on Monday.'

'How are you finding things?' And then without waiting for a reply, 'Nasty day, very gloomy, isn't it?'

I hate being asked two questions at once because I never know which one to answer first, so I settle for a 'Really good, thanks' and leave it at that.

'Not that I'm going to turn down a sale, but you could have hopped over the wall for these,' she says, brandishing the Bramleys, all three of them in one hand. I haven't a clue what she's talking about.

'I'm sorry?'

'The apples, love. They're from the estate. You could have nipped out the back gate in your garden and had a few while Mr McLennan was out doing whatever it is that he does.'

'Oh, I see,' I say, at a loss and not sure how to answer. I give a sort of half laugh, nodding my head for good measure. Mrs Tweedy, who has been scanning the contents of my basket, gives a triumphant snort.

'Serve him bloody right, that would, the silly man. I get mine for free, dear. I keep telling him to cut the branches down or lose his apples, but he won't listen. Half of them hang down right into my garden – and take the light from my herbaceous border, I might add. It's only fair; I've given him enough warning – isn't that right, Mrs Sullivan?'

The shopkeeper nods her head a fraction. 'I expect so, Mrs Tweedy, yes.'

My heart is sinking fast as I realise that my initial suspicions are correct; all three of these women clearly know exactly who I am and where I live, and not only that, but the tweed-clad OAP from hell just happens to live next door. Good job there's a nice brick wall at the end of my garden.

'Perhaps he doesn't mind you having the apples,' I venture, feeling somewhat inclined to stick up for Will. Mrs Tweedy is staring at me as if I'm deranged.

'Well, he should mind. It's no way to run a business. All that land and what does he do with it? Nothing. Lets it all go to pot. When I was first married, I used to go to the farm for all manner of things, and those were bad times then, just after the war. The farm kept the village going, and William – that's his father, God rest his soul – always had a kind word and a smile for everyone. He'd turn in his grave now, that poor man would.'

The egg-box lady to my left gives a wistful sigh. 'Well, it's true, Alice; I agree with you there. He's certainly not the man his father was.'

'No gentleman at all,' retorts Alice, leaning in. 'Or so I've heard. My husband was the local doctor, dear,' she adds for my benefit, 'and while Charles would never divulge a patient's confidence, you can't help but pick up the odd thing. Mr McLennan's wife was such a charming girl, really quite lovely, but very unhappy, I think. Desperate to have a child, but he wouldn't give her one, apparently. Such a sad business.'

I can feel my breath begin to hiss behind my teeth as I try to take in all this new information. 'Infertility is a very difficult and personal subject. I'm not sure it's right to—'

'Oh, I didn't say he *couldn't* give her a child; rather more that he *wouldn't*,' she says in a knowing fashion. 'Too busy *elsewhere*.'

I should have just paid for my things and left. I've practically goaded the woman on, and now look at the smug, satisfied look on her face. Christ, I only came into the shop for a few bits, and in the space of five minutes I've ended up discussing the intimate details of Will's marriage and a wife I didn't even know existed.

What is wrong with me? I can feel an ugly red flush creeping up my neck. I am mortified. What on earth will Will think when he finds out what we've been discussing? I need to get out of here as fast as possible. The longer I stay, the more I'm going to get embroiled in their gossip. I mutter something non-committal about not actually knowing Will all that well and pay for my shopping as quickly as I can. I practically run from the shop.

It's still raining and I've only gone a couple of steps when I realise that I need to repack my bag if my flour and sugar are going to make it home in this weather. I'm juggling apples and flour when I hear the shop door open behind me. I want the ground to swallow me up. Anything to avoid enduring another round with Mrs Tweedy.

'Didn't you want your cabbage, then?' comes the accusing tone. Typical. I can see that I'm going to have to brazen this out.

'Oh, sorry, I hadn't even realised I'd left it behind,' I reply, feigning foolishness. 'And I can't even blame it on being blonde, can I?'

For a couple of seconds, I think I might even get away with my pathetic attempt at levity, but then I realise that Mrs Tweedy is staring very hard at my hair, which has probably grown to twice its normal size in this weather. A hand holds out the cabbage.

'Have you spoken to Mr McLennan yet?'

'Oh yes, he's been very neighbourly,' I affirm, realising that he has.

'Well, a word to the wise. Don't be getting any clever ideas about him, will you?'

'I'm sorry, I'm not sure that I understand,' I say, trying to juggle the cabbage now as well.

'You young women are all the same. A single man in a big house and you all think you'll be the one to change his ways. Well, his wife never could, and she was something very special.'

At this point I drop the bag of flour. Mrs Tweedy, if she even noticed, has gone.

The bag has split down the middle, pouring a white drift onto the toe of my boot and across the pavement. I stare at it for a moment, unseeing. I'm not sure how long it is before I realise that someone is speaking to me.

'Are you okay? Vile old bat. Sorry, I couldn't help overhearing.'

I look to the new face in front of me. There's long blonde hair, a dimple and the sudden warmth of a smile. 'Here, I've got a carrier bag somewhere. Don't worry – it's clean. I always keep one in my pocket as a pooper scooper, but I haven't used it yet.'

I must give her a confused look. 'No dog today,' she adds in explanation. 'Couldn't face the wet smell in the house all afternoon.' And with that she bends and scoops up the flour bag, incredibly managing to retain some of its contents, and hands it to me, smiling.

'God, you're really not okay, are you?' she asks, realising it's not just rain streaming down my cheeks.

'I don't even know Will,' I falter, the necessity for speech finally kick-starting my brain into gear. 'I'm sorry – I don't know why I'm crying. I've only just moved here, and I don't know anyone yet. Well, I've met Will, but I don't know him, and I've only just met Mrs Tweedy. I can't believe the things she was saying.'

'Yes, well,' came the reply with a warm smile, 'that's her forte, I'm afraid – spreading vicious gossip. I'm not sure why. I haven't lived in the village for long, but it would seem she never used to be like that. Her husband suffered from dementia, I believe, and most people seem to think she's going the same way. I just try to keep out of her way; that way at least it's not me in the firing line.'

'I've just moved in next door to her,' I whisper.

'Ah,' comes the sympathetic reply. 'Look, why don't you come back to mine for a cuppa? I was on my way home anyway, and I've got a chap in at the moment doing my kitchen. I need an excuse not to hover.'

'I can't, really. It's very kind of you, but I think I should just get home and sort myself out.'

'It's no problem, honestly. Besides, I'm guessing you won't want to go back in there just now, and I can lend you some flour too, if you like.'

Jane isn't coming until about one thirty, so I've still got time. 'Thanks then.' I smile. 'That would be lovely. I'm Ellie, by the way.'

'I'm Helen,' she answers. 'It's good to meet you, Ellie.'

I've more or less pulled myself together by the time we near Helen's house, but it would seem to be a day for surprises. Beside the church, we turn up a little lane that I hadn't even noticed before. There's a white picket fence at the end of the lane, flanked by two ancient horse chestnut trees just waiting to be plundered, and then a beautiful sweep of a drive. At its end is an impressive and very handsome house of welcoming red brick. This is not a small house, but reassuringly there are children's toys on the front lawn. I have to bite back the low whistle that is trying to escape.

'I was wondering if your husband was the vicar when we turned down past the church . . . but I guess not.'

'He's a brain surgeon, actually,' she says, catching sight of the stunned look on my face. 'Well, in fact, he's a consultant neurosurgeon, which amounts to the same thing.' She laughs. 'Come on in.'

We enter through a door around the side into what should probably be described as a boot room. It holds an array of shoes, wellies, coats and the detritus of a busy life. From here we cross a huge hallway and enter the kitchen, at one end of which is a living room–cum–playroom, with toys on the floor and easy chairs, beside which stacks of books pile high. There are photos everywhere, both in this room and throughout the hallway, mainly of Helen's children, but also of her and her husband (whose name, I learn, is

Tom), Tom by himself or with the children, or all of them in large groups with lots of other laughing, happy people. If I am surprised by the size and grandeur of Helen's house, I am consoled by its unpretentious quality. It's warm and friendly, like its owner.

We settle in the kitchen, the builder chap evidently elsewhere, while Helen busies herself with the kettle. A Great Dane, stretched out on the floor in front of a range, gives a polite 'woof' as I look around me. The kitchen is gorgeous. I'm not quite sure whether this is the 'before' or the 'after,' but either way I'd be quite happy to replace my collection of bookcases and baskets with this.

'This is really very kind of you,' I begin. 'I'm not quite sure what happened back there.' I am, of course, but this is neither the time nor the place.

'Look, don't worry about it; it happens to us all sometimes. I've got over it now, but when I first had the children, I used to burst into tears all the time. I've embarrassed myself and complete strangers on countless occasions. Moving is such a stressful time, and I don't suppose being on the receiving end of Mrs Tweedy's brand of wisdom has helped you to feel settled. I've only been here six months, but it's a nice village. I hope you'll like it once you settle in.'

'I'm sure I will. It's very pretty. I'm from Cambridge, so all these hills are a bit of a novelty to me, but it's a beautiful part of the country. I have friends who live over by the Stiperstones . . . that's why I've moved up, really.' I pull a strand of hair thoughtfully through my fingers. 'I'm house-sitting for them for a while.'

'Are you up at the Lodge, then?' queries Helen, placing a mug in front of me. 'Is that why Mrs Tweedy was asking you about Will?'

I wait for her to join me before I reply, nodding an affirmative. 'I moved in on Monday, and I've only met Will the once. Well, that's not strictly true, but I didn't know he was married. All the women were talking about him, saying he was . . . well, they weren't exactly being very complimentary.'

Helen pushes a jug of milk towards me, together with a sugar bowl. 'I can imagine. I don't really know him either. In fact I could count on one hand the number of times I've seen him. I think he's very quiet, that's all. Supposedly it's his fault his wife left, but you never know, do you, what goes on in people's lives?'

'No, I guess not,' I reply slowly, trying to ignore the prickling in my nose and taking a sip of the hot tea, one of the best diversionary tactics I know.

'Listen, do you fancy a biscuit?' asks Helen, beautifully changing the subject. 'I've got a secret stash that the kids haven't found yet.'

After I leave Helen's with the promised bag of flour, I spend the rest of the morning baking like a thing possessed; partly so that everything will be ready when Jane arrives and partly so I won't have to think about the implications of my conversation in the village shop. It doesn't work, of course. I feel extremely uncomfortable knowing things about Will that he hasn't told me himself, especially since he had made reference to being 'fucked up' during our last conversation. I resolve never to mention what I've learned to anyone and to run in the opposite direction if I see Mrs Tweedy any time soon.

Jane arrives promptly, as usual, demanding the grand tour. 'It'll be a tour, Jane, not a grand tour. I really haven't done that much yet.'

'Hmm, maybe.' Jane smiles, knowing me better than that, and she shoves me out of the kitchen and into the lounge. 'Oh, this is lovely! What a beautiful screen,' she exclaims, crossing to the fireplace. 'Is it new?'

'To me, yes,' I reply. 'It was a housewarming present from my neighbour. He has several, apparently, so didn't need this one, which I find hard to believe, but still, it's beautiful, isn't it?'

'Gorgeous,' agrees Jane. 'I love proper fires.'

'And do you want to know what's really weird?'

'What?'

'You'll never guess who my new neighbour is.'

'I dunno – Julian Clary?'

'What?' I say, pulling a face.

'Sorry, first name that came into my head. Okay, I give up – who is it?'

'It's the guy from a year ago, the one that helped me when I had my accident.'

'What, Will? The one you couldn't stop going on about, he of *"the bluest eyes I've ever seen, Jane"*?'

'Okay, okay. I may have mentioned him once or twice, but in my defence I was in a lot of pain at the time. It's a bit of a spooky coincidence, though, don't you think?'

'Perhaps it's fate . . .' she trails off, smirking. 'But I thought you said he was a teacher. How did he get to be living on an estate like this?'

'I know,' I say, nodding. 'Not what you'd expect, is it? It's the family home; he doesn't teach now, just looks after the estate, apparently.'

'Yeah, I bet he does,' says Jane, rolling her eyes and tipping her head on one side. 'Bet he's married too.'

'Nope. He was, but not anymore.'

'And how do you know that?' Jane teases.

'Village gossip.' I take in her expression and shake my head. 'It's not good news, though. His wife left him quite recently, I think – well, since my accident.'

'You've spoken to him already, though?'

I nod, biting my lip. 'Actually I stormed into his house and accused him of trespassing, although I didn't know about his wife then. I'd been out, you see, and when I came back, someone had been in here and lit the fire and stuff, and I went a bit mad at him . . . I'm not sure why, really.'

'Oh, Ellie,' sighs Jane.

'We both got off on the wrong foot, but after that he was quite friendly. He showed me how to use the Aga too.'

'So don't worry about it. Just try and be a good neighbour. If it's a bad time for him as well, I expect he'll be keeping a low profile.'

'I know. Well I can't say anything about his wife. I mean he'll know I heard it in the village, and then he'll think I was gossiping about him, which I wasn't. I was set upon by this real old battleaxe who took great delight in telling me that he cheated on her . . .' I clap a hand over my mouth. 'Oh God, I can't believe I just said that. I swore to myself I wouldn't repeat it. Come on, let me show you upstairs before I say anything else I shouldn't.'

Back in the kitchen once more, I slide the kettle onto the hotplate to boil and bring out my offerings. 'Shortbread or apple cake?' I ask.

'Grief, Ellie, do I look like I haven't eaten for a week?' Jane grins, pointing at her rounded stomach.

I shake my head. 'Doesn't matter – not with cake. You know that saying – *"All things in moderation"*? Well, it doesn't apply to cakes; I know that for a fact. Doesn't apply to biscuits either, or Pringles for that matter.'

Jane's smile is wry. 'You're sure you're not making that up? Only I'm sure I've heard that things like this are laden with calories. It might be an old wives' tale, though.'

'Cross my heart. Anyway, if you're worried about that, just break one open and give it a shake; everyone knows that all the calories fall out then.'

It's nearly four by the time Jane goes, the dismal weather not having abated for a minute. It gets dark early now, and it's comforting to close the curtains against the rain. I catch a noise outside the window: more logs being dropped off. I cross to the door, flicking on the outside light, and pull it open.

'Will?' I call, trying to see beyond the pool of light that has thrown everything beyond it into relative darkness. A figure steps forward.

'Sorry,' says the voice, coming nearer. 'I didn't mean to disturb you.'

I can see that it's him, now. 'No, that's okay – I wanted to ask you something anyway. Would you mind coming in for a minute?' I hold the door open for him. 'God, aren't you cold?' I burst out, seeing his bare arms in just a T-shirt. Blue, like his eyes.

'No, I've been chopping logs,' he says with a slight smile, leaving me feeling stupid.

I forget what I was going to say and stumble over my words, finally managing to mumble, 'Look, sorry, I . . . er . . . wanted to ask you something about the logs. I know you said you didn't want anything for them, but I must pay you. I'm going through them like crazy.'

'They come with the house, always have,' he says simply.

'But that's not right, surely?'

'They're my logs. If I choose to give them to you, that's my decision. I don't want paying for them, I told you.' He thrusts his hands into the back pockets of his jeans, with a look that is not far off a glare. Our light-hearted conversation has stumbled off pitch somehow.

I try again, wincing inwardly when I hear my voice, which comes out sounding overly formal and polite.

'Well, that's very kind of you. Can I at least give you a thank-you gift in return? I made this earlier; I thought you might like it.'

I pick up the apple cake, still whole. 'It's an apple cake,' I say rather unnecessarily. 'I bought the apples from the village shop but was told they were from the estate, so hopefully it'll taste good.'

Will doesn't reply, merely nods and takes the cake with an odd little smirk. Unsettled, I babble on. 'In fact, the lady in the shop said I should have pinched them!'

I realise that I want to make Will smile, but he doesn't.

'You can have apples if you want them. Go and help yourself.'

'Oh, I didn't mean that,' I exclaim. 'That wasn't why I said it.'

'Why did you then?' he says, staring at me hard.

'I don't know,' I reply, flustered. 'It was just a comment; I didn't mean anything by it. Your other neighbour was there, Mrs Tweedy, and she joined in as well. Actually, she was rather rude. I thought it was a bit off, that's all.'

'I see.'

'Well, them discussing you like that – it didn't seem fair.'

Oh, for Pete's sake, Ellie, get your foot out of your mouth, I groan inwardly.

'And?' I have the distinct impression that I'm being toyed with.

'Doesn't it bother you what people are saying?'

Will drops his head for a moment and then looks up at me squarely. 'Not particularly, no.' He swallows. I can see his Adam's apple moving up and down.

'Well, sorry, but I'd mind if it were me being accused of chucking away my business. I mean, can't you prove them wrong and make cider or something?'

'Can you make cider out of cooking apples?'

'Jesus, I don't know,' I retort, angry now.

'Listen, I appreciate your concern, if that's what you call joining in with the village gossip,' says Will stiffly, 'but to be honest, I don't give a shit. If they're talking about me, at least they're leaving some other poor bastard alone. I haven't got the time or the inclination to don a pinny and make the whole village apple crumble just to prove a point. I've got more important things to do.'

He takes a step backwards. 'Thanks for the cake.'

I watch him go, abject misery flowing over me. 'Sod your bloody apples then,' I mutter at his retreating back. 'And sod you.'

Will raises a hand as if in acknowledgement, his back still towards me. 'When you change your mind, you're still very welcome to my apples.'

CHAPTER FIVE

The next day is amazingly bright and sunny, a perfect autumnal morning, full of delicious industry and optimism. Despite a distinct lack of sleep, I'm down the stairs early, determined that the thoughts that kept me up half the night will not be allowed to invade today as well. They'll still be there tonight, when I can brood on them at my leisure, after all. The kitchen is flooded with sunlight, blissfully warm and ripe for painting.

I pick up my log basket and go to fill it. On top of the pile outside, two small branches have been nailed together to form a cross, which has been pushed between the logs to stay in an upright position. A piece of paper has been pinned to it.

Cake was delicious – will don pinny immediately. I'm sorry. Will.

I walk back inside slowly, where I place the message down on the table. I don't know whether to smile or frown. Grumpy bastard one minute and purveyor of random acts of kindness the next. I look down at the note again, acknowledging the apology and the courage it took to make it, especially as the reason for it was my fault. Hell, he even likes my cake, unless he's just being polite. A voice comes from behind me then.

'Knock-knock?' It's Will, carrying the basket of logs I hadn't even realised I'd left outside.

'Were you spying on me?' I ask with a grin.

'No, no. Absolutely not . . . Well, alright then, yes, but only a little bit. I wanted to see if you got my note.'

'I did, yes,' I reply, turning around to pick up his message. 'Interesting analogy that, being nailed to a cross. Now which one of us is that supposed to be, do you think?'

Will ruffles the front of his hair. 'Christ, that's a bit deep for me this early in the morning. There's me thinking it was just two twigs bashed together, but now that you mention it, I can see my inner voice at work.'

'Mine kept me up half the night. It's me who needs to apologise. Somehow what I wanted to say didn't quite come out right.' I pull at a tendril of hair, running it through my fingers. It seems to mesmerise Will, and I wonder whether to go on. The silence between us is growing.

'You don't have to explain, Ellie, you really don't,' says Will gently. 'I'm sorry I went off the deep end, and I shouldn't have bitten your head off. I meant what I said about the cake too.' He takes a deep breath. 'So I'd be pleased if you'd come and take however many apples you want, any time, as long as you promise to keep me supplied with the proceeds. I could get used to coffee and cake for breakfast.'

I smile to show my consent and finally relax. I feel as though the air between us has been cleared.

Will comes and places the basket in front of the Aga, pops open the door and carefully places another couple of logs inside. It seems as familiar to him as drawing breath, and I remember how he'd come every day to check on Netty and lay the fires for her.

'Do you want the other room lit yet? I could do it for you, if you like.'

'I was popping out, actually, so thanks, but I'll do it later.'

'Sure.' He gives a quick glance at his watch. 'I must be off too. The day's too good to waste, isn't it?'

Muddy pea green is hard to suppress, but after three and a half hours of solid painting the (now cream-coloured) kitchen is beginning to breathe easier. The light looks like it wants to flow into the room now, and as I sit nursing a cup of tea and a brownie, a sense of real contentment steals over me. It's not a feeling I've been used to experiencing much lately, but I'm encouraged that I can still recognise its warm hug.

I pull the tin of brownies towards me, totting them up: there are six left, so definitely no more for me. I thought I'd pop them around to Helen to thank her for the flour – and, more importantly, the friendly face – yesterday.

It's as I'm walking through the village that I realise my timing is off. Just after three o'clock is simply the middle of the afternoon for me, but as the bustle of pushchairs, mums and children navigate around me, I realise that school has just finished.

I'm just rehearsing what to say that will make it clear to Helen that I'm not expecting to stay, when her door is yanked open and two boys race past me at speed. Helen's voice echoes behind them with a caution to keep track of time, and something about a barn and doors, as she follows to close the open door.

'Ellie, hi!' she exclaims, spotting me lurking, 'Come on in.'

'Thanks, Helen. I just popped round to bring you some brownies as a thank-you for yesterday. I know it's a busy time, so I won't keep you.'

Helen waves an airy hand, eyeing the tin. 'Oh, the boys will be gone until teatime; its conker-collecting season.' She practically drags me inside. 'Actually, it's quite possible that you've saved my life – I'm starving. That's the absolutely worst thing about having a builder in your kitchen; I mean how many biscuits can you legitimately eat in a day without looking like a massive greedy pig? I keep offering him some, but either he's too polite or too self-restrained, because he only ever has one a day, and it's driving me nuts. Come on, I'll put the kettle on.'

We cross the kitchen and go out into the hallway, Helen leading me towards a more formal sitting room at the back of the house. Part of it, she explains, was originally an old and rather battered garden room. When she and her husband, Tom, were renovating the house, they'd planned to have it removed for safety reasons, as most of the glass had gone. Instead, I can see how, with extraordinary vision, they knocked down the wall between the rooms and merged the two together, extending the overall size by about a third. The end result is a room that has nearly one whole wall of glass. The effect is simply beautiful, with the garden becoming part of the room's decor.

Incredible though it is, this isn't what takes my breath away. The room itself is full of texture, with a polished wood floor almost covered with an enormous earthy-coloured wool rug. The curtains are heavy and a contrast to the pale lemon walls. Three squishy sofas encircle the room, all different, but all striking the same eclectic tone. Along one wall, however, facing the garden, is the biggest wall hanging I have ever seen. It's a tapestry, but with an intricacy of stitching and colour that I've never seen before, and it grabs my attention just as surely as if it had reached out and touched me.

The design is abstract and it draws me in, my eyes following first one colour and nuance before being captured by another and led off in a different direction. I step closer and then back away, each angle providing something new. It is one of the most stunning pieces of art I have ever seen. I stand and stare, open-mouthed in wonder.

'This is beautiful, Helen,' I breathe. 'Where did you get it?' I ask, thinking that wherever it is, I'll rush straight there to buy one, if I can afford it.

'Oh, sign of a misspent youth. I was a very bored nanny for quite a few years. I had a tiny room with no telly, and there are only so many books you can read.'

'What?' I say, stunned, looking at Helen's impassive face. 'Are you telling me that you made this, all by hand? It must have taken you ages!'

'I suppose it did, really, on and off for about three years. It started as a Kaffe Fassett design that I found in an old library book, but the pattern was so mind numbing to follow that I sort of wandered off.' She walks over to me. 'It's actually two pieces joined together, if you look carefully. I was planning to make a huge floor cushion, but I never really knew what to do with it; it was Tom who suggested we put it up here.'

I stare at Helen's face as she views her work; she is clearly undecided about whether or not it should even be upon this wall. 'Helen, I'm not kidding. This is one of the most amazing pieces of art I've ever seen, and I'm not just being polite.'

Her face registers disbelief. 'But I did this ages ago. It's not really . . . well, it's not like I did it professionally or anything. It was just a bit of a hobby, nothing special. I haven't done anything else in years.' Her voice trails off, and I realise that an air of reticence has crept into it.

'But why did you stop?' I ask, and then, seeing Helen's shrug, add, 'I mean, did something else come along?'

Helen continues to stare at the wall hanging for a few moments more. 'I dunno, really. Life? Sort of gets in the way sometimes, doesn't it?' There's a flat tone to her voice that I recognize as sadness at the loss of a once-held dream. I need to tread carefully. She smiles again, almost by way of apology.

'Anyway, I'm still starving, so come on out with the brownies, and you can tell me how you're settling in. Not had any more fearsome encounters, I hope?'

I think back to my conversation with Will that morning and smile.

'No, no more immediate dramas, but I painted my kitchen this morning – well, made a start on it anyway, so I'm beginning to make headway, I think. The house needs a bit of work, so I'm expecting to be busy for a while.'

'And you've moved up from Cambridge, did you say? Was it a job move or something?'

I can feel the 'or something' hovering right in front of my face, and it takes me a second or two to answer.

Helen puts her brownie back down on her plate. 'I'm sorry. I didn't mean to pry; just tell me to mind my own business.'

'No, it's okay,' I begin. 'It's just a bit of a long story, that's all, and I'm not sure anyone needs to hear the gory details,' I finish, trying to smile.

Helen's reply is a warm dimpling of her cheeks. 'Oh, we've all got a long story in there somewhere, haven't we? And if my experience is anything to go by, almost all of them involve a man. You don't have to say another word, Ellie – not if you don't want to.' She motions to her plate then, adding, 'These are extraordinarily good, by the way.'

I'm grateful for her momentary diversion, which buys me a little more time.

'It's not that. It's just that I don't quite know how to begin this conversation. Do you know Little Fordham?'

'Not that well, but I buy my veg at the farm there, when I can. They have the most amazing shop – it's just before you get to the village.'

I know exactly where she means; after all I skidded to a halt just yards from its door. I nod. 'Well, about a year ago, I was driving through there on the way to visit my friends, and my car ran off the road – a bloody pheasant ran across the road in front of me – and I ended up in the ditch. A local chap came to my rescue and stayed with me the whole time until the ambulance came. I was in a lot of pain, probably more than I thought, because when they finally carted me off to hospital, all I could remember was that he had the most incredible blue eyes.'

Helen flaps her hand at me. 'Don't tell me, let me guess – he rode off into the sunset, you never saw him again and now you've come back to find him?' she exclaims wildly, her mouth open to carry on, before I jump in.

'Oh no, I've found him, but . . .'

'Sorry – just ignore me. I read far too many chick-lit novels, and my grasp on romantic reality is pretty slender.'

'Well, that's the weird thing. I didn't come up here to find him at all, but it's quite spooky, really: I've just moved in next door to him.'

Helen almost chokes. 'What – Will, you mean? Will McLennan is your knight in shining armour? I don't believe it!'

'I wouldn't put it quite like that, but I—'

A sudden noise from the doorway causes us both to look up.

'Ben!' I exclaim in surprise. 'I didn't know you were here.'

Helen looks incredulously from one to the other of us. 'What? You know him as well?'

'Yes . . . well, not really. We met the other week on a first aid course. You said you were working locally – didn't you, Ben? But I didn't know it was here. God, what are the chances of that?'

Ben has not said a word, but his eyes don't leave my face, and it shocks me suddenly to see the expression in his dark eyes.

'Are you okay . . . Ben?'

Helen sees it too. 'God, you're white as a sheet. What is it? Has something happened? Are you hurt?'

He drags his eyes away from me very slowly and rubs a hand over his face before turning to Helen. His mouth is working, but seconds tick by before the question comes. 'You mentioned a name just now; what was it?'

Helen looks to me in confusion and then back at Ben. 'Will, do you mean – Will McLennan?'

'Yeah, that's the one, that's what I thought you said.' His eyes are back on me. 'He lives locally, does he?'

'Just up the road, yes. Why? Is something wrong?'

The colour has returned a little to Ben's cheeks. 'No, nothing wrong. Just someone I used to know, that's all.' He gives a vague smile, his eyes flicking to mine. 'Sorry – I should get on. I just popped in to ask if it was okay for me to take a drink now.'

Helen smiles warmly. 'Ben, you don't need to ask; just help yourself. There's even a brownie left, if you want one. Ellie made them.'

Ben looks at me as if he's just been offered a grenade. 'Thanks, but I'm okay.' He swallows. 'I'll just get a quick drink and be away once I've tidied up, if that's okay. The light's gone now.' He hesitates for a moment. 'I'm sorry to interrupt,' he finishes, and backs out of the room.

Helen waits a moment or two to make sure he's out of earshot, before whispering, 'God, Ellie, whatever's the matter with him?'

I'm shaking my head in bemusement. 'I have absolutely no idea,' I whisper back.

'Perhaps you need to have a chat with your knight in shining armour and find out what's so mysterious.'

'I think I'll leave well alone. Life's been far too complicated recently.'

'You were just about to say why you came up this way. It wasn't because of Will, then?'

I shake my head vehemently. 'No – running away from a man – rather than running after one.' I pull a face at her before continuing. 'After my accident I rang my partner to let him know what had happened, but his mobile was switched off, so I rang the office of his client, where I knew he was working. Apparently, he was working from home that day . . .'

I think Helen can sense what's coming next; I can see it on her face. 'And yeah, when I rang the number, I got to speak to his wife.'

'No! You didn't know he was married?'

'Helen, we'd been together for six years. He got married to this woman eighteen months ago, about six months before my accident. Their daughter was born around the same time.'

'Oh my God, what an utter shit!' Her hand flies to her mouth. 'And you didn't have any idea that any of this was going on?'

'Sounds crazy, doesn't it? But no. No idea at all. He's an account manager for a big communications firm that has clients all over the world. It's one of the reasons we never got married – because he spent so much time away. He always said he wanted to carry on for a few years while he was flying high, and then he'd change jobs so we could settle down. I never questioned it, stupidly, but then it never occurred to me that I should. One of his main clients was in Edinburgh. He keeps a flat there, and that's where his wife and child are.'

'And don't tell me: another of his big clients is in Cambridge where you lived?'

I don't need to answer.

'And he truly thought he could get away with that? I was thinking what a clever man he was to be able to keep up that kind of pretence, but he's not clever at all, is he? Quite the opposite in fact.'

'Trouble is, he was getting away with it. If I hadn't had my accident, God knows how long it would have been before I found out. You know the worst thing was that when I confronted him, somehow it was all my fault. *I* was the reason he felt the need to keep a flat in Edinburgh. I was too grasping, too interfering, apparently. I'll spare you all the gory details, but needless to say, that wasn't my interpretation of it at all.'

'Oh Ellie . . . But you would have found out, at some point, I'm sure of that. I'm so sorry – what an awful thing to have to go through. I don't blame you for wanting to move away.'

'Now you know why I'm just after a quiet life at the moment. Somewhere to lick my wounds – and definitely no romantic entanglements.'

The warm smile returns. 'Well, you must come and talk to me, any time.'

I nod gratefully. 'I'm doing okay, I think. I mean, I managed to tell you without bursting into tears.' I grimace. 'The split wasn't pleasant at all, but I'm determined to make a new start here.'

'Good for you. I mean it – pop round any time you want to, especially if you need someone to save you from eating all the brownies yourself.'

'I will, thanks,' I laugh, grateful to her for lightening the mood. 'Anyway, I'd better get going.' A flash of colour hits the corner of my eye, and I remember what I wanted to ask her. 'Listen, Helen, the Lodge needs some serious cheering up . . . would you be willing to do a wall hanging for me?'

Helen stares at me incredulously.

'I mean, I'll pay you for it, of course.'

'I'm not sure what to say,' she replies, obviously at a loss. 'It's not really something I've ever thought about.'

'Well, I mean it. I'm not sure where I'd put it yet, but I really would like one of your pieces.'

A derisory noise echoes around the room.

'Seriously . . . people will part with huge sums of money to get their hands on exclusive pieces like yours. When I lived in

Cambridge, there were quite a few galleries there where you didn't ask the price of what was on display. I bet there are places around here where the same is true.'

'I haven't worked on anything in a long time, Ellie. I'm not sure I could anymore.'

'But you'd like to try?' I prompt.

'Maybe.' And then, with much more conviction, 'Yes. I think I would. I've even got some old pieces still up in the loft, if you wanted to look at those some time.'

'I would, yes, but as I'm all for new beginnings at the moment, I think I'd like to commission you to make something completely from scratch.'

'I'm not sure,' says Helen cautiously. 'It will take a long time.'

'That's okay. I won't go for something huge, I promise. And only on one condition.'

'Which is?'

'That I pay you the going rate,' I say, grinning.

Helen doesn't reply, but she's smiling.

CHAPTER SIX

October

October arrives with a cold, clear snap that sharpens the senses and makes your blood rush around in a glad-to-be-alive kind of way. The sky stays blue for days. The trees sing with burnished hues of gold, red and orange, and on the hills the dying bracken takes on the colour of fire with the sinking sun.

The grass is crisp underfoot this morning, and my feet lay a trail across the lacy white frosting. I walk most days – not far, but long enough that my cheeks turn rosy with the cold and my fingers long for a warm mug of tea to hug.

This morning I return to find a visitor on my step, mysteriously bearing a long cylindrical object wrapped in brown paper. I've seen Helen a few times in the last couple of weeks, but there's something different about her today, and it's not just the new hairdo she's sporting.

We peel off our outer layers and dump them on the kitchen table. Helen places her package carefully beside them. I give her a long look.

'I love your hair; it really suits you shorter.'

Helen twists the ends of her beautifully cut chiselled bob. 'Thanks. I thought it was time I changed one or two things. My hair has been the same since I was about six and a half, or it feels that way. I took the plunge – scared the hell out of my husband.'

'Didn't you tell him you were having it done?'

'Well, I did, but normally that just means half an inch off the bottom. Actually, it scared the hell out of me as well.'

'It's worth it, though – definitely. Very brave of you. So, any more surprises in store for me?' I ask, eyeing up the package.

'Hmm, maybe.' Helen's smile twinkles as she shoves me out of the kitchen and into the lounge. 'Is this the fire screen that you were telling me about?'

We chat about all manner of things over an impromptu lunch: Helen's children, my plans for the house, Helen's upcoming annual skiing holiday, the beautiful weather, until, as I bring out some cake for pudding, I can bear it no longer.

'Right then – no changing the subject – what's all the mystery about?'

'Mystery?' asks Helen, feigning ignorance.

'Yeah, all this "*I just wanted to change one or two things.*" There is something about you that's different – you're like a giddy schoolgirl. Besides which, you're not leaving here today until you tell me what's in that parcel,' I demand.

Helen looks like she's going to explode with the effort of keeping whatever it is bottled up inside her, but with supreme effort she manages to speak relatively calmly.

She explains that she has had an epiphany. Something that she'd been denying herself for many years, without really knowing why, had suddenly became blindingly obvious to her. The week after we spoke about her wall hanging, she went up to the attic to look at some of her old needlework books, thinking that she might look through them for some inspiration.

'To be honest, Ellie, I was getting a bit worried about making the wall hanging for you. Every time I began to think about what

I'd agreed to do, the enormity of the whole thing seemed almost overwhelming.' Taking in my concerned expression, she continues, 'Oh, don't worry – it has a happy ending.' She takes a tiny nibble of cake and carries on. 'So I was standing in the living room, staring at the hanging, when Tom came in and asked me what I was thinking. I had already told him about making something for you, and so I explained how I was feeling, and he said to me, "Do you know what I'm thinking?"'

Seeing Helen begin to grow flushed with excitement again, I egg her on. 'And what was he thinking?'

'He told me that I was still the most amazing woman he'd ever met, and he'd never understood why I'd stopped designing in the first place.'

'Wow!'

'And it gets better. He said I should do it again, whatever it takes. However much or however little I wanted to put into this thing, it didn't matter, just so long as it was what I wanted. I could do it all day, every day.'

'So what did you say?'

Helen looks a little embarrassed at this point. 'I didn't say anything, actually. I burst into tears.'

'Oh, Helen,' I say, feeling for my friend.

'And that's when it hit me, when it all became much, much clearer; what I've been doing all these years . . . compensating.'

I look a little confused at this. 'Compensating?' I ask. 'What for?'

'My life,' says Helen simply. 'It's never really sat easily with me the way we live.' She pauses for a moment. 'I mean, the way we *can* live,' she corrects herself. 'My husband is a very successful man, Ellie. I find it hard to admit, but he earns a staggering amount of money – well, to me it is. I never felt it was fair that I should have so much. Perhaps I didn't feel I deserved it. I mean, I was just a nanny when Tom met me, and over the years, I think I made myself believe that I couldn't – or shouldn't – share in what we had because it wasn't mine; I hadn't earned it. So I denied myself things, deliberately didn't work at the things I was good at, because I believed I had an unfair advantage. Any success I had would have been because of the money I could throw at it, not because I actually had any talent.' She trails off here now, uncertain how to continue.

'You have real talent, Helen. You shouldn't hide it. Don't you believe that?' I say gently.

'I didn't, no, but now I'm not so sure. I'd like to find out. I've been lucky enough to have been given an opportunity – I shouldn't waste it.' She stares at me, slightly breathless. 'Does that make any sense? Or do I just sound as mad as I feel?'

'From you, Helen, it makes perfect sense. So what have you decided to do?'

'I've already done it – well, some of it. I've begun a new job – I'm a textile artist!'

'Blimey.'

Helen is fizzing with excitement as she describes how she has spent the last couple of weeks sorting out all her old materials and books and looking at new ones, her head rapidly filling with new ideas, what type of work she wants to do, how she would promote it, maybe in time even getting a small workshop. I can feel my own sense of excitement mounting; Helen's mood is infectious.

Looking at my watch, I'm amazed to find it's nearly half past three, and Helen leaves a few minutes later, after pressing the mysterious package she had brought with her into my arms.

'Open it after I've gone, and see what you think. Let it sit with you for a bit, and call me in a day or two.'

I've barely waved Helen off down the drive when I rush inside and rip the packaging off the parcel. The day is losing the light, and as I spread the contents out on the table and turn on the overhead light, I frown. It's no good; I need pins. Rummaging through the basket on my bookcase, I find a box of drawing pins, and fix the large sheet of paper to the wall carefully, then stand there for several minutes, thinking.

CHAPTER SEVEN

Crossing to the back door to fill up my log basket, I stop mid-way, caught once again by the piece of paper I pinned to the wall the day before. It's more than just a piece of paper: it is part painting, part needlepoint sampler – a piece of canvas has been fixed over the paper to show how the paint rendering might transform once worked in wool. I'm not sure that I've hung it up the right way, but it's landed the way I see it.

The background to the piece is colour-washed in a creamy tone so that at first an expanse of it seems to be plain; then on the left-hand side, right at the bottom, a little bubble of colour begins, which swirls around as if caught in a current. The current grows stronger towards the centre of the piece, more colours colliding, merging and separating, until finally they explode out on to the whole of the right-hand side of the piece: reds, oranges, yellow, a small streak of blue, back to cream and on to red again. The painting itself is beautiful, but where Helen has worked stitches is perfect. A myriad of tiny strokes, each so carefully placed. Helen has worked over the flat one-dimensional base with accents in tiny embroidery so that the whole thing comes to life with depth and substance. As a centrepiece to the room, it will look stunning; as a work of art, it is inspired. For some reason, it makes me feel rather emotional.

I tear myself away, remembering that I want to get my jobs done early so that I can go out. I am determined to go into town today to find a birthday present for Grace, preferably of the fab princess variety.

Typically, just as I'm about ready, there's a knock at the door. It's Will with some post for me. For some reason, my bank cannot cope with my address: I don't quite fit their boxes. 'Rowan Hill, Wickford' they can do, but 'The Lodge, Rowan Hill, Wickford' seems to have one too many parts, so they simply leave it out, with the result that Will gets all my letters from them.

As he apologises for disturbing me, I realise his vision is no longer fixed on me but is hovering somewhere over my left shoulder. I half-turn, realising straight away what he is looking at.

'Do you like it?'

'Yes,' says Will slowly, flicking his gaze back to me and then away again. 'Sorry – do you mind?' He moves past me to stand in front of Helen's wall hanging.

'It's not finished, of course. This is just a working piece to show the idea of what it will be like.'

'I know, yes, but even so . . .' he trails off, reaching out a tentative hand towards it. I notice that his hand is shaking slightly. 'May I?'

'Of course,' I answer, allowing him to touch it. He is quite still for a moment.

He looks at me then, searching my face as if looking for clues. I can feel myself beginning to flush under his intensity. And then, like the wind changing direction, his clouded expression changes.

'Sorry, bit of a *"Twilight Zone"* moment there. It's just that' – he is struggling to find the words – 'it's just that this is really very good.

It reminds me of something I saw once.' He scratches his chin, a faint growth of stubble glinting copper in the sunlight. 'I had no idea you did this kind of work.'

'Me! God no,' I exclaim. 'I didn't do this. I've commissioned it from a friend of mine.' I am oddly touched that he finds me capable of such a thing and quickly push aside any further reflection in that direction. 'Actually, you may know her,' I continue. 'It's Helen Morgan – she lives in the village, up behind the church.'

Will shakes his head.

'This is the first thing she's worked on in a very long time, but she's just started to do it properly – you know, as a business. I think she'll do fantastically well.'

'She should do. She's clearly very talented,' says Will, his eyes never once leaving the canvas. 'She has a real feeling for colour and composition; the movement here is sublime.'

'I'm impressed. You seem to know your stuff.'

There isn't much change in his expression, but I sense a subtle shift, the shutters coming down again. Perhaps it's just that I know it's something I do myself, a wariness about giving too much away for fear of an awkward conversation. I try not to show that I've noticed as I wait for his reply.

'Oh, I'm no expert. I read a lot, that's all. If I like something or I'm interested in it, I try to find out about it.'

'Well, you obviously know a lot about art. That's good because I was beginning to wonder if the real reason is that you're a closet embroiderer.'

'Hardly. Haven't got the hands for it – look.' And he holds up his palms for me to see. He has small hands, which I can see are rough and callused. But they're neat, much like the rest of him. We're almost the same height; I'm quite tall for a woman, at five foot eight, and Will is quite compact for a bloke.

'I tell you what,' he adds. 'If you're not doing anything today, would you like to come out for a walk around the estate, have a little look at what I call art?'

I can feel my plans for the day sliding away from me. On the one hand, I feel quite excited at the prospect of looking around (after all, it isn't every day that you get to live next door to landed gentry). Besides, I don't exactly know why, but it means a lot to me to establish a friendship with Will, and I know how hard it is to issue an invitation and then have it refused. But I had made up my mind to go shopping today, and I know that it's this feeling of disappointment that will inevitably show on my face first, though I try to suppress it. Of course Will notices. He has the grace to look away, giving me the opportunity to come up with a plausible excuse, but I realise that I can't do it. A mended fence will surely break again if you keep crashing into it.

'I'd like that, but are you sure you're not too busy? I don't want to hijack your time.'

'It's the weekend. Even failed gentlemen farmers get the weekend off,' he says with a sardonic smile.

He knows, I think, but smile brightly, determined to gloss over any awkwardness. 'Great – well, I'll just go and grab my fleece.'

As we cross the courtyard, Will explains the original uses of the buildings surrounding the main house. My own cottage was originally inhabited by the head groom, while the lowly stable boys bunked in the loft above one of the stables. The carriage house, part of the main courtyard, is still hung with huge cartwheels, though it is now home to a couple of vehicles with considerably more horsepower. The whole space is neat and tidy, unlike a lot of farms I've seen.

An assortment of smaller rooms all face out onto the courtyard, which is cobbled in part, the cobbles themselves forming a central wheel pattern that interlaces with the red brick floor. Under a bell tower at the far end stand two white wooden doors, easily twelve foot high, and although we pass through a door of normal size that's been cut into one of them, the whole arrangement is clearly designed to give the impression of stature.

The world through the door is just as delightful, and I wonder how many, if any, of the villagers know that this is here. The garden would have been magnificent once, its high stone walls encircling the formal brick paths with their low privet hedge boundaries, which weave in a calculated design amongst the now somewhat riotous planting. Herbs of every variety tumble out onto the path, jostling for space with alpines and heathers. Stone benches sit low on each side of the square space, looking onto a central urn of impressive size, which houses a tiered fountain, now still. The garden walls themselves are hung with espaliered pear and apple trees, and are heavy with the blooms of rambling roses, still bright in the autumn sunshine.

At the centre of each wall is another white door. To the left, the door leads into an L-shaped garden room, which runs around the sitting room of the house. To the right lies the orchard, source of the infamous apples, and the back of both Mrs Tweedy's cottage and my own. To the far side of the orchard, rows and rows of polytunnels ripple like a breeze-blown lake. On this subject Will refuses to be drawn out, referring to them simply as one of his more unmitigated disasters.

We press on ahead through the doorway in the facing wall, which leads onto a gravel driveway that sweeps away in both directions. On the other side of this driveway runs a length of fence bisected by a five-bar gate, which Will casually hops over.

'Need a hand?' he offers as I swing a leg over the top of the gate. I'm torn between an odd desire to appear the fit and confident woman I recently was and not making a fool of myself. In the end I decide to preserve my dignity and take Will's proffered hand, feeling rather like a privileged customer of a tour guide.

So far, Will's manner has been informative and descriptive rather than that of the proud landowner I'd expected. He talks about the gardens as if they are a part of the estate that just happens to be there, as if he's never really given them any thought, but I can see that in earlier times they would have been its crowning glory. Formal traditional English gardens are not that common any longer, and at one time someone must obviously have paid these gardens a great deal of attention; now they've been allowed to assume an air of gentle but obvious neglect.

We walk through an area of woodland, away from the house. Many of the trees are quite young, and some have obviously been recently planted.

'Are you up for a bit of a hike?' asks Will, breaking into my thoughts. 'Only there's a bit of a trek up from here.'

I nod enthusiastically, realising how much I'm enjoying being outside again; I hadn't realised how cooped up I had been feeling. 'Where are we going?'

'I'm not saying,' answers Will mysteriously. 'You'll see when we get there. Come on.'

He sets off at a cracking pace, which has me wondering if I'll be able to keep up, but I stride on determinedly just the same. The woodland is not thick here, and the autumn sun is still very warm. Whether it's this or the climb that's making me hot, I don't know, but I'm certain I'm developing a rather unattractive sheen. I stop for a moment to take my fleece off and tie it around my waist. Will is smiling at me.

'Beautiful, isn't it?'

I have been intent on keeping up with Will, but now that I've stopped, I suddenly become aware of my surroundings and feel a rush of colour catch up with me. It is glorious; Will's right.

'You're very lucky having all this right on your doorstep. I'd forgotten how much I like woodland in the autumn.'

Will gives me a searching look. 'But now it's on your doorstep too. Just come on over any time you want. You'll notice I haven't put up any signs forbidding the lowly peasant villagers from entering.' There is a twinkle in his eye that I'm getting pleasantly used to. He carries on, more earnestly now. 'Seriously, though, I mean it: explore any time – you don't have to ask.'

We walk for twenty minutes or so, the terrain climbing all the while, until I have to admit that I'm out of puff. I'm about to reluctantly ask if we can have a breather, when Will forestalls me.

'It's only a couple minutes more, I promise, and then we can have a rest. It'll be worth it.'

Will doesn't look the slightest bit tired. He moves with an easy grace that probably comes from so much time spent outdoors. I redouble my efforts, seeing that the trees in front of us are thinning and I can sense sky ahead. We must have reached the top of the hill.

I break through the line of trees ahead of Will, squinting in the bright sunlight that suddenly floods my face. I become aware of many things in that moment: the sudden warmth, the beating of my heart and the stillness, but a different stillness from that of the cocoon of trees. This stillness is wide and expansive; it is borne on the wind that I can now feel tumbling about me, suddenly finding the wide open space. It's this space that strikes me the most vividly, as the ground drops away in front of me and my gaze extends out across the valley. I can see for miles. It's breathtaking.

Away to my left, a little in the distance, the side of the hill is thickly wooded. We're just above the line of trees that follows the slope of the hill down into the valley. The line is washed with red, and as I concentrate my vision, I realise why. I touch my hand to my mouth and turn to look at Will, who has come quietly to stand by my side.

'Oh my God,' I say slowly as realisation dawns. 'That's Rowan Hill.'

'Yes,' he says simply. 'It is.'

'And all this is yours?' My voice takes on an air of incredulity as I begin to understand the enormity of what lies beyond me. I turn around to look at Will, who is gazing out, lost in the scenery. He doesn't turn as he answers me, his voice barely above a whisper.

'Yes.' And then stronger, 'Well, mine and Finn's,' adding in explanation, 'my brother.'

I nod.

'And this is where you are all day.' It's a statement, I realise as I say it, not a question. Will touches my sleeve then, motioning to a bench which lies a little to our left.

Once we're seated, I realise I'm waiting expectantly for the explanation that I'm certain is coming. I wonder if I should say anything; I can sense Will struggling for a way to start the conversation.

'Do you like my bench?' he asks suddenly, running his hands along the smooth plank.

I look down at his handiwork. *Bench is slightly over-egging the pudding,* I think, considering it is a plank of wood resting on four round stumps, but then perhaps he's trying to catch me out. I look up, noticing the slight twitch at the corner of his mouth.

'I do,' I reply. 'Not short of a bit of wood, are you?'

He laughs, shaking his head in amusement. 'Apparently I'm short of many things,' he says wryly. 'I don't have a proper job or a sense of humour. I'm not half as nice or as good looking as my brother, or blessed with as many brains, if it comes to it, but what I do have, in plentiful supply, is wood.'

'That and a well-developed inferiority complex,' I venture boldly, thinking that this is the second time I've heard Will refer to his brother in similar tones.

'No, I'm just repeating some of the tosh that has reached my ears from the village. No doubt the same load of rubbish that you were trying to warn me about?' He waits for my answering nod of acknowledgement before continuing. 'Actually, Finn and I are very close, and despite the local view of the pair of us, he does share my vision for this place. It's in complete contradiction to what he does, obviously – throwing up soulless new buildings – but it's a means to an end. He works at one end earning the money to pay for what we do at this end.'

'So why not set the village straight?' I ask.

There is a pause. Will leans forward, resting his forearms on his knees and clasping his hands together.

'There's a bit more to it than that, I'm afraid. Let's just say that it suits me at the moment to have the village take a dim view.'

'Mrs Tweedy mentioned your wife,' I prompt gently and then trail off. 'I'm sorry. I didn't mean to pry.'

'Ah yes, the lovely Caroline,' answers Will, sounding more bitter than sad. 'And no doubt Mrs Tweedy also told you about my countless misdemeanours. They're some of her favourite stories.'

His look is very direct. I feel a rush of colour to my cheeks. 'She mentioned something, yes,' I say, quite ashamed now. 'But not in any detail.'

'And does that bother you?'

'I don't know,' I answer honestly. 'I prefer to make my own mind up about people, but I suspect things were rather more complicated than she made out. Most relationships are, in my experience.'

'Possibly, possibly not.' Will takes a huge breath. 'But I appreciate your honesty,' he says, smiling again. 'I'll tell you about it sometime . . . just not today.'

I'm intrigued but sense that now is not the time to question him further.

'So come on then. I know nothing about gardening and stuff. Tell me what your vision is.'

'I wouldn't exactly call it gardening – I don't know much about that either, as you can tell from the state of the gardens. Basically I'm clearing the woods.'

He tells me about the state of the woodland, which has been allowed to run its own course for many years, decades even. There is pride in his voice, and passion too, as he explains how a woodland should be managed to allow it to thrive, not only to benefit the trees but also the other living things that make the woodland their home: the plants that grow up under the shade of the trees, and the animals that only return and flourish given the right conditions. An ecosystem of its own.

The concept is not new to me, but Will makes it come alive. *He would have been an excellent teacher,* I think. He has a very expressive face and uses his hands a lot when speaking. Although I'm listening to him, I become aware at one point that I'm studying his face rather than taking in what he's saying. I pull myself up sharply and concentrate as I realise he's taking me into his confidence.

I doubt if many people have heard what he's telling me now, and I feel inordinately pleased that he's chosen to share his vision with me. He's spent the last year or so systematically working through the woodland, clearing out the dead and diseased wood, thinning sections that have become overcrowded and replanting where needed. It's a slow process, especially working alone, but already there are very encouraging signs.

'And you come up here every day, come rain or shine? Don't you ever get bored or just long to have people around you?'

'Not really. It's a great place to be. If I want to think, I can just drift, and if I don't want to, I work like stink, and that puts paid to that. Any time I feel I need people around me, I go and do my shopping, and that usually cures me pretty fast.'

'Don't you think that's a little sad?' I ask.

'That rather depends on your perspective, doesn't it?' replies Will, raising an eyebrow. 'I usually find it's other people that mind me being by myself.'

'Point taken, but it's an interesting thing – perspective, I mean,' I reply, thinking back to Robbie's accusations of me but saying nothing further. 'Why are you doing this, though? I'd like to know.'

'You're not going to let up, are you?' Will grins, giving me an exasperated, if amused, look. 'And worse, I'm not sure I can explain it properly. There is so little native woodland left in relative terms, and despite our best efforts to destroy it, it clings to life. I like that. Nature is so tenacious, and I feel like some things deserve to be the best they can – they just need to be, to exist. A bit like art, I suppose, just waiting to be created, brought to life, and then it belongs to everyone.'

'Is that what you want for this?' I affirm, spreading my hands in an expansive gesture. 'For this to belong to everyone?'

'I hope so, yes. I visited an arboretum last year, and I saw a dedication on a bench that read, "John, silent thoughts, as trees for company." I don't know who John was, but I'd like his spirit to come and visit my wood.'

Will's eyes are the clearest blue, I think, as I find tears suddenly welling up. I blink and look away, unable to speak. I sit looking out at the slope of the woodland before me, birds wheeling about the sky. Will, beside me, has not moved. We sit like this for some time before he gently straightens up.

'Shall we?' he says, and I nod, rising to follow him as we make our way back down the hill.

It's well past lunchtime when we reach the walled gardens again. We argue amicably as Will informs me that there is actually a track on the other side of the house that goes right by the point where we've been sitting and then on down Rowan Hill. He takes the pickup truck most days but didn't today; seeing as I'm a townie, he thought I could use the exercise. We laugh as we cross the stable yard.

As we near my cottage, Will repeats his offer that I should wander over the estate any time I like. One of the best things about it, he says, is that there's no one around for miles, especially up by the bench. You can laugh, cry, scream, shout, sing the Alleluia Chorus, and no one will hear. I should try it some time. And no, he won't come in for lunch, but thanks for the offer; he has some errands to run. He seems genuinely pleased by my assurance that I've really enjoyed myself.

That night, between the hours of one and two in the morning, Will chops logs for twenty-seven minutes. I'm not sure what time I fall asleep.

CHAPTER EIGHT

The last week in October sees the temperature plummet, and on Saturday night I light the fire in my bedroom for the first time. I'd gone for a long walk that afternoon, returning with the dying sun, tired but at peace. I'd had a long bath after tea, and by nine o'clock I am in bed with a book, blissfully warm and relaxed.

I read for perhaps twenty minutes, until I find my gaze drawn to the fire with increasing regularity, losing myself in its dance. I turn out the lamp and lie for a while, watching the flickering, enjoying the patterns and soothed by the dim warmth as I let myself drift.

I've been here for nearly two months now, and I'm beginning to feel a little more at home, with the Lodge slowly taking on some personality. I've seen Helen a few times – she's ecstatic about my reaction to her wall hanging and is working flat out to make progress. She is awash with ideas for her business, and although I take a second-hand pleasure in this, it does highlight my own lack of direction. Once or twice I've lain awake thinking about Rowan Hill and what I might do if it were mine. I know it's a pointless exercise, but I soon find my imagination starting to kick in, whereas thoughts about my own prospects tend to drift into nothing. Granted, I've been busy, and there is always enough to fill my day, but I still feel rootless and restless, particularly at night in the quiet dark.

Thoughts of tomorrow's house-warming lunch bring mixed feelings. Getting together with Jane and her family is always a pleasure, but this is the first time I've entertained anyone for a very long time. I'm not the domestic goddess that Jane is, and although I have a beautiful piece of lamb in the fridge, I'm a little nervous about pulling everything off. We might be best friends, but I still want to impress them. If I am troubled by these thoughts, it makes no difference; a few minutes after turning out the light, while imagining the white sauce for my leeks, I fall deeply asleep.

Next morning I light the fire downstairs quickly, snatching some toast and a hefty mug of tea before setting to making the pastry for the apple pie I'm going to serve for dessert. My mother always taught me to rest my pastry for half an hour before rolling it out, and so I do. I peel and core the apples while I watch the sun lift in the sky, gilding the already burnished trees. It's another beautiful day.

By mid-morning the veg are peeled, the white sauce is made and the apples and leeks are simmering gently in their respective pans. I move the kettle across to the boiling plate before going to get the rosemary from the larder. I'm nursing a welcome cuppa when my hand flies to my mouth.

'Oh, bugger!' I say with feeling.

I've forgotten the mint sauce. Not a major catastrophe, but it's the only thing that will persuade Tilly to eat her roast lamb (that and the temptation of a stickily sweet treat for pudding). I've ticked that box, I think, eyeing the saucepan that will soon hold caramel, but the loss of the mint sauce might just prove to be a deal breaker as far as Tilly is concerned.

I feel my balloon of contentment start to deflate. I stare out the window at the perfect day, willing a solution to come to me. The village shop doesn't open on a Sunday, and I haven't the time to drive to Church Stretton and back. I'm certainly not about to ask Alice Tweedy for some, which leaves Will. Although, it's silly to ask him, isn't it? . . . or is it? There's a slight chance he might be able to help, I think, and it's worth a try. I run out the door and across the stable courtyard, praying that he's in.

I tap tentatively on the door and, when there's no reply, tap a little louder.

'The door's open,' comes the shouted reply. I hesitate on the threshold.

'Will, it's Ellie,' I call out.

'Hello! Come on in.'

I would rather he come and open the door – it feels a little informal just walking in, but I do it all the same, trying to adjust to the relative dimness of the room compared with the brightness outside.

Will is sitting in an armchair at the far side of the Aga, one leg crossed at the ankle over his knee. A book is open on his lap. He's wearing jeans and a chunky cable knit jumper in a light colour. He looks like he hasn't moved for some time, except perhaps to refill his cup from the teapot that stands on a table beside him.

'I'm sorry to disturb you,' I begin. 'I've had a bit of a disaster.'

Will puts the book down and leans forward slightly. He smiles slowly. 'Tell me, Ellie, why is it that you always apologise for your presence?'

I had been expecting something along the lines of 'Oh dear, can I help at all?' and am thrown off course by his reply, flushing bright red.

'It's okay – I'm just teasing, so please don't say you can see I'm busy or something, because as you can see, I'm not. In fact this level of complete inertia is hard to come by.' He stands up, running a hand through his hair. 'Come on, sit down,' he says, indicating a squishy sofa that I hadn't noticed before. 'And you can tell me all about it. I'll get you some tea.'

Hearing the clock ticking in my mind, I stammer, 'Oh no, thanks, I'm fine.'

'What? You don't want to sit down? Or you don't want tea?' He pauses for a moment, considering my face. 'Or is it that you are in fact fine and have no disaster to tell me about?' He raises his eyes heavenward. 'You know, for an English teacher, you really are quite inarticulate.' He's trying hard not to laugh.

Catching his mood, I relax. 'Shut up. I only came to ask if you've got any mint sauce.'

'And that's a disaster?'

'It is when it's the only thing that will persuade the four-year-old who's coming to lunch to eat her food.'

Will nods wisely. 'Totally understand. Tell me, do you regularly entertain four-year-olds?'

'No,' I say. 'Her parents and older sister are coming too.'

'Oh I *see*. So this is one of those "I don't want to look like I've tried too hard because naturally I'm just an amazing cook" kind of dinners,' replies Will, summing it up perfectly.

I ignore him. 'Look, have you got any mint sauce or not?'

'Not,' says Will, looking crestfallen. 'Sorry.' Then he brightens suddenly. 'Although if the lady would care to wait a few moments, I might be able to oblige.'

Before I can reply, he disappears through a door. I'm not quite sure what I should do now, and I pull out a chair from the table, sitting down and feeling exhausted. Will has an uncanny way of being able to pick me apart, always seeming to know what's in my mind, and not just the bit on the surface that I allow people to see. The door flies open, and Will reappears carrying a small bunch of greenery, which he brandishes at me.

'Mint,' he says by way of explanation.

He runs the leaves under the tap, gives them a good shake and plonks them down on a chopping board. I realise what he's doing and get up, crossing over to where he's standing.

'Will, I didn't mean for you to go to so much trouble. You don't have to do this.'

He moves to a cupboard and takes down a bowl. 'It's ten minutes out of my day, Ellie. How much trouble can it be?' And with that he takes out the biggest knife I've ever seen and proceeds to chop the mint at lightning speed before sliding it into the bowl. Next, he adds a couple of teaspoons of sugar before pouring in a little hot water from the kettle. He hands me the bowl with a spoon. 'Keep stirring,' he says.

The hot water has released the scent from the mint even more, and I inhale deeply, stirring as instructed. Will returns to me with a bottle of vinegar and pours in a dash. He dips his finger into the bowl, sampling the contents.

'There you go,' he says with a broad smile. 'Mint sauce. Should be ready in about an hour.'

I return the smile, shaking my head in amazement. 'I'm seriously impressed. Where did you learn to do that?'

'Dunno, really,' says Will. 'I guess I just like lamb with mint sauce too.'

After that it seems the easiest thing in the world to invite Will to lunch, and to my surprise, he accepts immediately. I tell him that Jack would love the opportunity to thank him for what he'd done for Netty. He pulls a face at this but accepts just the same. We agree that he should come over about twelve thirty. It's eleven now, and I need to get a ripple on and finish my pudding. I leave, clutching the mint sauce before me like the Olympic flame.

Lunch goes superbly, and even Tilly, who liberally covered everything on her plate with mint sauce, eats steadily and without complaint.

Will proves to be a perfect guest: he arrives promptly, with wine, and immediately offers to lay the table. He appears a little reticent at first, after having been introduced to Jane and her family – their copious thanks for his unobtrusive care of Netty seems to make him uncomfortable – but he soon begins to chat easily and earns eternal gratitude from Jane by offering to sit between the two girls at lunch, even though I suspect he would much rather chat to Jack.

After lunch, Jane rather ominously declares that we have things to talk about, so we banish Jack and Will to the living room.

Jane pushes up her sleeves in a business-like fashion and begins to run water into the sink. 'You know the house is beginning to look really great, Ellie. I love this room.' She looks at the newly painted walls. 'How Netty managed to live with pea green I shall never know.'

She rinses a couple of glasses before continuing. 'I see you finally managed to get your bed together. Did Will have a hand in that too?'

I ignore the suggestive tone in her voice. 'He did, as a matter of fact, yes. He popped around one morning last week and noticed the two sides were still propped up against the wall. He asked me what they were for, and when I told him, he offered to help sort it out.'

Jane is watching me intently with a look that suggests she doesn't believe me at all.

'So you can stop looking at me like that!' I intone with a glance towards the lounge door.

Jane gives me an annoyingly serene smile. 'You've been drying that plate for an awfully long time, Ellie.'

She ducks as I flick the tea towel at her. 'Anyway, listen, I'm so pleased you're beginning to feel settled now. I can picture you here when I think of you. The place suits you.'

There is silence for a few minutes while I desperately try to think of something to change the subject, fearing what's coming next, and Jane tries hard to find a way of approaching what she knows is a delicate subject. She clears her throat and begins. 'And how are you feeling now? Ready to take on the world again?'

I take a proffered plate and try to make my voice light-hearted. 'Yeah, I'm okay, Jane. Maybe not quite the feisty young thing I was before, but I'm getting there. I still miss Robbie, of course, some times more than others, or maybe it's the thought of Robbie I miss – I don't know. But I think this place is going to be good for me.'

'Well that may be . . . I hope so, but look, Ellie, I have to ask' – she lays a hand on my arm – 'and you know I'm only saying it because I care so much, but what are you going to do, long term? You know, whenever we used to chat before, you always talked about your work, sometimes to have a moan, but mostly the good stuff, the laughs, your ambitions, achievements – always with passion. Since you've moved, granted you've had other things on your mind, but I haven't heard you mention work once, and that's not like you.'

I throw up my hands in a helpless gesture. 'I know it's not like me, I recognize that, but I don't know what to do about it.' A touch of anguish is beginning to creep into my voice. 'I've been a teacher most of my life – it's all I know how to do, but if I know anything now, it's that I absolutely cannot teach.' I give an involuntary shudder.

Jane puts down the dishcloth and hugs me, dripping suds onto the floor. She presses me tight, then pulls away to look into my face. 'I didn't mean to upset you, Ellie.'

'You didn't,' I reply, giving her a weak smile. 'It's just so weird,' I say sniffing. 'I don't know what I want to do. I feel like I want to do something completely different, but I don't know what. And when I try to tell myself to get my head out of the clouds and just buckle down to thinking about some proper work, I almost get palpitations.'

'Give it a little more time, then. It will come right, I'm sure, and don't mind me, I'm just an old mother hen.'

'You're a good friend, Jane – the best – and you have every right to be concerned, but I think things will come right, bit by bit. Anyway,' I carry on, brightening, 'it's been too nice a day to be all doom and gloom. Let's leave the pans to soak and put the kettle on. I expect the boys will need waking up soon.'

In fact, it's only Jack who is dozing, Will having taken up a place on the floor beside Grace and Tilly, who are doing a puzzle. He mirrors their position, stretched out on his stomach, propped up on his elbows with legs bent up at the knees. Jane nudges me as we walk into the room, muttering under her breath. 'Would you look at that? Grace will upgrade him to hero status for helping her do a puzzle.'

If any of them hear, they make no show, but Will looks up, smiling as we enter, and catches my eye. I feel unexpectedly pleased that he's scoring so many brownie points with my friends, and immediately think of the first weekend that I introduced Robbie to Jane and Jack. But this isn't the same thing at all, I remind myself. Robbie had been at his most witty and sparkling best that time, and I had been showing him off. Today, Will is here as a friend and nothing more.

'Come on, Jack,' says Jane. 'Stop pretending to be asleep. We're counting on you for some scintillating after-dinner conversation.'

Jack opens one eye slowly. 'Oh dear,' he mutters, both eyes closing once more, and then, 'That could be a problem.' But he struggles to a more upright position anyway, giving an apologetic shrug. 'Sorry, folks. Too much good food and this beautiful fire are a lethal combination for a man of my age.'

Jane makes a disapproving noise. 'Mmm, that and another late night in pursuit of the perfect plot twist.'

'Another late night? Ha! Anything past eight o'clock is a late night for you,' argues Jack amiably, all the while smiling affectionately at his wife. He takes a slurp from the mug of tea she has just handed him. 'Do you see what I have to put up with?' he asks no one in particular, but it is Will who replies, scrabbling to his feet and launching himself into a chair.

'I knew I'd seen your face before,' he exclaims. 'God, you even wrote to me, and I didn't connect the name at the time.' Will runs a hand through the top of his hair, pulling a contrite face. 'Sorry, I can't believe I didn't know you were *the* Jack Manning.'

'No reason why you should,' says Jack simply. 'There must be other Jack Mannings around.'

I see the tussle on his face: modesty and a degree of nonchalance vying with the desire to know just how big a fan Will is. His ego gets the better of him, but I smile, knowing how little Jack ever gets to talk about his work. He grins at Will. 'Now, I'm supposed to say something humble at this point, and self-deprecating, but actually' – and he pauses here for comic effect – 'I want to know exactly what you've read and what you thought of it. Don't hold back on the compliments either. I can handle it.'

Will doesn't. It's clear he thinks a lot of Jack's work, but beyond the initial general praise and admiration, he is clearly interested in what motivates Jack and how he writes. I think the world of Jack, and I'm keen to know what Will thinks too. In fact, I'm only too aware of my desire to see the world through his eyes. I wonder when that started to happen?

Jack is explaining how he first came to start writing and the sense of guilt he felt towards his growing family in giving up his secure job.

Will nods feverishly. Jack talks about his work in the same way that Will did, that day we sat overlooking Rowan Hill. He obviously understands Jack's point of view entirely; his own work is somewhat unconventional, and he has also felt under pressure to conform to what he feels others expect of him. I interrupt to fill Jack in on Will's plans for the estate, and he considers for a moment, looking thoughtful.

'And yet,' he says after a moment, 'you carry on doing it. Why? It's a very long-term project.'

There is a sudden stillness about Will as he answers. He looks down. When it comes, his voice is clear with conviction. 'Because right now it's the only thing that makes me feel alive.'

Jane is looking puzzled. 'I'm sure that Ellie said you were a teacher, though, Will.' She winks at me. 'You know, that time after her accident when she couldn't stop talking about the blue-eyed man who'd rescued her. Did I get that bit wrong?'

I could murder her sometimes, I really could. Will at least has the grace to blush.

'No, you're right; the forestry is a recent thing, really. I've done loads of things in the past. My brother was always the one who knew what he wanted to do, while I spent a lot of time kidding myself I could be all sorts of things. I've got a degree in fine art, believe it or not. I wanted to be a conservator, but it takes a while to get yourself established, and the income was a bit sporadic.'

I frown slightly at this. He is about to say something else, but I jump in first, determined to find out more. 'You don't strike me as particularly money driven, Will. How did you get from protecting art to teaching, and then to running an estate?'

Will pulls a face that verges on disgust. 'I'm not sure that I know. The long and short of it is that I met someone who convinced me that my conservation work was too unreliable to sustain a serious relationship, so I retrained as a teacher. I was never going to make a fortune, but at least it was a regular income. I'll spare you what followed, but teaching was never my thing, so I gave it up and turned my attention to Rowan Hill instead. It's restoration of a sort, I suppose.' He shrugs.

'Who are you trying to kid? I've heard you talk about your work with real passion,' I counter, playing devil's advocate.

Will looks at me for a moment, speechless, a slow smile eventually gathering. 'I know,' he agrees. 'It didn't happen quite the way I'd planned it, but the more I got into it, the more I found myself not wanting to do anything else.' He looks around at Jane and Jack, smiling.

You might say you're happy, Will McLennan, I think, *but something's keeping you awake at night.*

CHAPTER NINE

I take myself off the following day. I woke up in the strangest mood, one I couldn't understand that took me by surprise. Having gone to bed full of good intentions to seriously consider my work options, I had woken early, chasing remnants of bizarre dreams in which I found myself in a series of magnificent rooms, moving from one to another as new doors and staircases opened up for me. Coming to, I felt like I was standing on the verge of something, with butterflies of excitement fluttering around my stomach. The more I tried to think about it, the more tenuous the feeling became, and then when I got up to go to the loo, I found myself staring down into the courtyard of Rowan Hill for so long that I nearly wet myself.

I get ready quickly and go out, driving in the direction of Ludlow, where there is a bigger library than the local one. It isn't busy, and I commandeer a table. I open my pristine notebook and write a heading slowly across the page – *To Teach or Not to Teach* – and begin to fill the page.

I am interrupted by what sounds like twenty or so bangles crashing down the arm of the woman who comes to stand by my table. I look up to see a face that I recognize, although I can't remember where from. It's only when I see that her earrings are the same size as her bangles that I remember the waitress from the tea room in the village. She indicates the empty chair.

'I'm sorry, do you mind?'

'No, go ahead,' I say, motioning her to sit. 'I've forgotten your name, though – sorry. I'm spectacularly bad at that.'

She smiles. 'Yeah, me too. Your name, that is; obviously, I can remember my own.' She drops her bag onto the table, setting her bangles off again. 'It's Gina.'

I nod, and she flaps her hand at me, setting off another crescendo. 'Don't tell me; I know you're from the big house – it'll come to me in a minute.' She crashes her hand against her forehead. 'Evie, that's it. I've got it!'

'It's Ellie,' I laugh.

'Aw, hey, I was close wasn't I?' she replies, sitting down. 'Look, are you sure you don't mind me? I'm not exactly quiet.'

I shake my head with amusement, eyeing up the titles of her books, which are all on the subject of baking.

'Looking for inspiration?' I ask.

'Salvation more like. You've had my flapjack – it's bloody shite. I need something easy.'

The look on my face must have given me away.

'You're gonna tell me flapjack is easy, aren't you?' She pauses. 'Actually, don't answer that.'

'Scones?' I suggest.

'Like bricks.'

'Victoria sponge?'

'Sinks in the middle.'

I rack my brains. 'Shortbread?' I proffer.

'Yeah, mine's not bad, but it does have a tendency to shatter. It's not supposed to do that, is it?'

'Not usually, no.'

'I don't know what it is. I can do savoury stuff, no problem – soups, omelettes, perfect poached eggs – but I can't bake for love nor money.'

I wonder if Gina should be telling me this as a potential customer of hers, but it doesn't seem to bother her. She picks up one of the books and starts to flip through it at lightning speed. It's a *Good Housekeeping* title, and one I've got at home.

'That's quite a good book for traditional stuff. The recipes all work out well.'

'Yeah? Oh, right then.' She looks across to my notebook and the book that I was reading before she arrived.

'Hey, perhaps we should swap homework. You pick out my recipes, and I'll . . . what the bloody hell is that?' she exclaims as she picks up the book beside my notebook, reading the title. '*What Color Is Your Parachute?*' she intones. 'What the bloody hell does it matter what colour your parachute is anyway?'

I can't help laughing. 'Actually, it's got nothing to do with parachutes. It's quite an old book now, but it's supposed to help you look at what sort of person you are and what sort of job you should do.'

She peers more closely at my notebook. 'Teaching? Is that what you do?'

'Did do,' I answer. 'I'm trying to think of what else to do now, but I'm not doing very well, I'm afraid.'

Gina eyes my book suspiciously. 'Well, whatever you do, skip the page that tells you to buy a tea room and live happily ever after. Not when you've got a sodding husband trying to plug, anyway,' she mutters.

'Sorry?'

'Ah, never mind me, love. I'm just moaning 'cause my Derek's moving us on after Christmas. Going to somewhere in Lincolnshire. I'm not even sure if I bloody well know where that is. But he's got a new job, so that's that, and we're off.'

'Oh, I see,' I reply, not quite sure what to say. Gina doesn't strike me as the sort of person to let life get her down too much. In fact, she sounds quite cheerfully matter of fact.

'So what will you do?'

'Don't know. Probably sort something out,' she says fiercely, her earrings swinging violently. 'Derek only bought me the tea room to give me something to do all day – stop me from buying stuff and driving him mad forever cleaning the house. That's why I'm pissed off. I've made quite a go of it, and I didn't think I would. He didn't either, to be fair. Although, like I said, I expect he'll sort me something else out. I'll have to wait and see.'

Gina is, I realise, considerably older than I first thought, a little powerhouse of energy. Five foot nothing, and not an ounce of spare flesh on her.

'So why all the cookbooks then?' I ask. 'I mean, if you're selling the business, why go to all the trouble?'

She crosses her arms resolutely in front of her, crushing bangles ruthlessly. 'Because if I'm going to go out, I'm going out with a bang. It's not until after Christmas, and I'm damned if I'm going to give up after all I've done. Besides which, the place is up for sale, and for all I know, it will be crawling with people who aren't just there for the tea, if you know what I mean. I don't want anybody saying I served them a shite flapjack.'

I wish I had her determination. 'Good for you,' I say. 'In that case, go for the Delia and the good ladies of the Housekeeping Institute – they won't let you down.'

Gina springs up, looking at her watch. 'I will, thanks, love.' She smiles, and then taps my notebook. 'Come and have a cuppa in a day or two, and tell me what colour your parachute turned out.'

I watch her leave, balancing her bag and books under one arm. I look down at my page and the two columns of words, one considerably longer than the other. I slowly close the covers together. I think I'm done here.

The idea that has implanted itself in my brain sustains me all the way home. My mind seems peculiarly programmed to follow wild flights of fancy at the moment, probably to divert my attention from the things I should be focusing on.

As I dump my bag and book on the table, I think that perhaps Jane wouldn't be the best person to ask for advice. She might see my plan for what it is: a delusional smokescreen. She'd be sort of encouraging, but wouldn't totally convince me that what I had in mind for Gina's emporium might just work. I need to look elsewhere for a co-conspirator.

I should ring Helen. There's nothing like someone in the throes of their own creative process to be enthusiastic about someone else's. I've picked up the phone before I've even got my coat off. My stomach is rumbling, and an icy blast is coming from the lounge. I need to light the fire and have some lunch, but hopping around impatiently listening to Helen's ringing tone seems more important. She's out; I knew it was too good to be true. Will had better be in.

The answer to my knock is a long time coming. As I stand there, I realise that I have absolutely no idea what I'm going to say to Will. I'm still trying to come up with an opening gambit when the door opens. He is dishevelled, dusty and wearing an expression that could curdle milk. I'm mightily relieved to see the beginnings of a rather lopsided smile.

'Hi,' he says, wiping his hands down already filthy jeans. 'Come in.' He walks ahead of me, talking over his shoulder. 'I was going to come round this morning to say thanks for yesterday, but I saw you go out, and to be honest, I've got a bit of a sore head.'

'That's okay – no need.'

He goes to wash his hands in the big butler's sink. 'No, I wanted to say thanks. It's a long time since I spent an afternoon like that, and I enjoyed it. Your friends are nice people.'

He dries off his hands, and I suddenly feel shy. His back view is quite appealing. He drops the towel back beside the sink and turns to lean up against it, crossing his legs and raking both hands through his hair. I have to admit the front view is quite appealing as well; his jeans are pulled tighter across his thighs, and his T-shirt rests against what is obviously a flat stomach. I'm seriously beginning to doubt my sanity. I try to regain my composure. 'Yes, they are. I've known Jane since forever, and well, Jack – he's one of the good guys.'

'It makes a nice change for me to talk to someone with a less than conventional career. Most after-dinner conversations I've had result in me feeling inferior in the wake of everyone else's career ambitions. Either that or I'm offered the consolation of finding a "proper job" one day.'

'I'm glad you enjoyed it.' I smile. 'Sorry you've got a headache, though. I didn't think we drank that much.'

It was meant to be a light-hearted comment, but his face falls immediately.

'No, *we* didn't. Sadly, I managed to lay waste to a good part of a bottle of malt when I came home.'

Will doesn't look like he's joking. He scuffs at the floor with a toe. 'There were many and varied reasons for that, the most pressing of which was that I made a decision which meant that I was going to have a really awful day today. So call it Dutch courage if you like – just a little too much and a little too early.' Will's voice is still soft, and I realise that he's not looking to shock me or have me judge him, he's just telling it the way it is. There is no challenge being laid down here; my opinion is not what is required. I hold his look for a moment. 'Believe me, it made perfect sense at the time,' he says, shrugging.

'And have you had a really awful day?'

'Yes, thanks.'

'Great,' I mutter. 'Well, at least someone's happy, then.'

He flicks a finger around the corner of his mouth, as if to flatten the creasing that I know is appearing. 'So, have you had an awful day as well then?'

I think for a moment. 'No. Actually, I think I've had rather a good day.'

'I'm thrilled,' Will smirks. 'Thanks so much for coming round to share that with me.'

'You're very welcome.'

He smiles for a moment. 'Well? Are you going to tell me what you came around for, or had you just heard that there was a hung-over, morose man covered in dust here?'

'No, actually it's worse. I came to ask your advice about something.'

'Oh Christ, that's such a bad idea. I haven't made a good decision since I got up this morning.' Will is rubbing at his forehead.

My stomach is on the verge of making the most horrendous growling noise. 'Listen, have you had anything to eat yet?' I say, thinking quickly.

'No, breakfast didn't seem like a very good idea.'

'I don't mean breakfast,' I reply, pointedly looking at my watch; it's nearly two o'clock. 'Have you had any lunch?' I take in Will's vacant expression. 'Have you even got anything for lunch?'

'Um . . . I could go and look,' he says, misunderstanding me.

I give a patient smile. 'No, it's okay. I meant, would you like to come over for some lunch? I can pick your brains at the same time. That is, of course, if you're able to take a break from having a really bad day.'

'I think for the time being that I can. With any luck, by the time I get back, it may well have slid into mere mediocrity. Will there be cake?'

'There will,' I reply, thinking that this bodes well.

'I'll go and get changed.'

Twenty minutes later, when Will has lit my fire and I have made tea and sandwiches for us both, we sit basking in the warmth as I begin to recount my conversation with Gina and my idea to supply the tea shop with cakes.

'But even if she did say yes,' I venture, 'I'm not sure that they're good enough. I don't want to make a fool of myself.'

Will studies the fire for a moment. 'Do *you* think they're good enough?' he asks.

'I don't know. It's hard to be objective, isn't it, when it's something you've done yourself?'

'Mmm, but it's not a negative trait to have confidence in yourself,' he adds sagely, giving me a long and very telling look. 'Are you asking me whether I think they're good enough?'

I smile, found out. 'Probably,' I agree.

'In that case, then yes, I think they're good enough. Although on the basis of only ever having tried two of your cakes, I would say that more research was needed, wouldn't you?' He hands me his plate, which I dutifully refill.

'Plus, what you don't realise,' he says through a mouthful of carrot cake, 'is that I've tried Gina's flapjack, and it is, as she so eloquently puts it, shite.' He takes another bite. 'Anyway, what have you got to lose? If you've got the time and you enjoy it, do it. You don't have to just take one decision and then live with it forever. Make this decision, do this and then, when things need to change, make another decision and do that.'

'That's actually good advice.'

'I know. Sometimes I surprise myself.'

'She might say no, though.'

'She might, in which case I don't bloody know what to say. But Gina's not daft; I don't think she'll say no.' He pops the last piece of cake into his mouth.

'So is that what you do then – go with the flow? No big life plan all laid out?'

'No, I've tried that – several times actually – but I guess I just don't have the kind of life that wants to be planned. Right now, metaphorically speaking, I am most definitely flying by the seat of my pants.'

'Well then,' I say, raising my mug to him, 'here's to pant flying.'

'To pant flying,' he says, smiling.

It's only when Will gives himself an almost physical shake that I realise we've both fallen silent, staring into the fire. I'm lost, dreaming of recipes, and Will just looks knackered.

'Sorry,' he says, rousing himself. 'I was nodding off.' He looks exhausted, the dark circles under his eyes showing in the dimming light.

'So sleep,' I say, startling him. 'It won't bother me.'

'I can't do that. Thanks, but I'd better get going.'

'And do what? Find something to do, when what you look like you should do is sleep? Seriously, sit here; I'm just going to potter in the kitchen for a bit. If you're not asleep in ten minutes, you can go. Deal?'

'Okay,' mutters Will, throwing another log on the fire. But when I stick my head around the door a while later, he is fast asleep. He doesn't dribble or make strange noises or twitch – just breathes gently, his hands curled in his lap.

I sit in the chair opposite him and start to draw up a list of favourite cakes, flicking through my old cookbooks. I'm still engrossed when Will wakes a couple of hours later. He must have been watching me before he speaks.

'Drink your tea. It's getting cold,' he says, smiling lazily, and the fire glints off the coppery stubble on his chin. I smile back.

'Would you like a cup?'

'Thank you, but no,' he says, strangling a yawn and levering himself forward. 'I must leave you in peace after my inordinate rudeness. I can't believe I just did that. I haven't slept like that for a very long time. You didn't dope my cake, did you?'

'Nope,' I laugh.

He looks to the darkened window and checks his watch, pulling a face. 'Well, thanks again.'

I escort him to the door, not quite sure what to say after this strangely intimate moment. He seems a little uncertain too as he reaches the threshold, turning momentarily. 'Actually, I lied earlier, Ellie. I have made one good decision today.' And with that he drops a kiss on my cheek and slips through the door.

CHAPTER TEN

November

And so, as October slips into November, I become a part-time baker. It took me a couple more days before I went to see Gina, after whittling down the list I made, doing a few dummy runs and plucking up my courage. After that it was surprisingly easy. Gina listened carefully to my well-rehearsed but badly delivered sales pitch, studied me for a moment and then gave a huge cackle of laughter, asking if I could leave my trays of samples with her for a day or two.

Fortunately, she has a gaggle of mums who call in for a gossip and a cappuccino after dropping off their kids at the local playgroup each morning. It didn't take much to persuade them to call in for a gossip, a cappuccino and a slice of cake, and it just went from there.

Now I bake on a Sunday, deliver on a Monday, have a whole day off on Tuesday, bake on Wednesday, deliver on the Thursday, and by dint of Derek telling the local cycling club that his wife is no longer making the cakes, I also now bake on Friday for delivery on Saturday in time for Sunday's weekly club run.

It's not much, and it doesn't pay a great deal, but it has brought measure and routine to my week, and this is something I cannot put a price on.

I feel more like I belong now, like I'm legitimate. I am defined by my work. If anyone asks me what I am, what I do, I can answer them. I might not be a teacher now, or have a career, but I am the proud owner of a label, and that makes me feel better.

I'm sleeping better too. When I lie down at night, I think of the day ahead instead of the one just past (more often than not), and hopefully this will continue to improve. On some nights now I don't think about Will at all.

I've got a busy day ahead of me. I've promised Jane I'll go Christmas shopping with her this afternoon, but first I've got some serious baking to do. I'm on my way out of the shop with some eggs when I catch sight of a familiar figure climbing out of his pickup truck, which is parked outside.

'I thought it was you,' I say as Ben drops a banana skin in the bin.

He swings around. 'Hi,' he says, smiling warmly. 'How are you?'

'Bit cold.' I shiver. 'It's not a very nice day is it? But I'm fine, thanks. You?'

'Yeah, not bad.' He eyes the box of eggs I'm carrying. 'I remember your brownies,' he remarks. 'Are you making more?'

'Lemon drizzle this time. I've got a job making cakes for the little tea room up the road. But I thought you'd finished at Helen's house. Have you got more work here?'

'Well, I'm hoping to. Actually, I've just come from a cottage up by the school. There might be a bit of work there – looks hopeful anyway. I'm a bit stuffed at the moment.' He hunches his shoulders, jamming his hands into his jean's pockets.

'Is it the time of year?'

'Partly. It's the job too, though. Typically, it's either feast or famine. I've been working on a new development in Shrewsbury, which was fairly soulless, admittedly, but okay. Two new houses, with the next phase of three being rolled out straight away, but there's a problem with the right of way or something, so it's all on hold for the moment, possibly until the spring.'

I pull my coat around me a little more. 'I bet that's irritating. Still, I'm sure you'll find something.'

'Yes, I'm sure I will,' he replies, smiling again. 'You've just moved to the village, haven't you?'

'Yes.' I point beyond the church. 'Where the long stone wall runs along the other side of the road with the very grand house behind it – well, I'm the not-so-grand lodge just in front of it. I'm sort of doing it up a bit, but I'm supposed to be finding gainful employment as well. It's just that – well . . . it's a long story.'

Ben nods, sensing the natural stilling of our conversation. I'm not quite sure what to say next, but for some reason I don't want to just say goodbye.

'I'm really pushed for time today, Ben – I'm sorry – but I'm only up the road now. Would you like to stop by for a cup of something some time, and cake too?'

To my surprise Ben says that he would. He makes a small noise in his throat. 'Actually, I have to get back to Shrewsbury for something now which I can't do any other day, so it's no matter. But you never know: if I pick up this job, I'll be around a fair bit. Perhaps we could do it then?'

'Okay.' I hold out my hand. 'Nice to see you again anyway.' I grin. 'Take care.'

Ben takes my hand. His is freezing. 'I will, thanks, you too.'

I watch, pondering the coincidence of our meeting, as he disappears inside the shop. I've always believed that people cross your path in life for a reason – some for good, others for bad. But if they cross your path more than once, then you really do need to take note. I give a little shiver. That's two people now: first Will and then Ben.

By the time I get to Jane's house, she is panicking. There are thirty-one shopping days until Christmas, and by her calculations that is nowhere near enough.

I'm sitting in her kitchen flicking through the Argos catalogue, which the girls have thoughtfully annotated to show what they would like this year (there seem to be marks on every page).

Jane does Christmas like an eight-year-old, and it's brilliant. She cannot and will not see the need for restraint where decorations, food and party games are concerned. It's the one time her usual impeccable taste falls by the wayside. There will be no artfully arranged candles and swags of ivy, nor delicate monochrome fairy lights. Her basic philosophy is that everything looks better with the addition of tinsel.

I've just been offered an official invite for the big day, and as my options are somewhat limited this year, naturally I said yes. In previous years, I've either spent the festive season having a quiet but romantic time with Robbie or just a quiet time back home with my parents. It seems to be a year of firsts, though. My parents, who hardly ever surprise me, have booked a cruise, and Robbie – well, he sprung the biggest surprise of all.

In a few minutes we will be setting off for what is optimistically called a shopping trip but may in reality be more akin to a smash and grab raid, only with payment.

I have no great expectations for our trip, so I am rather taken aback when a couple of hours later I find myself having something of a eureka moment in the bookshop.

Jane is after a copy of the latest Jamie Oliver for her mother-in-law, and I have drifted past the cookbooks and come to a halt by a section on ecology, earth sciences and agriculture. I'm lured by as yet tentative thoughts that I might find something which Will would appreciate, but everything seems a little dry. I was thinking more coffee-table inspirational than kitchen-table instructional.

It is only when I start to move into agriculture that I catch sight of a title that I pull off the shelf immediately.

'Look what I found!' I exclaim when Jane is close enough to hear.

'*Undercover,*' she reads. '*A Guide for the Market Gardener.*' She gives me a wayward glance. 'Lovely.'

'I know, I know,' I say, batting away her accusations of insanity. 'It's not my usual reading material, but I've just had a brilliant idea. I met the Geoffreys in the tea shop this morning. Have I told you about them?' I don't wait for a reply. 'They are such a lovely couple. They've lived in the village for most of their lives, running their own business. They grow the most amazing veg and supply it to loads of places, even one of the Michelin-starred restaurants in Ludlow, but they're being kicked off the land they rent at the moment and are desperately trying to find some other space to move to.'

Jane looks totally bewildered. 'Sorry, Ellie, I'm not with you. What's that got to do with you?'

She has a point.

'Nothing, I know. Well, not as such, but you see Will has got loads of polytunnels he's not using. I bet the Geoffreys could use them. They'd pay him.'

'But if you say they can't find anywhere to rent, maybe they've already asked him and he said no.'

Another good point.

'Well, yes, I suppose so, but I doubt it. You see, I bet they don't even know that he's got them – no one does. It's like *Charlie and the Chocolate Factory* over there. You know, nobody ever goes in and nobody ever comes out. Besides, . . . how can I say it? Will is not exactly known in the village for being genial and approachable. He just keeps himself to himself, that's all. He won't know about their problem – I'm sure of it.'

'And you're going to be the one to enlighten him, are you?' says Jane drily.

I pause then, sucking in my breath. 'I don't know. I need to think about that one. But it seems such a shame. Will could do with the rent, and the Geoffreys are such nice people – very down to earth. They've been renting the same land for years, but the farmer it belongs to has just suddenly announced that he's got planning permission for holiday cottages, so they've got to go. No warning or anything. It's so unfair!'

'So, Ellie to the rescue?' says Jane, grinning.

That stops me in my tracks. 'Am I meddling again?' I ask, my stomach suddenly tightening into a knot.

Jane takes my arm and says firmly, 'Not meddling, no. You just want everyone to be happy, Ellie, and there's absolutely nothing wrong with that.' She lowers her voice before continuing. 'Just be careful. You don't want Will to get the wrong end of the stick, and he might not see it from your sunny point of view.'

So now I'm driving home, trying to come up with a suitable stick for Will to grab hold of. I probably shouldn't be doing this. It's none of my business; it's just that this feels like one of those serendipitous moments that should be allowed to come into being.

The house is frigid when I get in, and I nervously check the Aga. I live in fear of it going out, but so far, following Will's advice, it never has. I feed it its tea before I even start to think about mine. The weather is really cold now, and I've got into the habit of lighting a fire in both the lounge and the bedroom most days. My baking allows me to be at home most of the time, so it's pretty easy to keep the place warm. It's only on days like today, when I've been out, that I miss coming home to a warm house.

I carry my basket of paper spills upstairs to light the fire; a thought comes to me as, paper in hand, I return to the kitchen. I drop the day's offering onto the table and go through to my little utility area, where I keep a small pile of old newspapers. I know exactly what I'm looking for and pray that I haven't used it already. My eye alights on a likely candidate, and I pull it from the pile, flicking through the pages at speed. The article I'm looking for is a little way in.

I find the piece about the Geoffreys and read it again to make sure it says what I think it does. It's perfect, right down to the plea for help in the final paragraph. I offer up a silent vote of thanks. Now all I have to do is engineer a situation where I can bring it to Will's attention. Maybe I could pin it to his door, with a big red arrow pointing at the relevant article, and sign it *From a friend*. I leave the paper open on the table while I wait for inspiration to find its way to me.

In the end it's much easier than I could have hoped, and I can't help but take this as a sign that it was meant to be. I am just scrubbing my plate when I hear a tap at the door, alerting me to Will's presence. It can only be him – it's so utterly black outside, no one else would be able to find their way here. I usher him in out of the stinging cold.

'Another letter from your bank,' he says in greeting. 'I think it's a Christmas card.'

I place the letter on the table beside the paper.

'Thanks. I'll get on to them again to sort out my address.'

Will makes a dismissive gesture. 'Yeah, whenever. No hurry.'

I smile at this. 'Are you staying for tea? I've just eaten and was going to have a cup.' It's my best enticing smile. I feel a plan forming.

'Quick one.' Will grins. 'I haven't eaten yet, and I'm bloody starving. There's a jacket potato and a casserole in the oven with my name on.'

'Impressive. Puts my beans on toast to shame.'

'Ellie,' says Will drily. 'I live alone. I either cook or die. Besides, I didn't say it was a good casserole.'

'Bet it is, though,' I tease.

Will doesn't say anything at this but plonks himself down at the table. This is all working out so neatly, I can't quite believe it. I busy myself with the kettle and cups, deliberately turning my back to Will. I don't quite trust my facial expressions.

'I was just about to make a pile of spills for the fire. It takes me right back to my childhood. It's odd, isn't it, the things you remember?'

Will is silent for a minute, and I risk a glance. He is staring into space. 'Boot polish,' he announces. 'That's what I remember: polishing my dad's boots on the weekend. 'Course I didn't realise it was just child labour at the time. I think I'd been swung the line of being allowed to do it as a treat. It was my special job, you see. I still like polishing my own boots, though, even now. I love the smell of it.'

I place a mug in front of Will. 'It's kind of comforting I suppose,' I say, picking up *the* paper from the table. His blue eyes hold mine as he nods. I can feel a slow heat rising up my neck like I am being submerged in a pool of warm treacle. Any moment now it will hit my face. I remove the front two pages from the paper, making as if to roll them.

'Hey, look!' I exclaim, unrolling the paper again. 'Isn't that the couple from up the road? What's their name?' I make a show of examining the paper. Will looks on impassively.

'The Geoffreys, that's it. They supply the vegetables to Gina's, and the shop, I think.'

'I don't really know them,' says Will, who is forced to look as I shove the paper under his nose. I am on such thin ice here. He takes the pages and holds them away from him slightly to read.

'Looks like they need somewhere to move their business to. Their landlord is kicking them out,' he says. His gaze is steady.

'God, I shouldn't think that would be easy, would you?' I venture.

'Not a cat in hell's chance,' replies Will with, unless I'm imagining it, a bit more force than necessary. He rolls the pages up tight and passes the ends over one another in a fluid movement, dropping the knot into my basket. 'Although judging by the look on your face, you seem to feel it's my business somehow.'

I blush furiously. 'No, it's not that,' I stammer. 'I just wondered if perhaps they could use your polytunnels, that's all . . .'

'And why would I want them to do that?' Will glares at me. 'Thanks for the tea,' he says as he leaves. Except that he can't thank me for something he hasn't had. Shit.

CHAPTER ELEVEN

I don't so much sleep that night as fidget my way through hour after hour. Even Will's rhythmic log chopping doesn't soothe me. It takes all my willpower not to go out there and speak to him. I can't decide whether I want to yell at him or apologise. As one hour creeps into the next, I try to banish all thoughts of him, but I still can't sleep.

It isn't much of a surprise when I wake up in a foul mood. I look dreadful. My face is pale and blotchy, and the tension gripping my shoulders will doubtless creep up my neck and settle above one eye in the kind of headache that pounds with every move. It's bloody raining too, so any plans I might have made for my day free of baking are lost.

I am just returning *that* paper to the pile in the utility room when my slipper catches on a rucked-up piece of lino by the door. I drop to my knees. It's pulled right up; what was once a small curl is now a ripped triangle. *Just fabulous,* I think mutinously. *Another thing to sort out.*

The lino is old and fairly hideous, but something rusty red lying underneath it catches my eye. Having lived in older houses before, I think I know what it might be, and having scant regard for salvaging the lino, I pull. A whole piece comes away in my hand, revealing a pristine quarry tile. I was right.

Now I'm in a quandary. I can't look at the rest of the floor without taking the door bar off. Peering under the ripped area only gives me a limited view – not enough to determine the state of the rest of the floor. It would be a miracle if it were intact. My inner voice of reason tells me that the lino was probably put down to hide damaged tiles, but there is a slim possibility it might not have been.

Getting the lino up will be a bitch of a job. I'm going to have to move all the furniture around, then spend hours removing it, and God knows what I'll find underneath. I sit back and stare out the window. Rivulets of water are running down the pane. I stick my chin up grumpily; time is probably the one thing I do have today, and the mood I'm in means I'll probably enjoy a good wrestle. I go and get changed.

The door bar seems to have been in residence longer than I've been alive. The screw heads are buckled and dented, and on no account will it part company with the floor. I decide to leave it in place and instead manage to lever one side up enough to relinquish its grip on the lino, which I heave out with gritted teeth. So far so good: the tiles look okay.

Only the edges of the lino seem to have been stuck to the floor. The glue is old and brittle, dust-like in places, but it's made a real mess, leaving a crusty residue on the tiles.

I heave the table, chairs and sofa up towards the sink and manage to loosen a quantity of lino, which I try to roll, but any pliable qualities it once had have long since gone. The only way I can get it away from the tiles is by bending a section over and jumping along its length to crack it into a fold, a bit like a long strip of cardboard.

'It's okay. I think it's dead.'

I whirl around to find Will behind me, his coat dripping onto my newly revealed tiles. He's indicating the spot where I've been jumping.

'Ha bloody ha,' I say sarcastically.

'My God, look at these. They're beautiful. Are they all intact?' he says, looking down at the floor.

'I don't know,' I practically hiss, still trying to control the fold I'm working on. 'I'm trying to find out.'

Will looks around at the rest of what I've uncovered. 'It would be a miracle if they were. Can I help?' He shrugs off his jacket and hangs it on the door.

'I don't need any help,' I say coldly.

Will stuffs his hands into his pockets, his eyes searching mine.

'I see,' he says quietly. He looks like he's been slapped in the face. 'You're pissed off at me, I understand. I'll go then . . .' But he doesn't, and instead adds, 'I know you don't need any help, Ellie. But sometimes it's nice to accept help freely given – not because you need it, but because the other person wants to give it. It's a lesson I need to learn, apparently.' He shrugs.

What am I doing? This isn't like me. I set Will up yesterday and got found out. He had every right to be angry, and I'm just cross because he rained on my parade. The decent thing to do would be to admit it, but I can't, so instead I shrug too and point wordlessly at the other end of the room.

The next half hour passes in near silence, with instructions the only words spoken. The floor looks incredible. It's dirty, dusty and far from beautiful in its current state, but it still looks amazing. I don't know whether it's my mood or Will's that's infectious, but suddenly our pace picks up, and I'm desperate to see the rest of the floor.

It takes another hour of heaving and sweating before it's free. I suspect it would have taken me four times as long on my own.

I'm sitting on top of the lino 'log,' grinning, and Will has flopped back onto the floor, one hand over his head, the other resting on his stomach, where it rises and falls with his breathing. Neither of us speaks. After a few minutes of quiet but determined breathing, Will breaks the silence.

'Ellie? Can I have a cup of tea now, please?'

I laugh, climb off my makeshift chair and offer a dirty hand to Will, who levers himself off the floor. We stand in a now companionable silence and look around us in wonder. I can't believe it. Out of all the tiles we uncovered, only six are broken: two by the sink, three by the Aga, and one by the corner into the hallway. Will assures me that they can be replaced.

'You know what?' he says, plonking himself down on the settee and unhooking a chair from the table so that he can put his feet up. 'If you weren't going to keep that lino?' He looks to me for confirmation, and I shake my head. 'It would have made it one hell of a lot easier if we'd cut it down the middle, wouldn't it?' He reaches for the packet of biscuits on the table.

I stare at him, realisation dawning. Laughter rings out then, and I snatch the biscuits back, sitting beside him. 'Some bloody help you are!' I grin, elbowing him gently. He does it right back and leans across to fight for a biscuit.

I'm going to have to move. The weight of Will's body against mine is like a jump-start straight to my stomach, which drops away with a sweet, intense pull. I haven't thought about sex in a long time, but I'm thinking about it now. *Nice one, Ellie, really intelligent.* What on earth is wrong with me? I'm a rational, mature adult, I remind myself, one who knows better than to get all googly-eyed over a man I hardly know.

I can't say anything – my apology will have to wait. The tea is a bit too hot to drink comfortably, but I down it anyway and jump up with the fervour of someone who suddenly has to be somewhere else. Will fortunately mistakes my anxiety for eagerness and gulps his own tea down.

'Slave driver!' He grins, heading for the door. 'Back in a sec.'

Activity, I think, *that's what I need,* and I grab the broom out of the utility room, firmly closing my mind to any thoughts other than the state of the floor.

I'm still sweeping when Will returns, brandishing a tin of something that looks like it was bombed during the war, but is, I am assured, 'the business.' And so we sweep and mop and then start to buff. The hardened glue around the edges of the room responds well to the edge of a butter knife and scourer, and so it goes on. At some point I make another drink, and Will throws me a Mars bar he has smuggled in from home. I eat it in one continual motion, stuffing the wrapper into the back pocket of my jeans.

The tin of unction goes a long way, but it needs a lot of working in. By the time we finish, it's nearly three o'clock, and my hands are raw. My knees and back don't feel so good either. Standing up feels something of a novelty, but as I crank myself upright, I'm certain that it was worth it. One look at Will tells me I'm not wrong.

'Bloody hell!' he exclaims, hands on his hips. 'Pretty damned good, don't you think? Christ, I'm knackered, though.'

'I know – so am I. I don't know what to do now we've stopped. I think I'll be polishing floors in my sleep tonight.'

'Probably.'

I feel immensely happy. The day that started off so badly has become something of a triumph. I've enjoyed the challenge, the physical hard work, the single-minded purpose, working alongside someone, sharing a common goal, companionship. I've enjoyed being with Will. My head is so full of the things I want to say, and the different ways I could say them, that in the end the only thing I can do is grin and then grin some more.

A sudden toot cuts across my happy cloud. It sounds like a car horn, but I'm not expecting anyone.

Will looks at his watch and claps a hand across his forehead. 'Christ, I can't believe I'd forgotten about them. Come on!' he cries, catching me by the hand and hurtling towards the door.

The light is already fading outside, and the cold air catches at me as we run across the courtyard. A car has pulled up by its entrance, a figure climbing from it slowly. I can't see who it is yet, but Will doesn't let up, even though I'm still wearing my slippers. He's like an excited schoolboy. There's another figure getting out of the car now, and I recognize her. They are the last people I'm expecting to see.

Will is marching forward, a hand out-thrust.

'Hi! I'm sorry I wasn't here. I clean forgot the time. I've been over helping Ellie,' he says, shaking Mr Geoffreys by the hand warmly. 'And here she is.'

I am propelled forward.

'Well, young lady, I'm grateful to you, I really am. The missus too.' The hand shaking continues as I turn to look at Mrs Geoffreys, whose head is bouncing up and down in agreement.

'Bless me, though – I never thought this would happen. It just goes to show; you never can tell what's around the corner. I thought we'd had it right enough, and now' – he beams at Will and me – 'well, I just can't believe it.'

'Ellie?'

Will waits until he has my full attention before speaking. 'Bonnie and Richard are here because last night I officially became their new landlord. I've signed the Orchard Field over to them. I thought they might want to come over today and take a look.' He pauses for a moment before continuing in a still, calm voice. 'Of course, I made sure they knew whose idea this was. I'd like to thank you too.'

Will nods at me gently as if to acknowledge what I'm feeling, and I don't have to say a thing.

Later that evening, Will and I are sitting before a dancing fire, nursing a glass of particularly fine single malt (Will's words, not mine: I don't know a thing about whisky, and I don't actually like it, but it seems the right thing to drink somehow).

The Geoffreys stayed a little while, looking over the land, exclaiming over the polytunnels and generally behaving like villagers who had no idea what lay behind the high walls of Rowan Hill. Apparently, Will had no idea what the land should be rented for and, when told what the Geoffreys currently pay, laughed and said that he didn't need that much. What would be far more useful to him was if both households could be supplied with whatever they needed. It suited his view of the way of things. So the Geoffreys went away with big smiles on their faces, more money in their pockets and a pass to come and go as they pleased. I'm now also the grateful beneficiary of free veggies whenever I want them.

His living room is dark and red and rich and comfortable. I imagine that when you're in here at night, curtains drawn, it would be very easy to forget that the outside world exists at all. The colours are warm, and the room, full of texture. The curtains are of a crewel-work design, and there are tapestries on the walls; not exactly feminine, but not a typical bachelor pad either. A thought comes to me suddenly. 'Will?' He looks up from the fire. 'You know this morning, when you first came around? You know, the bit just before I was extremely rude to you? Well, what did you come around for? You never did say.'

As soon as I say it, I realise what the answer is. One look at Will's expression, a mixture of embarrassment and sheepish amusement, confirms my thoughts.

'You came to tell me about the Geoffreys, didn't you? Why the hell didn't you say so, you daft idiot? I made you stay the whole day, and you never even mentioned it.'

'You didn't make me stay; I offered, and I've had a nice day, Ellie. You know sometimes the journey is just as important as the destination.'

I think about his words for a moment, Robbie's accusations of trying to live others' lives for them still echoing in my mind. Will's right, of course; I've got a lot to learn about my own behaviour, shoving my idea down his throat yesterday when I could have achieved the same outcome with less acrimony and a lot more consideration for how Will might feel. Will kicks my foot then, which is resting inches from his own.

'Hey, don't be so hard on yourself,' he says gently. 'I meant what I said. I have had a really nice day. The floor looks fantastic, and this whole thing with the Geoffreys is just perfect all round. I only have you to thank for that. I'd never have known about their predicament if it wasn't for you. And I certainly wouldn't have done anything about it. I needed a good kick up the arse.' He pauses to take a reflective sip of his drink.

I can see the golden hairs on his arm in the firelight. 'Except that it wasn't really my place to do the arse kicking, was it?' I say. 'I'm sorry if I've interfered in how you do things here. That wasn't my intention.'

My words hang in the air between us for a moment. I am acutely aware of his eyes on my face.

'Is that what you think you were doing? Interfering?' he asks eventually.

My eyes drop to my lap. 'It seems to have become a bit of a habit of mine,' I mutter. 'This is your estate, Will. It really is none of my business what you do with it.'

'Maybe not, but as a friend, I value your opinion, Ellie. Besides which, it often takes someone who isn't quite so close to things to state the bleeding obvious, doesn't it? How can that be interfering? It was a brilliant idea, Ellie. Just sit back and take the credit.' He's grinning at me now as the silence stretches out once more.

'You're not very good at taking compliments, are you?' he adds, a teasing note to his voice. 'And that's the only thing you're not good at, by the way, so whoever told you otherwise got it very wrong.'

My heart gives a little flip; when they were handing out the perceptive gene, they certainly didn't miss out Will. I stare up at him, open-mouthed, wondering what to say now. Will simply stares back, a gentle smile on his face.

'Anyway, I have my own behaviour to apologise for. I took offence last night, and I shouldn't have.' I'm not very good with people since—' He breaks off for a moment, waving his hand as if searching for something to point at. 'Well, after Caroline left, I guess. I kind of shut myself away, and I've got so used to it, I find it hard to change.'

'How you feel is understandable surely. Anyone would be the same in that situation,' I say, thinking again of my own past history. Different circumstances maybe, but still a breakdown of a relationship all the same. I can recognize the symptoms. But Will is shaking his head.

'No, I just made things worse than they needed to be. I wasn't a very nice person at the time, so it was no surprise that people started backing away in droves. After that I didn't have to answer so many questions, and I suppose I preferred it that way.'

'And now?' I ask.

Will reflects on this for a moment. 'Now I've got too used to it. Most people around here think I'm a lazy, good-for-nothing, grumpy bastard. Can't say I blame them.'

'You talk as if you believe them, though. Isn't that what keeps folks away – you don't give them any reason to change their opinion?'

'Yes, well, like I say, maybe I prefer it that way.' His eyes are defying me, a bitter edge creeping into his voice. I hold his look for a moment. Too long. He looks away, embarrassed.

'I'm sorry,' I say finally. 'I just don't see you like that. These things are not reasons to dislike you. They might be your more negative characteristics, but they are your character. They make you what you are – bad things together with good things. Isn't that how we all are?'

'Yes, and I'm still a grumpy old bastard.'

At least he's not looking quite so fierce now.

'Not necessarily grumpy – just a little sad sometimes. Hard to get close to,' I finish, wondering why I just said that. I can feel the whole can of worms beginning to open as I finish speaking, and sure enough, the silence that follows is long enough for all the little critters to escape. I risk a glance at Will, who looks as if he's trying to swallow a length of barbed wire. There are a whole host of things both of us could say at this point, and neither of us do.

Any minute now one of us will change the subject.

'What are you doing for Christmas?' asks Will, right on cue.

'I'm off to Jane's. I usually go home to Mum and Dad, but they're off cruising this year. Jane's will be great, though. What about you?'

'Staying here, the same as usual. Finn's trying to get home, but he's busting a gut to get a big contract finished, so he's not sure if he'll make it.'

'Fairly quiet then?' I clarify.

Will laughs. 'Believe me, if Finn makes it home, quiet is the one thing it certainly won't be. Finn doesn't do reserved.'

The unspoken comparison dangles like an invitation in the air between us. I ignore it.

We lapse into silence again. A log shifts on the fire, and the sombre note of the clock swims gently into my consciousness. It's getting late and I should go. Will senses my signs and sits forward in his chair.

'Thanks for today, Ellie.'

I frown. 'What do you mean, "thanks"? It's me that should be thanking you for my beautiful floor.'

'Well, then I guess we're quits.' His smile is warm on my back as I rise and turn for the door.

'Hey, Ellie?' he says. 'Goodnight. Sweet dreams.'

CHAPTER TWELVE
December

At some point in the night, the skies must have cleared, I notice, as I open the curtains to a sharp frost and blue skies. I'm up early this morning – it's a baking day, but it's not just because of that. As soon as I wake, I can sense the brightness outside, and there's one place that really gets the sun in the early hours. The kitchen is glowing, and I marvel at how good it looks each morning.

I'm going all out on the Christmas theme today, making little spiced gingerbreads and cinnamon-sweet rugelach with their sticky sultana filling. If I have time later, I'll go out and try to buy a few more presents.

Instead, when it gets to late afternoon, I head outside to deal with my offending shrubbery, secateurs in hand. I've been meaning to do this for a while; it's grown so far over the path that every time it's wet, the postman or paperboy gets drenched.

As I prune, I suddenly realise that there have been voices talking for a little while. Once I tune in, they are quite distinct: it's Will and Alice Tweedy, which surprises me. I stand as still as I can to listen, unashamedly. Like most children, I was brought up not to eavesdrop. Eavesdroppers never hear anything good about themselves, said my mother, but I still did it, and I defy anyone not to earwig given the opportunity. Trouble is that it's a catch-22 situation: listen and you run the risk of having your character assassinated. Move and you're likely to be heard and accused of the very thing you were trying to avoid. You can't win, so I pin back my ears and do my level best not to let my teeth chatter.

'Are you sure you'll be okay?'

'Will, I'll be fine. I came through the Blitz, dear.'

'Yes, but you were all of seven years old and, as far as I know, didn't have an arthritic hip.'

'Oh, go on with you. You've got better things to do with your day than ferry me wood back and forth. I'll be perfectly warm.'

'I'll only be away for a few days.'

'I know, and you'll come and see me when you're back?'

'Promise.'

'You had better, or I shall want to know why. You're doing the right thing, you know.'

'I hope so. I'm nervous as hell.'

'Good. That means you understand why you need to do it. Caitlin will look after you, Will, and you'll be fine. Take care, won't you?'

'I will, and you behave yourself.'

'Wouldn't dream of it!' She chuckles.

Will laughs. 'Bye then.'

'Bye, love. Oh and one more thing: when you get back, you will tell her, won't you?'

'Yes, Alice I'll tell her. Now go inside before you freeze. I'll see you soon.'

I listen to the sound of the wheelbarrow squeaking in withdrawal and creep back into the house, stunned. I am surprised enough to hear any conversation between these two, let alone one full of what sounds like long-standing affection. The last time I heard Mrs Tweedy talking about Will, she was bad-mouthing him, but judging by what I just overheard, you'd think they were friends. I haven't a clue what they were talking about either. I've never heard Will mention anyone called Caitlin before.

I can see him out of my kitchen window now, coming back down into the courtyard and pausing by the log pile to refill the barrow. I know with the utmost certainty where he is headed for next, and throw the secateurs hurriedly back into the dresser drawer, ripping off my jacket and hanging it out of sight. When he appears by my door, he'll find me boxing up my gingerbread in a nonchalant fashion, no sign that I've ever been in the garden.

CHAPTER THIRTEEN

My mother was right (as always), and I spend the next couple of days doing penance for my moment of sin. Will came around to tell me that he was going away for a few days, just as I knew he would. He loaded up my woodpile and told me where I could find more in the courtyard if I needed it. He even left me the wheelbarrow. I thanked him and assured him that I would be fine, just as Alice Tweedy had done – but I didn't ask him about her. How could I? So now he's gone, and not only have I been left in an agony of curiosity about the conversation I overheard, but I've suddenly realised that I miss Will.

I catch myself looking for him whenever I pass a window, listening out for his car and checking whether his lights are on at night. I hadn't realised that I did this. It's not like we see each other that much, but I knew he was around, and now he's not. The big house is dark and quiet, and I suddenly feel very alone.

At the weekend I go up into the woods to gather holly to decorate the house. I find myself walking deeper and deeper, wondering whether Will has been working here and looking for signs that he has. What should have been half an hour's work turns out to take much longer, and it's only when I realise what I'm doing that I make for home.

I've decided not to get a Christmas tree this year as I'm going to Jane's. The holly will be enough decoration: it's covered in berries, and I've got some red ribbon to tie it up with, but the task that I would normally enjoy becomes fraught as I try to make head or tail of my emotions.

I can't have a relationship with Will that is anything other than friendship. I know that. In my heart of hearts, I know that I shouldn't even be contemplating having a relationship with any man. It's too soon after Robbie – I'm not ready to be in love again. I'm scared I don't really know what love is, and yet Will has got under my skin, plain and simple, and I don't know why. Every logical instinct tells me I'm being ridiculous; after all, I still don't know what happened between him and his wife, but I can't seem to settle for the friendship we have either. It feels like something is missing, and it strikes me that maybe it's the mystery of him that I find attractive; the reputed womaniser so at odds with the nature of the man I've come to know. Maybe it's the truth that's missing.

I bake like a thing possessed over the next few days. Rather fortuitously for me, Gina has been asked to provide a buffet for the local Over Sixties club Christmas get-together and she's put me in charge of desserts. I'm thinking that a few dozen mince pies doesn't sound that bad, until she explains that it's traditional for them to host a small tea party for the local schoolchildren afterwards, where Father Christmas is the guest of honour. I imagine seventy or so five- to eleven-year-olds can eat quite a large number of cakes.

Of course, although I am reluctant to acknowledge it, this industry is also eating into the time that Will is away. The Geoffreys have been over, but apart from a brief conversation with them, I've hardly spoken to a soul.

There's no sign of them this morning as I push the wheelbarrow across the courtyard to load up more logs. I'm conscious of the noise the barrow sounds into the still air. It seems to echo inordinately loudly across the brick floor, and I feel my invasion keenly. I've never been here when Will hasn't been around, and although I know it's fine, I feel as if I'm trespassing.

It's funny how you notice things differently when you're on your own, as if you're seeing them for the first time. I realise that when I've walked across the yard previously, I've missed things, small ornate details and doors where I thought there were just walls. The space here is incredible, and the scope for the use of it, more so. It sends my imagination into overdrive.

The wood is stacked in a lean-to, its tiled roof adjoining the main house. A pair of worn leather gloves hang on a hook protruding from the wall, and I put them on thoughtfully, my mind inevitably turning to the hands that previously wore them.

I load the barrow quickly, looking for smaller pieces of wood to go on top. What I could really do with is some kindling, but a swift cast about confirms that there is none here. A more detailed scout also confirms that there is no axe, but I know that this is where Will chops wood; I can see the block he uses on the floor in front of the woodpile. An axe must be somewhere close by.

There is a door in the back wall, but it's locked. Judging by the marks on the floor, it opens into this room, so I suppose the key is on the other side. Bugger. I am about to totally dismiss the possibility of finding any tools, when I realise that the timber roof beams rest on the ledge that the inner wall makes with the outer. It's like a little shelf. I wonder if Will is like most people around here, seeing little need for Fort Knox security. I stand on my tiptoes and gingerly run my fingers along the cobwebby ledge. I make contact with hard metal almost immediately. A key. I pull it down. It's one of those lovely iron ones – huge and probably as old as the house. I feel a little awkward, but I don't suppose that Will would mind me looking in his tool shed. But when I open the door, it isn't a tool shed that I find.

I expect a dark and dingy hole (well, a tool shed), but the space is flooded with light and of not inconsiderable size. As I step across the threshold, I realise it's a garden room.

There is glass *everywhere*, and not just making up the fabric of the room. There's a huge work surface running along the left-hand wall, with various pieces of machinery on top and vertical partitions underneath, separating the space into open-fronted cupboards. Each of these is filled with sheets of glass in a myriad of colours.

A workbench runs down the centre of the room, and I circle it warily, drawn to what lies on its surface. Somehow, I know not to pick it up. There are smaller pieces of glass beside it, and I lift one of these to the light: it's a beautiful swirl of greens. I lay it back down carefully.

The far wall has something stacked against it, and I'm attracted to the colours I can see there. The pieces are stacked together, leaning up against the wall, like canvases. I tip one towards me experimentally. It seems solid enough. I need to pick it up, I realise, to see it come to life, and wonder if I dare. I'm still wearing Will's gloves, so I lift it again, trying to gauge its weight. It feels okay, and I bend my knees to grasp the piece firmly on each side. I carry it carefully to the table, deliberately not looking at it properly until I'm ready. I lower the bottom edge until it makes contact and stand as far back as my arms will allow.

Good God! I suck in another breath, as mine seems to have left my body. I've seen stained glass before, but nothing like this. This is amazing. No, not just amazing: vibrant, shimmering, ethereal, haunting. My thoughts are pulled back to that first day after

I moved into the Lodge, when I came home to find my fire alight, to the screen dancing with the flames. I remember Will's offhand reticence when I thanked him for his gift. I know its maker now, but this piece is different somehow; it is so much more that it makes the fire screen look a bit pedestrian by comparison. I look back to the work stacked against the wall. There must be half a dozen pieces there. Why has Will just left them? Why hasn't he . . .?

'What the fuck do you think you're doing?'

The force of his voice from behind me takes the strength from my knees. A rush of adrenalin leaves my stomach behind as the blood rushes around my body, and my heartbeat clamours in my head. I'm acutely aware of the glass I'm still holding. I hear a strangled sound and realise that it's come from my lips; it doesn't sound like me at all.

Will strides over, bringing the smell of the cold with him. He grasps the piece from me and lays it down. The gentleness with which he handles the glass is in marked contrast to the rest of him, which is taut and shaking with anger. He steps away from me.

'Well?' he roars. 'I asked you a question.'

I can't speak. I feel sick and dizzy, and I can't bear to see the look of pain in his eyes. I stumble away from him, wanting to put distance between us and willing my legs to carry me through the door. I don't see the person standing there until I crash headlong into him.

'It's okay,' this man says, and again, 'hey, it's okay.' And then he's holding me, not in restraint, but in support. He is tall and solid, and without really knowing why, I let him take my weight. He speaks again.

'Will, what's going on?' His voice is deeper than Will's. 'I come home to find the house is freezing and all locked up, and you're terrorising the local womenfolk. What's the problem?'

'I've been away,' comes Will's flat reply. 'Only just this minute got back.'

'So?' There's a long pause where neither of them speaks.

'I don't want her to see them.'

'Well, Christ, it's not as if . . .' the voice trails off here, the arms around me loosening their hold a little.

'Jesus, Will,' he says, his voice catching in his throat, 'you're working again.' It's not a question.

His arms release me completely then, and I'm left standing. I turn around to see Will enveloped in an embrace that he returns needily.

The two pull apart slowly, nodding in answer to some unspoken question. Will is pressing the heel of his hand to his eyes.

The man turns towards me. 'You must be Ellie?' he says. 'Come on – let's get you home.' And the most gorgeous-looking man on the planet holds out his hand to me. 'I'm Finn, by the way.'

I don't remember the brief walk back home. Finn deposits me on the sofa and moves around the kitchen, making tea I suppose. I wonder what it is with the men around here, who all act like they own the place, before I remember who Finn is. I guess that, like Will, he's been in this room many times before. He doesn't speak until he's handed me a steaming mug.

'Bit of a shock?'

I press my mouth to the rim of the mug and inhale the warmth while trying to sort out my emotions. I am angry, indignant and also slightly relieved to discover that Will was hugging his brother, and not his lover as I had first thought. I'm cross with myself for straying where I shouldn't have, never having meant to upset Will, and I'm sad for blowing apart any chance I might have had of any kind of friendship with him. I nod mutely and then – much to my disgust – feel tears threatening to spill.

Finn sits beside me, taking my hand and clasping it in his own. The intimacy of this action is not lost on me.

'Can you forgive him, do you think?' he asks.

The question surprises me. I look at him quizzically.

'Forgive him?'

'Ellie, you have to know one thing,' he answers. 'I love my brother very much, and believe it or not, despite being away from home such a lot, I know him very well. He has a horrible tendency to let his mouth run away with him when he's feeling vulnerable or scared. On the basis that I've just flown halfway around the world and this wasn't exactly the homecoming I had in mind, I'm going to give him an almighty bollocking for his behaviour soon. That said, do you think you can forgive him?'

I give a slight nod.

'Good girl.'

'I didn't do anything!' I say finding my voice. 'I was only look- ing at the glass. I didn't break anything.'

'I know,' murmurs Finn.

'Have you seen it?' I shiver. 'It's beautiful. I've never seen any- thing like it before.'

'The fact that you think that makes you special.' He smiles. 'I don't believe Will has figured it all out yet, but he will.' He gives my hand a squeeze.

'I still don't understand what I've done,' I whisper. 'And you said he was scared, Finn. What on earth is he scared of?'

Finn's gaze is unrelenting. 'Himself . . . and the past.' He considers me for a moment, thoughtful. 'I know that you don't understand, Ellie – I'm not sure that any of us do, and maybe we don't need to yet. We just need to help Will have a little faith. Can you do that?'

He is quite extraordinarily good looking, I think. Taller than Will and more powerfully built, but with the same blue eyes, bright blonde hair and thick dark eyelashes. I can't help but think that at this moment I would do anything he asks.

I nod. Suddenly I very much want to be by myself.

'I'll be fine, honestly,' I lie, more confused than ever.

'Trust me, Ellie, you will be. Now excuse me. I need to go and find something to sharpen my tongue with.'

I never did find that axe.

CHAPTER FOURTEEN

I'm not quite sure what happened to the rest of the day, but somehow I turn out five dozen perfect fairy cakes, which I ice with little white stars. When I go outside at teatime to bring in a basket of logs for the night, the wind has risen sharply, and an icy rain drives at me. My log pile has been replenished, as has my store of kindling. I don't know why, but this upsets me beyond all comprehension. I lock the door behind me and return to the lounge, where, after feeding the fire, I watch the TV, unseeing, until I can legitimately crawl into bed.

Gina knows something's up when I drop off the cakes the next morning, but she doesn't press me. On a whim I offer to help her, a classic stalling tactic I know, but she accepts my offer with such gratitude that I feel a little better.

I've never been to the village hall before, and it's much like any other, but there's a huge tree, a ton of tinsel and hundreds of twinkling fairy lights, and it looks so pretty. By the time it's this close to Christmas, members of the Over Sixties have had so much turkey that anything resembling a traditional dinner has been banned. So, instead, Gina has made a wonderful feast of a huge dressed salmon, little caramelised onion and cranberry tarts, sausage rolls, bowls of assorted salads, a honeyed gammon, sandwiches and little cottage loaves. What with my cakes as well, they certainly won't starve.

The Over Sixties make a surprisingly riotous lot, but nothing compared to the children, whose noise level reflects their state of excitement. In a surprisingly short space of time, however, they are gathered together to be taken back to school, and I'm horrified to be dragged into the hall for a vote of thanks from the chair of the Over Sixties club, who leads a resounding round of applause for Gina and myself. I'm not sure it's deserved in my case, but I smile politely and slink away.

As I make my way out, a few of the club members are saying their goodbyes, muffling themselves against the cold before venturing out. I recognize one voice amongst the others: Alice Tweedy. I'm cornered, having to go through the cloaks area to return to the kitchen. I spied Alice earlier, but so far this afternoon she's remained at some distance from me. If I'm lucky, I might get away with a polite smile. I reach the kitchen door just as her voice floats past me.

'She is, isn't she? Not that I know her that well, of course; she seems a bit quiet. She can bake a good cake, I'll give her that, but like most young folk, she doesn't seem to know what neighbourly means. I could be dead in my bed, and they'd never know up at the house.'

The leap from relative normality to rage is instantaneous. It comes at me with such a rush, I can feel my hands shaking. My heart doubles its beat, adrenalin coursing around my body. Fight or flight? Fight definitely. I'm not running – not this time.

How dare she make accusations like that? It's so unfair, and I realise I'm angry, not just for myself, but for Will, who was clearly implicated in her last statement. I think back to the conversation I overheard in the garden and his obvious care of her. The whole thing was confusing enough, and now Mrs Tweedy has the gall to accuse him of something blatantly untrue. I'm not going to let her get away with her evil gossip this time. Someone has to set her straight.

Gina is just returning from another trip out to the car. There are a couple of boxes still to go, and we take one each. I'm not about to confront Mrs Tweedy here. She likes an audience, and I'm not about to give her the pleasure.

'Are you okay?' asks Gina, no doubt eyeing my flaming cheeks.

'Yes, fine,' I reply. 'Bit of a hot flush, I think.'

Gina rolls her eyes. 'You're far too young for that kind of thing, and believe me I know.'

I hand the final box to Gina with a smile. 'Are you okay if I get off now? I've got one or two things still to do today.'

Gina's reply is to give me a fierce hug. 'Of course it's okay. Listen, Ellie, thank you so much for everything. Not just for today. Your cakes have given things a real lift for me. I know it's not really what you want to be doing, but it's worked well, I think.'

'It has, hasn't it? I've really enjoyed it.'

'Well then, love, I'll see you in the New Year, and in the meantime' – she breaks off here to thrust something into my hand, closing her own hand over it – 'you have yourself a great Christmas.' She gives me another hug and then wafts her hands, motioning for me to go. I open my hand. 'Go on, not another word. Go!'

I curl my fingers back around the bundle of notes in my hand and return the hug. 'Thank you so much,' I breathe before returning to the warm fug of the kitchen to collect my coat.

I take a deep breath as I step out into the road, marshalling my nerve, my thoughts keeping time with my rapid steps. I can't be far behind Mrs Tweedy – she had better be in. My heart is pounding and my mouth dry. I think fleetingly that confrontation isn't my thing, but I've had enough. I hammer on the door.

Mrs Tweedy is still carrying her scarf as she opens the door. She's obviously just arrived home, and she doesn't look surprised to see me.

'Ellie,' she says, 'come on in,' and she opens the door wide. Whatever I expected her opening remark to be, it wasn't this. I step into the hall, which is wide and welcoming.

'I'm not stopping, Mrs Tweedy,' I say as steadily as I can. 'I just came to say—'

'Alice,' she corrects me. 'You should call me Alice.'

'Mrs Tweedy,' I reaffirm. 'I'm not quite sure what your problem is, but I thought it was about time someone put you straight. I heard what you said about Will and me up at the hall. How dare you say things like that? Don't you realise how hurtful they are?' I pause to gauge her reaction, but she simply nods her head, not in agreement, but indicating that I should go on. It infuriates me even more.

'I mean, I don't care what you think of me. I haven't lived here long, and why you think I would want to be neighbourly with someone who hasn't got a decent word to say about anyone else is beyond me, but I heard you and Will in the garden last week. You take the greatest delight in bad-mouthing him at every opportunity, and he might have his faults, but he doesn't deserve what you say about him. He's obviously very fond of you for some reason I've yet to fathom, and all you can do is spread the most disgraceful lies about him.'

I break off suddenly, panting. My anger has reached its peak and is now spent. I look at Mrs Tweedy, an elderly lady I've cornered in her own home, and I feel utterly wretched. My emotions, which have been up and down over the last couple of days, give way, and my control snaps. I burst into noisy, choking sobs.

'Oh my God, I'm so sorry. Sorry,' I manage, stumbling for the door, tears blurring my vision. I feel a hand on my arm.

'Ellie, child. Come and sit down. Come on.' And she pulls me away from the door, leading me down the corridor. Even in my distressed state, I am surprised. The room she leads me into is beautifully elegant, decorated in creams, browns and pinks, with Sanderson fabric at the window. It doesn't fit the picture of the fussily plaid-dressed pensioner. The fire is roaring in the grate, and either she's the fastest layer of fires in the West, or someone has been here before her. I cock my head towards the hearth.

'Will?' I question. She gives a simple nod in return. I cry some more then, sinking down onto the sofa and letting the confusion, anger and sadness of the last few days wash out of me.

Mrs Tweedy sits beside me in comforting acceptance, her arm around my shaking shoulders, tucking my hair back over my ear. It's such a soothing gesture, and although I'm twice her size, it doesn't seem to matter. For some reason I'm content to let her do this, and we sit together for a little while.

Eventually, I straighten, calmer, but beginning to feel more than a little embarrassed. Mrs Tweedy looks at me squarely, a kindly expression on her face. There is no anger there, none of the belligerence I expect to see.

'Perhaps it's time for some explanations if you're ready?' she asks quietly.

I inhale deeply, pulling myself together. 'I'm very sorry. I don't know what—'

'I didn't mean from you, Ellie.' She looks quite sad for a moment. 'I meant from me. I don't think any of us realised quite how upsetting and confusing this has been for you. That was never Will's intention, or mine. In the beginning I was just trying to protect him, just as I always have done, but now things are different.'

'I don't understand,' I say. 'Why are things different? I need to say sorry for shouting at you. I really shouldn't have done that, but it's just that somehow everybody seems to be party to some big secret. Even Finn knows.'

'Ellie, please, there's no need to apologise. I realised before Will went away that we needed to explain certain things. In fact, I made Will promise to explain everything to you as soon as he got back.'

I take a moment to digest this new information, thinking back to their conversation in the garden and then what happened yesterday when Will did arrive home. 'Things didn't go quite to plan, did they?' I ask ruefully.

'Not exactly, no, but that wasn't your fault, dear. You just caught Will off guard in the very place that he least expected to see you. Silly boy, his behaviour was quite unacceptable. You know, I could tan his backside sometimes.' She says, with a resigned smile.

'So, was it Will who told you what happened yesterday?'

'No, Finn, actually. He hotfooted it around here after he'd been to see you. Will is keeping a low profile. He's feeling quite disgusted with himself – as well he might.'

I frown. 'But I still don't understand what all the secrecy is about.'

Alice leans forward and gives my arm a brisk rub. 'I'm sorry, dear. I'm skipping bits quite dreadfully. Shall I get us a drink and then start at the beginning?'

She's gone for a moment or two, returning, not, as I'd thought, with a restorative cup of tea, but with a glass of clear liquid that turns out to be eye-watering neat gin. I notice that Alice's glass contains about a third of the volume of mine.

'I suppose I have to go back a bit to when the boys were both small,' begins Alice. 'You see, farming is a busy life, and there were no playgroups or nurseries back then, so the boys had to fend for themselves and make their own entertainment. They would spend all day outside if they could, thick as thieves, and when they were done with their mischief, they usually ended up here at some point or another. My door was always open. I came to love them both as my own in many ways.'

'You've lived here a long time, then?' I ask, beginning to picture the two little boys running around.

'Oh yes. I came to the village as a young bride, quite some while before Finn and Will were born. This was Charles's and my first house. It turned out that we couldn't have children of our own, so when the boys were born, we helped out as best we could – that's what people did back then. I watched them both grow up; very similar to look at with their bright blonde hair, but so very different in character.' She pauses, staring into her glass for a moment.

'Finn was always so sure of himself, a very confident young man growing up, whereas Will was much quieter even then. He was such a gentle child – not soppy, just thoughtful and generous. Whereas Finn could charm the birds out of the trees, Will preferred to ask them politely and wait patiently for them to come down.'

'He's younger, isn't he?'

'Yes, but not by much – not quite two years.' Alice drops her voice a little then, almost whispering to me. 'Don't you dare tell him this, but I've a bit of a soft spot for Will.'

I smile. 'I was beginning to think you might have.'

'They've always been very close, and although they're so different, there was one thing they always had in common, and that was their desire to do anything other than farming. Finn broke his parents' hearts when he told them he was going to university. That sounds odd, doesn't it, in this day and age? But although they were very proud of his academic achievements, they still believed he'd come back to run the farm one day. He didn't, though, and I think that's when it really became difficult for Will.'

'So what did he do?'

'He stayed here for a while, shying away from confrontation, and just tried to get on with what he saw as familial duty. He found it a burden, though, and his heart wasn't really in it. He's not a farmer, Ellie – he never was. His parents' disappointment in Finn inevitably transferred to him – unfairly I might add – something which he's always kept from his brother. After a couple of years, in an effort to finally stand up for himself, Will took off to art college against their wishes.'

'He mentioned he has a degree in fine art,' I recall, thinking back to our after-dinner conversation with Jack and Jane.

'Yes: a first-class degree, with honours. Not only that, but he became a supremely talented artist, Ellie. I think you can probably guess his area of expertise?'

'Of course!' I exclaim. 'The stained glass.'

'That's right,' she affirms, smiling now. 'He became interested in conservation when he was down in London, and it grew from there. He gained one or two commissions as word got round, and things were going well until he met Caroline.' She breaks off here, looking at me directly. 'I'm not boring you, am I, dear? Only, you know what us old folk are like for going on about the past.'

'No, not at all,' I hasten to say. I wait while she gets up and pokes the fire before returning to the sofa and taking a sip of her drink. She continues.

'I took an instant dislike to her. Will brought her back here the summer they met, and although he was clearly besotted with her, I thought her a very cold fish. Oh, she was beautiful to look at, tall and willowy with porcelain skin, but her smile never seemed to reach the depths of her beautiful eyes, and the way she always tossed her hair around was rather affected,

I thought. Of course I kept my thoughts from Will, and about a year later, they moved in together. I knew right away that something wasn't right. He'd always rung me you see, every week, just for a catch-up, but gradually the calls got further apart, and when he did ring, little sounds of dissension were creeping in about his work. He'd moan about colleagues and their work, or the money he was being paid, and that especially struck me as wrong. It just wasn't Will at all. Then he was persuaded to give it all up.'

'He became a teacher, didn't he?'

'Art for bored thirteen-year-olds – I ask you, how ridiculous! The only saving grace is that after his parents died, he came back home, having married Caroline first. I imagine that was part of the plan all along, to get her hands on the estate – that and a husband with a respectable, steady career.'

'But when we first met in the village shop, you told me Caroline was a lovely girl. In fact, more than that, Alice, you implied that Will had been having an affair and that they split up because he wouldn't father a child for her.'

Alice drops her gaze to her lap, where she removes a piece of lint. Her expression is pained when she looks up once more. 'I know, and for that I'm sorry. It's not true, Ellie. It was the story Caroline made up as the excuse for her leaving, and although she never said as much outright, she dropped enough hints to a few of her friends. Coupled with Will's surly behaviour and avoidance of people, I think most of the villagers put two and two together and came up with five. When I found out what people were saying, I thought at first I should try to put them straight, but in the end . . . well, it suited Will to have those lies repeated, and so that's what I did.'

'But why, Alice?' I shake my head in confusion. 'I don't understand.'

'Will had a breakdown of sorts, just over a year ago. I can't tell you why, dear; you must ask him yourself. But although I didn't like Caroline, I understand it must have been very difficult for her, living with the stranger that Will had become. She wasn't a fighter, though, and when she saw her rosy future wouldn't be quite so easily won, I think she decided it was too much like hard work. In her own way, I suppose, she thought she was helping Will. By letting people think he was having an affair, it gave her the perfect excuse to leave but also protected Will to some degree. People are so quick to judge, dear, and in believing that Will was an adulterer, they never thought to seek any other reason for the failure of their marriage.'

'But why didn't you tell people the truth about what happened? Surely they would have understood. Having a breakdown is nothing to be ashamed of.'

'Because Will couldn't face people knowing the truth behind it all. He didn't want people to know what happened, and he begged me to keep his secret. Rightly or wrongly, that's what I've done, what I've continued to do. I've been an angry, silly old woman this past year or so, Ellie. I've had my own reasons, but mostly because I was trying to protect Will. Since my husband died, he's become more like a son to me, and I couldn't bear to see him in so much pain. I thought I was helping him.'

'Alice, you did everything you could for him, I'm sure. Sometimes, though, in time, people have to start to make their own way through things.' I take her hand in mine. 'Is that why Will went to see this Caitlin person?'

Alice nods. 'She's an old friend of Will's from school. A psychologist. She's been helping him iron out a few things from his past. It's a rather tricky time for him at the moment.' She gives my hand a squeeze. 'You've seen his work, Ellie. He has such incredible talent, and yet he gave it all up for Caroline. Bit by bit, she took away all his passion for his work, all his joy – it all went. He became a different person to the one I knew. Finn and I tried our damnedest to get him to take up what he loved once more, knowing that this would help him to recover, and we were getting there, but then . . . one night a few months after Caroline left, he went into his workroom and tried to destroy everything. Completely obliterate it. How he didn't manage to kill himself with all that glass, I will never know.' She shudders. 'Finn hauled him out and calmed him down, but Will swore he would never set foot in there again, and up until a couple of months ago, he hadn't.'

I think back to the events of yesterday, and Finn's words to me later in the house. 'I know he's working again. Finn made it clear that it's a recent thing, but he said that Will just hadn't figured it out yet. Is that what he meant? That Will doesn't understand how important this is for him?'

Alice smiles at me gently. 'Partly,' she replies, 'but something else too.'

I look at her in confusion. 'And you want my help? Is that why you're telling me all this now?'

Alice tightens her grip on my hand and looks at me steadily, her eyes shockingly beginning to fill with tears. 'Oh, Ellie,' she says, 'I don't think you understand how much you have already helped. I'm telling you all this now simply because it's time you learnt the truth about what happened to Will. What Will hasn't figured out yet, but which is very clear to Finn and me, is that you, Ellie, are the reason he's started working again.'

My heart beats loud in the stillness. 'Oh' is all I can manage.

I feel my own eyes welling up then, my heart suddenly jumping around in my chest. Alice's last statement occupies a huge amount of space in the room, and I feel my cheeks grow hot at its touch.

'I see,' I say quietly, knowing that my response sounds limp. 'I don't know what to say.'

'I think,' says Alice, smiling at me warmly, 'that perhaps the things you might want to say are best saved for Will.'

I drain my glass, all rational thoughts scattered save one. My head feels a little fuggy, as if it's unable to cope with the onslaught of information I've just been given. It strikes me then that what surprises me most, apart from Alice's revelations, is Alice herself. The woman sitting before me has revealed a character full of warmth and compassion. She has watched over Will and Finn from infancy to manhood, a source of comfort and safety, a guide, a confidante and ultimately a true and loyal friend.

'You're a very special person, Alice,' I whisper. 'To have done all that for Will, just to protect him. But what I don't get is *you*. I understand you trying to protect Will, but if I'm not much mistaken, most of the village seems to think you're an evil old witch – I certainly did before tonight. Where's she gone?'

Alice sounds a low cackle worthy of any witch. 'Flown away on her broomstick!' She laughs but then takes a deep breath and sighs. 'It's like I said, Ellie. Over the last couple of years, I've been foolish, too full of anger and more than a little self-pity, and I let my behaviour get rather out of hand. It started out as something of a game, to prove a point to myself, and in a way I've used my shielding of Will as a further excuse to act the way I've done.'

'Go on.'

'My husband, Charles, died two and a half years ago. I was heartbroken: we were so close, even as old wrinklies. It was worse, you see, because he'd been suffering from Alzheimer's, and the night he died no one really knows what happened, but he took the car while I was out, and maybe he panicked, suddenly finding the road unfamiliar, but he lost control of the car, and it smashed into a tree. He was killed instantly.'

'Oh my God, Alice. That's awful.'

'There are others who have endured far worse than me, dear, but what made it so much more hurtful was the fact that in the last six months or so before he died, people had begun crossing the street rather than speak to us, as if his illness was catching.'

'He was the local doctor, wasn't he?'

'He was. You know, when we first came to the village all those years ago, medicine was a bit different. He thought nothing of making a house call on a sick child at eleven o'clock at night. He treated most of the folks around here at some time or another, and most of their children too. Even when he retired about seven years ago, he remained a pillar of the community. We considered everyone here to be our friends, but as soon as his illness became apparent, he was treated like a leper. Disgraceful.'

'People can be so cruel, can't they?' I sympathise.

Alice gives a rueful smile. 'I know now that lack of understanding about the illness was at the root of most of it, or just plain embarrassment, but at the time it really hurt. After the funeral, people stayed away, perhaps feeling guilty about how they'd behaved, and I was too bitter to care about the consequences of my own actions. I was determined to rub their noses in it and to prove to myself that what I thought about them all was right.'

Alice smoothes down her skirt, looking a little fidgety. 'But what I've realised is that I'm no better than they are. What you sow, you reap, my mother always used to say – so true. I know what people think of me.'

I lean across to take her hand in comfort now. 'I think you're actually very brave to admit all this. You're a very special person.'

'And so are you, Ellie. Do you know you are the only person who has ever stood up to me? Twice!' she exclaims. 'I hope you understand now why I behaved the way I did.'

I feel myself blushing, and nod.

'Anyway . . .' she tails off here, visibly straightening and drawing in a fresh breath, 'that's all in the past now; time for something different, I feel. Time to stop all this silly shenanigans and look to the future instead.' She cocks her head to one side.

'Now, as you know, old ladies are creatures of routine and need meals at regular intervals. I was planning to have cheese on toast for supper. Would you like to join me?'

I take my leave of Alice a little while later. We part with a hug and a promise to visit. It feels an age since I left the house this morning. So much has happened, but it's good to be back in my own undemanding space. The night has turned bitterly cold, but my sitting room is cosy and warm; Will might be keeping a low profile, but his unobtrusive care is still evident.

I sink wearily into a chair, holding my head. I feel as if I've had too much to drink – slightly giddy and unable to focus. I wonder if perhaps it's just that I've got too many thoughts clamouring for my attention, too many situations to reassess and too many conversations to replay. I can't keep up: I'm exhausted. All I want is to go to bed and sleep and have everything be simple again when I wake up, but I suspect it's like that old adage: you can't make an omelette without breaking eggs. Mine feel well and truly scrambled.

It's funny, but over the years I've found that when I've got something important to think about, it's best not to think about it at all. My brain seems to do its own sifting and reasoning, and eventually a clear thought or emotion comes floating to the surface. Some may call it cowardly; some may call it bottling things up. But for me this non-confrontational method seems to work.

So it's something of a shock when I wake groggily the next morning, feeling even worse than the day before. My head is pounding, and there's an ominous tightness to the back of my eyes. My throat doesn't feel too great either. It seems that the Christmas

Fairy has decided to bring me the common cold this year. At least it's three days until the big one, so I should have time to get over it, though I've still got a few tasks to do before I pack to go to Jane's tomorrow.

By lunchtime, my throat is edging from sore to raw, and by teatime, although I'm desperately trying to deny it, I can hardly lift my head. I feel like I've been hit by a truck, but I plough on regardless. I should go and see Will. I wrapped his present earlier, and although I understand why he's keeping out of my way, there's so much I want to say to him. But the thought of going outside nearly undoes me. I can take it round tomorrow before I leave.

The temperature must have plummeted, because the house is freezing, and I just can't seem to get warm. I swallow another couple of paracetamol with my tomato soup, fighting to get them down my throat. At eight o'clock, I go to bed with a hot water bottle, thinking that the early night will do me good.

I don't remember Sunday at all.

CHAPTER FIFTEEN

It's Finn who first notices Ellie's car as he crosses the courtyard. He kicks open the back door unceremoniusly and dumps his bags on the table with a grunt. Thank heaven for Sunday opening. He'd been abroad since the summer, and it wasn't until last week that he'd been sure that he'd actually be able to make it home for Christmas. At least he'd finished the shopping now, so there would be a Christmas dinner after all. Perhaps he'd be able to have a chat with Will about his future plans then.

There's no sign of his brother now. He pulls open the workroom door, but Will isn't there either. A shout into the hall and up the stairs also proves fruitless. Will's probably still out, no doubt venting his angst on some tree that would damn well be coppiced whether it wanted it or not.

Finn is frying bacon and eggs when Will returns, his face red from the cold, and practically falling down with exhaustion.

'Christ, it's freezing out there. Alice says the forecast is for minus four or five tonight. I reckon it's freezing now.'

'Is she okay?'

'Yeah, fine. You know her; her heating is turned up to at least thirty-two, and she's got plenty of wood.'

'Well, I remembered her box of Newberry Fruits, so we're all set for Christmas lunch. Is she coming for morning sherry as usual?'

'Try and stop her,' Will mutters wryly. 'She's bringing our stockings over tomorrow, so we can have them Christmas morning. Although I might add that she's not at all sure I deserve mine,' he finishes, sitting down glumly.

Finn catches his brother's eye. 'I was wondering if we shouldn't invite Ellie over,' he ventures.

Will returns the look squarely, seeing straight through the supposedly casual remark. 'We can't,' he answers flatly. 'She went to Jane's this morning.'

'Well, her car is still there.'

'Is it? That's odd,' he replies, crossing to the window. 'Only she was supposed to be leaving this morning. Alice said something about her taking Jane's children to see Father Christmas. There's a light on upstairs, but nothing downstairs.'

Finn comes to stand beside him. 'Maybe Jane came over to collect her.'

'Hmm, maybe,' Will answers, sounding unconvinced, 'I might just pop over and see that everything is all right. Even if she's not there, she won't want the lights left on all over Christmas.' He looks to Finn for affirmation.

'It wouldn't hurt, just to be on the safe side,' he agrees, returning his attention to the frying pan. 'Do you want me to come with you? Only—' He breaks off, eyeing his tea.

'No, you eat. I'll get something later. I probably won't be long anyway.'

'What if she's there?'

'Well, I dunno, Finn,' he says sarcastically. 'I guess I'll just have to talk to her.'

Finn watches Will go, smiling. It's been a long time since he's seen his brother look like this. When the phone rings ten minutes later, he doesn't expect to hear Will's voice, breathless.

'Finn, it's me.'

'You okay?'

'Yes. Listen, I'm going to stay here for a bit. Ellie is here, but she's really sick. I don't know what's wrong, but she's curled up in bed, shivering like crazy.'

'Do you want me to come over?'

'No . . . Yes? Christ, I don't know. I think she's got a fever or something; she's mumbling about weird stuff.' There's a long pause, and Finn hears him pulling himself together. 'Look, I'm going to light the fires again and see if that helps; it's bloody freezing in here. I'll call you, yeah?'

'Okay, but maybe she needs to see a doctor, Will.'

'It's Sunday night. You're never going to get anyone to come out, and she's not going anywhere at the moment. I'm sure she just needs to sleep it off. I just . . . Finn, I just think I should stay here.'

'Yes, okay, mate. Call me if you need to.'

There is a murmured assent from the other end before the connection clicks off. Finn holds the receiver thoughtfully for a moment before gently replacing it. He kicks about the kitchen for a bit and then watches TV, marvelling that however long he's away, the programmes are always the same when he returns. At half-past nine, he figures that Will isn't coming home and heads to bed.

Will isn't sure what he's going to find as he crosses the courtyard. He half expects a mouthful from Ellie, either for his disgraceful behaviour the last time they saw each other or for interfering now and offering help where none is probably needed. Despite this, he desperately wants to speak to her. There is a lot he needs to explain, and although he knows Alice has talked over much of it with her, it's his responsibility. He has behaved badly, and as Finn and Alice have both bawled him out, it's only fair that he let Ellie do the same. At least it would mean she was still talking to him.

The door is locked when he reaches it. Nothing unusual about that, particularly if she's away. He takes out his spare key to let himself in. At first he thinks he has the wrong key as he can't get it in the lock, but then, as he shines his torch on the keyhole, he realises that there's already a key on the inside. This is strange. Ellie must still be here, but there are no lights on downstairs, even though it's pitch black outside.

He gives a tentative knock, but there's no answer. He knocks again, louder this time, his pulse beginning to quicken. Nothing. He is beginning to worry now.

Although Alice hadn't seen Ellie yesterday, she'd seemed to be fine when she'd left on Friday. Will had taken this as a hopeful sign, reassuring himself that maybe she'd accept his apology. He hadn't dared to think further than that. Perhaps Alice had got it wrong, though, and Ellie really had taken it to heart. He had never got to the bottom of what happened in her last relationship, but Ellie had a fragility about her at times, and he hadn't pushed it. Maybe the way he'd acted had been the last straw for her, coming from someone that maybe she had begun to think of as a friend.

He thinks about shouldering the door. The hinges will splinter easily, but he restrains the impulse – far too dramatic. Instead, he shines the torch beam around, looking for something long and thin. He finds a stick in the kindling pile and tests it for size. Fortunately these old keyholes are bigger than modern ones, and the stick slides in easily. He gives the key a good shove, hoping that its weight will cause it to drop. Thirty seconds later he is inside the house.

He flicks on the lights hurriedly, taking in the half-eaten plate of food by the sink. A single wrapped present sits on the table, the tag turned up. He traces his fingers across the parcel briefly as he strides into the lounge. The fire is dead, a smattering of ash coating the hearth. For a moment, he looks at the fire screen carefully placed across the opening. He remembers the day he made it, who he made it for and the arguments that followed. Things weren't right with Caroline, even back then, yet in its wrongness it was still better than the nightmare that followed, and he'd have given anything to have so much as half a life back at that point. It all seems such a long time ago now.

He finds his voice and calls out to Ellie, but there is no reply. He takes the stairs two at a time.

The bed is a jumble of blankets and clothing, and a soft light glows from the lamp beside the bed. At first he thinks that she is not there, but then the blankets move, a low moan sounds and a hand clutches the top of a blanket.

Ellie lies curled in a ball, her face turned inwards, her mouth parting in noisy breaths. Will kneels by the bed and lays a hand across her cheek. She is burning. She turns at his touch, her eyelids fluttering, her long damp hair stuck to her neck, and shivers violently. She mutters something then, and Will leans in, his lips brushing her hair to catch her words. He could stay like that forever.

With a wrench he pulls away, fumbling for his mobile and hurrying downstairs. After he calls Finn, he throws the back door open, ferrying logs and armfuls of kindling into the house. The Aga is still lit, mercifully, but he throws more wood into it, opening the vent until it is roaring. He slips the kettle across to boil and goes to relight the lounge fire.

He feels uncomfortable returning to the bedroom. After all, it is not somewhere he's that familiar with, but now that his sense of urgency has diminished somewhat, he is able to take in more of the intimate details of this very private space of Ellie's. A tortoiseshell hair clip that she often wears lies on the dressing table, with an amber pendant beside it. The green shirt that makes her eyes dance is slung over a chair in the corner of the room. Will tries not to let his thoughts linger on these items for too long and sets to making a fire to bring some warmth to the chilly room.

Eventually, a whistle from downstairs summons him to make a hot drink. Alice always used to bring him camomile tea with honey when he was sick, and although he teased her by saying it looked and tasted like cat's pee, somewhere between childhood and his more recent past it had become one of his stock remedies. He can think of nothing better now anyway, and the very act of brewing it makes him feel useful. He knows Ellie keeps some in the house: she had offered him a cup one evening, but he had politely declined it. She'd laughed, saying she wasn't sure if she liked it either but that it made her feel virtuous.

He tops up the tea with cold water and carries it upstairs, placing it carefully on Ellie's bedside table. He goes through into the bathroom and runs some cool water into the sink, soaking the facecloth that he finds draped carefully over the side of the bath.

Ellie is lying on her back now, one arm flung up onto the pillow, palm side up, her fingers opening and closing gently like the fronds of a sea anemone. Will gently pulls back the hair that is plastered across her forehead and smoothes it. He lays the cloth against her forehead for a moment before carefully wiping her face and neck. She moves slightly, turning at his touch, and Will is buried under an emotion so strong that his throat constricts violently, forcing him to cough. It wakes her, of course, but even as she looks at him, her eyes become unfocused, and she hovers between waking and sleep. Will pulls her against him, cradling her weight, and holds the mug to her lips, speaking softly. She drinks a little, her nose wrinkling at the taste, before she pulls away. Will turns her pillow cool side up before he releases her, letting his fingers slide through her hair as he sweeps it off her face once more. He watches her for a moment before leaving.

It is warming up downstairs, and he sheds his jacket, hanging it over one of the kitchen chairs before he collapses onto it, holding his head in his hands. He doesn't want to think further than the moment at hand. Above all, he is desperate to keep himself from foraging deeper into his thoughts. The things to focus on now are necessity, function, movement.

Wearily, he gets to his feet and makes himself a drink, then devours slice after slice of toast, plundering the pot of jam with his sticky butter-laden knife. He lays his crockery carefully by the sink before relocking the back door and banking up the living room fire for the night. He breathes deeply, then climbs the stairs to the bed-room, where he stokes the fire before arranging himself carefully on the bed beside Ellie, without touching her but close enough so that even with his eyes closed, he can feel her presence.

She'll be okay; he knows that. Her fever will break soon. But this is one night when he does not have to sleep alone, and perhaps he can dare to remember what Caitlin had said he must. As he listens to Ellie's breathing, he closes his eyes and softens the edges of his mind, allowing the memories to come – at last. Hardly worn by use, they are as fresh as the night they were created. The physi-cal pain overwhelming all else, the revulsion, anger, disgust, shame. The sour taste of bile in his mouth as he retched endlessly in the damp grass. The smell of the earth pressed up against his face and afterwards the kind hands that sought to help, but whose touch felt like fire on his skin.

He thinks then of the weeks that followed, of the all-pervading numbness and recriminatory disbelief that tumbled round and round, repeating themselves with their endless questions to which he had no answers. The weeks that became months, punctuated by bitter arguments with Caroline as he sought to make sense of a life that had suddenly deserted him, and Caroline, unable to cope with this stranger in her midst, seeing a way out and taking it. And now he is here, lying beside a young woman who has, unaccountably, made a difference, who makes him feel like he can be who he once was but whom he has deceived in order to protect himself from those very memories now flowing through him. He grieves then – for all the things he has lost and for the things he has not allowed himself to find.

Towards three in the morning, he becomes aware that Ellie's breathing has eased. He slides his hand next to hers and feels her fingers close softly over his own, and he sleeps.

CHAPTER SIXTEEN

I'm not the kind of girl who wakes up in strange places or (worse) with strange men, and even though I am struggling to work out if I am alive, I panic at finding a body lying on the bed beside me. I realise pretty quickly that it's Will, but I'm not able to take that particular thought any further. I have more pressing things to work out.

My mouth feels like something has crawled inside it and died, and the rest of my body feels like it met a rather large truck down a very dark alley. I try to pull myself towards the side of the bed, but even this is incredibly difficult. The bedcovers weigh a ton, and I feel like I'm trying to move through glue.

I lie back on my pillows for a moment and turn to look at Will. I register that he's fully clothed, curled towards me with one hand flung out so that it rests only centimetres from me. He looks very peaceful. I have no idea what time it is, although it's light outside, but I suppose I should be up and about. I stagger to the bathroom, holding the walls for support. I return to bed with a crash. There's a soft sigh beside me.

'Good morning,' whispers Will. He hasn't moved, but there is a sleepy smile on his face. 'How are you feeling?'

I struggle to find the words. They don't come, so I settle for a weak 'Okay.'

'You sure about that?' replies Will. 'Because you look like shit.'

I feel a smile form. 'So do you,' I retort, and it's true, actually. He looks tired and something else, something deeper. I can't hold the thought, though.

Will looks at his watch. 'Christ! It's nearly eleven. I can't believe I've slept for eight hours solid.'

'Oh my God, I'm supposed to be going to Jane's today,' I groan, realising that this might not be possible.

'Ellie, it's Monday.'

'What?'

'It's Monday. Christmas Eve. You were supposed to go to Jane's yesterday.' He studies my face, which must look both bewildered and horrified. 'It's okay, though. I spoke to Jane yesterday and explained. She was quite worried when she hadn't heard from you, but I've signed you off Christmas duties . . . and don't look at me like that. Jane wouldn't hear of you going over. You're really not very well.'

I close my eyes, feeling teary. I'm never ill. I struggle to make sense of Will's words. 'So when did you arrive?'

'Teatime yesterday. Finn noticed you had a light on, so I came over to investigate. Bloody good job too. I'm guessing you weren't able to make it out of bed yesterday. You were burning up when I got here, so I stayed' – he swallows – 'just to make sure you were all right.'

I'm aware of something as he speaks. 'Christ. I stink.'

Will smiles but makes no comment. He slides a lock of hair away from my cheek and then suddenly rolls off the bed and pads through to the bathroom. I hear water start to splash into the bath.

'Back in a moment,' he says as he breezes back through the room and jogs down the stairs. I lie back and listen to the soothing sound of the water flowing. I hear the back door open and close, and Will moving around in the room below. It's oddly comforting. He appears after a few minutes, carrying a mug, and goes back to the bathroom to turn off the taps.

I'm ushered into the bathroom, a solicitous arm around my shoulders, and am handed a couple of paracetamol and a mug.

'Drink this; it'll help.'

I sip through the steam cautiously. It's sweet and soothing, and I sip some more. Will is taking armfuls of linen out of the cupboard.

'Do you need a hand?' he asks.

I shake my head quickly, suddenly conscious of the way I must look.

'Okay,' he says slowly, 'if you're sure.' He pauses for a moment. 'Only can I just point out that although I may not have had sex in over a year, I'm pretty sure I can restrain myself.'

There's that twinkle again.

'I'll be fine,' I reply, reaching for the clip on the windowsill to put my hair up. He bows, walking backwards out of the room, and pulls the door closed.

I emerge a short while later, more exhausted than I can ever remember feeling, to find the fire roaring once more in the grate and the bed freshly made. Will is sitting cross-legged on the floor, facing the fire, with his back against the foot of the bed. He's cradling a mug in his lap, his head bent. He's so still, he could be asleep. He looks up as I approach.

'Better?' he enquires.

'Loads,' I say. 'Thank you.'

'Come on then, back to bed.'

I haven't the strength to argue. He's by my side as I climb between the smooth sheets.

'Can I get you something to eat? Some toast maybe?'

'No thanks,' I mutter into the pillow.

He pours another drink from the teapot on the table by the bed. 'Try and drink this, then.'

I nod, feeling my eyes begin to close against the swimming tide in my head. The last thing I remember for a while is the softness of his lips against my cheek.

I am vaguely aware that Will reappears at intervals during the day, and Finn too, but it's dark when I come to properly, suddenly aware of movement in the room. Drawers are being opened and closed.

'What are you doing?' I croak.

'Rifling shamelessly through your underwear drawer,' says Finn, holding up a pair of my knickers as proof. I can't believe he just did that.

'Too much information, Finn,' comes another voice to my rescue. 'Just packing up a few of your bits, Ellie, that's all.'

I've only been awake two minutes, and they've lost me. I struggle to sit up. 'Why are you packing my stuff?'

'Just so that you can come to us for a few days,' answers Will, coming around to the side of the bed. 'It's Christmas Day tomorrow. You're not staying here by yourself,' he adds firmly, handing me my dressing gown.

I shake my head with as much strength as I can muster. 'I'll be okay.'

'No, you won't. You're coming where we can keep an eye on you. Besides – we have two things that you don't.'

I give Will a quizzical look.

'Food and central heating.'

I realise then just how much of a pain I must have been over the last two days – probably the busiest days of the year. Will has been babysitting me instead of all the things he should have been doing, and now all I can do is argue, wanting to stay here in my own space. I feel awful. And I can't help it – the tears begin to flow down my cheeks.

Will is making *come on, let's get you into this dressing gown* gestures. He pauses to wipe away my tears with his thumbs, hardly missing a beat.

'Hey now, Finn's cooking isn't that bad,' he says gently. 'Come on – pop this on?'

I do as I'm told.

Will looks to Finn. 'All set?' There is an answering nod.

'Right!'

Before I know it, I'm lifted from the bed, covers trailing in my wake. I clutch at Will wildly, thrown off balance, but his grip is firm. I can feel the hardness of his muscles against my back and legs. He smiles down at me apologetically.

'I could probably walk, you know,' I manage.

'Probably, but it's bitter out there. You'd have hypothermia before you reached the back door. Besides, this will be much more fun.' He grins, trying not to bash either of our heads as he descends the stairs.

'Fun?'

'Oh yes! It is Christmas Eve after all.'

I'm trying to work out what could possibly be fun about being hoisted unceremoniously to Will's, when my dignity takes a further step backwards as Finn throws a blanket over me. I groan with embarrassment as he tucks it around my feet and up underneath me. I bury my face in the folds of jumper across Will's chest, which feels so good I'm tempted to stay that way, until I remember the book.

I point at the kitchen table. 'Could you bring that present for me, please?'

'What, this one?' says Finn, clutching it theatrically to his chest.

'Hands off, mate,' responds Will. 'That's mine!' He looks down at me. 'Sorry, but I checked it out earlier,' he whispers.

I feel rather pleased.

'So where's mine then?' demands Finn, acting like he's put out. I'm about to answer, when he grins again. 'Don't worry, I'm just kidding. Anyway, is the reindeer express ready?'

'It is,' replies Will solemnly.

'Then headgear on, and let's away!' exclaims Finn, bending to retrieve something else from a bag on the table. He pulls out a pair of bright red felt antlers which, after a moment's manipulation, start to flash. He places them on Will's head and then retrieves a second pair, which he dons.

'Course and trajectory plotted and confirmed?'

'Check.'

'Then let's fly!'

I am 'galloped' across the cold dark space between the two houses, and I'm still laughing as we crash into the kitchen.

'Oh my God . . . I've got to put you down,' splutters Will, staggering through to the lounge, where I am lowered onto the sofa. 'Sorry,' he says, grinning and breathing hard. 'I couldn't hold you anymore. I'm laughing too much.'

Finn bursts into the room. 'Man, what a ride!' he laughs, antlers awry.

They both stand there looking down at me, chests heaving. I think I may have died and gone to heaven. Finn is like a huge, gangly puppy. A very well-groomed, beautiful, pedigree puppy. I wouldn't be at all surprised if his tongue lolled out. Will looks . . . well, just happy. His smile, which has come right up from his boots, stays on mine for a moment.

'Is he always like this?' I ask him, nodding towards Finn.

Will grins at his brother, throwing an affectionate arm around his shoulder. 'Most of the time, yes,' he replies, knocking Finn's antlers off.

Finn wriggles out from under Will's arm. 'Wait – there's more!' he exclaims and rapidly turns off both lamps, which are the room's only light apart from the fire. It takes a moment for my vision to readjust.

'Are you ready?' asks Finn.

There is a loud ta-da, and I suck in my breath as the room is lit by what seem to be a million twinkling white fairy lights. A huge tree, which had been standing unadorned in one corner, springs to dancing life; so does the ceiling, which is criss-crossed with lights, the mantelpiece and a large bowl-shaped vase. It's beautiful. Enchanting.

'Finn, it's just lovely. Did you do all this?'

'Well, it's kind of a tradition,' he replies modestly, not quite answering my question.

Will comes to my side once more. 'We've probably worn you out now, haven't we? Get yourself comfy, and we'll go and finish off the tea, okay?'

I nod in agreement at his well-placed concern, aware once more of the throb in my head.

The sofa is piled high at one end with pillows and an eiderdown. Not a duvet, but a real, old-fashioned eiderdown stuffed with feathers.

I breathe in the soothing semi-darkness, suddenly still now, the currents of air settling about me gently. I lay my head against the back of the sofa, smiling to myself at the memory of the last few moments. The warmth in the room is delicious, and I pull off my dressing gown, slightly self-conscious to be sitting in my pyjamas. I move the pillows towards me and prod at them experimentally. They're beautifully soft – I knew they would be.

I stretch out then, the eiderdown around me, and lie back to look at the 'stars.'

I wonder what Jane and her family are doing now. No doubt the girls are a mass of exuberant excitement. I would have been a part of that, and I can see the little tableaux of their evening so clearly that I could almost be there. I'm glad to be here, though. No worries of the past, no anxieties of the future, just the slow movements of the present, demanding nothing from me save my passage through them. I feel almost giddy with the sensation.

Soft footsteps announce Will's presence once more. He crouches beside the sofa, straightening the eiderdown.

'Could you manage some soup, do you think?'

'I'll give it a go, but just a little please . . . and as long as it's not pea.' I shudder.

'Leek and potato, very gentle I promise.'

The soup, when it comes, is thick and comforting. I don't quite manage the bowlful, but pass my compliments to the chef, who turns out to be Finn. He stays with me a moment while Will clears away the dishes.

'Are you feeling any better?' he asks.

'I'll be fine,' I reply, feeling more than a little sleepy.

'I'm being purely mercenary, you understand. My motives aren't as pure as Will's. I just want to know if you're going to be able to do justice to my Christmas dinner.'

I laugh. 'Well, I can't promise that, but I'll do my best.'

'Glad to hear it,' he says, moving to sit on the edge of the sofa. I move my legs to make room for him. 'Can I stand Will down to amber alert now, do you think?'

'I should think so, yes,' I giggle. 'He's been very kind – you both have.'

Finn gives me a disconcertingly direct look. 'Charming bedside manner from the original grumpy bastard – I don't think so.

162

Kindness has got nothing to do with it, Ellie. Now, promise me something?' He cocks his head at me. 'When you're feeling up to it, make sure you have a proper chat with him. There are things you two need to sort out.'

I nod meekly, not sure what to say. To my horror, he leans forward and very gently places a soft, slow kiss on my forehead.

'And just in case you were wondering,' he whispers, 'I'm the wrong tree.' He winks at me then and springs up from the sofa. Evidently, his hearing is better than mine, as Will enters the room seconds later. My head is spinning. What on earth was he talking about?

'Now what would you like to do, Ellie? I can show you your room upstairs if you want to sleep, or you can stay down here – if you prefer?'

'Won't I be in the way?'

'Nope. You can supervise. Finn and I are going to carry out at least three Christmas Eve traditions. One is to decorate the tree, and—'

'Two and three,' interrupts Finn, 'are to lay waste to these.' He finishes by brandishing a bottle of whisky and a tin of Quality Street chocolates that he has removed from a cupboard.

I seriously thought they were joking, but an hour and a half later, as the pile of glinting foil papers attests, they have indeed laid waste to the tin of Quality Street. Neither of them is on their first glass of whisky either.

'God, I feel sick,' groans Will, sinking into a chair. 'Remind me not to do this again.'

'Didn't we say that last year?' answers Finn, following suit. 'The tree looks good, though.'

The tree looks amazing. It's decorated with pinecones and strings of popcorn, little stars made out of twigs sprayed gold and silver and bound with scarlet wool, slices of orange dried to a burnished hue and smelling divine, and ginger biscuits iced with little silver balls.

'It's beautiful, Finn,' I agree. 'Did you make all these yourself? Only it's not what I pictured at all. It looks really . . .'

'If you say "girly," you're toast,' remarks Will drily.

'I was going to say natural, sort of homely. I guess I just had you figured for chuck-a-bucket-load-of-tinsel-at-it kind of guys.'

Finn looks positively outraged. Will just smiles. 'Definitely no tinsel allowed. The tree is beautiful all by itself, don't you think?'

I have to agree with him that it is, and think of my present to Will, nestled under its branches.

CHAPTER SEVENTEEN

My room is beautiful, not large, but big enough to feel airy and restful. It has windows set up high in the eaves, the sloping ceiling giving the room character. Almost everything in it is white, apart from the red rag rug on the floor and the bedspread, which is a mixture of red, white, blue and yellow patchwork. The sun is glancing across the corner of it this morning. Dancing.

I realise that my head is clear as I lie cocooned in the white cotton sheets, my mind drifting lazily. I fell asleep in seconds last night, too tired to think about anything much, but this morning there seems to be enough space in my head, and it would appear that my thoughts all seem to be converging in one direction: Will.

There's a flurry of doors opening and closing, and moments later the sound of voices floats my way. Christmas Day has obviously started. I am determined to get up today, but wonder how long I can reasonably leave it before making an appearance: I don't want to peak too soon. In fact, I'm not too sure what kind of an appearance I will be making – I'm viewing what Will and Finn packed me to wear with some trepidation.

There's a soft knock on the door, and Will comes in wearing a floppy Santa hat with a white pom-pom on the end.

'You're looking brighter,' he says, placing a mug on the bedside table. 'Much more like your normal radiant self.'

I bet I don't. I bet I look like death.

'Thanks. I do feel better today. My head at least feels partly connected to my body.'

'Glad to hear it. Finn is somewhat anxious that you join us for lunch. Otherwise, we'll have to eat at least another fifteen sprouts each.'

I laugh. 'Actually I'm quite fond of sprouts, but I don't think I've ever eaten thirty in one sitting.'

'Well, there will be four of us around the table, so naturally Finn is cooking enough for twenty-eight. I'm counting on you.'

'I'll be there, I promise. What time is it now?'

'Only just ten. Lunch won't be until two, so I should stay here for a bit and rest. Have a long bath or whatever you want. Alice is coming about noon.'

'Oh lovely. We got on great, well . . . after a while we did; did she tell you? Quite a surprise considering I thought she was an evil old witch!'

'She did tell me.' He pauses for a moment, looking down at his hands, and I realise that I've made reference to something that I hadn't intended to. Not just yet.

'I don't know what I'd do without Alice, really,' he says simply. 'I know she explained a lot of things to you, Ellie, and that likewise there are things I need to tell you, things I need to say, but—'

I cut him off, anxious to reassure him. 'I'm not angry with you, Will. I was, but not anymore. How can I be after everything you've done for me the last few days? We do need to talk about what happened, but let's not do it today. I've completely hijacked your Christmas, after all, and it would only spoil it.'

I'm pleased to see he looks a little more relaxed, so I decide to leave it there.

His face suddenly brightens again. 'Hey, looks like you've had a visitor in the night,' he says, moving to the end of the bedpost and unhooking something which had been hidden from my view. It's a Christmas stocking of rather generous proportions and, judging by its appearance, some age.

'Happy Christmas!' Will says, grinning and dumping the stocking on the bed, then plonking himself down beside it. 'Go on, let's see what the big man's brought you.'

I take a quick swig of tea, rather embarrassed. After all, the only thing I've bought Will is a book, and I've nothing for Finn or Alice.

I pull the stocking towards me, hearing the crackle and rustle of the gifts within, and my embarrassment gives way to childlike excitement. I remove the first present and rip off the paper, intrigued by the rattling noise it makes. It's a tub of paracetamol. The second and third gifts reveal a pack of tissues and some throat lozenges.

'I'm beginning to sense a bit of a theme,' I laugh. Will says nothing, just smiles.

I pull out a pair of bright red socks with Christmas puddings on them, a beautifully soft knitted hat and scarf, a couple of bath bombs with little flowers pressed into them, and the newest novel by one of my favourite authors. I feel a lump form in my throat.

'I don't know what to say . . . I never expected any of this.' I'm trying hard not to become mushy.

'Good job Father Christmas knew where to find you then,' he says gently.

'Well, he's made some excellent choices, I must say.'

'Yeah, me too – look, I got socks as well,' he affirms, pulling up the leg of his jeans to reveal a bright blue pair with holly sprigs on them. 'Finn's have reindeer on.'

'Did Father Christmas lend you his hat as well?' I ask, wrinkling my nose.

He slides it off his head, raking his fingers through his hair. 'No, that would be one of Finn's optional extras.' He grins, his blue eyes catching the slant of sunlight.

'He doesn't stop, does he?' I retort.

'Not often, no.' He checks me for a moment. 'Is it too much for you? I can ask him to wind it in a bit.'

'God no, don't do that. I think it's lovely,' I say, laying my hand over his. 'Really.'

'Well, okay. Finn's always been a bit of a clown, but I know he really misses home, especially now he's away working for months at a time. I think he just goes into overdrive when he gets back, especially at this time of year.'

'I just hope he doesn't think I'm a party pooper, that's all. I'm not sure I can keep up at the moment.'

'There are no expectations, Ellie, from either of us.' He gives my fingers a little squeeze. 'Listen, I think I'm supposed to be chopping or peeling something. I'd better go. Take your time, okay?'

I nod, feeling a bit useless and a bit jittery until Will drops a kiss on my forehead and breathes 'Happy Christmas' in my ear, and then I just feel jittery.

There's a collective groan as spoons are rested back in bowls, and various people declare that they couldn't eat another thing. I think I did fairly well considering I haven't eaten anything more than a bowl of soup over the last three days, but I'm beginning to feel the effects. I take another sip of my water before speaking.

'It's quite possible that I might actually explode, but that was fabulous, Finn. Thank you.'

'Oh yes, hear, hear,' agrees Alice, raising her glass to him.

'You're very welcome,' says Finn warmly. 'I can't believe I managed to fill you up, though, Alice. I thought you'd be good for another three roast potatoes at least,' he adds, winking in my direction.

'Less of your cheek, young man!' she scolds with mock fierceness. 'I've had to wait all year for this.'

'Bloody good job I managed to make it home then,' he retorts. 'Otherwise, Will would have had to cook.' He mimes clutching at his throat as though poisoned and slumps sideways in his chair, with his tongue lolling out.

Will slaps his brother on the arm. 'Oi!' he exclaims indignantly.

He gets up and slides the kettle across onto the plate to boil. 'Job well done, though, mate,' he agrees, returning to the table. 'In fact, so well done, we'll be eating it for the next week or so.'

'I deliberately over-catered so that there would be plenty left for bubble and squeak tomorrow.'

'Yeah, yeah,' Will says, smiling broadly and then feigning a bored yawn.

I let the banter wash over me for a few minutes, feeling tired but peaceful. 'How long are you home for, Finn?' I ask. 'Will mentioned that you're often away for months.'

'Actually, I'm not going back. I'm home for good,' he says softly.

There is a sudden stillness to the room. Will, who is playing idly with a puzzle from his cracker, looks up sharply.

'Since when?' he asks abruptly.

'Since about four days ago, when I quit. I've sold my soul for long enough, Will. I'm not doing it anymore.'

'So you just up and left?'

'No, Will,' he says as if talking to a small child, 'I talked this over with Gus a while back. I made it clear the last time I went out that this stint would be my last. He renegotiated my contract for me so that, provided I brought the project in on time, I was free to go. I did, so here I am.'

'But you didn't feel the need to discuss any of this with me over the last – what – six months or so?'

Finn sits back in his chair, looking levelly at Will. 'No, I didn't. I'm thirty-nine years old, Will. I can make my own decisions.'

I look between the two brothers. I've just totally ruined things. The kettle starts to whine on the hotplate, but nobody moves. Alice is watching Will like a hawk. He looks like the rug has been pulled out from under him. Eventually, he gets up and slides the kettle off the heat, turning to lean against the Aga, where he scuffs the floor with his foot.

'I'm so sorry,' I manage to say to no one in particular. 'I've obviously put my foot in it . . . I didn't mean to upset anyone.'

Alice pats my hand reassuringly.

Will lets out a long breath. 'Jesus,' he sighs. 'The only thing you did was underestimate what a selfish bastard I can be sometimes. It's not your fault.' He comes back to the table then and holds out his hand to Finn. 'I'm sorry, mate. That was a really shit way to react, and you didn't deserve it. I was just a bit shocked, I guess.'

'Well, there never was going to be a good time to tell you,' Finn replies drily, taking Will's hand and grasping it. 'I do understand, you know. It changes a lot of things, but we can talk about it some more later, and I'll accept your apology on one condition.'

'Which is?'

'That you've bought me a really great present.'

Will laughs and seems to relax. 'I have, actually.'

'Cool, well come on then; we've sat here long enough. To the living room, ladies!'

Relief washes over me, and I begin to pull my chair out. 'Shouldn't we wash up first, though?' I say in an attempt to reclaim the role of well-behaved guest.

'No, leave it,' says Will. 'The washing-up fairy will do it later.'

'Don't push your bloody luck,' mutters Finn.

'You know, my dear,' Alice confides in me, 'they were just the same when they were little. Will was always the first to apologise. Finn used to sulk dreadfully; he—'

'Yes, thank you, Alice. That's enough of that.'

I lean towards her, ignoring Finn. 'I'd love to hear all about it. You can tell me all the gory details later.'

'Oh, I shall, dear.'

It takes a few moments before we are all seated, waiting for Will, who settles himself cross-legged in front of the tree, to begin to hand out the small pile of presents next to it. I sit back and watch as the pile of wrapping paper grows. It's a modest pile; they're a small family, and soon there are just three presents left under the tree, mine to Will, another tiny one and the other, considerably bigger. Finn pulls this towards him.

'This had *so* better be mine.' He grins, looking for confirmation at Will, who nods in return. He doesn't waste any time in ripping off the paper.

'Christ, where did you find this?' he exclaims, brandishing what looks to be an old violin, of all things.

'At an auction house in Leominster,' answers Will, trying to gauge if his present has been a good choice.

Finn is turning the instrument over and studying it, smoothing his hands down its back. 'God, it's fabulous. Thanks, Will – really, this is great. I collect old instruments, Ellie,' he adds for my benefit. 'Violins, violas, guitars mainly.'

'Really? Do you play?'

'I do, yeah – how well is a matter for debate. Not this, though – not yet anyway. It wouldn't sound very pretty, but I like to get them into working order if I can. I'll have to play one for you some time.'

'He's nauseatingly talented, I'm afraid,' says Will warmly.

'As are you,' answers Finn. 'Speaking of which, you may have noticed that there's no gift from me under the tree, which is because I was a little pushed for time out in Dubai, so my options were somewhat limited. This was a bit last minute, but I hope it helps.' He fishes in his back pocket for something and passes Will a sheet of paper, a little crumpled now. 'You're either going to think it's a good idea or deck me one, I'm not sure which.'

He sits back on his heels, waiting for Will to unfold the paper. A rather expectant hush has descended on the room. Will is now sitting on the floor and is silent for a moment longer before slowly raising his head to look up at Finn, an unspoken query on his face.

'I've seen your sketches, Will,' says Finn in reply.

'Yes, but—'

'No "buts." I can only begin to see what's in your head, but from what you've already got down on paper? You should do this, Will, you really should.'

Will is struggling to make a coherent reply. 'It's too much, Finn. I can't accept this.'

'Yes, you can,' replies Finn with force. 'And you're bloody well going to. This piece looks special, Will. I know you could probably make do with the materials you've got, but that's not what you see, is it? It's not what you want. This time make it the best you can.'

Will looks down again at the sheet. His hands are shaking. 'Thank you,' he whispers, emotion catching at his throat. 'I will.' And inexplicably he turns and looks at me full on. 'Thank you,' he says again, and I'm not sure whether he's speaking to Finn or to me.

Gradually, bit by bit, the sound comes back into the room. Alice clears her throat.

'May I?' she asks Will, holding out her hand. He looks dazed now. 'Oh, I see,' says Alice, light dawning as she reads.

I lean towards her until I can see the words 'Graves and Cookson' across the top of the page. Actually it looks like a bill.

'That is such a lovely idea, Will. Graves and Cookson are glass suppliers, Ellie. I'm guessing Will had an account with them a while back, which he probably hasn't used in a while?' Will nods mutely. 'It would appear that Finn's present to Will is to put the account into credit, and by rather a generous amount, it would appear.' She taps the bottom of the page. I can't help but draw in a quick breath.

'Is it something special that you're working on, Will?' she asks gently.

'Oh yes,' he answers, swallowing and looking at me again. 'But it will take a long time. I'm not sure that I . . .' He trails off, leaving the thought unfinished – out loud at least.

'But with Finn home now, that will help surely?' I comment.

Will looks at me, indecision written across his face, 'Yeah, maybe,' he agrees. 'We'll sort something out.'

I want to ask why having Finn around would be a problem, but I daren't. I've already put my foot in it once today. On the surface the brothers seem to get on well; in fact, I would say they're pretty close. Perhaps it's just that Will is used to having his own space.

'Come on then, Will, last presents and then charades, I think,' Finn announces.

I look at Alice with horror, feeling decidedly jaded now.

'I think he's joking,' she says reassuringly. 'Finn knows I don't play charades under any circumstances, don't you, Finn?'

Finn sticks his tongue out at her. 'I won't do any rude ones, I promise!'

'Do you two mind?' asks Will, exasperated. 'There do happen to be two last presents left, and as one's for Ellie, you two can both be quiet.' He turns to scoop up the little box left under the tree.

I give him a nervous look. 'Actually, can I give you your present next, Will? It's not much, and I feel bad that I haven't got anything for Finn or Alice.'

'Not required,' replies Finn immediately. 'Anyway, Ellie, if I'm not much mistaken, Alice and I have already had our present.' He shoots a complicit look at Alice, who beams back at him.

'Go on, Ellie,' she encourages. 'Let's see what you bought Will.'

I hand him my little gift as my heart starts to pound. I just hope he'll like my choice; after the well-thought-out gifts that have been opened so far, it seems a little ordinary now by comparison.

Will seems to take an extraordinarily long time to get the thing free of the paper, and when he does finally unwrap it, I can hardly look at his face.

A small smile starts to play around his mouth, and he even gives a low chuckle, turning the book over and back, and then dipping into the pages inside. I must remember to breathe.

Will's head comes up. 'You know it's been a while since anybody took me seriously, Ellie, which is what makes this all the more special. Thank you.'

Okay . . . and breathe.

'And so this is for you,' he says in such a way as to leave me with no doubt as to who it's from.

174

The card is not signed, but simply reads *With love* and is annotated with two kisses.

I remove the lid of the box. There's a flash of silver and orange as I lift my gift from the tissue paper. It's a hair barrette, a perfect silver oval inlaid with amber nuggets of every hue of orange, yellow and red.

'Oh my God,' I say to the accompaniment of a low whistle from Finn. 'I've never seen anything like this before. It's stunning.'

'I hope you like it,' answers an anxious Will. 'I can take it back if you don't.'

I still Will's hands with one of my own. 'How could I not like it? It's perfect. Can I put it in?'

Will nods. 'Here, let me help.'

I twist my hair up into a loose knot and let Will place the silver oval over the top. Suddenly, bizarrely, in a room full of people, the feel of his hands in my hair and his breath on my neck is the most erotic sensation I've ever felt. I can feel the hairs rise along my arms as every nerve in my body seems to stand to attention, waiting, pulsing. I feel him gently draw away.

'You look very pretty, dear,' says Alice, touching my arm.

'Can't argue with that,' agrees Finn. Will shoots him a look that has him holding up his hands in a *who me?* manner.

What?' he says indignantly, 'I know what you're thinking. Big brother is about to make some toe-curling remark that will have you looking for the hole to swallow you up, but I'm not going to. Nope, no smart remarks.'

He pauses for a moment then, to wink at Alice.

'After all,' he adds blithely, 'I'm adult enough to recognize a situation where it would be appropriate to be more tactful than I usually am. I mean Will has obviously given Ellie's present a very great deal of thought. No doubt when he chose it, he hoped it would convey to her the strength of his feelings, and to make fun of his bravery in giving such a gift in front of two other people would be insensitive and childish in the extreme. Shall I go and make some tea?' He doesn't skip a beat. Will just puts his head in his hands and groans.

CHAPTER EIGHTEEN

The bath bomb fizzles itself away to nothing as I watch, releasing a delicious scent of rose and geranium. Every molecule in my body is aching to get into the water. It's been quite a day: a lovely, relaxed, heart-warming and – let's face it – thought-provoking day. I reach up to touch my hair clip as if to check it's still there, which it is, of course. I've been touching it to check repeatedly ever since I got it.

I spoke to Jane earlier. They've had a lovely day too. The girls have gone to get ready for bed, so she's anticipating being able to put her feet up with a mug of Baileys and a box of Black Magic. I can't tell her too much as I'm in the kitchen while Finn is making a mountain of turkey sandwiches, but I'm able to mention my present, and knowing me the way she does, she's quick to catch on, asking me if I've snogged Will yet. Honestly, she's as bad as Finn (not that the thought hasn't crossed my mind in glorious technicolour). I was thinking that I could still go over to see them, but Jane's sister broke her arm on Christmas Eve, and they're all decamping to her house tomorrow to help out. Besides which, says Jane apologetically, if I think about it, I might find that I prefer to stay where I am.

I'm a little confused, or maybe it's just that I'm disappointed. I know Jane was only teasing when she asked me if I'd snogged Will, but I had thought he might have tried to kiss me. I've been alone with him a few times, and he's been caring, charming, funny and attentive, and his gift was certainly romantic, but so far, nothing.

For goodness sake, I think to myself angrily, sloshing water about, *this is ridiculous.* It's making my head hurt. It's only early, but I've said goodnight to everyone already. The last couple of hours have been a struggle, and I'm ready to take some paracetamol and go to sleep.

I don't notice Will as I come out of the bathroom, mainly because he's doing what can only be described as skulking – walking up and down the corridor, trying to look nonchalant instead of like he's lying in wait for me. At least I hope that's what he's doing.

'Will, are you okay?' I ask. 'You look a bit lost.'

He looks rather ill at ease. 'May I come in for a moment?'

I move back from my door to let him pass. We both stand there for a moment, a rather uncomfortable silence growing.

'I brought you up some paracetamol and a drink, in case you want them,' he says eventually.

'Thanks, I think that's just what I need. I'm feeling a little worse for wear.'

'It's been too much for you, hasn't it?'

'Well, I felt better after my little nap, but I think it was the game of Pictionary that finished me off. Let's face it, against a structural engineer and an artist, Alice and I were never going to win, were we?' I laugh.

'It was Alice's boat that did it for me,' he says. 'I can't remember the last time I laughed so much. My sides still hurt.'

What I remember is how Will's eyes sought out mine as he started to laugh, and as he struggled to bring himself under control, he went to Alice and gave her a hug, telling her what an amazing woman she was. I realised that he'd done this to make it clear that he was laughing with her, and not at her. This was the moment when it occurred to me that I was in very great danger of falling in love with Will.

I look up at him now, smiling at the memory.

'I've had the best day, Will. In fact, it's probably the best Christmas I can remember in years. You and Finn have made me so welcome, and I want to thank you for looking after me the way you have.' I'm suddenly nervous and try to choose my words carefully. Will looks so serious, his eyes dark and locked on mine.

'I want to thank you for this as well,' I add, reaching up to touch my hair and present. 'I never expected anything like this, and you must have—' I stop suddenly as Will reaches across to me, closing the space between us.

'May I?' he asks somewhat hoarsely, moving his hands up to my hair.

I have trouble finding my voice and murmur an assent, starting to turn around. Will catches my shoulders softly and holds me facing him, reaching up to gently remove the clip. I can feel his fingers against my head, running through the curls in my hair, lowering them onto my back and shoulders, pulling tendrils around to frame my face. I don't move, aware that I'm trembling slightly.

'Oh God, Ellie, you're so beautiful,' he whispers and moves his hands to the back of my head, pulling me to rest against his chest.

I'm trying hard to savour each sensation, and the feeling of his warmth fills up my brain.

I'm not sure who moves first, but we're pressed together, tentative at first, questioning, seeking assurance, then becoming more urgent as we find it. I'm not sure whether it's me who is shaking or Will.

His erection is hard against my hip, his flesh pressing against the two layers of material that separate us, and I return the pressure. My legs feel like jelly. Will gives a low groan somewhere deep in his throat, his breathing ragged, but I can't sustain this and feel myself begin to pull away.

'I think I need to sit down,' I gasp, leaning my full weight against him.

He chuckles, and as I feel his chest heaving, he scoops me up and hobbles to the bed, hampered by his laughter and mine. We crash onto the bed in an ungainly heap and bounce there for a moment or two.

'I'm so sorry,' splutters Will, trying to compose himself.

I pull myself upright. 'William McLennan,' I say with mock severity, 'what are you apologising for?'

'I'm such a bloke – wilfully trying to take advantage of a girl with flu. In my defence, though, I've wanted to do that for such a long time, Ellie, I really have.'

He's looking up at me through his lashes, his head slightly bent as if genuinely contrite. I take a deep breath.

He runs a hand through his hair. 'I'm a bad bet, Ellie,' he says quietly.

I don't say anything at first but lean into him, listening to him breathe steadily in and out, the very action of his breathing the only real guarantee we have in life.

'Who isn't?' I reply. 'We all have issues. The trick is not to let them become a barrier to something beyond.'

'You're never going to let me get away with my crap are you?'

'Nope.'

His eyes crinkle then as he touches his lips to mine briefly. 'We need to talk, though, Ellie. There are things I want you to know, cards-on-the-table kind of stuff. Alice told you some of it, which is just like her, coming to my rescue again. I know it should have been me talking to you, but let's face it, I was pretty incoherent at the time. I don't believe that I've been let off the hook, though; you need to know what happened to me and the reason why Caroline left, and it needs to be me that tells you . . .'

'She mentioned you had a breakdown . . .'

'Of sorts, yes . . . but I'm sorry, Ellie, I just can't do this right now.' He falters. 'Today has been so lovely – I don't want to spoil things, and I'm not sure that you're completely up to it now.' His eyes drop to his lap, closing momentarily.

He's right. I'm not processing information at all well today. I'm still trying to grasp the fact that we just kissed. I don't think I'm ready to take in anything else yet. The thought of what he has to tell me makes me nervous, but one thing at a time, I remind myself.

'That's okay, Will, honestly . . . I'm sure you're right.'

'But you think I'm a massive wimp?'

'No,' I say slowly, 'I think you're just being as considerate as you always are. Part of me wants to say, "Oh sod it, let's just rip our clothes off now," but on balance I think my head would probably explode.'

Will takes hold of my hand, shaking his head gently in amusement. 'I don't know what I've done to deserve you. This is important to me, Ellie – too important to get it wrong, and I promise you I will get it right. I'm not going to stay with you tonight, Ellie. I want to, but you need to sleep, and I need to . . . calm down.'

'I know.' I nod, not wanting to crawl out from under his arm, but knowing I have to.

'And you'll be okay?'

'I'll be fine, really.' I smile, looking up at him, letting him go. 'Happy Christmas, Will.'

He drops a sweet kiss on my forehead. 'Happy Christmas, Ellie. It's been a perfect day – thank you.'

It has now.

CHAPTER NINETEEN

It's said that the Inuit have over a hundred words for snow. Finn is rather less eloquent. 'Fuck me,' he says, crossing to the kitchen window.

It's the morning of New Year's Eve, and Will and I are having breakfast. Finn has joined us rather later than usual, adding his sparkling repartee to our conversation.

I still haven't gone home. If you asked Will why, he'd give you several highly plausible reasons for this, not least the fact that following Christmas Day I had a mini relapse and have spent the last few days largely in bed. This has propelled Will into a state of guilty attentiveness which, though lovely, hasn't allowed our relationship to progress any further.

The winter is Will's busiest time of year, but he declared that he's off duty until the New Year (apart from ferrying wood about).

He and Finn obviously have a lot to talk about, but strangely, Finn seems vague and somewhat unwilling to commit to any meaningful discussion. Despite this, or perhaps because of it, the last few days have been filled with good-humoured walks to test my legs, returning to warm fires, thick soups and slabs of cake. I even managed to make one of my own to add to the proceedings.

I've enjoyed myself immensely, but I'm becoming acutely conscious that the day after tomorrow will see a shift back to normality – one that I'm not really looking forward to now. I'd like to stay in this suspended state for a while longer.

Will senses it too, I think. He seems a little distracted this morning, though delighted by the unexpected snow.

Finn drops to the table opposite us, with a huge mug of coffee, looking, oddly for him, tired. Will always seems to have a lot of energy, but Finn? Finn is usually off the scale.

'Still half-asleep?' I ask.

Finn rubs at his eyes. 'Yeah, I couldn't sleep and then dropped off about four o'clock – typical – and now I could sleep for Britain. I didn't realise it was so late.' He winks at me. 'Precious snowman-building time wasted.'

'Not like you,' adds Will carefully, ignoring the comment about the snowman.

'No, not like me at all, but then I've never been unemployed before. I started thinking about it and then boom – wide awake. I take it we're going up to the seat tonight?'

'Want to?'

''Course – it wouldn't be New Year's Eve otherwise, but I need a hand here, guys, I really do.'

Will is quiet for a moment. 'I thought you had it all planned. Earlier this week you talked about some ideas you were mulling over,' he says, looking puzzled.

'Yes, I did, didn't I? Big fat fraud, I'm afraid. Honestly? I haven't got a fucking clue.' He pulls at his eyebrow. 'You know the last couple of months have been pretty tough for me since I knew there was a chance I might get to come home for good. It became the only thing that kept me going. Thinking about what I was going to do once I got home was beyond me. A bit bloody naïve, to say the least.'

'We'll sort something out, Finn – it's okay. Just enjoy being home,' answers Will reassuringly. 'There's no major rush, is there? And there's plenty of work in the wood meanwhile.'

'Yes, but long term?' counters Finn, looking surprised.

'Things might not be as difficult now as you'd imagined.' Will nods, with a slight glance at me, and then shoots Finn a look which silences him.

Finn drains his coffee in one go, still looking apologetic.

'So, what am I going to put on my plane?' he asks.

I haven't a bloody clue what they're talking about.

'Excuse me,' I sound. 'Would one of you like to translate? I know the two of you are related and can talk quite happily in code, but you've totally lost me.'

Will breaks into a grin and apologises. 'When we were younger, we used to go up to the top of Rowan Hill and fly paper aeroplanes off the top, right by where the seat is that I took you to. One year we went up on New Year's Eve 'cause we were pissed, and wrote what we wanted for the coming year on our planes and then chucked them off.'

'And all your dreams came true?' I tease.

'Some foolish romantic claptrap like that, yes, though mostly they just crashed and burned,' imparts Finn. 'The pissed part is optional, although at the time it seemed to help.'

'Now it's become something of a tradition,' carries on Will. 'We go up there every year, if we can.'

'But you need something good to write on your plane,' moans Finn, dropping his head in his hands and then looking up again sharply. 'Hey, Ellie, you should do a plane too.'

'I could,' I say, thinking. 'Except I don't know what to put on mine either.' I look to Finn. 'I'm kind of in between things at the moment too.'

'We should brainstorm,' he answers, staring at me, or rather through me, as if seeking inspiration from the world outside.

'It's snowing, look!' he says excitedly and then snaps his fingers, announcing the arrival of an idea. 'I've got it! We should brainstorm in a snowstorm! Come on, I bet I can build a better snowman than either of you.'

'I should bloody hope so,' laughs Will. 'You're a structural engineer.'

'Not anymore, I'm not!'

In the end we declare it a draw. Will's is the biggest snowman, whilst Finn's wins the aesthetic prize, and mine is awarded the most original design because its head is only marginally smaller than its body.

We tumble back into the warmth of the kitchen, like heat-seeking missiles, and gather around the Aga, waiting for the kettle to boil.

'So what did you do out in Dubai, Finn?' I ask, trying to rub some feeling back into my fingers. He's looking better now.

'Specifically, I worked as project manager for a large conglomerate, trying to work out if their designs for evermore wayward buildings were in any way possible, and then making sure they got built to appease the local god, otherwise known as the tourist dollar.' He looks at Will then, who rolls his eyes, I suspect because he knows what comes next. 'Actually, what I did in practice was deal with all the shit that happens.'

'Sounds fun,' I comment drily. 'And is that what you're good at?'

'Oh yeah, I kick arse with the best of them.'

I bash his arm. 'Be serious for a minute.' I think I might be asking the impossible, but to my surprise Finn's face falls, and his answer takes me aback.

'I'm a good engineer. I've worked hard, and I've taken the opportunities that have allowed me to be up there with the best. Along the way I've learnt how to get results quick, and on the job

I'm known as something of a ball-breaker – I make a lot of money for other people. Problem is I don't always treat people the way I'd like to, and I've turned into a foul-mouthed, cynical bastard, which I cover up with tomfoolery and humour.'

I've never heard him sound so cold. 'Jesus,' I say weakly. Will is frowning at him hard.

'Well, you did ask.'

I did, didn't I? But as I look up at him, feeling rather shocked, I notice the small beginnings of the trademark McLennan wrinkle at the corner of his mouth.

'You bastard!' I exclaim, punching his arm again as his face dissolves into a wide grin. 'Was any of that true?'

Finn waves his hands. 'Actually, it all was. A rather melodramatic version of it, granted, but in essence, yes, it's true. Don't worry, though; I'm not about to slit my throat. I've just had enough of behaving the way I've had to. It goes against the grain, and I need to recharge the old batteries is all.'

'Which is why you came home?'

He nods. 'Which is why I came home, yes.'

We move to the table as Will fills the teapot, ready for our slab of mid-morning cake.

'So are you going to look for new job opportunities around here, or do you fancy trying something completely different now?' I continue, helping myself to a slice of the lemon drizzle.

'Neither. It's more a complete change of lifestyle I'm after. I need to inject some meaning into what I do, and that's not a new concept – we both decided to focus on Rowan Hill a few years back, to put a few things in place, a few pounds in the bank, and then draw up some sustainable plans for the estate's future. It's just that I seem to have changed our plans now.'

Will looks up as he clasps his hand around his mug. 'Let's get the facts straight, shall we?' he says softly. 'We took the decisions we did based on two things. One, a genuine desire to conserve the estate, and two, to get me out of the hole I'd fallen into. I got to play in the woods while dropping out of the real world, and you got to graft for a living. It was never a fair division of labour, Finn; you got the bum deal – I know that. I'd say we both knew that a change was long overdue.'

Finn looks a little uncomfortable at this. But Will's face isn't angry; in fact, he looks very relaxed, cutting off slivers of cake and idly eating them, though it's clear he feels strongly about his last words.

'Maybe,' ponders Finn. 'But I wasn't labouring the point, Will. You're determined to feel guilty about this.'

'Ah, but I do it so well,' quips Will in reply, popping a piece of cake into his mouth. 'I can see things so much more clearly now my head is finally coming free from my arse.'

Finn gives an exasperated sigh. 'Look, will you give me the knife or bloody well cut me a piece of cake before there's none left?' he says, his words belying his frustration. 'We're going around in circles here. You have no reason to feel guilty about my work: nobody forced me to go out there. Yes, the last few months seemed endless, but only because once there was the possibility I might be able to come home, it was all I could think about.'

I draw my chair back slightly, causing both of them to look at me. Will is instantly contrite.

'Sorry, Ellie. We should save this discussion for another time.' He reaches across the table to take hold of my hand. It's warm. I am quick in my denial.

'No, no. I don't think you should. This is clearly something that means a great deal to both of you.' I pause to tuck a piece of hair back behind my ear. 'Maybe you don't realise it, but from where I'm sitting, you make a great team, not least because you're prepared to work together and make sacrifices for something you both believe in.' I stop for a moment, drawing a slow, steadying breath, taking courage from the expression on Will's face, which is one of acceptance and warmth.

I turn my attention to my left. 'Finn, I haven't known you for very long, but you strike me as a very thoughtful and resourceful person. You may not have liked all the decisions that you've had to take, but you've stood by them and worked to the best of your ability – something which has clearly been appreciated by other people. Christ, it's New Year's Eve; if you two can't come up with something to forge ahead with, today of all days, I'll bash your bloody heads together!'

'I wish you were my teacher,' simpers Finn, who can't help himself. But then he jumps up, crying, 'Paper!' excitedly, and brings several sheets back to the table.

The discussion ranges back and forth for a few minutes while I refill the teapot, looking for an excuse to take a back seat.

'See, we need to stick to our original thoughts on this,' opens Will. 'That Rowan Hill shouldn't just belong to us, or it will die with us. It's not a farm anymore. No one comes here, and we have no involvement with anyone outside. Basically, no one gives a fig about the heritage of this place.'

'Well, I agree we're not farmers, but we need to make a live-lihood somehow. In theory we should be able to sustain both ourselves and the local community with what we have here.'

'What, a bit like the Geoffreys?' I interject, thinking back to the polytunnels. 'They get to run their business, but it benefits you as well – free produce and a bit of rent to help maintain the estate.'

'That's exactly it,' agrees Finn excitedly.

'There's the firewood to sell,' says Will, pulling at his lip, 'but it's a pity that the woodland can't be more productive than it is at the moment. The process of coppicing the trees is relatively slow, and there's still so much land to be cleared. It takes up too much of my time as it is, and that's before you start to factor in making products from the wood and selling them. If someone else came on board to take on that side of our work, it would allow me to concentrate on other things. We could still take back a little of the profit from the wood, and we'd be getting help with the clearing at the same time.'

I think I can sense what Will wants to say.

'Will, you have to carry on with your glasswork. You need to be able to throw everything you have at it.'

'Write it down, Will,' says Finn in agreement. 'I know your glasswork will sell. It would more than make up for what we would lose from the logs, and the coppice products are so seasonal anyway, I'm sure we can still do both. It's a pity we don't have more diversity of land here, really.'

My mind has been running at full pelt for the last few minutes. I have lain awake so many nights, letting my imagination fill up the spaces of Rowan Hill, that I know exactly what I would do. It was solely an exercise to help me fall asleep, but I realise that my inner ramblings may not be so inane after all, if I have the courage to share them.

'You have got the buildings, though,' I volunteer. Finn's eyes land on my face, a question forming, but it's Will who grabs my hands.

'Come on, on your feet, Ellie. Up!'

I'm dragged towards the door, Finn following behind. Will leads us into the centre of the courtyard and turns me to face the bell tower at its rear. He drops my arm, standing still beside me.

'Tell us what you see, Ellie.'

And so, standing there in the scuffed-up snow, I tell them about the people who might like to come and work at Rowan Hill. People like Helen, who need a workspace and somewhere for potential customers to browse. Somewhere fairly small because they're never going to be running a multinational, but nevertheless people whose small business means the world to them.

I tell them about the people who value the rural economy and who might want to buy something of real individual value, not mass produced, who want to build up a relationship with the person they buy from and not be treated like an anonymous irrelevance. People who, while they're here, might also take a walk in the woods because it's such a beautiful day and life's too short not to.

People who might stop for a cup of tea or to meet a friend for a natter before collecting their children from school, the same children who might one day come and experience the unique learning environment of a Forest School and maybe come back at the weekend because *'Wow, Dad, it's just so cool.'*

And then I'm finished, out of steam, standing there feeling rather foolish amid the snowmen, the fresh flakes of snow catching in my hair. I don't know what to say (I've said far too much already), but though I wait for Will and Finn to laugh at me, they don't. Instead, I'm caught up by them both and whirled around, with Will's voice singing in my ear. 'I'm going to show you how to make the best paper aeroplane you've ever seen.'

CHAPTER TWENTY

I never expected it to be so light up here by the seat, but there's moonlight bouncing off the snow, giving everything a shimmering glow. It's bitterly cold, but the sky has cleared, and while I'm grateful that Will brought the truck up, the hundred-or-so-yard walk wasn't long enough to warm me up.

I feel a bit of a lemon, to tell the truth, not really sure what to expect, but it's still beautiful up here, even at night, standing on the edge of a sense of space that seems to seep right through you.

Will's arms wrap around me from behind, and I lean back into his solid warmth. He dips his head against mine, holding it there for a moment quietly before whispering, 'You okay?'

I breathe a reply, suddenly feeling utterly fantastic.

Finn has been moving around behind us, taking things from the rucksack he brought up. A couple of lanterns now stand beside the bench. In the stillness a champagne cork sounds like a gunshot.

'Ladies and gentlemen,' says Finn, 'time to charge your glasses, please.'

I can't believe he's brought champagne. I glance at my watch. There's only about ten minutes to go until midnight.

'Do we synchronise watches?' I ask as I hold out my hand for the glass Finn passes to me.

'We should be able to hear the church bells from up here; that's what we usually wait for. It's amazing how the sound travels up.'

'So, what do you think then, Finn?' asks Will. Like me, he defers to Finn as master of ceremonies.

Finn considers the question for a moment. 'I think, all things considered, that the year is ending rather better than it started. I'm looking forward to the next one.'

Will takes a swallow of his drink. 'Yeah.' He pauses, looking at me. 'I think I'd agree with that.'

I flush bright red, grateful that it won't be obvious in the dim light. I'm excited too, I realise. The whole afternoon has been spent talking of plans for the estate and things that need putting in place for the coming year. As early evening approached, some of these thoughts were committed to the paper planes, my own included.

I'm not sure I've ever done anything like this at New Year before, and if I did, it's too long ago to remember. I went to parties, yes – whooped and sang 'Auld Lang Syne' along with the rest of them. But I'm not sure I ever gave much thought to the year just passed or made such plans for the one to follow. I almost feel ashamed of my lack of direction, allowing one year to drift into the next, and maybe it's the company I'm keeping, or maybe it's where we are, but I feel as if I'm standing on the edge of something that is way bigger than I am.

I return Will's smile, nodding in agreement. I'm not quite sure what there is between us yet, but whatever it is feels good right now.

'Well, no prizes for guessing what else you two wrote down,' observes Finn, giving us both a searching look but grinning benignly.

It strikes me then how accepting he has been of me: arriving home to find me well and truly in his midst, but never showing me anything other than generosity. As a matter of fact, he has been openly encouraging of our fledging romance.

'So what about you, Finn?' I ask, teasing. 'Are you going to tell us what else is on your plane?'

'Not bloody likely!' he sends back, quick as a flash.

'Seriously, though,' butts in Will, 'do you think what we discussed can work, Finn? Are you okay with it?'

I watch Finn's reaction carefully. I know this is important to Will, and I'm pleased to see Finn measuring his response. He slowly holds out his hand, his palm facing upwards.

'It'll be hard work, and its success depends on a lot of things, many of which may be out of our control, but I think it's the best shot we have at finally getting it right. In all sorts of ways, I'm in.'

A slow smile creeps across Will's face as he grasps Finn's hand and gives it a firm shake, pulling him into a hug which threatens to spill the contents of both their glasses. Will pulls away first.

'We should drink a toast,' he says, motioning with his glass for us all to follow suit. 'Come on, Ellie, what do you propose?'

There's only one thing I can propose, really, as I stand looking out across the valley of snow-covered hills and trees.

'To Rowan Hill,' I say firmly. Two glasses crash against my own.

'To Rowan Hill,' chorus both brothers.

'Good choice, Ellie,' adds Finn and then, 'Christ, look at the time!'

I snatch a hurried sip of my drink, barely having time to register its icy bubbles before my paper plane is thrust into my hand.

We stand in waiting silence, breathing, listening, and then a single clear note flies up to us as the church bell begins its heralding chime.

'Happy New Year!' yells Finn, launching his plane upwards in a high arc that sends it sailing out over the slope.

Will catches my arm. 'Come on, Ellie, on three!'

I wait for his signal and throw my plane as hard as I can. It catches the breeze and glides out into space, carrying my hopes and dreams for the coming year with it. I daren't hope that they might come true.

We collapse into a giggling heap, high on the moment, as the chimes continue to ring out amid a flurry of staccato bursts, fireworks from some distant place, some other party.

We take up our glasses once more and drink. None of us want to say it, but we all want to go home. It's too cold now; the warmth of anticipation is no longer with us, and the release of the nervous tension that we've been holding all day brings tiredness in its wake.

Finn upturns his glass, draining the last drops of liquid out onto the snow. 'Well, boys and girls, that's me done, I'm afraid. Way past my bedtime, and I fear I shall be turning into a pumpkin sometime soon.' He looks to Will for assent.

'Yes, come on, let's get back,' he agrees. 'We can always have a nightcap back at home. It's been quite a day one way or another. A good day, but I'm knackered too.'

I murmur my own affirmative. 'I'm so glad we came up here, though,' I say. 'It's a brilliant tradition.'

Will puts his arm around my shoulders. 'Think you'll come next year then?' he asks playfully.

'If I'm invited, yes,' I shoot back.

'Well, I guess that rather depends on what you both wrote on your planes, doesn't it?' grins Finn. 'Especially yours,' he adds, looking at me. 'Your plane went the furthest, so whatever you wrote has to come true.'

'Is that a fact?' I counter, pausing. 'You're so full of shit, Finn.'

'I know, but I'm just so good at it,' he says, winking.

'It's a nice thought, though, mate,' says Will, slapping him on the back. 'I hope we all get what we want.'

Finn rolls the rucksack up onto his back and groans with longing. 'God, I hope so,' he says, walking past us back towards the truck. ''Cause I really would like to get laid sometime soon.'

CHAPTER TWENTY-ONE

I wish Finn hadn't made that comment earlier in the wood. We're back in the kitchen now, Finn having gone up to bed as soon as we got home, while Will is ostensibly making cocoa for us both. We're both in no doubt that the next stage in our relationship is looming, but the distance to that from where we are now seems like a gulf. After Finn's comment it's as if a huge spotlight has suddenly been shone on us, and whilst its light is warming, the glare is a little harsh.

Will senses me behind him, turning in an instant, one hand holding the base of my neck gently as he pulls me towards him. A small tickle flicks around the base of my spine. I can feel him growing hard almost immediately, and I slide my hand down to rub against him, eliciting a sharp change in his breathing. He pushes against me, but then almost immediately I feel him pull back.

He removes the pan of milk from the heat and turns back to look at me, breathing raggedly.

He swallows hard. 'I have something to tell you, Ellie.'

It's said in such a way that I'm left in no doubt as to how serious it will be. Apprehension catches in my throat as I suddenly realise that it is this thing – whatever it is – that has been keeping us apart. Until Will has unburdened himself, there can be no moving forward. I just hope that the price is not too dear.

My feelings for Will have solidified into something more intense than I intended, but the one thing I am certain about is the need that I sense from him right now, both physically and emotionally. For all that his friendship has come to mean to me, I cannot deny him that.

'Let's go upstairs,' I tell him.

There's an odd moment of indecision on the landing as we do that (bizarre in the circumstances) your-place-or-mine routine. The proximity of the room I've been sleeping in to Finn's soon resolves the question.

Neither of us speaks as we undress, nor do we touch, but the atmosphere is so charged that I feel as if I have been undressed with the greatest care and attention.

Will climbs into bed first, opening his arms wide to welcome me, enfolding me warmly until we're lying, bodies touching. We lie quietly for a moment, soaking up each other's skin. I don't want to speak; I just want to lie there safe in our cocoon, where no words can break through, but I know they must.

I can't imagine what he's going to tell me that can be so awful, but his demeanour is one of guilt and shame. The possibilities that occur to me are stark in their awfulness. Maybe he's been to prison for some hideous crime – perhaps in a fit of mad rage he hit his wife. It's hard to contemplate Will being capable of any of these things, but they run through my mind anyway. I wonder how I will react. Will I be shocked, angry, hurt, disbelieving?

I'm so busy sifting through the possibilities that I almost miss what Will quietly says. I don't want to make him repeat it, and I struggle to take in the words I heard, putting them into an order that will make some sort of sense. When I think I've grasped what my brain is trying to deny, he says it again. Four words that I know cost him dearly.

'I was raped, Ellie.'

I clamp my mouth, determined that the stunned *what?* that wants to be said won't get out. Instead, I raise myself onto my elbows to look into his face and see his skin, wet with tears, and a raw pain that is made up of so many things. As he fights to hold my gaze when I know that all he wants to do is look away, what I see most is fear. Fear that I might reject him, push him away, belittle him, and although I know my own reaction is clamouring for attention, his need is so much greater than my own.

My touch releases a shuddering sob. I hold his shaking body to me, stroking his hair, whispering to calm his ragged breathing. 'Can you tell me?' I ask. I listen, my salty tears mixing with his own, as he tells me about the night a little over eighteen months ago when his world was cleaved in two.

He tells me about the attack that came from nowhere, two men with knives who knocked him to the ground and used every part of his body for their own gratification. He tells me how he offered no resistance, but lay there as they each took their turn with a knife at his neck and a hand over his mouth, unable to make a sound, but screaming inside with pain, in shame and disgust. He would have been happy to die, but a stranger came then. A stranger who took a knife wound to save him, hauling the men off him. A stranger who undoubtedly saved his life but who somehow also made it worse – who saw him stripped bare of everything, his soul openly on view. This other man, bleeding and in pain himself, cared for Will as best he could until help came.

It takes a long time, Will's story, spilling from him in fits and starts, sometimes a whisper, sometimes almost a shout, until he has said all he can say for now.

'It's okay, it's okay,' I say over and over again, taking his face in my hands so that he has to look at me. I tell him silently that although his choice of words at times made me wince and beat a pulse in my stomach as it dropped away in shock, I understand now. I know why he's said and done the things he has to protect himself. I understand the emotions that have changed him, but which have also made him who he is today. Despite all this, or maybe because of it, it really is okay. He is still the man who befriended me when all was new and strange, the man I fell in love with.

'I'm not sure I can do this, Ellie,' murmurs Will, fluttering kisses across my stomach. 'It's been a long time since I made love to anyone.' He pauses, looking up at me, his lashes still wet. 'I'm serious, Ellie. I need you to know this. I'm not using you as a bandage, a quick fix to make me feel better. I need to know how to touch and be touched again. God, at times I thought I'd never want this ever again, but now . . .' His expression takes on a sharper look. 'It's not about sex either – Christ, I can do that myself.' He looks away now as if in disgust. 'That's not what I want for us . . . and I need you to know that this is only because of you, because it's *you*, but I just don't know if I can make it okay.'

I pull him to me then, cutting off his words. 'You will. Maybe not tonight, but you will.'

Will's clock is showing five when I wake, casting a soft green glow into the room. I can only have been asleep for a couple of hours. The memory of last night is still fresh; my body remembers it too, and I smile realising that Will's arm is still around me, just as it was when we fell asleep, just as it was when he told me he loved me.

Our climax had brought tears again for both of us.

I can't imagine how Will must have been feeling. I tried, but I know I can't even get close. He was physically hurt, yes, but his mental anguish has nearly destroyed him. My torment over Robbie seems pale and insignificant in comparison, and yet at one time it seemed to have such a hold on me, I thought I would always be under its shadow. I realise now what I've found these past few months: joy, wonderment, admiration, honesty and friendship. And, more recently: passion, tenderness and love. All things I thought I'd lost or that maybe I'd never had, certainly not for a long time. I'd let my relationship with Robbie carry on these last few years without any of these things, and I never even realised. How could I have been so complacent, so lazy? I've given the last few months of my life over to my hatred of him, such a futile emotion and so misplaced. I see now that all he'd been was a coward for deceiving me instead of coming clean about how he felt about our relationship.

'You're frowning,' comes a voice from beside me. I look up to see Will's gentle smile.

'I was thinking,' I say, smiling back sleepily.

Will nods, thinking he understands. 'You must have a list of questions as long as your arm,' he says, looking resigned but resolute.

I think about his words for a moment, wondering why, when I probably should have a myriad number of things to ask him, I can't think of any. I shake my head.

'No,' I answer truthfully. 'And anyway,' I tease, 'I wasn't thinking about you.'

'Well, why the bloody hell not!' he replies.

I snuggle deeper into the crook of his arm. 'Sorry, I shall start again immediately.'

We lie quietly for a moment, savouring just being together.

'You know, I don't mind if you want to ask me something. There must be things you want to know about what happened.'

'Such as?' I ask, wondering whether in fact it is Will who needs to hear the questions more than I do, Will who needs the opportunity to give the answers. He wastes no time in replying.

'Like how come I was such a wuss? Why didn't I try and fight them off? I'm a reasonably strong bloke, so why did I just take it?'

I reach up to touch Will's hair, turning so that I can see him squarely. I choose my words with care. 'I don't think that you took the easy way out at all. If you had tried to fight them off, you probably wouldn't be here now. Yes, maybe what you did kept you alive, but what it also did was sentence you to self-doubt and recrimination. Hardly the easy option. You know, bravery isn't always measured by heroic deeds.'

Will nods almost imperceptibly. I realise I'm probably not the first person to tell him this.

'There have been times when I've wondered if I picked the wrong option that night. I didn't want to die, but in the days that followed I often thought that maybe I didn't need to stick with the decision to choose life at all.' He pauses then, catching the alarm in my eyes, and is quick to reassure me. 'But I guess in the end I realised that I'd never just give in. I'm too much of a stubborn bugger for that.' He gives a wry smile before continuing. 'And as Finn has delighted in pointing out to me, I'd much rather enjoy being miserable.'

I trace the line of his smile to the corner of his mouth, thinking very much about kissing it.

It occurs to me then that actually I do have a question. 'How come no one knows what happened? Wouldn't it have been in the news?'

Will's voice is flat. 'They're dead.'

'Dead?'

'Yeah, the guys that did it died in a car accident the night it happened, full of drink and drugs; they crashed their car into a concrete bridge support. I couldn't give the police a proper description of them. All they had to go on were the patchy details the other bloke supplied, but something about the accident must have made them suspicious, because they tried for a match from the DNA samples, and bingo. Case closed.'

'Jesus.'

'I was in hospital for a while, and Finn just told everyone I'd had an accident. Both the stories were reported, but in separate articles, and no names were ever mentioned. It ended there, and there was no reason to connect the two events as far as people were concerned. There was no court case and nothing to contradict what was in the newspapers, so people believed Finn's story – why wouldn't they?'

'And people still don't know?'

'No.' Will looks ashamed now. 'Finn and Alice just tried to protect me as best they could – Caroline did too to start with. They closed ranks, I suppose, but the more time passed, the harder it was to tell the truth, and then things between Caroline and me fell apart, and she paraded her version of events around the village. I think I was an embarrassment to her.'

'Perhaps she just wasn't a very strong person,' I say, trying to be generous.

'She was strong enough when she was getting her own way,' he replies bitterly. Her solution to the state I was in was to give me something else to think about. She wanted a child, and she thought dragging me into bed every five minutes would cure me of my complete revulsion towards sex. It didn't, needless to say, which just left her with the tricky problem of extricating herself from our marriage whilst managing to save face – hence my supposed philandering. Better that than admit that her husband couldn't make love to her.'

I reach my hand up to stroke his face once more. 'Will, none of that was your fault. No one will blame you for what Caroline did or said, just as they won't blame you for anything else. I think you've suffered enough already, without having to worry what other people think.'

Will shifts suddenly, more onto his side, now able to reach his hand across to lay it gently across my neck, his thumb moving against my cheek.

'Thank you,' he says simply; then, 'We should really go back to sleep, I suppose,' he adds, moving his hand south.

'We should,' I murmur in agreement, although not, of course, to the suggestion of sleep.

He hasn't forgotten much, Will.

CHAPTER TWENTY-TWO

I instantly know he's not there when I wake again. It's not so much the warmth that's gone, but the hole he himself seems to have left. It throws me for a minute. It is nearly eleven, though, which might explain it.

I sneak back into my room, smiling like a guilty teenager at my unslept-in bed. I dress hurriedly and pad downstairs.

Finn is sitting at the kitchen table, a large notebook in front of him, a quick hand committing detail to paper. There's no sign of Will.

He doesn't look up. 'Afternoon,' he quips, but then looks up to fix me with a beaming smile. 'Happy New Year!'

I realise belatedly that he's right. It is New Year's Day, even though our time back in the woods at midnight seems like an age away.

'Happy New Year, Finn,' I say warmly, taking up a seat opposite to him.

He hefts the teapot in front of him and starts pouring. He waits until the mug is nearly full before speaking again.

'And was it?' he asks, pushing the mug towards me and directing me to the jug of milk with a look.

'Sorry? Was it what?'

'A happy New Year?'

'Oh!' I say, and blush.

Finn winks. 'No need to answer that one then.'

I take a hasty sip of tea as Finn leans back, studying me, taking his time as he taps the end of his pencil against the page. Thank Christ, the tea's not too hot as I hide in gulping another mouthful.

'He's told you, hasn't he?' says Finn suddenly, all the easy jocularity gone from his face. Instead, he's leaning forward again, arms braced against the table, but his expression is warm, compassionate.

I'm not as surprised as I thought I'd be under the circumstances. Finn has an extraordinary ability to sum up situations in an instant.

'How do you know?' I whisper, as if the walls themselves might suddenly transmit this knowledge to the outside world.

'Because you have the same scattered look as I did when I first found out. Like you're trying to think of too many things at once. One: Oh my God, I can't believe what he's just told me. Two: I can't imagine how he must be feeling. And three: What can I do to help him? Then it goes back to one again, and so on and so on. I can keep that little trio going for days.'

He takes my hand then, the one that's not holding onto my mug for dear life. 'Are you okay?'

I nod, and then again more confidently. 'I am actually,' I affirm.

Finn's wide smile is back. 'Good girl,' he says. 'You know, I am so very, very glad that he's told you. You know why?'

I don't get to answer. 'Because you are the only person he's ever told, aside from me, Alice and Caroline, and yet he bounded out of here this morning like a kangaroo on speed, talking nineteen to the dozen about his work, plans for this place and you; then a bit more about you, going to see Alice, a list of people he needed to ring and obviously more about you.' He pauses for a minute to catch his breath. 'Are you getting the picture?'

'I am,' I laugh, touched by Finn's words. 'Is that where he's gone then? To see Alice?'

'He has. "Bring her up to speed" was the phrase he used, I think. He's always been the same: anything happens – go tell Alice,' he says, using his hands to make an underlining motion. 'He tells her everything.'

I nearly choke on my tea, catching the glint in Finn's eye. 'Everything?' I say weakly.

'Absolutely. Although in this case I suspect he won't need to tell her about you two doing the wild thing – she'll probably guess.'

'Finn!' I groan. 'Will you stop it!'

Finn just winks and turns his attention back to his drawing, adding in a few lighter strokes.

'Ellie, you should know that I'm here if you want to talk about anything, any time – you know, about Will?' His voice is light-hearted, but I cannot fail to miss the 'serious content' alert.

'Thanks, Finn,' I say, smiling. 'I know how hard this is going to be. Things like this don't just go away, and while it's the last thing I want to think about right now, I guess it's just the beginning, really.'

'Will gets . . . *stuck* sometimes. It's the only word I can use to describe it, but it helps if you know where he's coming from.'

'And you've seen all this before?'

'I have, in a way, but Ellie you really do make a difference; please, just remember that. This is the best I've ever seen him, and while it might not be all plain sailing, I think we're leaving the past behind, bit by bit.'

He carries on drawing, but I still his hand. 'It must have been hard for you, Finn, after Caroline left, being the only one here.'

Slowly, his gaze comes up. He draws in a breath. 'It was. It's hard seeing someone you care about in so much pain. Personally, it was easier when Caroline left . . . we didn't exactly see eye to eye.' He stares off into space. 'Actually, if I remember rightly, she called me a self-indulgent, weak-minded tosspot.'

'Bloody hell, that's a bit strong,' I reply, shocked.

'Don't worry – the feeling was entirely mutual. And even though her leaving was yet another stick for Will to beat himself with, I was glad she went. Her staying would just have caused more problems for all of us.'

'You really didn't like her, did you?'

'No,' he replies vehemently, 'and neither did Alice.'

'I know Alice didn't like her much – she told me – but I thought she was just being protective, you know, maternal even, thinking perhaps that Caroline wasn't good enough for him.'

'That was partly it, I suppose, to start with at least,' agrees Finn. 'But once it became clear what she was really like, the only one who was ever going to get hurt was Will.'

'He must have seen something in her, though. He doesn't strike me as a particularly bad judge of character.'

'Present company excepted?' Finn smiles then, looking down and pushing his pencil around.

'I don't think Will could believe his luck,' he says slowly. 'Somehow I always seemed to get in his way when we were younger. Leaving the farm when I did made it almost impossible for Will to leave himself, and then when he finally did, he met Caroline, and like I said, I don't think he could believe that a girl like that could fall for him, and so he snapped her up.'

'Was she very pretty, then?'

Finn nods. 'I never met anyone like her, Ellie. She was absolutely stunning. Too beautiful for her own good, possibly. Maybe it was her upbringing, but she had a way of assuming that whatever she wanted would just fall into her lap without her ever having to try too hard. It was a horrible time when Will came out of hospital, granted, but she just couldn't deal with it. She had no means of coping with something so difficult. I needed her help, but she just couldn't give it. We had an argument about something one day, and I lost my temper with her; that's when she called me a tosspot, and she left not long after.'

'And is that why you went away too?' I surmise.

'Partly.' He shrugs. 'I stayed about six months before I bailed out. I felt somehow that I should have been able to help Will, but I couldn't seem to. He alternated between periods of burning anger and withdrawing to such a point that he wouldn't speak. He shunned any physical contact, and I couldn't find a level on which to reach him. I felt so guilty about Caroline leaving. Even though I knew it wasn't my fault she left, it was still something else for Will to contend with. In the end the stress of dealing with Will by myself was driving me mad. When the chance came up of a job overseas, I took it in a minute.'

'But you think you did the wrong thing?'

Finn scratches the end of his chin, running his fingers over the stubble of his beard line, catching a patch of hairs that must be slightly longer than the rest and playing with them for a moment. He moves his gaze up from the table.

'At the time I did, but with hindsight I know it was the right thing to do. It gave us both some space. Will didn't have to deal with me constantly trying to make things right, and I didn't have to cope with my guilt at not being able to. Time is a great healer after all. We took to emailing one another, and gradually Will was able to write down some of the things he couldn't say out loud. It was a kind of therapy, I guess, and time just moved on.' He takes a deep, refreshing breath. 'And here we all are.'

The back door clatters then, followed by a stamping of feet as snow is removed from boots. It's still beautifully white outside.

Will crosses the threshold first, a rush of energy with a 'Hey, you're up' in greeting. He comes to me, planting a kiss that lingers just a little longer than the casual greeting mannerisms his body displays. I nod slightly in response to the unspoken *are you okay?* in his eyes. I am kissed again.

'Bloody hell!' cries Finn unceremoniously, and I pull away, looking around Will to see the cause of his outburst. It can't be us, surely? The same two words ring through my mind then as I catch sight of the other person who has entered the room.

'Alice!' I exclaim, scrambling up to give her a hug. She returns my hug fiercely, as if we hadn't met for years. She may be in her seventies, but she's a woman, and she's felt what I'm feeling now. I can tell she's pleased.

'You look incredible,' I remark, holding her at arm's length to see her better. 'What have you done?'

I take in her dark-grey tailored trousers, which, combined with a scarlet jumper, reveal a hitherto unguessed-at trim figure. A pale grey scarf is wound elegantly around her neck. Of the dreaded square tweed, there is no sign.

'I've been shopping,' she says delightedly, excitement showing in her brown eyes. 'I told you it was time for a change. Do you like it? All in the sales, dear, and quite a bargain.'

'I think you look amazing, Alice,' I answer truthfully. 'People won't recognize you.'

'Which may well be no bad thing, the way I've been carrying on. I must say, you look very bonny too, dear. Something has given you a lovely glow,' she teases. 'Finn, dear, whatever is the matter?'

Finn, whose mouth gaped the minute Alice came into the room, is still sitting, mouth wide open, a stunned expression on his face.

'Is that a wig?' he asks in wonder.

'No, it is not!' replies Alice hotly, putting up a hand to feel her now straight and beautifully cut hair. 'Less of your cheek, young man.' She waves an airy hand. 'I just thought rollers were rather passé. All that palaver twice a week. This is so much easier.'

'It's lovely, Alice,' soothes Will, coming to her side and throwing Finn a dark look.

'I didn't say it wasn't lovely,' argues Finn, trying furiously not to dig himself an even bigger hole. 'I just wondered if it was real, that's all. It's so different from your usual style. I'm just very pleasantly surprised,' he finishes, giving Will a *so there* look. He pats the chair beside him.

'Come and have a look at these, Alice. See what you think,' he says, moving the paper out from under his arm so that she can see.

It's the first time I'm able to take in what Finn has been drawing. Our conversation about Will monopolised my attention, pulling it away from what I'd assumed were just sketches. They're not just sketches; they're fully formed artist's impressions of life at Rowan Hill, the type of thing you often see for new housing developments or hotel complexes. Little cameos of life and small moments of time in the future: a mother and child buying vegetables from a farm shop, burgeoning baskets of produce laid out around them; two men in what looks like a workshop, looking at plans spread out on a table; a potter giving a demonstration of her work to a group of schoolchildren; the courtyard at Rowan Hill; the closed-off rooms with their frontages enticingly open. The whole area vibrant, restored and energised. The bell tower stands surveying the scene, a beautiful sign hanging beneath it on a wrought-iron frame, its huge gates open to show a tantalising glimpse of the gardens beyond.

Nobody says anything for quite some time, the moments ticking by as we take time to gaze at Finn's vision. It's idealistic, yes, but it looks attainable. It looks like it could all so easily happen, just metres from where we're sitting, and I can sense what we're all thinking in turn. It represents an enormous amount of work, but ultimately, what an opportunity, what a journey and what a chance for all of us to change our lives if we can make it work.

I look up to see Will watching me, looking for the fire that is burning in his own eyes. It catches hold as Finn's gaze meets ours, and the three of us grin inanely at one another, feeling the excitement of our common purpose. Still, we say nothing. I know that we are waiting for the one thing that, whether they acknowledge it or not, means a lot to Finn and Will: Alice's approval.

She fingers the scarf at her neck thoughtfully. 'And you can provide plans for all of this?' she asks Finn, who nods briefly.

'And a business plan?' This to Will. He grimaces but nods firmly.

'And of course more of your brilliant ideas?' To my amazement, she is looking at me, and I feel a little thrill of pleasure in my stomach. What else can I do but nod?

'Well then,' she says slowly, somewhat theatrically, knowing that we are all hanging on her every word, 'I think we must deliver this lot to Graham with all haste.'

Finn raises his hand in the air for a high five, which we all slap with gusto, almost knocking him off balance.

I lean in towards Will. 'Who's Graham?' I whisper. Will holds a hand to the side of his mouth to whisper back conspiratorially, 'Alice's nephew in the planning office.' He winks.

'Oh, I see,' I say, realising now why Alice's approval was so important.

Will sits down now, pulling the tin of biscuits that's on the table towards him. He cranks off the lid, taking a digestive and cramming half of it into his mouth, pushing the tin back into the middle of the table.

'We'll need a loan for the building works, but I would think with the house as collateral, we should be okay,' he says, pushing the other half of the biscuit into his mouth.

I can't believe I didn't think about this. It seems unimportant, I suppose, when you're sitting in the middle of a huge estate. It never occurred to me that Will and Finn might not have the money for this project. Their heating bill alone must be astronomical, and the overall cost of running the estate is probably huge. Like a lot of landowners, they're property rich, cash poor.

I had felt proud when Alice named me as the instigator of ideas, but now I'm feeling ashamed that it never even crossed my mind how Will and Finn would pay for the work. I think of my own pot of savings: money from the sale of my house that I will almost certainly need when my time comes to move on from the Lodge. I have to offer some of this money now if I'm to be treated like a partner in this venture. I should be prepared to put my money where my mouth is.

'How much will it cost?' I ask, directing my question towards Finn, who, I'm assuming, is the one able to answer it.

'That rather depends,' he says thoughtfully, 'on what we want: the final design, what level of finish, et cetera.'

'But you must have a rough idea, a ballpark figure?'

Finn looks at me steadily with an amused expression on his face. Perhaps he's sensed the note of panic that I can hear in my voice. I feel a vague sense of irritation that he can treat the subject so light-heartedly. All this hope, all this excitement, and it might not even be possible. I have to tell myself to relax: Finn knows all about this; it's what he's good at. He can probably estimate what it's going to cost down to the last pound.

'The trouble is that it could be anywhere from here,' he says, holding up one hand, 'to here,' he finishes, holding up his other hand some distance from the first.

I can't understand why he's being so deliberately obtuse. I frown and am about to interrogate him further when he cuts across me.

'It will also depend on whether this is true,' he adds, twisting in his chair to fish something out of his back pocket. He produces it finally and places it in the centre of the table, like a ticking time bomb. It's a folded piece of paper.

'What is it?' asks Will, reaching forward to pick it up.

'An email from Gus, confirming my bonus – what you might call a farewell handshake.'

I watch as Will's expression changes from one of casual enquiry to stunned incredulity.

'Jesus H. Christ, Finn. I thought you were talking out of your arse before,' he exclaims, looking up sharply.

'I might still be. Check the date on the email. The money won't reach my account until tomorrow. I'm not counting my chickens just yet.'

'Still, that's an awful lot of chickens.'

I hardly dare ask, not yet feeling familiar enough to be privy to the family's finances. Alice has no such qualms. She picks up the email, scans it and hands it to me.

I look at Finn in horror. 'It's not going to cost that much, is it?' I ask, thinking of the amount I could offer, which now seems paltry by comparison.

Finn shakes his head, laughing. 'No. Good to have a little to fall back on, though, don't you think?'

'I can't take this in,' mutters Will. 'I don't know what to say. Are you absolutely sure you want to do this, Finn?'

'Yes,' he replies firmly. 'Totally.'

Alice chips in then. 'You know, for once I know the perfect thing to say. I heard this quite some while ago now, and what makes it seem even more appropriate is that it was Graham who said it.' She's beginning to smile at the memory of it now.

'Naturally, I ticked him off about it at the time. He didn't always work in the planning department you know, Ellie. At one time before he married and became respectable and middle-aged over-night, he was really quite a rebel. He drove my sister mad with his antics.'

'Come on, Alice, what did he say?' badgers Finn.

Alice tut-tuts, determined to tell the story at her own speed. 'Well, I was telling him off one day – not badly you understand, just trying to get him to see that he should calm down a little, and he told me that he was trying to get it right.'

'Get it right? But what's *it*?'

'That's what I'm trying to tell you,' says Alice in exasperation. 'Just listen. I asked him what getting *it* right meant, and he said, "Getting it right, Auntie Alice – life I mean. You only get one crack at it after all; you'd better make sure you nail the fucker the first time around."'

CHAPTER TWENTY-THREE
February

I can't help smiling to myself. It's such a foul day out there, and Finn is having to be endlessly nice, cooperative, patient and polite – never mind the fact that he's cold and very wet. I know for a fact that what he'd like to be is impatient, irritated and probably rude, but he won't be. He's had a smile plastered to his face for the past forty minutes or so, ever since Graham arrived, and I know that as soon as he's gone, Finn will come tumbling in here, expletives firing, seeking warmth and cake like his life depended on it.

They must be nearly finished by now, surely. They've criss-crossed that courtyard fifty times, in and out of every room time and again, Finn's plans becoming more and more sodden by the minute. After today we can do no more. The meeting is on Friday, and if the plans are passed, it's all systems go. If not – well, I'd rather not think about that. I open the oven door and manoeuvre another tray of muffins inside, setting the first tray down on the table to cool.

I moved back home after New Year's Day, just over a month ago now, despite Will's suggestion that I should stay. I still have my job baking for Gina, of course, and despite what had certainly been a momentous holiday, it *was* a holiday, and it was time to get back to normal – and time to see if my relationship with Will could continue to flourish outside of that extraordinary Christmas.

I find myself smiling again at the memory of the last few weeks and the emerging pattern to our days. The woodland keeps the boys at their busiest this time of year, and they're up and out early, even before it's light, putting in long hours before the night falls. I've taken to cooking for them in the evening, giving them back the hour or so it would have taken them to prepare a meal.

I don't know how they do it, but they seem to have boundless energy, getting up after dinner to carry on with work of another kind: Finn covers the table with endless sketches and plans, his laptop permanently emitting tiny clicks, and Will sketches, colours, buries his head in catalogues. Some nights it seems we hardly even speak, but no one minds: the silence is warm and comfortable, and when Will does pull me towards him, it's either with the most gentle of caresses or with a fierce ignition of passion, and both are equally wonderful.

On more than one occasion, I hear Will's pickup slew gravel across the drive as he arrives at speed, ostensibly having come to get something from the house, but in reality rushing in for a drop-everything, frantic, sweaty quickie. More than one batch of cakes has been burnt in this way.

Hands are being shaken now. Finn is edging out of the courtyard towards Graham's car, trying to signal the conclusion of their business, and then suddenly Graham gives Finn a final slap on the back and rushes to his car as if he's only just realised it's raining.

I slide the kettle over the hot plate to boil. Finn walks back to stand in the courtyard. He's thinking he could have done better. Graham might be our man on the inside, but it's by no means a done deal. Will and I have helped where we can, with suggestions, ideas and refinements. The plans are a collaboration of all our thoughts, but this is still Finn's baby. He's the only one who could present these plans, show their detail, explain their reasoning, and I can see him carrying the weight of this responsibility now as he comes towards me.

I slather butter and jam onto a scone and place it on the table. Finn gives me a weak smile as he comes in, his blonde hair darkly plastered against his head. His eyes flicker towards the Aga and then settle on the mug in my hand. He's too polite to ask me to make him a drink, but his smile deepens in gratitude when he sees that I have.

I let him sit for a few moments, both cooling off and warming up, his hands wrapped around his mug. He takes a bite of the scone, which I know is still warm. His eyes close. He is, I think idly, one of the most beautiful creatures I've ever seen. Not that I think of him in that way, obviously; he's like the older brother I always wished I had and, increasingly, a very good friend, but for some reason (for which I am eternally grateful), I'm quite happy to leave it there.

'You know, ten years ago Graham was an irritating, irresponsible prick. Now he's a pedantic arsehole. I'm not sure which is worse.'

I bring my own mug over and sit opposite Finn. 'Didn't it go well?' I ask gently.

'No . . . yes . . . I mean, it was fine. Graham is paid to be a pedantic arsehole anyway, and it's not like I haven't come across his kind before. My working life was usually knee-deep in them. It's just that this is more . . .'

'Personal?' I suggest, cutting across him, understanding how he's feeling.

'Something like that.' He gives a rueful smile. 'I should learn to keep my ego in its box, that's all.'

'Rubbish. You should be proud of what you've done. I know it's not on the same level, but I'd feel exactly the same if someone had one of my cakes and said it was crap.'

Finn, his mouth full, waves his scone. 'These are most definitely not crap.'

I smile. 'I wasn't fishing for compliments.'

Finn returns it. 'No, neither was I,' he retorts, the trademark McLennan twinkle back in place.

'Graham has asked for a few tweaks. He thinks we should go all out on the heritage angle and make a big issue out of the restoration. As you know, I planned to change the roof on the large barn because the beams aren't that sound, but Graham wants it reinstated, which will mean going about things in a very different way.' He pulls a face. 'He's right, though – it will look better. I was just trying to save a few bob.'

I nod, understanding his dilemma.

Finn stands up, draining his mug. 'Tell Will I'll speak to him later. I've got some designs to reinvent.'

It's getting late, and I should start thinking about tea. I look at my watch, glancing up and across at the big house. The kitchen light has glowed steadily all afternoon, and I expect Finn is still working.

I don't bother knocking; it's become the accepted norm to walk in and out of each other's houses, and Finn is right where I expected to find him, at the kitchen table, staring morosely at a pile of papers. His laptop sits to one side, tiny points of light flying through space on his screensaver. I suspect it's much how his brain feels.

'How's it going?' I ask.

Finn throws his pencil down onto the pile and leans back in the chair, stretching. I'm not even sure he knows what day it is anymore.

He gives me a blank look, his eyes flicking between me and outside, then finally to his watch, before back to me again, this time looking slightly more focused.

'Sorry,' he says, unnecessarily.

'Have you eaten?'

'Yes, I had . . .' He trails off, looking towards the draining board for inspiration, clearly unable to remember what, if anything, he's had. His eyes return to the table. '. . . an apple,' he finishes lamely, spying the core.

'And lunch?'

Finn catches on. 'I had a lovely scone, nice little place, not far from here.'

'That,' I reply pointedly, 'was not lunch.' I start to pull out his chair. 'Come on – move! Up!' I command, yanking at the chair. He staggers to his feet. 'Right – go and wash your hands and face,' I add, shooing him out with my hands.

Twenty minutes and several slices of toast later, and Finn is tucking into a mushroom and cheese omelette, looking much better.

'So, what's the problem?' I ask when he's settled.

'I don't know exactly,' he says, grimacing. 'I think I've got it right, and then – I dunno.' He shrugs. 'Something's not right anymore.'

'Okay, well, let me be your client then. I know the brief. Pretend I don't know anything about building, which shouldn't be difficult, and show me your very first design, the one you started work on when you left me earlier.'

Finn shoves in the last of his supper, pushes his plate aside and fishes for a piece of paper under all the others. He smooths it out.

'You see the barn has a cruck frame, which is pretty rare, really. These are huge timbers that go all the way down to the ground. Replacing them is a mammoth task, but the whole structure depends on them. In this drawing, I've left the whole thing pretty much as it was originally. See? It preserves the original roofline, and if you look at this sketch here . . . this is what you'd see if you were inside the building.'

I look to where Finn has directed. You have to imagine you're lying on your back, looking up, a strong graceful arching of timbers above you. Finn has shown the room open to the rafters rather than as it is now with its false ceiling. I never realised there was so much hidden, but suddenly the room has leapt from a rather large but fairly boring space to a celebration of its structure. I look at another detail on the page where Finn has sketched the elevations, examining the difference between the front and the side of the building.

'What's this?' I query, pointing to the side, the wall split by the two enormous arms of the cruck.

'It's glass,' offers Finn simply, and as I look at the drawing again, I can see what Finn has done. The end wall of the barn looks out onto the garden, standing as it does at the top left of the courtyard. A door sits in the middle of this wall, serving as an entrance to the garden; and above it and to the sides, glass extends right to the roof. Once I grasp this fact, the vision of how it will look comes to me at speed.

'It's beautiful, Finn, like a cathedral,' I say, tracing my fingers over the glass arches.

Finn rubs his chin. 'I was hoping I could get Will to fill in a little magic in between.'

'Oh yes!' I breathe. 'Is all this possible?'

'Not impossible,' says Finn, considering it carefully. 'But difficult, yes. Time-consuming, costly and requiring someone with real skill.'

'Ah,' I say, looking around the table, 'I see. That would explain all the other drawings, then?'

Finn nods wearily. He is, I think, caught between a rock and a hard place.

'Can you afford this?'

'Yes, but it might mean economising elsewhere. The other units are relatively straightforward. It's this one that is going to be the most expensive to fit out, as well as converting it in the first place.'

'Then let the building speak for itself, be its own decoration. Everything else can be very simple.'

Finn looks at me steadily, his own thoughts racing, catching up with mine and exploring the possibilities of what I've just said. He gives a rather rueful smile.

'I wish you'd come over three hours earlier,' he says, his eyes sweeping over all the other papers on the table.

'I think that's what's known as due process,' I say. 'You probably had to do all of these to confirm what you already know, that this plan is the right one.'

'But don't you want to see any of the others?'

'No.'

'Why not?' asks Finn, frowning at me.

'Because – correct me if I'm wrong – but when you came over here with Graham's words about the changes you needed to make fresh in your head, you didn't sit down and think, *Righto, I'll make a really mediocre plan to start with and then work up to it*, did you? Of course you didn't. You sat down to create a vision that was the very best it could be.' I tap the plan. 'Which is why this is the right one.'

'Oh bloody hell!' groans Finn, and then laughs, with a final flourish holding up the paper as if proclaiming it to be the winner.

'Right then. Let's get this emailed. Christ, I need a beer.'

CHAPTER TWENTY-FOUR

I think that Friday may well have been the longest day of my life. We've spent the rest of the week trying to be normal, trying to do anything but wait for *the* phone call. I've been baking, shopping, cleaning, visiting Jane and Helen (who, having survived the family skiing trip intact, has thrown herself into finishing her piece for me), the usual diversionary tactics, all the while feeling a little off balance, and with a little thought skittering about in the back of my head that pops up with monotonous regularity: *how long is it until Friday?*

Will says he's fine. He's been cloistered away in his workshop, busy drawing up plans for the barn, hoping he'll need them. I'm not even allowed in. It's maddening. He's not fine, though. He's playing the waiting game too.

Now it's Friday and the phone hasn't stopped bloody ringing. I drop my cakes off at Gina's early. The planning meeting starts at eleven, and I'm keeping vigil in the big house's kitchen, talking about anything other than getting the call.

The first call is from the oil company, to say that they'll deliver on Monday. The second is from the dentist, asking whether they can change Finn's check-up, as they've had a cancellation.

('No,' says Finn, 'they can't.') The third is a wrong number, and the fourth is from a company selling kitchens. There is a slight lull over lunch, and then the fifth call comes in from the wood-yard in Bishops Castle, with the name of a chap they know who might be interested in taking on the woodland work. Will duly writes his name down, saying he'll give the guy a ring. None of us say it, but we're all thinking that it's beginning to look like a superfluous call.

By three o'clock the kitchen is doom-laden; by half past four it's settled into a deeply despondent *well, that's that then* feeling, and I start to make noises about what to have for tea. Finn mutters something about a large malt, and Will, looking morose, declares that he will ring Alice.

I'm staring into the fridge, looking for inspiration, when there's a ferocious expletive from behind me. A stunned-looking Will is holding the phone receiver.

'There's a bloody message on here.'

I stand up as Finn magically materialises back into the room, both of us watching Will's finger press the button on the phone. Finn's been up and down all day, checking to see if any messages had been left while the line was engaged. None of us can remember if he did so after the call from the woodyard. I guess it doesn't matter much now. Will's face is expressionless, and then he grins, a huge transforming grin that radiates across the kitchen as he listens to the last of the message. He drops the receiver, flying across the space to throw his arms around me and then Finn, who comes to join us, until all three of us are locked together, jumping up and down and whooping like small children.

We stop for a moment, out of breath, looking at one another and laughing, all the tension of the day dissipated. Will gives Finn a hearty slap on the back.

'Well done, mate. Bloody well done.' He grins at his brother.

Finn almost chokes. 'Hey! It's not just me,' he protests, but I can see he's relieved, the implicit weight he carried for all of us lifted. 'It's all of us. The vision, the ideas—'

I cut across him. 'But nothing without your drawings and plans. They brought it all to life, much more so than words could do.' Finn is struggling to interrupt. 'So just shut up, stop being so modest and say thank you.'

Finn turns ever so slightly pink. 'Thank you,' he says, managing to look both pleased and bashful at the same time.

The enormity of what we've got to do strikes us then. It's not just lists on paper anymore, it's an actual thing that we have to make happen. It's an awful lot of work. Will goes to sit at the table. He looks stunned.

'I'm not sure what to do now,' he says. 'Part of me wants to get out there and start, and the other part wants to celebrate, do something mad.'

Finn goes to join him. 'I'm not sure I've got the energy for either,' he groans. 'I don't feel like I've slept for days. Can I just go to bed, please?' he adds, a pleading tone in his voice, but I can tell he doesn't really mean it. He looks tired, but way too wired to sleep.

'Well, at the very least we should go and wet the baby's head, so to speak,' I say, looking at them both.

Will flicks his eyes towards Finn, who returns the look steadily. I'm certain that the last time Will set foot inside the village pub was quite some while ago. I'm equally certain that it's the right thing to do. I decide to cut off Will's protestations before he can make them.

'We should, you know, just for a quick one, and perhaps a bite to eat. We don't have to stay long.' I smile at Will encouragingly, letting him know that he won't be on his own.

'Or we could go up to the bright lights of the big town?' Finn suggests, perhaps seeking a compromise.

Will snorts derisively. 'What – Shrewsbury? It's hardly the metropolis, Finn. Besides which, on a Friday night I suspect we're all about twenty years too old.'

Finn pulls a face, acknowledging his point. I'm determined to make a point of my own, though.

'We should go to The Bull, really. I mean, this is a community project, isn't it? We're going to need the community's support.' I cock my head at Will. 'Got to do it sometime,' I add.

A smile is playing around the corners of his mouth. I watch as the realisation that he's not going to get away with this one dawns.

Finn shrugs. 'I'm easy,' he says, now firmly putting the ball in Will's court.

The hand goes through the hair again as Will breaks into a gentle smile. 'I think I might enjoy showing you off after all. Come on then, let's go get our glad rags on.'

CHAPTER TWENTY-FIVE

Gina takes one look at me on Monday morning and loads up my mug with hot chocolate, cream and marshmallows, pushing it towards me with a lengthy sigh.

'You see, now I feel terrible,' she says. 'I knew this would happen and right at the wrong time too.' She eyes me steadily. 'Don't worry; I've let Derek know how bloody annoyed I am. Not that it'll make any difference, of course, but I've told him I shan't be going quietly.'

Gina's earrings swing vehemently as she talks. I've never met Derek, and I can't picture the man who is married to this little stick of dynamite at all, but I hope that at least *he* knows what she's talking about.

I fish out a little pink marshmallow, sucking on it. 'This is lovely, Gina,' I mutter, 'but I haven't got a clue what you're talking about.'

'Me selling up, love. It can't have come at a worse time for you, can it?' she answers. 'I know you haven't been making my cakes for long, but it's a bit of something, isn't it? I'm so sorry.'

'Oh God, I see what you mean,' I reply, finally understanding. 'You've got a buyer for the business?'

'Yes, sorry, didn't I say? It's all a bit sudden, really. I knew it was coming, of course, but when it does it makes you think. I don't bloody want to move to Lincolnshire, wherever that is. I like it here, and I like this place, so like I said to Derek, I don't have to be happy about it.'

'No, I don't suppose you do,' I sympathise, keeping a very firm lid on my own news for a moment. 'How long have you got left?'

Gina looks at me carefully, obviously weighing up the need to be both indignant at her situation and considerate of mine at the same time. She takes the lid off one of the large plastic boxes I delivered that morning, inhaling the rich ginger scent.

'We got a letter from our solicitor this morning. They've set the completion date for the fifteenth of March, but I was thinking maybe I should close at the end of the month,' she says sadly, starting to remove the cake and get it ready for her customers.

I touch her arm gently and take the lid off the next box, following her lead. 'Gina, that's only a couple of weeks away. How horrible for you.'

'Too bloody right, it is! I dunno – it's sort of snuck up on me, but there's not much point in staying open. The lease transfer on this place won't take long; it's fairly straightforward, but the new people don't want it as a tea room, so there's nothing to even hand over. I've got to clear it all out. I'm really sorry, Ellie.'

I wave a pair of tongs at her. 'Hey, don't you worry about me. You've got more important things to think about.'

'Not *more* important things to think about,' she admonishes. 'It's such bad timing. I've got nicely used to our arrangement. I mean, I knew this was going to happen when we started, but shit, I'd even started thinking about what else we might do – you know, functions and stuff. How stupid is that?'

I smile. 'I think you suffer from the same overactive imagination that I do. It's not stupid, though. It's probably what got you this far, and it'll do the same for you again when you move, I bet.'

Gina waves her own set of tongs at me with mock ferocity. 'Okay, that's enough sympathy for me. I'll only get maudlin.'

She grimaces. 'But what about you, Ellie? What are you going to do now?'

This is the crunch part. I'm glad that my own news will seem like letting her off the hook. She'll have nothing to feel guilty about as I'm going to be all too busy very shortly, but I'm fully aware that our plans to open a tea room at Rowan Hill will be a very obvious rubbing of salt into the wound. Even though when we made those plans, we knew she was closing, I still feel like it's a betrayal of sorts. I was nervous as hell coming here this morning, but I promised Will and Finn I'd let her know what's going to happen so there are no hard feelings. The fact that the place isn't going to remain a tea room is better news than I dared to hope for.

I take a calming breath before telling Gina of our plan's approval.

'Okay, now I'm super-jealous,' she admits, grinning. 'I'll even put in a good word for you, if you like, with the new owner. She's going to be opening a bridal boutique. In your current loved-up state, you might like a discount!'

I look around for something to throw at her and have to settle for a tea towel. 'Don't mock the afflicted,' I laugh. 'I was going to offer to help you clear the place out, but I'm not sure you deserve it now. Is that right, that it's going to be a bridal shop? God, how awful. It seems an odd choice, don't you think?'

'I'm not sure, really. I thought so at first, but the lady who is taking it on is a friend of Amanda Kendrick – you know, the woman who runs the dress shop at the end of the village. I think they're planning some sort of joint venture. Amanda does very well – real niche market stuff, but you never know.'

'Ah well, time will tell, I suppose,' I reply, looking at my watch. 'Speaking of which, I should get going; I have to see a man about some cabbages. Give me a ring, though, and let me know when you need help, won't you?' I wait for her answering nod as the doorbell tinkles, announcing her first customer. 'And if you need a buyer for any of your equipment, I might know of someone.' I grin, walking out into the seating area of the tea room.

Gina follows close on my heels, to see me out. A dark-haired chap is standing in the middle of the room, looking about him. He looks as surprised to see me as I am him.

'Ben!' I exclaim. 'Hello again.'

He returns my warm greeting and then, glancing at the piece of paper in his hand, looks from me to Gina. 'Er, Mrs Henderson? Hi, I'm Ben Carter. I think Mrs Cunningham called you to say I'd pop over? She's asked me to measure up for some new fittings I'm making for her.'

By the time Ben knocks on my door later that afternoon, I've ticked another little job off my list, and even I have to admit that the day has gone much better than I'd expected.

Mr and Mrs Geoffreys seem genuinely pleased with our proposal that they expand their business by taking one of the stable units and turning it into a farm shop. In fact I'd go so far as to say they were touched that we'd ask them. They were a little bemused when I explained that Will sees the site operating like a cooperative, only charging a peppercorn rent for the units. After that everyone would pay a percentage of their profit into a central pool that would be used to pay for the overall costs of running the site. Apparently, anything other than megalomania is considered odd in today's society.

'Refreshing,' said Mr Geoffreys, but judging by the expression on his face, he meant 'odd.' I like them, though. They are what you'd describe as salt of the earth, never expecting too much but genuinely grateful when offered more, and never, ever with a bad word to say about anyone.

I'm so pleased that Ben accepted my offer of a coffee. We got on so well at the first aid course, and yet when we met outside the village shop that time, he seemed rather edgy, as if he needed to get away. The first thing he does as he sits down is apologise, putting his odd manner that day down to a tense situation at home, and now he chatters away as if the past five months have never happened.

I'm amazed to learn that he's been working in the village since before Christmas. What started out as a few kitchen cupboards turned into a bespoke kitchen with proper furniture and has shifted slightly to include the shop fittings for his client's new business venture.

'I can't believe I never saw you around,' I comment, passing Ben a mug.

Ben gives a sheepish shrug. 'In my defence I haven't actually been in the village all that much. I've got a workshop back home where I make most of the furniture. For some reason most folks aren't that keen on me sawing bits of wood in their kitchen.'

'No, I suppose not,' I laugh. 'But I didn't think you made much furniture. I thought it was all the big stuff, house builds and so on.'

'Well, it has been for a few years, mainly because that's what pays the bills. I can make more money on building work.' He runs a hand over the smooth hair on top of his head, still pulled back into a band. 'I love that side of things – don't get me wrong. The furniture has only ever been a bit of a hobby, but it's been good for me taking on these couple of jobs and doing something different. I've really enjoyed it. Different challenges.'

'Enough to want to keep on doing it? I mean all the time?' I ask as naturally as possible, trying to keep the innermost workings of my mind from showing. Do I have the nerve to talk to Ben about the units at Rowan Hill and maybe even get him to take a look at them? They'd be the perfect showcase for his kind of work.

'I'm not sure,' says Ben slowly, obviously revisiting his own well-worn arguments. 'It's too complicated, really. With the furniture, most of the work I've done has been through word of mouth. It takes a long time to get your name known, and advertising is so damned expensive; plus you need somewhere to sell from. If I had a clone, then maybe I could manage to work all day and still have time to devote to the furniture, but I don't, so for now I carry on with the status quo. I save what money I can, though, so maybe one day, who knows?'

He doesn't look like he's about to change his mind. Now doesn't seem like quite the right time for my sales pitch.

Ben traces the grain on my table with a finger. 'Anyway, after this job it's back to the hard graft. A job I was working on before got put on hold, but it's all go again in a couple of weeks. No time for any more fanciful stuff. It's on the other side of Shrewsbury. A bit further to go now I've moved, but it's not too far.' Ben nods with an easy smile. 'After all everywhere is closer to somewhere, isn't it?'

'I didn't know you'd moved. Where are you living now, then?'

'I'm up at Lower Turnham,' he says, naming a small village a couple of miles away. 'I'm renting the gatehouse at the Manor, which is amazing. I live one side, and my workshop is on the other. I have to cross over the arch above the gates to get into it. It's just a little storeroom, really – well, it was – but I was lucky to get it. It's a beautiful place.'

'Oh wow!' I exclaim. 'I know where you mean. It's got those little leaded windows across the top, hasn't it?'

I watch him nod in reply.

'I bet it's a bit of a change from Shrewsbury,' I note, thinking of the remote setting of the cottage. 'The nearest house must be a mile away.'

'It's certainly that,' agrees Ben. 'Although I don't feel quite so guilty now when I'm making a huge row into the evening; woodwork is not exactly a quiet hobby,' he finishes with a pained expression.

'Doesn't Alex mind?'

Ben's brown eyes seek out mine for a moment, as if weighing something up. He holds my look for a second before looking away.

'Alex was often out in the evening, so it was never really an issue.' He looks back to me with an apologetic shrug. 'But, anyway, we're not together anymore.'

'I'm sorry,' I say automatically. 'I didn't know.'

Ben gently acknowledges my discomfort. 'No reason why you should. We had a bit of a parting of the ways, I'm afraid – that's why I moved. The house was Alex's place, you see – no way I could stay.' Ben drains his coffee, putting down the mug on the table but leaving both hands laced around it.

'Had you been together long?'

'Only a year or so. Things had drifted a bit for a while, really, but it was long enough, you know?'

'Long enough to still hurt like hell; yes, I know,' I sympathise.

Ben merely smiles. 'So anyway, enough about me. What have you been up to?'

'Oh, busy,' I reply. 'In fact, where are my manners? Would you like something? I think I've got some lemon drizzle on the go.'

'I better had, hadn't I, to make up for my past failures. But what will you do when the tea shop closes. That's soon isn't it?'

'Yes, at the end of the month, so only a couple more weeks to go.' I can feel small bubbles of excitement welling up. 'It's only a temporary halt, though. I've got involved in a project here, and I'll be running a tea room when we've finished.'

Ben looks out of the window, trying to see into the dimming light outside. 'So what's here, then? I drove by a big house – is that where you mean?'

'Yes. I'm just a poor tenant, actually. This place is my friend's house, if you remember; it was originally the lodge to the main house. It got sold off from the main estate years ago, but the whole estate is huge. There's the house that you can see, but loads of stabling and acres of woodland as well, and it's all this that we're going to be developing.'

'Into what?'

'I'm not sure what to call it, really.' I pause, swallowing the remaining piece of cake in my mouth. 'It's kind of a community thing – an artisan community. The stables are going to be offered to local craftspeople to use as workshops and showrooms. We'll have a farm shop too as we've got a market gardener using some of the land here at the moment. There'll be the tea room, of course, and the woodland is going to be developed further, opened up to the public for walks and perhaps to create a Forest School in time.'

The fork which Ben is holding suddenly stops midway to his mouth, the piece of cake there wavering slightly. He swallows. 'That's quite some project. I had no idea all that was here.'

I laugh wryly. 'No, neither do most folks. It's going to be a surprise for quite a few people, I'd imagine.'

The cake finally makes its way into Ben's mouth, where he chews thoughtfully for a moment. He waves his fork nonchalantly in the air. 'I don't suppose it crossed your mind to offer me one of the workshops, did it?'

'It did,' I agree, 'but I thought better of it. It didn't seem like the right moment for you.'

He eyes me steadily. 'Mmm. Actually the timing is spectacularly bad, which is a real shame. I could have been quite interested.'

The corner of the room lights up as a car's headlights sweep around. Finn must be home.

'You could still have a look around if you wanted to. It might be something to bear in mind for the future.'

Ben looks to the outside once more, mulling things over. 'I might,' he says finally. 'It wouldn't hurt, I suppose, although perhaps it would be better in daylight,' he adds, looking rather disappointed.

I'm about to suggest another time when there is a perfunctory knock at the door, and Finn immediately comes in, still muffled against the cold, a smile of greeting on his face.

'Hi,' he says brightly, taking in the presence of another person, pausing automatically for me to make introductions.

I've hardly opened my mouth when Finn crosses the room, and there's a hideous scraping noise as chair leg meets floor. Ben struggles up from the table.

There's a moment when the two men look at one another, unsure, before Finn laughs and shoots out his hand, which Ben takes, pulling Finn into a hug and that back-slapping thing that men seem to do.

Finn is the first to speak. 'Christ, Ben!' he exclaims. 'What are you doing here?'

'Catching up with Ellie. Do you live here? I had no idea. Ellie's just been telling me about your development plans. They sound fantastic.'

Finn ignores this last statement. 'I didn't realise you knew Ellie.' He turns to me then for confirmation.

'Ben and I met doing some first aid training just before I moved up here,' I reply. 'We bumped into each other again a few months ago, and now Ben's doing some work at Gina's for the new owners. It seemed like a good opportunity for a catch-up.' I look between the two of them. 'Small world, isn't it? I didn't realise that you knew each other either.'

Finn nods, although he's not looking at me.

The atmosphere between the two has cooled considerably. Finn drags a smile back onto his face, remembering his manners. 'It's good to see you again, Ben. How are you?' he says, as if the previous minute or so had never happened, and ignoring my question.

'I'm good thanks. You?' he replies brightly, taking Finn's cue. 'This is great stuff you've got going on here.'

'Yeah, well, we're only just getting going, but it's exciting, you know. I hope it all works out. It's a bit of a change of direction, for me especially. I've been working overseas for a bit. I came home just before Christmas myself, but yes, things are really good right now.'

'And you've roped Ellie into this as well?' he asks. I'm glad to see at least one of them has remembered I'm still in the room. I don't get a chance to answer, though.

'Actually, it was sort of Ellie's idea to develop all the stabling, and the market gardening – that was her idea too. She and Will are . . . um . . .' He turns to me, an apologetic look on his face, as if he didn't mean to reveal our relationship to Ben.

'Oh, I see,' says Ben slowly, looking between us repeatedly to see if his assumption is correct. His eyes flick to the window. 'And Will? Is he—?' Again the question is not asked of me.

'Yes, he's here,' confirms Finn. 'Funny, but he never mentioned he'd seen you.'

'I don't know that he has. I certainly haven't seen him. But how is he? Is he okay?'

'Pretty good at the minute. He's taken up his glasswork again – must be the love of a good woman,' he jokes.

I'm determined to get the conversation back into a place where I can join in with it, and I ignore his last remark.

'I was telling Ben about the units, Finn. He thought he might like to have a look at one, perhaps in the daylight, though,' I say somewhat forcefully. 'He's a carpenter,' I add, realising as I say it that it's probably superfluous information. 'As you two know one another, perhaps you should show him around one day?'

Finn coughs as Ben looks at his watch and mutters, 'I'm not sure when I'll be free. I've got a bit on at the moment, like I said. Maybe I could let you know, though. I expect I'll see you at Gina's sometime?' he says, turning to me, and then, 'I really should be going. Thanks so much for the coffee, Ellie. It was nice catching up.' He comes across to give me a kiss on the cheek.

'It was good to see you again, Finn,' he adds, holding out his hand. 'It's like I said, though: probably the timing is a bit off for me just now – sorry,' he says apologetically.

Finn nods. 'No worries. Good to see you too.'

I move to escort Ben to the door, but he stops me. 'I'll see myself out, Ellie. Thanks again.' He smiles and is gone, leaving Finn and me looking at each other. Finn looks away first.

'Are you going to tell me what the bloody hell that was all about?' I demand.

'Nope,' answers Finn, moving past me to the Aga. He lifts the kettle, testing its weight before placing it over the hot plate to boil. He turns back, a challenging look on his face.

'You greet one another like long-lost friends, and then all of a sudden Ben can't wait to get away.'

'Yeah, well, maybe that's exactly what we are: lost friends,' he says, sounding bitter. 'And it needs to stay that way.'

'I don't understand.'

'Ellie,' replies Finn more gently. 'You don't need to understand. Just please trust me on this and let it drop.'

'I could ask Will,' I challenge, still angry.

'You could,' he replies, his voice soft against the rising noise from the kettle. 'But I'm asking you now: nothing to do with Will. Please drop it,' he pleads. 'Please.'

I can't fight against Finn; he looks utterly defeated. 'You know I do trust you, Finn, but even now I get the feeling that there are things you aren't telling me, things that you're deliberately keeping me in the dark about. You know, if you trusted me too, maybe I could help.'

Finn rubs his face with his palms. 'It's not about trust, Ellie, and I know you'd like to help, but mentioning this to Will is a complication you two don't need, and it'll blow the lid off things for me – things I haven't the energy for right now. I want to get this place up and running – that's what's important at the moment. I'm sorry, I know it seems unfair, but please try and understand.'

The kettle begins to shriek its alert, and Finn swings to remove it from the heat.

'Are you having tea or coffee?' I ask, signalling an end to my questioning. Finn looks visibly relieved.

'I'm gasping for a coffee, thanks, if that's okay. Then I'll get out of your hair. Where is Will anyway?'

'Still in the workroom, I think. I've been banned. But tea won't be long; I'll fish him out then.'

'Good, I've a few things to catch up with him about. I think I've found a bloke who's interested in working the woodland. His name is Patrick, and he's very keen. He's going to come over tomorrow for a look-see. Better than that, though, he's got a mate who works for a company that builds timber-frame houses. The chap does a bit of private work too, so Patrick's bringing him along as well.'

'I'm impressed. Not that I've been slacking myself, of course.'

'Oh?'

I tell him about my day's own successes as he drinks his coffee, both of us mindful to keep the conversation on work as we run through the small things already achieved and the plans we have for the next couple of days. Finn would like me to be around when the builders arrive, he explains, so that I can hear how things will progress. It'll help me answer questions from potential occupiers.

He appears relaxed, and I try hard to act normally. At length Finn stretches languorously and announces that he should be going.

'I'd better go and catch up with Will,' he says as he stands, ready to leave.

'Okay. Listen, I won't say anything to Will – about Ben, I mean.'

Finn reaches forward to offer a hug goodbye, as is his custom. 'Thanks, Ellie,' he says in parting.

He looks unbelievably sad.

CHAPTER TWENTY-SIX

April

The weather has been balmy for weeks now, with clear sunny days and little wind to drag the temperatures down. In fact, it's been perfect building weather, and the stables are being transformed at a rate I never thought possible. All of them have been cleared now, reduced to bare canvases ready to be primed for their new life. The windows are going in along the orchard side, and then the stonework will need to be repointed, but the structures are sound, so most of the work is relatively minor, except, of course, for the end barn.

The roof is off this now, exposing its wooden frame as a surgeon might peel back the scalp to expose the innermost workings of the brain. It's a sorry sight, in a way, to see it stripped, but on a day like today, the sun slants right through into the garden, which is waking up beautifully from its winter rest. It's in a state right now, but so full of promise, and I'm hoping that help in that department might be arriving very soon.

The woman who's going to give me the verdict of just how ebullient we're going to be (as opposed to an overblown mess) is a herbalist by the name of Patience Connelly, whom Helen met at a craft fair recently and has been persuading to come on board ever since. Their visit this morning will be the first time I meet her, and I'll admit I'm a little nervous.

Helen has told me a little about her work with the rider: *'Whatever you think she's going to be like, think again.'* So now I've been going through every scenario I can think of for what a forty-eight-year-old herbalist might look like.

I don't even come close.

It's the legs I notice first. Clad in skin-tight white jeans and punctuated by three-inch-high red stilettos, they float towards me down the gravel, carrying their mysterious owner ever closer. The legs go on for quite some time before meeting a scarlet trench coat, cinched at the waist and with a deep revere collar showing a glimpse of white T-shirt. A jaunty spotted scarf is tied at the neck amid a tumble of rich dark hair that hangs down well past her shoulders. 'Vamp' is the first word that springs to mind. I slap it down, a smile of welcome on my face as I look between her and Helen, who, I'm relieved to see, is bringing up the rear. I feel like a nervous wall-flower before this woman. I'm working out what to say, when a hand is thrust towards me.

'If that gorgeous sex on legs works here,' comes a low, husky voice, 'then show me the dotted line; I'll sign up today.'

I take the proffered hand, looking helplessly to Helen for assistance.

'We met Finn out the front,' she exclaims, grinning.

'Oh, I see.' I smile, trying to match the firm handshake I'm being given. 'He is quite nice, isn't he?'

'Nice!' roars the husky voice, 'Christ, did you see the arse on him? I sincerely hope he's *not* nice. I sincerely hope he's a very bad boy.'

I smile weakly, swallowing and mentally apologising to Finn. What on earth have I done?

Helen clears her throat slightly. 'Ellie, this is Patience, who I've been telling you about,' she says, turning back to Patience and poking her in the ribs. 'May I remind you that Ellie is going out with Finn's brother?'

Patience merely bats her eyelids. 'A brother? Is he just as gorgeous? Or presumably more so?'

I have to laugh. 'I can't possibly answer that. Finn is lovely, but he doesn't do it for me, I'm afraid.'

'What! Are you blind?' She laughs, a full-throated belly of a laugh. 'It's nice to meet you, Ellie. This is quite some set-up here. Very impressive.'

'It's not bad, is it? Although you came around the posh way,' I say, knowing that they walked up along the drive and around the house rather than coming through the stable yard. I incline my head backwards towards the shell of the building behind me.

'The new units are through there. I'll show you around in a minute, if that's okay,' I suggest, looking carefully at Helen, whose expression gives nothing away. Patience is looking around her, giving off a rather distracted air. She swings her attention back to me.

'That's fine, Ellie – whatever you think. But first, do you mind if I take a look around here?' She makes an expansive gesture towards the garden, looking a little nervous.

'Be my guest,' I say, waving her onward, then turning to Helen. 'Hello,' I say, marking the first opportunity I've had to greet her. She giggles, giving me a hug and waiting until Patience moves away, before adding, 'I told you she wouldn't be what you expected.'

'You got that right,' I whisper back drily.

'Well, you know what they say about appearances being deceptive. In Patience's case, it's most definitely true. Bizarre, admittedly, but what that woman doesn't know about plants you could write on the back of a mint leaf.'

I arch my eyebrows. 'As opposed to on the back of a postage stamp?'

'I thought it was more appropriate,' she says, grinning. 'Anyway, look.' She points to the retreating figure of Patience, who is now, to my surprise, standing in one of the flower beds, heels and all, lifting plants, touching them, smelling them and tasting them. She hops from bed to bed like an inquisitive scarlet blackbird, until she has more or less toured the whole garden.

'She has a certain something, doesn't she?' remarks Helen. 'Just wait till you get talking with her. She's fascinating.'

'I'm not sure Finn will see it that way,' I mutter, wondering what he's going to say when I tell him he's been described as 'sex on legs.' Perhaps I won't tell him. On the other hand, I'd quite like to see his face.

'Just wait and see,' says Helen gently. 'Take my word for it.'

We watch as Patience makes her way back to us.

'Christ, I wore the wrong bloody shoes, didn't I?' she swears, holding out a foot in front of her. 'I didn't think I'd be getting in amongst it just yet.'

I'm not sure quite what to say to her; agreeing would seem rather rude. I try another tack.

'I think Helen has told you what we're all about here, but I'll admit the garden is a little subterfuge on my part. I know I should be showing you the stable units, but I wondered if I could pick your brains for a few minutes first. You seem quite interested in our garden.'

Patience turns to look around her slowly, and I follow her gaze. The gathered light inside the walls is warm, reflected off the red brick. There are patches of bright colour from the spring bulbs and fledgling greens everywhere. She turns back to me. 'Do you know who planted the garden, Ellie?' she asks finally. Her question surprises me.

'Er, no I don't, I'm afraid. I don't know much about the house's history at all. Will or Finn might know, I suppose. It was probably one of their relatives.'

'That's okay – don't worry. It doesn't really matter. It's just that whoever did plant it certainly knew what they were doing. You don't know what you have here, do you?' She smiles.

I slide a glance towards Helen. 'Er . . . no?'

Patience smooths down her coat a little before speaking. 'Can I be perfectly honest with you, Ellie?' she asks directly. I nod in reply.

'I am fully aware that I talk straight out of the gutter and dress like a common tart.' She holds up a hand to forestall my protest. I close my mouth again. 'But I'm nearly fifty, and these little foibles make me laugh. They are my "fuck you" – oops, there I go again – to the life I left behind.' She laughs, then pauses for a moment to check that we're both still with her. Helen looks as astonished as I suspect I do.

'Quite a number of years ago, I trained with the Royal Horticultural Society and became a qualified horticulturalist and garden designer. I designed gardens for some very rich and very famous people until I realised one day that I had become almost as arrogant, shallow, grasping and ignorant as they were. Quite by chance, I read a wonderful book on the healing uses of plants, and it changed my life. I have spent the last twelve years of my life learning just how special plants really are.'

Helen shakes her head in amazement. 'You never told me that. And there's me telling Ellie that you might be able to offer her a little advice. I got that wrong, didn't I?'

'I don't usually bore people with all my crap. Besides, Helen, correct me if I'm wrong, but the last time we met up, the conversation turned rather quickly from a good oil to use on stiff shoulders to an erotic massage with George Clooney.'

'Helen!' I snort loudly, suddenly warming to this vibrant character and feeling more relaxed.

'I've only told you this, Ellie,' continues Patience, 'so that you'll know I understand what I'm talking about when I say that this garden is an absolute gem – a veritable apothecary, no less. It's extraordinary, but almost every plant here has some kind of medicinal or healing use. There are plants here that I rarely see.' She breaks off again now, her face flushed with excitement, before pausing slightly and taking another look around her. 'If you're looking for some help with the garden, Ellie, I'd be honoured.'

I feel my smile growing wider. 'Time for some tea,' I say, feeling an agreement shaping up. 'And then I'll go and find Finn, and we can have a look around.'

Patience winks in an exaggerated fashion, laden with meaning. 'Nothing I'd like better,' she drawls.

It feels quite dark in the kitchen after the brightness of the day in the garden. It makes me realise how much I enjoy being outside now, closer to things, the physical work more satisfying. I can understand why Will and Finn are so passionate about the estate. It's such a beautiful place to be. It would seem that I'm not the only one who thinks so, and Patience wastes no time in letting me know.

'I would love to work here, Ellie,' she says directly. 'I've looked at other places before – although, admittedly, only half-heartedly – but the combination of things here would be perfect for me.'

I finish pouring tea in an assortment of mugs that now reside more or less permanently on the table.

'So how do you work?' I ask. 'Helen has told me some of what you do, but I'm not sure how you do things exactly.'

'At heart I suppose I'm a practitioner,' explains Patience. 'I started off looking into how herbs and plants could provide health benefits, and once I qualified, I started seeing clients, advising them and providing remedies. It grew from there, really.' She takes a huge gulp of tea, which must be really hot, but she doesn't seem to mind.

'This is great, thanks. God, I miss real tea,' she groans. 'When I'm working, I drink a lot of herbal teas, and – don't get me wrong – they're fine too, but you know, try as I might, some of them still taste like cat's piss to me.' She swings her hair back over her shoulder, laughing like a drain. 'Sorry,' she adds unnecessarily.

Patience takes another gulp before continuing. 'I found after a while that I just couldn't find the things I wanted for my clients: a salve with a different combination of ingredients, for example. So I started experimenting with making my own, and that's how Patience's Little Pots of Goodness was born. Hang on a minute.' And with that she rummages in her bag until she finds what she's looking for and places it on the table triumphantly. She pushes it towards me. 'If you don't mind my saying so, I couldn't help noticing that you could use some of this.'

I pick up the pot. It's beautifully shaped glass in the darkest green. A circular label on the top bears a leaf emblem encircled with the words 'Patience's Little Pots of Goodness.' Another white label runs around the side of the pot, which reads 'Little Pot of Hand Healing.' I take off the lid and inhale.

The scent is pungent, but gorgeous, redolent of living things and outside spaces. Knowing that it was what Patience intended, I go to poke a finger into the pot's creaminess. Instead, my action is interrupted as Patience takes my hand.

'May I?' she asks, unfurling my fingers. I hand her the pot. She scoops out a little cream and places it into the palm of her own hand.

'Now we let it warm a little in the hand before we rub it in. It's very important for you to get the full benefit of the cream; it allows the oils to be more readily absorbed by the skin.'

Her skin against mine is soft as she begins to massage the cream into my hand. It feels cool and silky and utterly delicious. Gently, Patience uses both hands to rub first the back of my hand and then my palm in wide circles, pushing against the heel of my thumb, spreading my palm before grasping each finger in turn, making pulling and twisting motions along its length, until finally smoothing around each nail. I feel reborn. She lays this hand back down on the table, again palm uppermost, before turning her attention to the other hand. I sneak a glance at Helen, who is sitting back in her chair wearing a very pronounced *I told you so* expression.

When Patience has finished, it seems like time itself has slowed to a stop. Even the light in the room has ceased its endless rushing. If I laid my head on the table right now, I would probably be asleep in minutes.

'Wow,' I say simply, looking at my hands in amazement as if I'd never seen them before.

'Feels good, doesn't it?' whispers Helen, not wanting to sound harsh in a world that has suddenly had its edges softened.

'What else can you do?' I ask Patience, somewhat in awe. 'That was just amazing.'

Patience smiles warmly. 'I'm glad you liked it. Perhaps it's given you a little insight into what I do, enough maybe that you might want me to stick around?' She winks lasciviously. 'Enough maybe for you to convince Finn it would be good for me to stick around?'

'Do you want to go and meet him now?' I laugh. 'I think he's out in the yard with Patrick somewhere.'

'God, yes,' comes the quick reply.

I'm not sure that Finn will be ready for the onslaught that is coming his way, but I can see how good it will be to have Patience on board, in more ways than one, and I hope that Finn will too. He's pretty astute when it comes to sussing people out. Patience might make him a little nervous, but I'm sure he'll see the benefit. He's never questioned my judgement before, after all.

In the end I needn't have worried. When I finally root out Finn, Patience is supremely well behaved. She is warm and friendly, charm personified, and extremely complimentary about the site. It doesn't take Finn long to declare that he'd be delighted for Patience to join us, and the formalities are a breeze after that. Within minutes it seems we're talking about the garden and how Patience would love to help us get it ready. Finn instantly agrees to her offer, saying that they'll come to an arrangement to reimburse her, something which she bats away without a second thought.

Very soon, both Finn and Patience give agonising groans after looking at their watches and apologise, saying that they have to be somewhere else. Finn shakes Patience's hand warmly and gives her a peck on the cheek as he dashes off, leaving her in a mock swoon.

After saying goodbye to Patience, Helen and I wander over to her little corner of the site, which is now nearly finished. She's chosen to take over the corner stable with the mezzanine floor. It's calm and soothing after the bustle outside. I can't compliment Helen enough on her design ideas. The interior walls have been left as bare stone, but sealed and painted bright white. A turned wooden staircase will rise up to the mezzanine level, where she plans to have her drawings and meet with clients, and from this balcony will hang a massive piece of her art, which will act partly as a room divider, sectioning off her gallery to the rear from the working space towards the front of her studio. It is this piece that visitors will see first upon entering. It's not up yet, but it will be breathtaking. Helen is looking at it now in her mind's eye. I can almost see her thoughts as she looks around the room, deciding what colour here, what texture there. I give her hand a little squeeze. She returns the gesture, turning to me, her eyes shining.

'I can't believe all of this, Ellie,' she breathes with excitement. 'Just a few months ago none of this had even been considered, and now' – she pauses for a moment to best explain what I know she's feeling, for I'm feeling it too – 'my whole life has changed. I've never felt this way before,' she rushes on, 'well, except when I met Tom. In a way it's a bit like falling in love, isn't it? The same rush of feelings.' She stops then, looking at me as I try to look innocent. 'And don't try and tell me you don't know what I mean.' She squeezes my hand again. 'I'm so very grateful to you, Ellie, for giving me all this.'

'Oh, don't be daft,' I argue. 'I haven't given you anything. Helen, you are so flaming talented, and you always have been. It's just that now you finally believe it, and you're doing something about it, that's all.'

'And who was it that pointed this out to me?'

'Only one of many, I'm sure,' I observe. 'Perhaps it's just that out of all your friends, I'm the only one who's an interfering old bat.'

Helen holds up a finger and waggles it at me in a stern manner. 'None of that,' she admonishes. 'You're a true friend, Ellie,' she adds softly, giving me a hug, 'and don't you ever forget it.'

CHAPTER TWENTY-SEVEN

I wander back through the courtyard a little later. It's in absolute disarray. There's rubble everywhere and discarded building materials, the debris that's the result of weeks of fevered activity. I know it will all get cleared, and I'm certain it will look fabulous when it's finished, but just now a huge leap of faith is called for.

My watch confirms that it's time to get back to work. I'm tired, but there's a lot of light left in the day, and I should get on. Will has been called to London for the weekend to see his old professor about a potential new project, and Finn won't be slacking either. Oddly, there doesn't seem to be much going on in the end barn today. Usually it's out of bounds without a pre-announced visit and a hard hat, but as I cross over towards it, I begin to wonder where everyone is.

I stand in the doorway, looking around as I always do, in awe of the amazing structure of this building. Even with half of it missing, and scaffolding and supports everywhere, it commands attention. It's only after a minute or two that I realise I'm not alone. Finn is standing at the far end underneath where the massive cruck frame that will support the resurrected building will go. He's looking at the plans, standing perfectly still.

'Hi,' I say brightly, moving to join him.

He looks up, frowning. 'Hi,' he replies quietly, and turns his attention to the plans once more. He doesn't say anything else. Now I'm closer, I can see how angry he looks, but knowing Finn, whatever it is that's riled him will be the last thing he'll want to talk about.

'Patience seems to be a great find, doesn't she?' I say, hoping to have landed on neutral ground. Finn seems to consider this for a moment before very slowly lowering his plans.

'As always, Ellie, a perfect call,' he says. The statement is loaded. It's heavy with sarcasm, and I know Finn doesn't mean it this way, not really, but it doesn't make me feel great. He registers the hurt look on my face but doesn't flinch or look away. The gauntlet is being thrown down. Maybe Finn does want to talk about it after all.

'Would you like a cup of tea?' I say coldly, feeling my mood begin to turn. I feel an overwhelming need to get us both out of here, to retreat to the privacy of the kitchen before whatever Finn is barely containing comes spilling out.

'No,' answers Finn bluntly. 'Despite popular opinion to the contrary, tea is not the panacea for all things that people seem to think it is.'

I try a different tack, snatching the plans out of his hands. 'Right, you and me, in the kitchen, now,' I snarl, turning on my heel and stalking from the building as best I can and hoping that Finn will follow me.

Reaching the kitchen, I busy myself, rinsing out the mugs we used earlier, pushing the kettle to boil and gathering what I need to make more tea. I'm killing time, and there seems a lot of it before I finally hear the back door slam and Finn enters the room. I add milk to the tea, hearing him sit at the table behind me. I place the steaming mug in front of him.

'As you well know, it isn't the tea that is the panacea for all things; it's the opportunity it provides for the angry, frustrated, upset, despairing and just plain bloody-minded to have some time out, take a step back, do a little thinking and then start talking – usually to the person who's made the tea,' I snap at him. 'In your own time, Finn.'

I sit quietly beside him, hands in my lap, contemplating my own cup of tea. I daren't risk another look at Finn, feeling rather ashamed that I hadn't noticed the state he was in before. I've been too busy, I think, searching for an excuse.

Maybe, now that I think about it, that's Finn's problem. He's running around taking care of everything and everyone to do with this project. We agreed from the onset that Finn would take the lead on the build. It made sense given his background, and Will needed the time for his work – but I can see what it has meant for Finn. He's patient and encouraging, cheerful and accommodating. The list is endless as he moves about each day, checking with us: Are we okay? Do we need anything? Any problems? What can he do to help? And he's still doing his own work, of course, out in the woodland with Patrick – hard physical work, day in, day out. He's tired – exhausted even – but there's something else beneath what I have come to realise is a very carefully contrived exterior, something that has been niggling away at him these last few days, something that he's been unable to talk to Will about, and I realise belatedly that I've scarcely seen them together recently.

The plans for Finn's redesign of the barn are still on the table where I left them. Finn leans forward to take them, expelling a huge vent of frustration as he does so.

'Will is going to fucking kill me,' he confides, smoothing out the paper, a note of real despair in his voice. He looks at me then, no longer angry, and I can see the weight of his burden, heavy in his eyes.

'What's the matter, Finn?'

'I can't believe I let this happen. Jesus, of all the things I could have ignored, it had to be this one I took my eye off. I knew something was wrong, dammit, and I didn't do anything about it. What the hell is the matter with me?' he pleads.

'Too many balls in the air?' I suggest gently.

Finn gives a mirthless laugh. 'I won't have any left when Will gets home; he'll have mine on a platter.'

I can't help but smile at his analogy. 'Well then, we have a couple of days to find a way for you to keep your tackle intact.'

'It's not funny, Ellie,' returns Finn. 'This is serious.'

I lay a hand over his. 'I know it is, Finn, so why don't you tell me why it's so serious instead of just beating yourself up over it? What exactly has gone wrong?'

He throws himself back in his chair, stretching out his long limbs, and places his hands behind his head.

'James has pissed off, that's what's happened. He's been taking the mick for a couple of days now, never around, this or that excuse for where he's been, and whenever I tried to get hold of him, I couldn't. The lads tried to cover for him – why I don't know – but now that I've bollocked them too, I've found out that what he's actually done is get another job and, like I said, pissed off.'

This is not good news. James is the carpenter in charge of the barn and the building of the new cruck frame. It's central to the whole project.

'And what's more, he won't speak to me or return my calls, spineless bastard. He's really left us in the shit.'

'So you don't even know why he's gone?'

'Well, I suspect it's because that now I've actually got off my arse and checked, he's totally fucked up some of the frames he's already put in. They're going to have to come out and be redone. I'm not sure he actually knew what he was doing at all.'

'Finn, none of this is your fault. You didn't know that.'

'But it was my job to check it all out. How can it not be my fault? I'm the only one who could have done something about it, and I didn't. I just sat back and hoped it would all be okay, like a rank amateur, until it was too bloody late.'

'Even so, you can't shoulder all the responsibility for this. It's not fair.'

'Why not? There's no question about fairness at all, Ellie. The responsibility was mine, plain and simple. You know it's what we agreed, and for some reason that even I can't understand, I chose to let this go. This is what I do for a living, for Christ's sake. I wouldn't normally let anyone get away with what James was doing. It was my responsibility, and no one is going to see it as anything but, least of all Will.'

I give him a longer appraising glance. He looks totally disgusted with himself. I suspect I'm not going to get an answer to my next question, but I ask it anyway.

'What is it with you two?'

Finn's gaze flicks up and then away.

'What do you mean?' he asks as if he doesn't know. Except he does.

'I mean that there are plenty of people who might have something to say about the delay to the barn being finished, myself included, but I don't see you falling at *my* feet begging forgiveness. I'm curious as to why you think you're going to be in so much trouble with Will, and in particular why you would care. Will's your brother; wouldn't he, of all people, understand?'

Finn stares at me, rankled, a grim expression on his face.

'Which of those questions would you like me to answer, Ellie?' he says stonily.

254

I return the look. 'Any of them would be a start,' I challenge. Eye contact is maintained for a minute, but then Finn looks away, and I know that nothing will be revealed. A sigh comes then.

'Look, I'm just worried, that's all. This is important to Will – to all of us I know, but especially to Will. You know how things are with him, what he's been through. He's finally finding his feet again, and on a professional level the barn is going to be a real showcase of his work. I'm cross with myself for not picking up on this sooner, and I'd really rather not have to let anyone down.'

This is as far as I can push it, I know. I lean towards Finn so that he senses my reaching out to him, even if he doesn't want to acknowledge it.

'We'll sort it out, Finn, and I mean *we*. There's no reason for you to have to shoulder this yourself, and like I said, we've got the weekend to exercise some damage limitation.' I cock my head on one side. 'You hungry?' I ask.

There is a sullen answering nod. 'Starving.'

'Good, because I've had a thought, but I can't do anything about it until later, so I suggest we have something to eat and take it from there. That sound okay?'

Finn drains his mug of tea. A slight gathering is taking place at the corners of his mouth. 'Do I have a choice?'

'Not really, no,' I agree.

'Right. I might as well go and have a shower then, if that's alright. Are you okay with doing tea?'

Ever the gentleman. 'Yes, Finn,' I smile. 'I'm okay with doing tea.'

I could probably make the carbonara sauce for the spaghetti in my sleep, which is just as well, as I realise halfway through its preparation that I've been on autopilot. I can't decide what to do for the best: ring Ben and check if he's in or just pitch up with Finn in tow. And there's no guarantee that Ben will even be at home. He'll probably still be working, and if he is at home, no guarantee that he'll want to see Finn. I'm still not sure what was going on the last time they met.

The one thing I am sure about is the necessity to contact Ben. His name popped into my head the minute Finn told me about James leaving. I very much need Finn to see that there might be a way out of this situation, but I can't offer him a glimpse of hope and then pull it away again. I should probably just come clean with Ben and explain everything. Problem is, I have a sneaky suspicion that I won't even get the chance to explain before Ben says no, a knee-jerk reaction born out of some past history between them.

I add the cream and watch it bubble, wafts of garlic making my stomach growl in anticipation. I'm going to have to lie. Well, not *lie* exactly, but a certain economy of detail will be called for. I push the pan almost off the heat on hearing Finn moving around upstairs. The spaghetti is nearly done; I haven't got long if I'm going to go through with this.

The phone only rings a couple of times before it's answered.

'Ben Carter.' The voice is businesslike and a little abrupt. I sit down.

'Ben, it's Ellie,' I announce. 'Sorry, are you busy?'

'No, it's fine,' he lies, and then, 'How are you?'

'Not bad, thanks.' I falter. 'I wasn't sure if you'd be at home.' A second or two skips by before the reply comes.

'No, well, I had a bit of a slow day, so I bumped off early. I've been working on something here.'

This is never going to work. I take a deep breath.

'Ben, I'm sorry to disturb you. I just wondered if I could pop over and see you. There's something I wanted to ask you.'

I can hear him smiling. 'Sounds mysterious.'

'Not really. I just wanted to have a chat about a bit of work – some furniture,' I clarify. 'I wondered if you might be able to make something for me.'

'I'm here all evening, Ellie. Pop over any time you like.'

I do a quick mental tot-up. 'Would about an hour's time suit you?'

'Sure. I'll see you then. I'll be in my workshop, so when you get here, knock on the door to the right of the arch, not the left.'

I click off with a slightly shaky hand.

When Finn reappears, I'm nonchalantly draining the pasta.

It's turned into a beautiful evening. The days are stretching out now, sunlit and calm. The hedgerows are burgeoning along the lanes, fields just turning to yellow as the rapeseed ripens. It should be a lovely drive, but I don't really see anything around me as I chatter away inanely to Finn, whose mood has improved somewhat but who is still very quiet.

He's asked me several times where we're going and who we're going to see, but I've been as non-committal as I possibly can. It hasn't improved his mood, but at least he's come along with me.

I knock on the door to the left as directed, suddenly wishing I could run away.

All credit due, Ben manages to keep the smile on his face as he takes in not one, but two visitors. Finn is rather less discreet as he regards me mutinously, muttering, 'I might have bloody well known,' but he still slopes in behind me.

Ben's workshop isn't huge, but it's filled with industry. Tools hang on every spare bit of wall space, and wood shavings litter the floor around a table that Ben has clearly been working on. The table itself is a perfect circle, plain but beautifully so. Instinctively, I reach out as I catch sight of the design that Ben is working around its edge, an intricate Celtic knot work that seems almost impossible to follow. My fingers trace the dents and ridges in wonder. I can feel Ben's eyes on me.

'Do you like it?' he asks, brushing down his T-shirt, which is covered in little curls of wood.

'It's gorgeous, Ben,' I exclaim, looking to Finn for confirmation. Finn is silent.

Ben looks from him to me and then back again.

'Ah . . . I see,' he says slowly. 'This is not about furniture at all, is it?' he surmises, quite correctly. 'I should ask you both to leave,' he continues, 'but actually I'm curious. I'd quite like to know what has made you bring Finn to my door, and I'd really like to know what on earth you think I could possibly do to help.'

Ouch. I risk a nervous glance at Finn, who has said nothing. His teeth are clenched, and I can see a muscle working in his cheek.

'Ben, I'm sorry. I should explain. You're right – this is not about furniture, but Finn didn't know we were coming to see you; the subterfuge is all mine. I wasn't sure if I told you the truth up front that you would see us. Well, me possibly, but maybe not Finn.' I've obviously hit a nerve. 'Will you at least let me tell you why we came, now that we're here?' If I have any feminine charms at all, I could really use them now.

Ben studies me for a minute, and then, with a final look at Finn, I see a subtle shift, a softening of his expression.

'No, my apologies, Ellie. I can see Finn had no idea he was coming here. Whatever it is you need to say, you'd better come in and tell me about it properly. I'll get us a drink.' He points to the stairway in the corner of the room. 'We'll go next door.'

We cross over the arch of the gatehouse and drop down again into a sitting room on the other side. After the bustle of the workshop, this place is neat as a pin, airy and full of the evening sun. Finn and I perch on the edge of an enormous sofa while we wait for Ben to reappear. He does so shortly, handing me a mug, and Finn, a large glass full of red wine. He looks stunned for a moment but accepts the proffered glass with an odd smile and takes a large swallow. Ben takes up a place in a chair towards the fireplace.

'Before you start, Ellie,' he begins, 'there's something I need to know.' He angles himself towards Finn. 'Does she know about Will?'

An answering nod.

'And me?'

An almost imperceptible shake of the head.

Ben actually laughs then, a hollow sound.

'That's rather unfair, Finn, don't you think?' he says. 'Ellie hasn't a clue what's going on, I'll bet. She's come here hoping to help you out, hasn't she? In fact, both you and Will, and you're too cowardly to even tell her the truth.'

Finn starts violently, slopping his wine, and struggles to get to his feet. 'You bastard!' he spits, his face ashen.

I grab hold of Finn's arm. 'Sit down!' I yell. 'Christ, what is the matter with you two? This is the second time I've been in a room with you both, and you've talked like I wasn't even in it. I'm sorry, Ben, but I thought you could help. Clearly I'm delusional.' I bang my mug down onto the coffee table. 'I'm going home, Finn. I don't care what you do.'

This time it's Finn's turn to grab my arm. 'Ellie, wait. Listen, I'm sorry. You're right – both of you are right. This has all got to stop.' He releases my arm, slumping back in the chair. He looks exhausted. He takes another gulp of wine and then another. It's a while before he starts speaking again.

'Ben, firstly, I'm sorry. I shouldn't have spoken to you like that. You've suffered as much as I have through all this – more so – and I have no right to ask you to keep my secrets. I had no idea that you were back in the area again until I saw you that day at Ellie's, and Will still doesn't know.'

He smiles at me then, a soft warm smile, the Finn I first met, but his eyes are tinged with regret and apology.

'Will still doesn't know, and I'm scared shitless of telling him,' he continues, 'Because since Ellie arrived, the change in Will has been more than I could ever dare hope for. This project as well – it means more to me than anything I've ever done. I don't want either of those things to change, but, Ben, if you do what I know Ellie came here tonight to ask you, I cannot see how they can stay the same.'

There are questions dancing about my head. Endless questions. My mouth keeps opening and closing like a goldfish's, but Finn's hands are splayed towards me, warning me to let him finish.

'Ellie wants you to rebuild the barn, Ben.' His voice catches a little then. '*I* want you to,' he sighs. 'It's a long story, but our guy has blown us out. We can't finish unless we find someone else who can help, but Ellie has to know why this can never work. Show her, Ben.'

The look is held between the two of them for a few beats, Ben's face full of concern now.

'What about you, though, Finn? Or me for that matter? If I show Ellie, what then? You're asking me to reveal everything, but are you really prepared for the whole truth to come out?'

The breath slides out of Finn. 'What I want is to stop pretending, for us both to stop pretending. I know you're only trying to protect Ellie, Ben, but it's time she understood. Tell her what happened. I'm in enough trouble as it is; I might as well go the whole nine yards.'

Ben studies us both for a moment, weighing up his choice. The blood is pounding in my ears as he slowly begins to roll up the sleeve of his T-shirt. I gasp when it reaches his elbow and

I see a mass of twisted and scarred flesh. He continues rolling the sleeve, the scar tissue stark white and hairless against Ben's normal skin tone.

'I got this pulling two guys off Will the night he was raped.'

I probably knew this was coming, deep down. Somehow it seemed like the only thing Ben could say. But even so, to hear him voice it out loud takes all the breath from my body. 'Does it hurt?' is all I can think of to say.

'Not anymore.'

And it hits me then why Will wasn't to know that Ben was around, why there had to be distance between them.

Ben's voice sounds weary. 'The difficulty is that I put Will in the curious position of simultaneously having to feel grateful to me for saving his life and hating my guts because I'm a constant reminder of what happened to him. The worst thing is that I was there: Will can choose what he wants to remember, what he wants to tell any-one else, but he can't hide anything from me. I was there, and he'll never forgive me for that.'

My nostrils flare as a sudden burning heralds a stinging rush of tears. I clamp my back teeth together in an effort not to cry. This is so unfair. Ben would have been the perfect solution to our problem, and as I feel Finn's arm go around me, I realise that he knew the problems that a meeting between Will and Ben could mean for me all along. He even tried to warn me, calling Ben a complication Will and I didn't need, and something else. What did he say? Something about blowing the lid off things. The trouble is that, all these things aside, Ben is still the perfect solution to our problem.

I shrug away from Finn's comfort, watching Ben carefully and thinking about what he has said.

'So just where exactly do you fit into all of this, Finn? I mean really fit in. Just how will Ben "blow the lid off things" for you?'

I demand, suddenly recalling Finn's actual words. 'Beyond a brotherly concern for Will's well-being, which is all very noble, I'm sure, what's the real issue for you here?'

I'd expected Finn to look surprised at my question, or at the very least thrown off balance. The fact that he doesn't only lends more weight to what comes next. I think perhaps that he's been waiting to say this for a very long time.

'Only that very soon Will is going to remember why it is that he hates having me around.' His eyes are a dark blue in the evening sunshine as he looks first to me and then to Ben.

'I've spent the last year or so of my life running away from things, running away from a life at Rowan Hill because I believed the things I wanted were just never going to happen. But now, far from seeming impossible, those things that seemed so out of reach before are just inches away from actually becoming reality. It's made me realise that I don't want to settle for half a life anymore.' He stops suddenly, something catching in his throat. He takes a swallow of wine, nearly finished now.

I'm so busy watching Finn that I hardly notice Ben has moved forward in his chair and is now sitting almost on the edge. He reaches towards me to attract my attention.

'Ellie, there's something about me which, perhaps understandably under the circumstances, doesn't bring out the best in Will.'

I look at him in puzzlement.

'I'm gay, Ellie,' he clarifies.

Okay, I think, *that makes sense, sort of.* I can see how Ben would be a constant reminder of what happened to Will, how his sexuality would make it worse, how . . . and then my head does one of those double-take things as I look between Ben and Finn and back again, and the last penny finally drops.

'I'm sorry, Ellie. I should have told you,' says Finn quietly, and finally now it all makes sense: the comment between the brothers about Finn's presence causing Will anxiety – it was no different to having Ben around. This was the real reason why Finn felt he had to go away before and why Ben coming back now would blow the lid off things for Finn. It put both of them in an impossible situation. I have to know.

'Were you lovers?' I ask.

'No,' answers Finn, swallowing, 'but the way things were going between us, becoming lovers would have been inevitable. Under the circumstances, though, maintaining any kind of relationship would have been difficult at best. Ben was right; in reality it could never have worked, so we walked away. I walked away.'

'But maybe if you came and worked at Rowan Hill, Ben, things could be different. Maybe Will would see that—'

'Ellie,' cautions Finn, cutting across me. 'Let's not get carried away here. Not everything turns out happily ever after.'

He's right, of course. I'm meddling again, but I don't want to believe him. There has to be something better than this. I can see the problems just as well as Finn can, but looking at the pair of them, it's so obvious how they feel about each other.

There's just one thing I need to clear up. I hold up a hand, acknowledging Finn's point. 'I understand why having Ben around would be a constant reminder of all that's happened to him, but surely if Will got to know him, he would feel better about things. Why would your relationship make things any worse?'

Finn raises his eyes heavenward and groans. 'That's what I love about you, Ellie. You're so wonderfully naïve. It's all black and white to you, but some people, and that includes Will, can't help but let their feelings colour their judgement.' He rubs his forehead distractedly. 'Will has known about my sexuality for years, and it was never a problem before. He's certainly not homophobic, but look at it from his point of view. Here is a man who will always be a constant reminder of what happened, and like I said before, it's as if Will gets stuck. He can't separate in his mind what happened before with what's happening now – it's like they're the same thing. Can you imagine how he'd feel if I had any kind of a relationship with Ben?'

'So you just ran away from it.'

'Ellie, you have no idea what it's like.'

'Try me.'

There's a very long pause at this point, during which Ben whispers, 'Jesus,' clearly aimed in my direction. Finn and I glare at one another.

'I can't believe you'd be happy to throw everything away, just for an easy life. Why don't we all stick around long enough to find out what happens this time? You know, we might surprise ourselves.'

'Why are you doing this?' demands Finn. 'You and Will could just ride off into the sunset. Piss off together and leave all this mess behind. Why are you so intent on doing it the hard way?'

'I'm not, though, Finn. Don't you get it? This way it all fits. Whether you like it or not, our lives have become intertwined. We're all pieces of the same jigsaw now, and we need each other to finish the puzzle. If one of us goes, there'll always be a piece missing. I never imagined that we'd all end up so involved with one another. You could say it's all just a coincidence, but can't you see how we all fit together?'

Finn makes a barely disguised snort of derision.

'Don't you believe in things happening for a reason?'

Finn's gesture is now more non-committal than anything. 'I prefer to make my own fate,' he shrugs.

Ben smiles, rubbing the end of his chin. 'Presumably, when making this fate, you use the scenery and cast of characters already to hand?'

Finn can see where this is leading only too well. He knows Ben is teasing him, and after struggling for a few minutes to find a suitably pithy reply, he gives up.

'Perhaps we should just tell you what exactly the problem with the barn is,' he says.

CHAPTER TWENTY-EIGHT

I leave them to it after about half an hour, guessing they prob-ably have quite a few things to talk about. Ben says he'll drop Finn home later. I'm not sure I believe him, but he returns just before eleven, at which point I fall into an almost catatonic state until about six this morning. It is now nearly eight, and I'm seri-ously contemplating dragging Finn out of bed to find out what happened, when the kitchen door opens and Finn comes in, plonking himself down at the table and automatically picking up the teapot.

'Morning,' he says. There's a grin behind his eyes. Somewhere.

'Morning,' I mirror. 'You look better.'

The grin comes then. 'You know, you are the most wonderfully, irritatingly stubborn person I know.'

'And you are one of the most beautiful. I never could figure out why I didn't fancy you.'

'Yeah, sorry about that.'

'No, don't be. It's just that I didn't figure it out. I mean, you don't come across as a—'

'What, raging poof?'

'Something like that.' I smile wryly.

'Come on, how many blokes do you know who are fastidiously tidy and like decorating Christmas trees?'

'You might have a point there,' I concede.

'I am sorry I didn't tell you before, though. I probably should have done, but it's just one of those things – well, you know, if you don't look for it, you don't see it, and we're not exactly the type to advertise, either of us.'

'It's none of my business, Finn, really,' I reply, wondering what he's thinking. 'You don't have to talk about it if you don't want to. It's just that I thought Ben had a girlfriend – he talked about her when we first met.'

'Alex?'

'Yes, she . . . Oh, duh!' I exclaim, bashing my forehead. 'I fell right into that one, didn't I?'

Finn chuckles. 'Ben thought you might mention that. We had quite a lot to catch up on last night, including the mysterious Alex, who – yes, you guessed it – is actually a bloke, not Alex as in short for Alexandra.'

'I'm sorry. I just assumed. But they've split up, haven't they?'

'So I believe.' Finn studies me for a moment. 'You wouldn't be shamelessly fishing for information, would you?'

I blush, caught out, but Finn continues. 'Actually, I don't mind. It's probably time I filled in a few of the blanks for you. Besides which, despite your rather stereotypical fantasy that everyone's going to live happily ever after, I like you, Ellie. You're good for Will, and I also happen to think you understand what I'm about. I had a hard time when I was younger, understanding that being gay doesn't make me any different as a person, and I thank you for respecting that.'

I like that – it makes me feel slightly less interfering.

'In fact, I'm no different from anyone else, Ellie. I want the same things from a relationship as most people: friendship, commitment, love, security.'

'Mind-blowing sex?'

'Yes,' he laughs, 'that too.'

I contemplate him for a moment, his hair still damp from the shower, and wearing jeans and an old T-shirt. He looks, if anything, more relaxed than I've seen him in a while.

'And have you fallen in love with Ben?' I ask.

There's a sigh and a small smile. 'I think I fell in love with Ben the minute I met him.'

I let the sentence hang in the air for a while, both of us thinking about lost opportunities.

'So what next?' I ask eventually.

'Breakfast?'

'Finn, I'm being serious.'

'I know. Honestly? I have no idea.'

'But Ben knows how you feel?'

Finn nods. 'It's mutual, sadly. I'm not sure which is worse, unrequited love or something that has no chance of ever going anywhere.'

'And Will knows nothing about it?'

'I'm not actually sure – we tried to be as discreet as possible, but unfortunately Caroline didn't feel able to share our stance.'

'What? She told Will?'

'She threatened to. That's why we had a massive fight. She found out that I was seeing Ben and told me that I had to stop meeting him. I knew the relationship was wrong, and like I said, Ben and I both knew in our hearts it couldn't go anywhere, but I didn't like being told what to do, and that's when I lost my temper with her. She got angry too and threatened that if the relationship didn't end, she'd tell Will. She knew I couldn't risk that; imagine what it would have done to him. I was never completely sure whether she told him or not, but somehow I think he knew. Maybe he just guessed.'

I wince. 'I'm so sorry, Finn.'

'It was an impossible situation. So I ran away, just like you said, and I've spent the last year working my arse off in an effort to try and forget Ben, to erase all the memories of that time. That's why I came home, because I thought maybe I was ready to pick up my life here at Rowan Hill again. That's why it's so hard for me now, the thought of having Ben back again, getting the chance to explain, but knowing that I might have to go through watching him walk away one more time.'

I can feel tears threatening once more. I reach forward to take Finn's hand.

'I'm so sorry for interfering. I know I've made things difficult for you,' I say, totally inadequately. 'I just wanted to help,' I add, knowing the burden of guilt I'm letting myself in for. 'It's the very thing Robbie accused me of and something I've been trying so hard not to do. He said I was trying to control his life by offering to move with him, but I never saw it that way. I wanted to be with him. I thought I was helping, and now I'm doing it all over again.'

'Trying to help is not interfering, Ellie. Not when we all need a bit of a kick up the backside. Running away from problems is never the right solution, but most of us are too cowardly to stay and fight them. Don't let that bastard colour your judgement now – it's not the same thing at all.'

'Isn't it?'

'No,' says Finn firmly, and lets go of my hand, pushing himself to his feet. 'Come on – let's get the day started. Have you had breakfast yet?'

It's Saturday, so the site is quiet, and the sound of tyres is loud against our breakfast taking. If part of Finn's anatomy is turning somersaults, he hides it well as he looks up casually. It's a Toyota pickup.

'Will he want a bacon sandwich, do you think?'

'I don't know.' Finn grins, getting up to let Ben in. 'I'll go find out.'

I know there's a soppy grin on my face, but I just can't help it. I still don't know how things were left between them last night, but I hope that Finn got the chance to explain to Ben what really happened before. I'm assuming that Ben's appearance this morning can only be a good thing.

Finn walks outside to greet Ben as I watch through the window unashamedly. There are nods and smiles and hand gestures on both sides as Finn stands on one side of the truck and Ben on the other. I don't expect them to fall into each other's arms; that would just be ridiculous, but there is a gentle reticence there, a wariness that is offered up like a protective shield, a poignant signpost to past history. It's all rather sad, really.

Ben has already eaten, so no more bacon sandwiches are required. I make a start on the washing-up. This has nothing to do with any desire to restore order to the kitchen, but removes me from the equation as Finn offers to show Ben the barn.

'These are the plans?' asks Ben now, picking them up from the table. He smooths them out, standing for a moment to absorb their content.

'You don't believe in making things easy for yourself, do you?' he remarks eventually, an amused note to his voice.

'I didn't want to compromise. I know the tolerances are tight, Ben. That's why we need someone who knows what they're doing.'

Ben's look is steady. 'Are you paying me a compliment or asking me if I'm up to the job?'

Finn thrusts his hands into his jeans pockets. His look is equally direct. 'I don't know yet.'

'Well then, let's go take a look, shall we?'

They're not gone long, returning deep in conversation, which doesn't skip a beat as they come back into the kitchen to sit at the table once more. It's not an argument exactly, more of an exchange of views as each tries to make the other understand his opinion. Ben starts sketching furiously, quick and decisive strokes. He pushes the piece of paper towards Finn.

'See? It's purer; it shows off the design better.'

'But it'll take longer?'

'Two weeks maybe, a bit less if we're lucky, but the cruck timber is flawed. It's not obvious, and you're just going to have to trust me on this one, Finn, but carry on as you are and put that baby up, and you'll have a serious problem with the join. It needs recutting.'

'It's just the time factor here, Ben. I don't want to push back the opening of the centre, but this extra work could kill it.'

Ben's expression doesn't alter. He doesn't look impressed. 'We'll recoup a little time with the alterations I've suggested, and I'm repeating myself here, but I don't believe this design is a compromise. I honestly think it'll look better. I can turn this project in on time, Finn, but we need to cut the new cruck now.'

There is no answer from Finn, who, if anything, looks slightly amused. He looks between Ben and the piece of paper. It's clear what Ben's argument is: you got me over here to ask my advice, and now you'd better bloody well listen to it. I know Finn is equally passionate about his own point of view. There is a shift then as Ben catches my eye and winks.

'Still think I'm the man for the job?' he asks, now equally amused.

Finn lets out air between his teeth. 'Yes, actually,' he agrees, looking at the paper again. 'These are really good, Ben. Though it pains me greatly to say it, the design is better than mine.' He smiles warmly.

'Different,' replies Ben. 'You know architecture; I know wood, that's all.'

'So, do you want to go get a tree?' Finn grins. 'I'll ring Patrick to come and give us a hand – only I could kind of do with getting something underway before the weekend is out.'

'What? Now?'

'Why? You didn't have anything else planned this weekend, did you?'

'No,' replies Ben blithely. 'Not a thing.'

CHAPTER TWENTY-NINE

May

I have argued endlessly that I should be the one to tell Will. After all, speaking to Ben was my idea, even if I didn't exactly have all the facts at my disposal, but Finn won't hear of it. He says that it's about time this issue between him and Will was sorted out, and that aside, they have to stay focused on the real issue of the barn. Will surely will be able to see the business sense, even though, as Finn so eloquently puts it, it's the personal side that's going to prove to be the ball-breaker.

Alice has come over to offer moral support, although as this entails actually entering into a discussion about the one thing that Finn does not want to talk about, all it does is wind him up further.

'Do you think you should ring him, Finn, dear? At least to forewarn him about the problem with the beam? That way, when he's back on Monday, he'll only have one thing to take in, not two. You know how Will is going to feel when he finds out, don't you?'

Finn makes a strangled sound. 'I know exactly how he's going to feel, Alice,' he retorts, his temper flaring. 'I can't think of any- thing else at the minute, but I can't think how telling him sooner would make things any better either. I want to tell him the news face-to-face; otherwise, it will just be another item on Will's long list of reasons to hate me.'

My heart goes out to Finn.

'Alice, it's not Finn's fault,' I say quietly. 'None of this was his idea. And I agree with him about not telling Will just yet.'

'I know, Ellie. I understand it's a difficult situation.' She sighs. 'Just ignore me, Finn. I can't help thinking that this is just prolonging the agony, though.'

'Prolonging the agony?' hisses Finn. 'Jesus, my agony is so fucking prolonged, it's going to meet me one day coming back the other way.' He glares, struggling to unfold his long legs from under the table. 'I'm going to get a drink,' he adds, stalking off, either to the kitchen or the drinks cupboard, I'm not sure which.

Alice turns to look at me. 'Oh dear,' she murmurs, 'I didn't mean to upset him like that.'

'I know. I know,' I croon. 'He'll be okay in a while. We're both a bit on edge at the moment. Let him just calm down a bit – he'll be fine.'

'Oh, it's all such a dreadful pickle at the moment, isn't it? I just don't know what should be done for the best, to try and avoid some of this upset for everyone.'

'Maybe we can't, Alice, and that's the fact of it. I feel dreadfully responsible for all of this. It was my suggestion that Ben rebuild the barn, but I had no idea who he was.'

'Well no, of course not, dear.'

'And I know Finn feels responsible too, even though it was me who egged him on. It's just that there seemed no other way around the problem, and even now I still feel it was the right thing to do, asking Ben to help.'

I pause for a moment, chewing my lip. 'I want this for Finn too, if I'm honest. I think he deserves a break, but I'm torn between him and Will right now. If I do the decent thing by Finn, then Will suffers; and if I protect Will, then Finn will lose what might be the only chance he has with Ben. How can I possibly choose, Alice? Whatever I do, I land myself in the mire.'

'It would seem that way, yes,' she agrees, watching me carefully. 'But very brave of you also, don't you think?'

'Or very stupid.'

She smiles for a moment, fishing in her handbag. 'No, brave, I think, and selfless. It would be very easy for you to try and preserve what you have with Will, to keep the status quo, but I think it's very mature of you to see your relationship with him as something subject to change and alteration. You're not afraid of it, dear, which is very commendable.'

I look at her incredulously. 'Alice, I'm blooming petrified.'

'But you're sticking with your decision?'

I nod mutely.

'Well then, we must trust that what we believe to be right will come right. A little faith is called for.'

'Yes, and a miracle or two.'

There is a ripple of amusement. 'I'm off to church in a bit, dear. I'll see what I can do.'

CHAPTER THIRTY

The door to the workroom is open as I enter the kitchen, and I can see Will's silhouette there, bathed in the golden light that floods the room this time in the morning. Master of all he surveys. I cross the threshold.

This thing that he does is in his blood now; it's hardwired to his heart.

'Can't wait, can you?' I observe.

Will strokes the central table, which is currently empty. 'Just savouring it,' he remarks softly. 'I love the workroom like this, the calm-before-the-storm moment. It's the most delicious feeling.' He looks around him then, out into the garden and beyond. 'What was it that Finn wanted to talk to me about?'

I can't make any sort of reply. I'm not sure what to say, and in any case I've just spied Finn sitting on a bench in the garden, ostensibly enjoying the sunshine. Will spots him too. He opens the double doors, sticks two fingers in his mouth and gives an almighty whistle, followed by a beckoning wave. Finn can hardly pretend not to hear, and comes ambling in.

'I'm all yours, Finn,' states Will.

Finn looks like he's being slowly disembowelled.

'I just wanted a bit of a catch-up. I thought I could show you what the woodland trail is looking like.' He pauses to flick a green-fly off his arm. 'Patrick has been working like a man possessed. He's managed to lay a trail right through the coppiced area, up to Rayner's Field and along back down through the oaks, to the bottom of the bank.' He starts to jiggle in his pocket for the keys to the truck and is about to carry on when he stops, rethinking. 'Let's walk it, though. It's such a beautiful day, and that way you'll get the feel of it better.'

I look to Finn, nodding. I know exactly why he's chosen this route. It's beautiful – it's what visitors to Rowan Hill will see when they choose to follow one of the woodland walks. It's a central part of Will's vision for this place, and one of the things he holds dearest. It will settle him, put him in a good mood, something I know Finn is banking on.

It only takes a few minutes to reach the gate that will take us through to the woods. The gate is closed at the moment, but in a few short weeks it will be almost permanently open. Beside it, newly inserted into the ground, is about four foot of tree trunk, stripped of its bark, on top of which will rest a dedication plaque with a little reminder from both Will and Yeats: 'Tread softly because you tread on my dreams.'

We pick up the trail and start walking, the small markers discreet and yet obvious enough to guide a route through the woods. In time I know that Will would like to lay a flat surfaced trail to make it accessible to everyone, but at the moment it's too big a job for the manpower and funds we have available. Some things will have to wait.

It's beautiful here: light and dappled shade, rich verdant greens and carpets of ferns and wild flowers where the trees have been coppiced and the new light has woken the woodland floor. The most miraculous thing is that it will never be the same on any two days.

There will be some slight change in the light, some new colour or form appearing, and the once familiar will be renewed.

There are no plans to carry the trail up to the lookout point: both brothers wish this to remain a little more private. It won't be out of bounds, but people won't be pointed in that direction. Instead, the path will skirt around the bottom of the hill, rising gently, crossing over the access road and then down through the rowans that lie to its side. The path will double back on itself then and finish up to the left of the house, where a small car parking area will be. Patrick has offered to make some sculptures to lie along the route, an idea that Will readily agrees to. The fact that Ben has also agreed to make some carvings is not mentioned.

We don't rush, taking our time to enjoy the surroundings, all of us acknowledging that downtime has been a little hard to come by lately. The conversation flows easily, until we come full circle back to the house and the barns.

Little bubbles of apprehension are beginning to rise from the pit of my stomach. Will is excited by the tour. His pace quickens as we pass the front of the house and enter through the massive arches into the courtyard. The work in the barn is not easy to miss: with its roof off, it gapes open to the sky. Although the rest of the stables are by no means finished, by comparison this is like a jagged wound. If the roof – or lack of roof – doesn't invite comment, then the monumental tree lying to one side of the courtyard definitely does.

It draws Will like a magnet. He runs a hand along its length, grinning.

'It's beautiful, isn't it,' he remarks happily. 'Huge when you see it like this.'

Neither of us comments. We're waiting for the inevitable question.

'Aren't we a bit behind on this, though, Finn? I thought the crucks were supposed to be up by now.'

'We are, yeah,' answers Finn, unsure how to continue. 'We hit a bit of a snag and had to do a pretty rapid rethink.'

Will, who is sitting astride the beam, smoothing its contours, looks up sharply.

'Oh?'

I can almost smell the fear, and I try to smile reassuringly.

Finn draws a breath. 'Well, basically James pissed us around. It's probably my fault. I didn't pick up on things until it was too late. He's buggered off, though, and left us in the shit. Not only that, but he's done a spectacularly crap job: the cruck was flawed.'

Will is generous. 'I doubt it's your fault, Finn,' he replies evenly, and then looks down at the trunk on which he's sitting, a little confused. 'But this hasn't been cut yet. Which one are you talking about?'

'This is a replacement for the one James cut,' says Finn, swallowing. 'We found another guy who could help. He's recutting part of the frame as well, but that's what's put us behind. We had to alter a couple of things slightly to try and make up the time, but it'll work well, I think.'

'Bloody hell, Finn, I can see why you're project manager and not me. Any other major catastrophes averted that you need to tell me about?' asks Will, still smiling.

'No,' answers Finn truthfully, studying his feet.

'Well, if we get this one cut, we should be fine. You've found someone who knows what they're doing now, so don't worry, Finn,' Will reassures. His face falls a little when he realises that Finn looks anything but okay or reassured.

'What? It's not going to be okay?'

There is no immediate answer. Will's tone is patient.

'Finn?'

'I don't know.'

'What do you mean you don't know? What else aren't you telling me?'

Finn thrusts his hands into his pockets as if for ballast. He's taller than Will and, as his brother is seated, he towers over him.

'The bloke who's cutting the frame, Will – it's Ben.'

No need to supply the second name then.

Will is silent for a moment, studying the back of his hand for some reason. He looks at me then. He's trying to work out what I know, whether he can make some sort of reply to Finn without giving the game away. Trying to protect himself even now, as we knew he would. He's trying to work out if this is a fight he can win.

He looks back to Finn, his eyes clear, regarding his brother squarely.

'An interesting choice,' he remarks mildly.

Finn's face registers surprise. He'd expected to get it with both barrels. Will might look relaxed, but Finn's been through this too many times before to count his chickens before he's finished walking over their eggshells. He composes his answer carefully.

'It wasn't much of a choice at all, not if we wanted to keep this project going. I thought James was decent, but I realise now it's not just about being a good carpenter; it's about knowing the wood inside and out, knowing where it will trip you up and how to bring out the best in it. I think Ben is possibly the only one who can get us out of the hole I let us slide into.'

'He's clearly very talented,' agrees Will. 'Does he wear his pants on the outside of his trousers, I wonder? That's twice now he's come to the rescue. I hadn't realised that you two were in contact with one another,' he adds, pinning Finn with a stare.

'We're not,' he manages to say, trying to keep the edge out of his voice.

'No, that was me.' I jump in, anxious to do what I can. 'I met Ben a while back, but I bumped into him again a couple of months ago, and we got talking. It was just a coincidence. I had no idea who he was, Will.'

'And now you know better?'

I nod slowly. 'When Finn told me about the problems in the barn, I immediately thought of Ben. I dragged Finn over to see him – only because I thought he could help. It was all my idea. Finn knew nothing about it until we got there.'

'But he told you all about Ben anyway, behind my back, when I wasn't even around.'

'It wasn't salacious gossip, Will. They only told me to shut me up, to try and convince me why it was such a bad idea.'

A few beats of my heart skip by as Will weighs up what I've told him. He doesn't look at either of us but focuses his gaze across the courtyard to the barn beyond. A slight breeze whisks over my back, suddenly cold, and I realise I'm sweating.

'How far behind are we?' he asks Finn, turning his head back towards him. His expression is hard to read.

'About two weeks, max. Hopefully less.'

'And you're absolutely confident that Ben can pull this off?'

A rapid nod.

A hand reaches out towards me then, pulling me down onto the beam beside Will.

'What am I going to do with you, Ellie?' he sighs, but there's a slight twitching at the corner of his mouth. 'Christ, you two must have been pissing yourselves this morning. How come he drew the short straw, then?'

'I didn't,' replies Finn. 'I volunteered to tell you.'

'Ballsy, mate. I'll give you that.'

Finn gives a tiny smile, doubtless remembering previous conversations about the state of his tackle. Will looks up again.

He catches both my hands and stands, pulling me with him as we swing our legs over the broad beam. His hand goes out to Finn.

'Thank you,' he says simply. 'I know this isn't easy for you either,' he says with a grin. 'Anyway, you and Ben—'

'No,' shoots back Finn, cutting across him.

'What no, as in "no, not yet"? Or no, as in "no"?'

There's no way Finn can possibly answer that.

CHAPTER THIRTY-ONE

I'm not sure we realised we were still holding it, but over the next few days our collective breath seeps out of us like air from a balloon, turning nerves that were taut and stretched into something more relaxed.

Ben duly arrives for work each morning, and Will is perfectly civil, not gushing exactly, but appreciative nonetheless of Ben's expertise and help. He asks a few relevant questions and is complimentary about the work done so far. He is far from relaxed, but then none of us are to start with.

It comes over us gently as we move about our work each day – a settling, an acceptance, a new status quo, but a comfortable one.

I've come into the kitchen to make everyone a drink. It's not officially lunchtime, but the last couple of days have been unseasonably hot, and Patience and I are dying out there. Helen is here as well, as she is most days now. Her workshop is virtually finished, and although she's trying to get as much work done as possible, she's become the site's unofficial style guru. Her ideas for display and design are so effective that everyone has been asking her advice about their own projects. The vision of community that Will and Finn had for this place is magically happening all by itself, and I'm smiling as I pour orange juice into a glass pitcher.

As I walk across the courtyard, I see Helen and Bonnie chatting like they've known one another since birth, Helen holding up what looks like asparagus, no doubt illustrating some idea or other. Patrick is in a deckchair, minus his shirt, doing what can only be described as whittling. There's no idleness here, though. It's all moving inexorably towards a common purpose, and I feel a little thrill in my stomach as I remember that we officially open to the public at the beginning of July: only six weeks or so away.

Patience has been such a help getting the garden ready. In fact, she's been a one-woman whirlwind. I almost didn't recognise her the first time she came to help. Gone were the heels, skin-tight clothes and tumbling curls. Instead, the tattiest pair of jeans I've ever seen, clogs and baggy T-shirt, topped with scragged-up hair thrust under a baseball cap. She launched herself into the garden with undisguised glee and has worked like a Trojan ever since. I'm not sure how much help I've been to her – I suspect I'm more of a hindrance – but what I've lacked in knowledge I've made up in hard labour.

Even though it's so warm today, Patience hasn't let the pace drop for a minute. I've been suggesting that I make a drink for the last hour, and Patience has merely smiled, suggesting we just finish this or that little bit.

It's cool here in the kitchen, and for that I'm grateful. I take a bottle of lemonade out the fridge and empty most of it into the pitcher, mixing it a little with the juice. I add some ice that Patience insisted I make up. It's got tiny sprigs of mint and borage in it, and it's quite lovely in drinks, once you get used to straining the bits through your teeth.

I give a tap on the workroom door, which is deliberately closed. I'm not allowed in there. It's all a bit secretive. There's no reply, so

I cautiously and slowly push the door open a little. Will is standing in a patch of sunlight, holding up two pieces of pink glass, looking first at one and then the other. The room is stifling. It's beautifully light, of course, but even with the outside doors open, it heats up unmercifully.

Will turns at the sound of the door and immediately puts the glass down, walking towards me. A smile transforms his face.

'You know the rules.' He grins. 'No peeking.'

I catch the arms he holds out to me, sliding in for a cuddle.

'Are you okay?' I ask. 'It's blooming hot in here.'

He pulls away for a moment, as if to check whether what I've said is true. 'It is a bit, isn't it? I'm okay, though, I promise . . . and before you ask, yes, I have had a drink.' He smiles, forestalling me.

The cup of tea I brought him this morning is still on the table, cold and untouched. I look at it pointedly, to which Will, by way of reply, moves to a side bench and picks up a two-litre bottle of water that is only half full, waving it at me. Of course, it may have been there since a week last Wednesday. I make a disparaging noise, but Will is already hustling me out, flapping his hands at me and moving me backwards towards the door.

'Come on, woman, some of us have got work to do. Stop snooping – out you go!' And with that he crushes me to him and finds my lips with his own, surprisingly soft and gentle, a kiss that sets my heat rising again.

'Lunch will be in an hour, Will,' I add as he releases me. 'You know, that thing where you stop work and put food in your mouth?'

'Okay, in an hour,' he repeats, but his attention is already drifting, turning back to the pieces of pink glass on the table. I shake my head in proud amusement and close the door.

I arrive back in the courtyard just as Jane's car pulls up outside my house. I stop to wait for her, knowing that she's brought something for us. I'm dying to see it. She reaches over to pick something off the passenger seat before climbing out and crossing the few metres to where I'm standing.

Jane flaps the envelope she's holding at her face like a fan. 'God, can I have one of those?' she asks, indicating the tray of drinks I'm carrying.

'Of course. Come on. I'll get everyone together, and you can show us what Jack's done.'

A makeshift table of two huge straw bales has been set up in the middle of the courtyard, courtesy of Patrick, and I rest the tray of refreshments on it now, waving him over and pouring him the first glass.

'Help yourself, Jane. I'll just go and round the others up.'

There's hardly any need, as my appearance draws everyone out like a magnet, ready for a welcome break. I cross through the huge door at the top of the courtyard, skirting around to the garden, where I know Patience will not have stopped for a minute. She's pretty much where I left her, in fact. She looks up, though, as she sees me approach, straightens up, easing her back, and takes off her cap, shaking out her hair. She lifts it up again as if this will remove the heat gathered there and slowly lets it fall. I don't need to say anything. She starts towards me, no doubt anticipating a long cool drink.

As she joins me, I nod towards the barn. 'I'll just go and rouse these two,' I tell her. Finn has the same workaholic tendencies as his brother. 'I'll catch you up.'

Patience merely smiles and follows me. She's dropped the sex goddess act around Finn now, but she still takes advantage of any opportunity to feast her eyes. I haven't the heart to tell her that her voluptuous figure is wasted on Finn.

I pause in the doorway, checking that it's safe to enter, but today the space inside is still. I spot Ben and Finn sitting at one

of the worktables towards the other end of the barn. Ben is drawing something, a book open in front of him, while Finn watches.
If there is any space between them it's millimetres, the length of
their forearms touching as Finn leans in to see what's been drawn.
I smile to myself, wondering if anyone else has noticed what to me
seems to be increasingly obvious, but with Patience in tow I daren't
say anything.

'Come on, guys, drinks up!' I yell, moving through at speed and
out the other door without a second glance, hoping that Patience is
behind me. She catches my arm as we reach the outside, sadly not
to tell me to slow down.

'And there's me thinking I was losing my touch,' she whispers
in my ear.

I decide to feign ignorance. 'Sorry, what?'

She nudges my arm. 'Those two in there. I was wondering
why my come-to-bed eyes weren't working on Finn. Clearly my
charms are nothing compared with Ben's. Talk about barking up
the wrong tree.'

I laugh then, remembering Finn's words to me from what
seems like a very long time ago, when he himself told me that
he was the wrong tree. Finally I understand what he meant.
Clearly, Patience catches on faster than I do. Now that she's
said it, I can hardly refute her comment. 'Ah,' I say slowly, 'you
noticed then.'

Patience taps the side of her nose in a knowing fashion. 'I'm a
very wise woman, Ellie. My radar misses nothing, particularly when
it comes to eminently fuckable younger men.' She giggles as my
hand flies to my mouth in shock. 'Bloody shame, although not for
Ben, alas. Lucky bastard.'

'Shh, Patience, they'll hear you,' I caution, laughing with her.

She rolls her eyes. 'Anyway, I can be discreet. Don't look at me
like that – I can, honestly. I won't say anything to anyone.'

'It's not a secret as such; it's just that I'm not even sure they're together, if you know what I mean. I'd rather not broadcast the fact, that's all.'

'Girl, you are so naïve. They are most definitely together, believe me, but I swear my lips are sealed. I know it's a bit of a touchy subject.'

I look at her quizzically, not sure what she means by this last statement. 'What do you mean, "touchy"?' I clarify: 'It doesn't bother me.'

There's a flicker of alarm in her eyes as she realises she's strayed into murky waters. She looks at me for a second or two before answering. 'No, I know – sorry. Just something Will said once. Ignore me; it's none of my business,' she says, linking her arm through mine.

I want to ask her what she meant, what Will said, but somehow it's easier just to walk out to the waiting group of friends whose relaxed chatter I can already hear drifting up the courtyard. I know that Jane will have waited for me to reappear before showing the others what she's brought.

She picks up the envelope from the makeshift table as she sees me coming.

'Come on, Jane, let's have a look,' I start, wiping the moisture from my glass of juice down my jeans.

Wordlessly, Jane hands me a folded paper from within the envelope. She wants me to see it first. I look at Rowan Hill's first-ever brochure, excitement mounting. It's beautifully simple.

The front cover shows a stylised pen-and-ink drawing of a Rowan tree, colour washed, with simple lines. It's modern but has a traditional feel to it somehow. The whole thing has been printed on recycled paper, and the uneven texture and colour deliberately adds to this. Hand-drawn lettering reads 'Rowan Hill,' and I smile to myself, knowing how right Will was.

We thought long and hard about what to call ourselves, end-lessly bandying about words like 'centre,' 'workshop,' 'co-operative,' 'community,' but not one ever quite felt right. It was too defining, Will argued. He wanted the name to mean different things to different people. He wanted people to come with an open mind, and so in the end we agreed that Rowan Hill was all that was needed. As I read Jack's perfect words underneath our name, I see how clever his ideas were.

'Come first out of curiosity. Explore as our guest. Return as a friend.'

It's just brilliant. Well, there's no point in having a friend who's a writer and former ad man if he can't come up with a hook like that, is there?

I unfold the brochure like a map, looking at the outside and motioning for Jane to hand copies to the others. Out of the corner of my eye, I see Finn and Ben coming to join us. The inside pages give little potted histories of everything that you can expect to find here. Everyone had their own ideas of what they wanted to say, and Jack has turned these into a brilliant mix of quotes and factual information. Each area has been illustrated by a sketched tableau just like the ones that Finn drew that day in the kitchen when all this was just an idea on paper. I feel a lump form in my throat. I can hear the others exclaiming in delight around me.

'Jane, this is just wonderful!' I throw my arms around her. 'I love it. Jack is such a hero for doing this for us.'

She beams. 'It was the least we could do.'

I can hear Finn receiving congratulations for his drawings. I catch his eye. 'Finn, go and get Will; he's got to see this.' I'm interested in his reaction, and sadly, yet all too predictably, he throws me a *why me?* look, but he goes anyway. I notice Ben move around to the other side of the table, ostensibly to talk to Patrick but also so that when Finn returns, if he takes up his original position, Ben will be nowhere near him. Perhaps I'm just being overly suspicious.

I'm glad to see the two brothers talking animatedly as they reappear from the house, Finn's hands gesturing wildly as usual. I can't hear what they're saying, but it seems relaxed enough.

Will comes over to give Jane a hug and a kiss. 'I hear the old man's done us proud, Jane,' he greets her, smiling broadly.

She returns his smile, handing him a brochure. 'He wanted to come over himself, but he's chained to the desk, I'm afraid.'

Will is scanning through the brochure but looks up. 'Maybe at the weekend then? You could all come over, so we can say thank you properly.'

I nod enthusiastically. 'That's a brilliant idea. Please say you'll come,' I plead, realising just how little time I've spent with my friend recently.

'We'd love to,' Jane affirms, taking a drink. 'So what do you think of Ellie's picture then, Will? Doesn't she look beautiful?'

Will looks straight at me. 'She is very beautiful . . . and this really is superb, Jane. It hits just the right spot.'

I return my attention to the brochure, looking for the picture I'd obviously missed before. Will helps me out by turning it over and tapping the paper. How could I have missed it? The whole of the back is a map of the site, showing the walks, the woodland, the barn with its historic cruck frame and, of course, Will's work. By its side is an invitation to have tea and stay awhile. A smiling woman hands a customer a cup, her head thrown back in laughter. Corkscrew curls tumble over her shoulders, her face animated. This can hardly be me. I look up to find Will's eyes on me. He raises his glass in a silent toast.

'Gone a little overboard with the artistic license there, Finn,' I suggest.

'Really? Do you think so?'

'I don't,' sounds Will, pulling me to him. 'You're right, Jane, she looks beautiful, and, Finn, thank you – these drawings are just right.' He nods at his brother, smiling warmly. There are murmurs of assent from all round.

'Well, folks,' continues Will, 'we're nearly there. Just a few more weeks and we'll be up and running. I'm amazed how well it's all coming together, and I don't know about you lot, but I'm scared shitless. I'm still not sure it's sunk in properly yet. I have to pinch myself when I think how different things were just six months ago.'

'I think it's the same for everyone here, Will. I know it is for me,' puts in Helen. 'Still, I can't wait to get open and see all this come to life.'

Will throws back the last of his drink, running his hand through his hair. 'I'm in serious danger of holding you all up if I'm not careful, so excuse me, but I better get my nose back to the grindstone.' He gives my shoulder a squeeze. 'Jane, please thank Jack for me, won't you? And I'll see you soon.' He drops a kiss on her cheek and turns back towards his workshop.

Jane gives his back a disapproving glance. 'You're all working far too hard, I've decided,' she states. 'So I think you should have a little respite. How about I bring over a picnic on Friday afternoon, and we have a little jolly?'

'Jane, you can't do that,' I declare.

'I wasn't planning a Victorian feast resplendent with butler. It's just a few sandwiches, Ellie.'

'Okay, but even so—'

'Why don't we all help?' butts in Helen, bless her. 'I mean we could all bring something – you know, salad, cake, whatever – wouldn't that help?'

'That would be lovely, Helen, thank you. I'll take you up on that, if you don't mind. I'll leave you to decide amongst yourselves, shall I?' She nods and then checks her watch. 'Listen, Ellie, I'll ring you, okay? I'd better get going.' She smiles at everyone. 'See you soon.'

I give her a thumbs up.

CHAPTER THIRTY-TWO

I am so looking forward to sitting down. Some days I don't feel so bad, but tonight every fibre in my body is protesting. We're all feeling it. Finn got up after tea and went to watch the telly, something that happens very rarely. Even Will said he wouldn't be long working. I'm just collecting the last few bits to wash up, and then I am definitely going to stop. I stick my head around the workroom door to see if any glasses are being harboured there, only to find Will standing by the open doors to the garden, glass in hand and deep in thought.

'Penny for them?' I ask gently, not wanting to break the peace and quiet.

Will swings round and gives that lazy, slow smile that transforms his whole face. A little stubble glints off his chin in the evening sun.

'Sorry,' he says unnecessarily. 'I'm not even sure I was thinking about anything, actually. I seem to have ground to a halt.'

'I think we all have. Come on. Stop now. Come and sit down.'

He thinks about it, but then something else crosses his face, and he waves his glass slightly. 'I will in a minute. I just need to work something out first; it's bugging me.'

'Can I help?'

'Probably, but maybe not tonight.' He looks almost apologetic and waves his glass again. 'Do you want a drink?'

I eye the bottle of whisky on the table. 'God no, that'll finish me off completely. I might have a glass of wine.'

'I probably shouldn't be drinking this either. It's just been that sort of a day. Do you want to see if Finn wants one?'

I know when I'm not wanted. 'Okay, I get the message. I'll leave you to your conundrum. Just don't be long; you look knackered,' I warn, picking up the bottle.

'I won't, I promise.'

The telly is still on when I reach the lounge, but Finn has flaked out, still in his work clothes. Well, at least he got as far as taking his boots off. I put the bottle down on the table and go to switch off the TV. Almost immediately, as though he were a small child, one of Finn's feet gives a twitch as he wakes up and looks around in shock at the sudden lack of sound.

'Oh God,' he mutters, rubbing his face with both hands.

'I know,' I agree. 'Do you want a drink?' I ask, motioning towards the bottle.

It takes a few beats for him to process this information. 'Yeah,' he says eventually. 'Not that, though – that's a really bad idea.'

'Glass of wine?' I suggest, and then when I get no reply, 'Tea? Beer? Glass of water?' He stares at me vacantly. Dear God. 'Hot chocolate?'

His face lights up at this. 'Is that weird,' he asks, 'on a boiling hot day?'

'Probably,' I say, 'but what the hell. I'll have one as well.'

Finn struggles to his feet. 'I'll make them, Ellie. You've been running around after us all day.'

I curl into a corner of the sofa, reaching for my book. In the distance the church bells are ringing out eight o'clock. It's later than I thought. Finn reappears after a few moments, putting two mugs down on the coffee table before crashing back down on the chair and giving an almighty sigh.

'Is it too early to go to bed?' He smiles weakly.

'Not necessarily, but then you'll never sleep. You were up at some ungodly hour this morning, though.'

'I had a lot of energy, then,' he protests.

'You're not off out tonight, then?' I muse.

Finn looks at me carefully, knowing exactly what I'm driving at. 'No,' he says slowly, weighing up just how much he wants to tell me. 'We're having an off day.'

I lower the book onto my lap. 'What, "off" as in "not on"? Or "off" as in you've had a tiff?'

He pauses for a moment, clearly amused. 'Actually I meant "off" as in "not on." We haven't had a row.'

'So things are good, then?'

'Yes, Ellie, things are good,' he intones patiently.

He's obviously not going to say more. I get the distinct impression I'm being toyed with. I ball up a piece of paper I've been using as a bookmark and throw it at him. 'Come on, you rotten sod, tell me! You know I'm dying to get the low-down.'

'The low-down on what?' he asks, deliberately obtuse.

'Are you and Ben together?' I growl slowly, enunciating every syllable.

Finn can't contain himself any longer, and his face cracks wide into a grin. 'Yes.' He says. Full stop.

I wriggle further forward on the settee. 'And?'

Finn chuckles. 'What, you want me to draw you a diagram?'

I flush bright red. 'Sorry, I didn't mean it like that. Stop giving me a hard time, Finn. You know I'm not making fun of you. I just want to know if things have turned out the way you wanted.'

'I'd say that things are . . .' – he struggles to find the right word – 'profound.'

'Wow. Profound is good.'

'Yup.'

'So how come you're having an off day, then?'

'Ah,' answers Finn succinctly. 'That would be because I'm knackered, he's knackered and we're trying to be a little low key, that's all.' His face has dropped a little.

And there it is: the elephant in the room.

'Because of Will?' I suggest. I have to know.

There's a small answering nod. 'Can you imagine what he'd say if I brought Ben around here, Ellie, or what he'd do if he stayed over?' He's keeping his voice deliberately low. He doesn't want Will to hear him, but there's real force behind these words.

'But do you honestly think that's the case?' I argue. 'I think Will's pretty cool about it.'

'No, he isn't. He just wants you to think that he is. You're the only one he listens to, Ellie, and he doesn't want to hear what you've got to say. He's keeping you sweet, that's all.'

I wish I'd never asked. I can see the immediate apology in Finn's eyes, but I don't know what to say. Trouble is, deep down I know he's right, and so does Finn. I try a weak smile.

'I'm still glad you two have finally got things going.'

Finn swallows hard. 'So am I, Ellie; I've waited a long time for this. Actually I can't begin to find the words to describe how I feel about Ben. I've never felt this way before.' He studies my face, which I know looks troubled. 'Maybe we just need to give things a little more time with Will. You know, it was when I looked at you two and how good you were together that I realised what I'd been missing. Don't worry, Ellie – it'll be fine.'

'I hope so,' I whisper.

When I turn over in the night, I realise that Will is no longer beside me. I'm not sure how long he's been gone, but I count another forty-two minutes before he comes back to bed. It's not until I'm washing up the breakfast things that I realise the whisky bottle is back in the workroom.

CHAPTER THIRTY-THREE

June

The temperature soars, and by Friday afternoon I'm looking forward to the break in routine and the opportunity to get out of the stifling heat. At the last minute Finn and Patrick cry off the picnic, claiming they want to get the last of the trail poles in before the weekend. This gives Will the perfect excuse to carry on working too, and so in the end it's just us girls plus Ben and Richard, who have chivalrously offered to carry the bulk of our food, including the early strawberries that Richard and Bonnie picked this morning.

Helen and Patience are ahead, nattering away, and judging by the shrieks of laughter coming our way, Patience's sense of humour is in full flow. Jane and I hang back, talking about the weekend. Jane's worried that I've got enough to do without cooking Sunday lunch for everyone. Quite frankly, I'm more worried that, given the amount of single malt he seems to be getting through, Will might not make it to lunch sober.

I'm lying on my back in a patch of dappled sunshine, staring up through the canopy of leaves and feeling a gorgeous, sleepy peace wash over me. A gentle breeze is rustling the undergrowth every now and again, and aside from the odd murmured comment or noise as

Patience steals another strawberry, the air is soft and soundless. It hangs with the sort of vibrating stillness that you often get in the middle of a summer's day, strangely both enervating and calming at the same time. I love these moments of suspended animation, just adrift. There is absolutely nothing better for the soul, and I tell myself that everything will be fine.

By late afternoon the sun has gone, and the still air hangs heavy. It's time to be heading home; the best of the day is behind us.

As we cross back into the courtyard, a sudden wind whips up, chasing the dust. We look to the skies, where threatening clouds are rolling overhead. Our goodbyes are quick.

I take the picnic detritus back into the kitchen, leaving Ben to put away some of the equipment that's still outside before the rain comes in earnest.

The workroom door is open, but there's no sign of Will. The only indication of his presence is an empty bottle on the table.

I eventually find him in the barn, standing in front of the huge cruck frame and the space where his window will fit. He's staring into the tumbler of whisky that he's brought in with him. He takes a sip now, a bitter expression crossing his face as he slowly upends the glass and pours the rest of the liquid onto the dirt floor. He transfers the glass to his other hand and very slowly, with deliberate care, places it down on the workbench.

I hadn't realised he'd heard me come in until he speaks.

'I can't do it anymore,' he says, his voice only just above a whisper.

I watch the coloured liquid disperse, but say nothing. I want Will to fill in the blanks.

'I shouldn't do this anymore,' he says again, only slightly differently this time, I notice. 'The drink,' he clarifies. 'I've been drinking again.' He's asking me if I've noticed.

'I know,' I say. 'Does it help?'

He wasn't expecting that. He wants to be told off so that he can defend his actions, at least make himself feel a little more justified by them. He doesn't answer, but then he doesn't need to. He and I both know that this is not about his drinking – not really. Something about today has opened up another crack in Will's carefully constructed wall, and we both need to dig out the loose mortar.

After Will told me about his attack, I had thought that certain issues had been resolved, and to some extent I was right. He's got his work back. His passion for something that he had given up so many years ago has been reignited, and he's finally allowed himself to accept that the pursuit of his art is worthwhile.

Ben's reappearance probably couldn't have come at a worse time. The one person who makes it almost impossible to forget what happened is now a constant reminder of everything he's trying to leave behind.

I move my foot against Will's to attract his attention.

'I'm very proud of you, you know,' I say, smiling.

Will rakes a hand through his hair, heaving air into his body, his hand shaking slightly. 'I had quite a lot to drink this afternoon, Ellie. Christ, when I think what could have happened.'

'Yeah, you know if you were very lucky, you might have dropped a piece of glass and slit your wrist.'

'Don't make fun of me, Ellie. This window is probably the single most important piece of work I've ever done, and today I came this close to ruining it completely. I'd have been quite happy if all I'd done was slit my wrist.'

I shake my head. 'Listen, Will,' – I break off to wind my fingers around his – 'nothing happened. You had the sense to stop when you realised it was dangerous, so don't beat yourself up. You do need to stop drinking, Will, but not because of anything that might have happened this afternoon. You need to stop because you're hiding behind it, and you and I both know it.'

There's a look of slight acceptance.

'Why do you do it, anyway?'

Will shrugs. 'Because no one wants any logs at this time of year,' he says, not actually answering my question.

It's a throwaway remark, but there's a lot of truth in what he says. He chopped logs because he had trouble sleeping, and he chopped logs to stop himself from drinking when he couldn't sleep. The hard part comes when you have to admit that neither the drink nor the lack of sleep was actually the problem. The problem is what lies beneath both these things. And it hasn't gone away.

'I get that,' I say slowly, measuring my response. 'I get that nothing's really changed. You're drinking again because you don't need to chop logs at the moment, but I'm not interested in your justifications. I'm interested in why you drink at all. So I'll ask the question again – only answer me this time: why do you do it?'

Another shrug as Will looks away, hunted.

I want to hold him, to make this easier for him, but I know that if I do, the answer may never come. I wait out the moments until Will's answer comes, unyielding.

'Because I have questions – questions to which I will never get answers.'

'Why? Because the people you need to ask aren't here?' I probe gently.

A release of breath. 'Something like that.'

'And you can't just let those questions go?'

'I can't. I've tried,' answers Will, his eyes returning to seek out mine. The bitterness is gone. He's asking for help now.

'What happened today, Will? What was it that started you drinking?'

His hand goes to his jeans pocket, fishing out a piece of paper that he hands to me, a look of abject misery on his face.

'I found this in the bin – it's a letter. I've not seen it before, so I'm guessing Finn put it there.'

I look down at the note, written in flowing handwriting, a few lines on a page. As I scan it, I realise that reading it is not required. The only thing that seems important to me about his letter is the two solitary words on the bottom of the page, which read *Love, Caroline*.

My head jerks up sharply, the bottom of my stomach falling away in shock.

'I haven't seen it, Ellie. I didn't know she'd written,' sounds Will's voice quickly, defensive, but angry too.

'So why has she then?'

'It's written to Finn, not me.'

'And? Come on – you've obviously read it.'

'She wants to come and see me.'

'Well, that's just fantastic isn't it, Will,' I say sarcastically, my own temper flaring at my hurt. 'At least Finn had the sense to throw it in the bin where it belongs, not moon about and drink himself senseless.'

Will's eyes flash in response. 'Yeah, you take his side, why don't you. I suppose it never occurred to you that Finn might not be the innocent party in this? That the reason he didn't want me to see the letter is because he's got too much to hide.'

'Well, what the hell do you mean by that? Jesus, Will, now you're just being ridiculous! Have you not noticed what's been going on around you for the last few weeks?'

'What – Finn and Ben you mean?' he bites back, his voice heavy with bile. 'I suppose you think they're in love?'

I try to swallow some of my anger. 'Why can't they be? You know, being homophobic is a little old fashioned in this day and age, Will. How come you think you're the only one that can be in love, anyway? That's if you actually are; I'm beginning to doubt that.'

Will stares at me, open-mouthed. 'I don't give a shit that Finn's gay, if that's what he is. I just wish he'd make up his mind which team he's playing for.'

Now I'm really confused. I sit down on the edge of the workbench for stability. 'What do you mean? Have you actually spoken to him about Ben, about how he feels? Well?'

There's a moment of reflection. 'I think that Finn sometimes makes use of whatever's available,' he answers carefully.

I register the rush of movement to my side just a little too late, as Ben knocks Will sprawling to the floor.

'You bastard!' he spits.

I have to say I agree with him.

CHAPTER THIRTY-FOUR

It's six o'clock now, and Will and I are sitting alone in the kitchen, Will holding a long since melted ice pack to his cheek. The words dried up a while ago. We are both lost in our own thoughts, and we've hardly moved for the past half hour.

My mood is so dark, I've hardly noticed that the room is too, until a sudden flash that could only be lightning cuts across my thoughts, and a tumult of rain begins to pound against the window. The day has finally had its release too.

I don't even hear the kitchen door open, accompanied as it is by a huge sounding of thunder, but as my thought processes, which have previously slowed almost to a standstill, struggle to gain speed, I become aware of a hulking figure in the gloom, dark, wet and suddenly very loud against the previous stillness of the room. It might as well be Frankenstein.

'Christ!' shouts Finn, shaking off water like a dog. 'What a fucking great end to an utterly shitty day.' He drags out a chair from the table, making me wince. 'Glad you two are nice and dry. I've worked my arse off this afternoon, trying to get the flaming trail poles in: the ground is so fucking hard.' He pauses a moment to wipe rain from the end of his nose. 'And now I'm bloody soaked as well as knackered.'

Will passes a hand over his eyes, rubbing them gently and expelling a huge sigh, slowly raising his head. Finn looks at him and then at me.

'What's wrong with you two?' he demands, glaring. 'Somebody die or something?'

At any other time, I think, that would have been absurdly funny. I'm contemplating laughing in a masochistic kind of way, when Finn catches sight of Will's face.

'What the hell happened to you?'

I might as well tell him. It's unlikely the day is going to get any better. 'Ben hit him,' I say quietly.

I thought that Finn would explode, but he doesn't. Instead, he joins us at the table, where he sits in silence for a moment or two, watching Will.

'Would you like to tell me what happened, Will,' he says coldly, 'before I thump you as well?'

'I told Ben about you and Caroline,' he says bluntly. 'Well, not exactly . . . I found the letter, Finn, from Caroline, the one you'd hidden from me. It would seem the past is catching up with you. I think you'd better decide which team you're playing on.'

Finn stares incredulously at me, wondering no doubt where my allegiances lie. There are tears in my eyes. I think he'll work it out.

'You unmitigated bastard,' he hisses, launching to his feet and beginning to pace the room. 'You know, I never realised quite what a number she'd done on you, Will. I spent hours in the past, agonising over whether to tell you or not. In the end I didn't because I wanted to protect you – I thought you had enough to deal with,' he shouts bitterly. 'And what's worse is I'm still doing it now.'

'Finished?' spits Will sarcastically.

Finn glares at his brother, water still dripping off his hair onto the floor. 'No, actually, maybe I'll tell you the whole story. You don't seem to care about the consequences of what you say, so why should I? Read the letter again, Will, but this time in the knowledge that the person Caroline refers to in it is Ben.' He takes in Will's startled expression. 'Yes, that's right, not herself, but Ben. The person I was supposed to be having an affair with. I gave him up for you, Will – the only man I have ever loved, and I did that for you, to spare you any more pain. Then when you've finished reading, you can sit and think about how you're going to live the rest of your life knowing that you've just thrown away everything and everyone in it.'

He comes to my side then, holding out a hand to gently stroke my cheek. 'I'm sorry, Ellie,' he whispers, and creeps from the room.

My throat is so tight from holding on to too much emotion, I don't think I can speak. I look to Will, whose face, even in the dim light, is ashen. He'd better say something soon because right now my resolve is very much on the fence. I'm hanging on to the last ten per cent of me that wants to hold him and get to the bottom of this; the other ninety per cent just wants to run.

There is so much guilt here, so much misunderstanding. I reach out to take Will's hand, marvelling at this thing we humans do, such a small thing, really, the reassurance of touch, but at times feeling so very big. In fact, just as it felt to me the first time I met Will, alone and in pain, when the very first thing he did was seek to comfort me.

His look of gratitude spills the tears from my eyes. I tighten my hand over his. 'I'll read it, shall I?'

Finn,

I read in a newspaper recently about the changes going on at Rowan Hill, and I must say they sound amazing. I'm so glad that the place is finally going to be on the map; you know how much I loved it, and I've missed it so much, as I have Will.

I wonder how he is now and thought that I should come and see him. I only ever wanted what was best for him, as you know, and it strikes me that now, with me at his side, he could really go places.

I think we misunderstood one another, you and I, but I hope by now that you've overcome your silly infatuation. I never did tell Will about the affair, you know, so I hope there's no hard feelings. Anyway, I'd be grateful if you could put in a good word for me with Will, and let me know when I could come and see him.

Love, Caroline xx

Will has lowered his head to the table. He's still gripping my hand, but his shoulders are heaving silently with the weight of guilt and blame that has now settled upon them.

We sit like this for some while until he eventually speaks.

'What am I going to do, Ellie?'

I wipe my own tears away. 'Take one day at a time, Will, and try finally to leave this all behind.'

'I didn't know. Why didn't Finn tell me?'

'How could he, Will? It would have tortured you even more.'

'But I never gave them a chance. Finn's right; everything I have now is gone too.'

'Not everything,' I reply.

There's confusion in his eyes now. 'You'd stay with me, after all this?'

'I'll stay, Will, because I think what you've been is a victim, in every sense of the word. It's this that's haunted you, and until you can lay down your guilt too and realise that you did nothing wrong that day, you won't move on. I think that maybe now, finally, is the time to do it.' I squeeze his hand.

Reluctantly I move away and cross to fill the kettle, the mundane task giving me time to think.

I hear the back door reopen and, to my surprise, the figures of Ben and Finn appear, hands clasped together. They go and sit silently at the table, both resolute and fearful.

I stay beside the Aga a little longer, breathing calmly, drawing strength from what I know to be right.

'Will, there's something else I never told you,' Finn begins.

I place the drinks on the table, acknowledging Finn's desolate expression.

'Where were you, Will, on the night you were attacked?'

Will's look is puzzled. 'On Blackwood Heath, but you know that. What's that got to do with anything?'

'Why were you there?'

'Walking, that's all. I went to get some fresh air.' He looks embarrassed now. 'I'd had an argument with Caroline and needed to clear my head.'

'No, I meant why go there?'

'No particular reason. I remembered you saying how nice it was, and I just ended up there.'

Finn starts to fidget I notice, but he stays silent. Ben gives him a slight nod.

'So you didn't know that it's a place where young gay blokes hang out in the hope of meeting other young gay blokes?'

Will's look is sharp. 'No, of course not!' he exclaims, flicking a glance at me. 'What's that got to do with anything?'

'Only that it's the reason why I've always blamed myself for your attack. It was me who told you about Blackwood Heath. It's my fault you were there.'

Will stares at Finn then, his jaw working furiously. 'But that's absurd!' he splutters.

'No, Will, it's guilt, plain and simple.'

'It's time to sort things out, Will,' I say. 'You've both spent far too long letting your perception of things colour your actions. Now it's time to deal in the truth. With everything that's going on here, let's finally put this right.'

Will reaches out his hand once more towards mine, tentative.

'I told you I was a bad bet, Ellie.'

'So ask yourself why I'm still here?' I counter. 'Ask yourself why we're all still here, Will. The chances are the odds are actually pretty good.'

CHAPTER THIRTY-FIVE
July

It's hard to hear Will's voice above the cacophony of noise. Finn insisted that he do the honours, claiming that he had far more experience of public speaking, but it's not the only reason Will has been elected host for the ceremony. This day belongs to all of us, but to Will most of all perhaps, whose journey has been the hardest.

Finn joked earlier that it would probably only involve a handful of people anyway, a comment designed to put Will at his ease, though this has backfired somewhat now that the courtyard is massed with people.

We officially opened at 10 a.m., but with the opening ceremony not starting until two o'clock, we thought people wouldn't start arriving until lunchtime. We were still stringing up masses of fairy lights for tonight's party when we heard the first cars arriving, and since then it's gone ballistic. By eleven, the courtyard, the workshops and the tea room were all full of people.

The courtyard looks amazing. I never dreamed it could look so good all those months ago when I lay in bed, letting my imagination run riot. The reality has surpassed all our visions. The community that we hoped would grow in time is already flourishing, and the hard work of the last few weeks has brought us even closer. Each and every person here has proved themselves worthy of their place, and today their work is clear to see.

A beautiful carved Rowan tree stands at the entrance to the courtyard, courtesy of Ben and Patrick, and planters that Patience filled with riotous colour have sprung up everywhere. Over the doorway to her workshop, a swag of herbs wafts glorious scents into the summer heat.

Helen has wound jam jars with a tumble of coloured wools and stuffed them with roses for every table in the tea shop. So simple and yet so stunning. I've had as many comments about those today as I've had about my cakes. Even Bonnie and Richard (whose shop is so full of produce that it's hanging from the ceiling too) have touched us all by presenting us each with a little basket of fruit for the day, in case we forget to eat. A table stands outside their space with a display, the like of which you would never see in our supermarket convenience–focused world. It's almost a mosaic – edible artwork. With incredible imagination, Bonnie has also taken a huge display book and filled it with recipes to transform the ordinary carrot or the more unusual fruit or vegetable. Her handwritten recipes have been reproduced for people to take away with them.

I'm constantly in awe of these incredible and talented people; they have made Rowan Hill, quite simply, perfect.

Its nearly two o'clock now, and the press have just arrived to officially record the unveiling of Will's window. None of us have seen it, of course, except Finn, and I've tried every arsenal in my book to get him to reveal a detail or two, but he's remained tight-lipped.

I strain to hear what Will is saying now. I look around anxiously for Jane, and she is beside me in an instant. Together we scoop up my nerves and go join the crowds.

Inside the barn, the tea-room tables have all been pushed to one end to make room for us all, the window hung with drapes until the time comes to reveal what lies beneath. A small stage has been set up for Will to stand on so that he can be seen clearly, and I can see him looking nervous and wondering quite how to begin. I squeeze myself forward, trying to find a space where I can make eye contact.

The general rustle of conversation slowly fades as people catch sight of Will's desire to proceed. Finn is by his side, smiling encouragement.

'I'd like to start by welcoming you all here,' begins Will, giving an apologetic smile. 'I didn't actually think that quite so many of you would come to see us today, but then I've been surprised by a lot of things recently, not least of all by Rowan Hill itself. What you see here today has been a long time in the making, but I hope that the longer you stay with us, the more you will come to see what a special place it is. After our parents died, my brother, Finn, and I hoped we could bring Rowan Hill back into the community, but we weren't sure how to go about it. It's taken some very special people to bring it back to life, and I'd like to thank them now.'

Will shifts his weight from one foot to the other, clasping his hands together, his thumb absently rubbing the top of his knuckles.

'I'm not going to thank them all individually, which they'll be very pleased to hear,' he says, waiting as a polite ripple of amusement passes through the crowd. 'Instead, I'm going to ask you to visit their work and let them explain to you what they are all about. They'll do it much better than me, and only then will you begin to understand how talented they really are. Please take your time to wander around, through the woodland also if you'd like. It will always be here for you.'

Appreciative noises are being made, and I hope Will takes encouragement from them. He clears his throat before continuing. 'I am however going to mention one or two people.' He raises his hands to the rafters now, directing people to look upwards. 'We are,

I'm sure you'll agree, standing in the most magnificent building, and I'd like you all to put your hands together for my brother, Finn, whose vision this is.'

There is thunderous applause and a stamping of feet. Finn hops up onto the stage, receiving a huge hug from Will.

'Finn has redesigned this space, transforming it from a boring barn into the magnificent tribute to its heritage that you see today, and with acute cunning he's also provided me with a wonderful space from which to show off.' He turns slightly towards the window at the end and the cruck frame still shrouded in cloth.

'I'm going to need Ben up here now . . . don't groan,' he says, grinning. 'Listen, if we've got to stand up here cringing in embarrassment, so have you.' He waits until Ben takes up the stage, slapping him on the back.

'Ben here is our master craftsman, who literally put this baby back together. Behind this cloth is the historic cruck frame of the building that holds everything up. It's a replica of the original that Ben has skilfully recut, and if you look up, you'll see what a huge amount of work he's had to do.' He starts to clap then, a slow, strong clap that Finn instantly picks up, a little faster, holding his hands up in the air, until in seconds the whole room is resounding with the noise.

Gradually, as it dies down, Will raises his voice once more. 'I know what you're all thinking now: hurry up and get on with it. But before I do, I have to thank the person who has made everything possible, and the only person missing up here.'

Will's eyes fly to mine, winking. 'I promised I wouldn't get her up here, but I lied I'm afraid, Ellie.' He opens his arms, beckoning me forward as I feel Jane's hands in the small of my back, firmly pushing me on.

I make my way through the throng, heart beating like the clappers until I am up there and I can feel Will's arms go around me.

I'm nervous for so many reasons. This day has got to work for all of us: it's our future.

Will starts to speak. 'I've realised recently that life, like art, is all about perception – a lot depends on how you look at it. My own point of view has changed dramatically over the last few months, and I only have one person to thank for that.'

A loud 'Hear, hear' rises up from the crowd.

Will grins. 'As you can hear, I'm not the only one who thinks so. There's a good reason for that. As I said before, there are many people here today who have put in a tremendous amount of work to get Rowan Hill open, but it was Ellie whose idea this was, Ellie who brought us all together, Ellie who convinced us all that what we had was special and Ellie who finds the best in everyone but refuses to believe it about herself.'

Will holds up a hand to still the noise that is beginning to bubble up. 'Can I ask you to hold off on your appreciation just a moment longer? You see, I thought long and hard how to convince Ellie what we all know to be true, and in the end I came up with this.'

Will gently takes hold of my shoulders and guides me to a spot in the centre of the space so that I'm standing just under the still-shrouded window. What's he doing? This wasn't what we planned at all.

'Someone once told Ellie something about herself that she came to believe was the truth. It wasn't – it was only ever their perception of the truth, and so I hope that this will convince her that we see her very differently. Like I said, it is all about perception, and, Ellie, far from interfering, you've shown us all how to dream dreams again. You've shown us how to fight for the things we love, and I hope you never stop. I'm so glad that the sun is shining today. It will make it so much easier to see that sometimes it's not only windows that let in the light.'

I'm aware of movement to my side as Finn and Ben disappear. Will himself releases me and takes a step sideways, putting distance between us. I'm left alone, facing a sea of faces. A waft of air gushes against the back of my legs, and dust motes rise up in front of me in the brilliant light as the shrouds fall away from the window. I can feel the sun on the back of my head as a flow of colour washes over me. It races out across the room, across the people standing before me, over the whitewashed walls, instantly decorating them, magical in their transformation. I look up, and even to the rafters I can see its colours, rose and copper and gold.

And that's when it hits me, the stillness in the room – not just a lack of sound, but a space where for a second there is nothing else but a profound awe. For just as I am gazing out into the room, everyone else is gazing back, looking not, as I am, at the light flowing outwards, but at the point at which it flows inwards. I hardly dare to turn around.

A voice beside me sounds out across the space. 'Oh my word!' Three simple words of honest astonishment.

Thoughts are finding voices now, and a swirl of noise is born. A single clap rings out, followed by another, then another, until the whole building is thundering with their sound. I look at Will, whose face is wrought with emotion as he stands there receiving a standing ovation for his window, washing us with its brilliance.

I am open-mouthed as I try to take in what Will has created, revelling not only in my own emotion but that of those around me. We stand as one collective body of wonder, lost in the myriad colours and patterns.

The piece is abstract, modern and bold. It has none of the embellishment of a traditional window, no paint or etching, but its strength is in its design and use of colour. At the base a turmoil of dark blues, greys and mauves are swirling, moody and oppressive, but split in one corner by a tiny tendril of the brightest coppery red, which weaves itself upwards like molten lava through the smoke that swirls on either side – smoke that billows up to arch over itself like a wave, a wave that becomes a hand, reaching out to the spark in its midst. A tiny finger touches it, and an explosion of colour– reds, oranges and yellows – bursts upwards like a firework, dissipating the smoke, curling to caress the darkness which thins gradually, taking on the new colours until it reaches the top of the window, now ablaze with richness, a rose and copper sky.

I can see that Will wants to say more, but although he holds his hands up, he has to wait some time before his voice can be heard.

'Ladies and gentlemen, thank you, thank you.' He pauses until there is relative quiet. He gives a little cough. 'I'm not sure I can speak, actually. I really wasn't expecting this, and well . . . I'm glad you like the window. The piece is called *Into the Light*, and if you haven't guessed by now what kind of declaration this is, then I will have to say it out loud as well. This is for you, Ellie, my inspiration, with all my love.'

A low whistle from Finn reaches me, but my eyes remain on Will, as do his on mine. I'm vaguely aware of heads around me craning to get a better view, but the room might as well be empty, and Will's words, spoken to me alone. I'm going to need a tissue.

The air is soft out here tonight. It's getting late, but there's still light left in the sky. A gentle breeze sends notes of music my way every now and again, a violin, I think, or a banjo maybe. Some of Ben's friends came down for the evening to provide the entertainment, and Finn joined in too, on an ancient fiddle, partner to Ben's guitar, and the group of them have serenaded us with haunting folk ballads or had us in hysterics trying to dance the dizzyingly fast jigs. How they're still managing to play, I don't know; I'm dead on my feet.

The public have long gone; now it's just family and friends, but even they are starting to drift away too. The public will be back tomorrow, and the day after, maybe not in such numbers, but they'll be back. I'm certain of it. There will always be people at Rowan Hill now.

I'm hiding, I guess, tucked into a corner of the garden. An ages-old yew tree fills the space. Careful pruning of it and the apple tree that sits next to it has formed a natural arbour, instantly filled with one of Patrick's benches.

If I'm still, I might not be noticed at all. It's been quite a day – wonderful, but I need a little time to take in all that has happened. It's been exhilarating, tiring, satisfying, uplifting and undoubtedly emotional.

I look down at my hand again, all other thoughts gone, save those of Will. I've never had a ring on that finger before, and as I touch the single stone, I feel the most magical sense of peace wash over me. The last few weeks have been difficult as Will and Finn learned to trust one another again and remember how close they really are. That day back in June was the start of it, but since then bonds have been forged, stronger than ever before.

I can hear footsteps now, headed in my direction. I've probably been missed, but it's so lovely and quiet here in the dim coolness.

'I thought you might have snuck in here,' Will says, grinning and peeping around the tree branches. 'Can I sneak in with you?'

'I'm knackered,' he adds, as I move over to make room for him.

I lean my head against his shoulder. 'Hmm, me too. Happy, though.'

'Happy,' he affirms. 'Very happy indeed, Mrs McLennan.'

'Hey, I'm not Mrs McLennan yet. It's still Miss Hesketh to you,' I giggle.

'It has a nice sound to it, though, don't you think?'

'Perfect,' I reply, snuggling closer. 'But I'm going to have to go to bed soon, Will. Do you think people will mind?'

'People don't necessarily need to know, Miss Hesketh. Besides which, when has going to bed ever been a problem?' He laughs, arching his eyebrows. 'Come on, let's sneak off.'

I scramble to my feet just as Will pushes me back down on the bench.

'Shh, someone's coming,' he warns, pulling us both back out of sight.

'It's okay – it's Finn,' I say. I'm just about to call out to him, when Will pulls me back once more.

'Don't Ellie – look.'

I follow to where he points as Ben appears, joining Finn on the bench over by the fountain.

Helplessly, we watch as Finn pulls Ben into a gentle embrace. After a moment, though, they pull apart reluctantly, kissing again before Finn breaks off and walks away.

'What are they doing?' he whispers.

'Saying goodnight, Will; they're saying goodnight,' I say sadly.

Will looks at me for a moment, confusion written across his face. He frowns gently, 'But why?' he asks. 'Is Ben going home?'

There's a change then as Will registers the meaning of what he's just said. He smiles at me gently. 'Then I'll just have to convince him otherwise, won't I?' he adds, getting to his feet.

I follow him across the garden to where Ben is still sitting, no doubt staring wistfully into the distance. He looks up with a start as he sees us.

'Hi,' he says, smiling. 'I'm just taking the air for a minute. It's been a mad day hasn't it?'

'It has,' agrees Will. 'But don't lie, Ben; we saw you saying goodbye to Finn.'

Ben stares at him, open-mouthed.

'So I thought you might be needing these?' he adds, giving Ben a warm smile. He fishes in his pocket for a moment, pulling out a bunch of keys.

'I thought I might stay over at Ellie's tonight.' He winks, placing the keys in Ben's hand as Ben stares at them in bemusement.

He catches hold of my hand and starts to walk away before turning back for a moment.

'Oh, and Ben? Finn's room – it's the second on the left.'

ACKNOWLEDGEMENTS

It is a beautiful summer's day as I write this, sitting on a bench in the shade of a willow tree, but I have written in times of rain, snow, floods, storms – and a large chunk of time was spent at the local swimming pool as I waited for my children to finish their lessons. In fact, my writing has been with me through many seasons and many changes, not only to my life but also to the lives of those around me. It has been a source of comfort, as familiar as a favourite seat by the fire.

My characters are a loyal bunch too, for only they truly know how long this book has been inside my head as I've juggled and struggled to get their story down on paper. They never gave up on me, and they too have been a part of my life for so long now, I'm really going to miss them. I would also like to thank all my favourite authors for their wonderful books; after all, what more inspiration could you ask for? I've been transported to new places and met wonderful new people, and my life has been so much richer because of the power of words. It's something I could never give up.

Finally, I'd like to thank my wonderful agent, Peta Nightingale, whose first email to me on that sunny August day quite literally changed my life. It's meant lots of excitement and new challenges, but ultimately dreams fulfilled. Since that time new life has also been breathed into *Letting in Light* and I'd like to thank the team at Amazon, especially my editor, Sophie Missing, for helping me be better than I ever thought I could be.

P.S. Lynne, if you're reading this, the biggest thank you ever – you know why! Will you be available for my next book?

ABOUT THE AUTHOR

 Emma Davies once worked for a design studio, where she was asked to write an autobiographical note. 'I am a bestselling novelist,' she began, 'currently masquerading as a thirty-something mother of three.' That job didn't work out, but she's now a forty-something mother of three, and she's working on the rest. For years Emma was a finance manager who spent her days looking at numbers, so at night she would throw them away and play with words, practising putting them together into sentences. She now writes in all the gaps between real life. Visit her website, www.emmadaviesauthor.com, where, amongst other things, you can read about her passion for Pringles and singing loudly in the car. You can also find Emma at www.facebook.com/emmadaviesauthor and www.twitter.com/emdavies68.